International acclaim for Beware this Boy

"Writing with all senses on high alert, Jennings creates a flaw-less approximation of a typical day in the life of all the girls who worked on weapons assembly lines, their skin yellow and their hair orange from the cordite. And when she takes the story underground during an air raid, those bombs she starts dropping come so close that readers might want to duck their heads and take cover."

– *New York Times Book Review*

"*Beware this Boy* works best when Jennings makes room for her characters, from Tyler to visiting filmmaker Lev Kaplan to Eileen Abbott, a factory worker observing events in her diary, to express their inner feelings in concordance with the wartime tumult. . . . The times were tough, and Jennings reminds us exactly how, in the way she's best done for her entire career."

– *National Post*

"It's among Jennings' gifts that all her people are painted in full colours, each comprehensibly human, even the nastiest with their own sorrowful, if not quite mitigating, histories. And Tom Tyler is the most complete and human of them all – smart, empathetic, yearning, mournful and fair. [Jennings's Murdoch] novels are compelling in character and plot, and historically valuable, but her efforts with her new protagonist in a more recent period are possibly even more sterling – may, in fact, be verging on classic war-fiction status."

– *London Free Press*

Beware this Boy

Beware this Boy

A Detective Inspector Tom Tyler Mystery

MAUREEN JENNINGS

McCLELLAND & STEWART

First edition published 2012
This edition published 2014

Library and Archives Canada Cataloguing in Publication

Jennings, Maureen
Beware this boy / Maureen Jennings.

ISBN 978-0-7710-4319-2

I. Title.

PS8569.E562B48 2013   c813'.54   C2013-900658-3

Published simultaneously in the United States of America by McClelland & Stewart, a division of Random House of Canada Limited, P.O. Box 1030, Plattsburgh, New York 12901

Library of Congress Control Number: 2013931603

Typeset in Caslon by M&S, Toronto
Printed and bound in the United States of America

McClelland & Stewart,
a division of Random House of Canada Limited
A Penguin Random House Company
One Toronto Street, Suite 300
Toronto, Ontario
M5C 2V6
www.randomhouse.ca

1 2 3 4 5   18 17 16 15 14

Always for Iden, my best supporter.

Also to my mother, the late Betty Jennings,
who endured it all.

To all those Brummies who went through the bombing
and the war with courage and steadfastness.

He'd waited patiently, knowing everything had been set in motion. There was nothing more for him to do. At six o'clock, he switched on the wireless. A slight crackle, then the announcer's voice came on. "This is the BBC Home Service. Here is the six o'clock news and this is Alvar Liddell reading it. There was an explosion in a Midlands factory this afternoon. Three fatalities have been reported. Four other workers, two men and two women, were also injured, one of them seriously. However, work is expected to resume within a few days."

That was enough. The rest of the news didn't interest him. He turned it off and sat back. "Work is going to resume, is it indeed? We'll see about that."

CHARLES ENDICOTT LIKED TO RUN WHAT HE CALLED a tight ship, and his employees had learned to be punctual. However, when the workers on the afternoon shift, Danger Sections A and B, arrived, they were held up for a good fifteen minutes. The women's changing room was unaccountably locked. The first shift had already cleared out, but the precious transition time allocated to the incoming group was used up while Mrs. Castleford, the supervisor, went off to find a key. The twelve women stood waiting in the drafty entrance hall where the clocking-in machine was located.

"I wish she'd hurry up. I need to go to the toilet," murmured Sylvia Sumner to the girl standing beside her. Sylvia was the youngest of the group, shy and sweet, new to factory work. She still retained the fresh complexion of a country girl.

"Why don't you go through and use the men's," said the other girl. "Apparently, it's open."

"Ooh, I couldn't do that, Tess."

"Don't be such a silly goose. A loo is a loo. What's the difference?"

"No good asking her," said another girl.

Tess grinned. "You'd better take her under your wing, Prue, before it's too late."

Of all of them, Prue McDermott, with her lush lips and perfectly applied makeup, came closest to being a "woman of the world." She was also funny and good-hearted, so nobody was overly judgemental about her way of life.

Sylvia ducked her head. She was always being ribbed about being an innocent.

Unexpectedly, Irma Dimble, who rarely laughed these days, joined in the teasing. "She'll know soon enough." But she patted Sylvia's arm affectionately to take away any sting from her words. She knew Sylvia was counting the days until her fiancé would come home and they could get married.

"Speaking of which, you'll never guess what happened to me on the way here," said Audrey Sandilands. But before she could tell her story, a flustered Mrs. Castleford reappeared.

"Situation resolved. You can come in. No shoving now, we're not on a bus."

The girls surged through the double doors separating the cloakrooms from the main floor. There were already women working at the lathes, and some of them broke into cheers and hoots when they saw them.

"Make sure you don't claim that on your overtime, McDermott," one woman called out.

"Shut it," Prue yelled back.

"What happened, Mrs. Castleford?" asked Sylvia. "What was the delay?"

"I really don't know. Fortunately Mr. Riley has located another key."

The magazine-keeper was standing at the changing room door. He threw up his hands. "Don't ask me," he said. "I *know* it's not supposed to be locked. I'll look into it."

He opened the door and stood aside to let them in. Prue positioned herself at the threshold as they jostled past. "Tickets, please. Have your tickets ready. Next stop, Hell."

Mrs. Castleford frowned at her. "Miss McDermott, please!"

Audrey nudged Tess and whispered, "Mr. Riley, indeed. No wonder it took so bleeding long to find a key. They had to search *everywhere*."

They both burst out laughing, drawing another frown of disapproval from the supervisor.

The girls went to the lockers and began to disrobe. The factory provided white cotton turbans, blue overalls, and the special soft leather shoes they had to wear.

"Ooh, those are posh," remarked Audrey as Prue undressed to reveal peach-coloured silk cami-knicks.

"Must have cost a week's wages," added Tess. She was the youngest of a large family, and her own style of dress was hand-me-downs. All from a taller, older sister.

"A week's? Try a fortnight's," retorted Prue.

"I hope you're saving them for his eyes only," said Audrey.

Prue shrugged provocatively. "Some things are too good not to be shared."

She took her compact from her handbag and handed it to Sylvia. "Hold this for me, there's a pet. I can't get a look in edgewise with the ugly sisters over there."

One of the Section A operatives, a chunky brunette, had stationed herself in front of the small mirror on the wall and was applying her lipstick. Her skin had a yellowish tinge and the front of her hair was bright orange. All the girls who handled the cordite ended up like that.

"I heard that," she said over her shoulder. "Who's calling us ugly?"

"Nobody, dearie," said Prue. "Just an expression." She checked herself in the compact mirror, pulled out a strand of hair from beneath her white turban, and studied the result. She had only recently transferred from Section A and her normally brown hair was still an orangey yellow. "Draws the blokes," she whispered to Sylvia, who was watching. "They get hot and bothered at the thought we might be blown to smithereens any moment."

"Don't tease the child," piped up Audrey. "She doesn't know what you're talking about."

"Speaking of smithereens, I still haven't got over that damn raid on Friday," interjected Tess. "The worst yet. Our entire family stuck in our Anderson shelter for eleven bloody hours. Eleven hours. Bombs falling all around us. Can you imagine me and my sister together for that long? Christ! I thought it would never be over."

"Better that than dead," said Irma Dimble. A recent widow, she knew what she was talking about.

"Quite right, Mrs. Dimble," said Mrs. Castleford. "Let's have no more gloomy talk, girls. That won't win us the war. And no more swearing from you, Miss Deacon, or I'll dock your wages." She clapped her hands. "Chop-chop, girls. Let's not dilly-dally. We have absentees today, which means more work for the rest of you. We don't want to fall behind, do we."

"Or on our behinds, for that matter," said Prue, winking.

"Speaking of which," said Audrey, as she tied on her turban, "I never got to tell you my story."

"Never mind that now," interrupted the supervisor. "Section A ready? All clear?"

"All clear, Mrs. Castleford," came back the chorus. One by one they hopped over the low barrier into the clean area beyond the lockers and headed for the far door.

"Get down to work right away, you lot," called Prue. "You've kept us waiting lately. Falling asleep, are you? Too many late nights?"

The little brunette, the one who'd been looking in the mirror, cocked a snoot at her behind Mrs. Castleford's back.

The supervisor turned to the remaining five girls. "Let's get a move on. Miss Sumner? Mrs. Dimble? Did you remove your rings?"

"We've put sticking plasters over them," said Irma.

Althought the ASA powder they worked with was so volatile

that anything that could create a spark was a worry, everybody knew how important it was for her to keep her wedding ring on. Mrs. Castleford nodded.

"Just let me see." She inspected their hands. "Yes, that's acceptable." Her glance swivelled over to the others. "Miss McDermott, how many times must I remind you? *All* of your hair must be covered. You have some hanging out."

"Sorry, Mrs. Castleford." Prue tucked away the strand.

The supervisor waved her hands as if she were shooing chickens. "Now then, off we go. Miss Sandilands, I don't need to check you for cigarettes again, do I?"

"No, you don't." Audrey's voice was demure. She was on warning and she knew she would be fired if she was found a second time with contraband.

"Are we all clear, then?"

"All clear," the girls chorused.

Just as the others had done, they all stepped over the low barricade. Mrs. Castleford hustled them through the door and into the passageway that connected with their section.

The two danger areas were new additions to the old factory and were strictly practical. Squat and square, they were built of brick painted battleship grey. Official word was that this prevented the Jerry bombers from seeing them in the fog. However, the employees joked that the real reason was Mr. Endicott had got a bargain on grey paint.

"Have you decided whether or not to evacuate the kiddies?" Tess asked Irma as they scurried along. The passageway was roofed but open-sided, and the damp fog had settled in.

Irma shook her head. "I can't bear to be without them is the truth. Not with Dick gone."

Tess linked her arm through that of the older woman.

"That's understandable. You probably should have taken more time off."

Irma's husband had been killed at Dunkirk seven months ago, leaving her with two young children.

That same fog followed them as they pushed open the heavy fire doors and entered the section. There were no windows, and the narrow, shed-like building was bathed in the bluish light of mercury lamps. There were two benches, each covered with rubberized linoleum, also grey coloured. Buckets of sand lined the walls.

Two men were working at one of the benches, which had the covering torn up.

"What are you fellows doing here?" demanded Mrs. Castleford. "You know it's against regulations to be doing repairs when the shift starts."

"Sorry, ma'am, won't be much longer," said the older one. "We had to replace the lino."

"Well, please hurry. We're losing far too much time as it is."

"You're late today, aren't you?"

"Yes, we are." She regarded her charges. "Take your places, girls. Miss McDermott and Miss Sandilands, you can sit with the others until the men have finished."

The two girls settled themselves onto wooden stools at the adjacent bench.

Mrs. Castleford glanced around. "Where are the carrying boxes? Don't say there aren't any fuses ready?"

One of the men indicated a wooden box on the floor between the benches.

"There's one there. The first shift didn't quite finish its quota."

Mrs. Castleford sighed and turned to the girls. "Mr. Riley says there's a miscount from the morning shift. I really must help him sort out the problem."

"We can start up by ourselves," said Audrey.

The supervisor hesitated. "You're not supposed to."

"We know what to do," added Irma.

"Oh, all right, seeing that we're so late."

She went over to the box, which was about the size of a small suitcase and had rope handles on each end. Both of the workers flicked her an appreciative quick glance. Mrs. Castleford was as plump as a robin but firmly corseted.

"Here, let me do it," said Doug Aston, the younger man.

"Why, thank you. Just be careful."

He took the box by the handles and placed it on the bench between Irma and Tess, who were at the far end.

"Mrs. Dimble, I'm leaving you in charge for now," said Mrs. Castleford. "I won't be long."

She bustled off and Audrey started to sing softly, "*I'm in the mood for love, simply because you're near me . . .*"

"Shush. You're so wicked, Audrey Sandilands," said Tess with a grin.

"I wonder why they had a miscount on the red shift," said Sylvia.

Audrey made a guffawing noise. "That's a bit of malarkey, if you ask me. It's an excuse for Mrs. C. and Phil Riley to have a little shag. Or search for some more missing keys."

"But they're both married," exclaimed Sylvia.

Irma looked disapproving. "Let's not get into gossiping, shall we."

The girls subsided into a chastised silence that was only half sincere.

Tess lifted out one of the cylindrical papier-mâché pots from the box. She began to count out her quota of fuses, placing each one in her tray.

"I keep trying to tell you what happened to me as I was coming here," Audrey said as she watched.

"What happened to you on the way here?" chorused Tess and Prue.

"Well, this bloke bumps into me, see. Suddenly I feel his hands all over my bottom. 'Oi, what do you think you're doing?' I says. 'Sorry, miss,' says he, 'it's this fog. I mistook you for a lamppost.' What cheek."

The others all laughed. Audrey was as thin as a stick.

"Too bad for him he didn't collide with our Sylvia here," said Tess. She gestured with her hands, making curving movements. "He'd have thought he'd died and gone to heaven."

Sylvia blushed. For a young girl, she had a full figure. The two workmen were pretending not to listen in, but they were. They grinned at each other.

Tess went back to counting out the fuses as she removed them from the pot.

"Fifteen . . . sixteen . . . and never been kissed . . . seventeen . . . eighteen, wished she had been . . ."

"Hurry up, slowcoach," said Audrey, drumming her fingers.

"I can't rush today. I didn't get home until one o'clock. I was at a dance."

"Did you meet anybody interesting?" asked Prue.

"I did indeed. A Canadian bloke. He joined the RAF. Ever so smashing, he is. He's going to meet me tonight after work."

"I don't understand how you can go out dancing at times like this," interjected Irma. "What if there's a raid?"

Tess shrugged. "I'd rather be done in having a good time than be sitting shivering in a shelter when the bomb lands. Friday was enough for me."

"I feel the same as you, Tess," said Prue.

They were silent for a moment, then Prue clapped her hands in a good imitation of the supervisor.

"Now, girls, no gloomy thoughts. Chins up."

"She's the one should talk about chins, not me," said Audrey, patting her own lean jaw.

There were two rectangular boxes in the middle of the bench. One contained plugs, the other specially designed brass holders. Having finished her count, Tess removed one of the plugs and inserted a fuse from her tray.

"Here you go. Here's baby." She passed both plug and fuse along to Prue.

"Here comes some screwing," said Prue with a lewd grin. She had one of the holders at the ready to engage the threads of the plug.

Audrey yawned. "Stop playing around, you two. Oh, what the hell, I might as well tray up too."

Impatiently she reached for the papier-mâché pot and started to pull it towards her.

"Oops, why is it so wobbly . . . ?"

"Audrey, be careful," Irma cried out in alarm. "Don't! Don't move it like that!"

***

The meagre fire in Detective Inspector Tom Tyler's office seemed to be in its death throes, smoking continuously. The old police station, with its ill-fitting window frames and doors, couldn't cope. Tyler knew he shouldn't use up his coal ration all at one go, but he was very tempted. He was dressed warmly enough, but he craved brightness and warmth.

He got up from his desk, where he'd been trying to justify being at the station on a Sunday afternoon by filling out the endless forms that the government required these days. They were mostly requests to replace missing ration books or identity cards. Each had to be considered carefully. Not exactly an exciting task, but being at home with Vera was so painful, he avoided it as often as possible. It's not that they squabbled anymore; they didn't. It was just that there was a silence between them that he found impossible to bridge. Had he even tried? Perhaps at first after the tragedy, but Vera had made it clear she didn't want to. So he'd stopped and they remained locked each in their own loneliness and sorrow.

He went over to the window. Outside, a fine drizzle was falling on the empty streets. Even before the war, the shops and pubs in the little country town were always closed on the Sabbath, but today everything looked bleak and uncared for. Flowers gone from the front gardens, few displays in the shop windows. The weak afternoon light was fading fast but there were no lights showing in the houses. It was the hour for blackout. Whitchurch had not so far experienced the bombing that the big Midlands cities of Birmingham and Liverpool had, but the townsfolk were conscientious. For a brief moment, Tyler leaned his forehead against the cold windowpane. Then he turned around and stepped away.

"For heaven's sake, Tyler," he said to himself. "Moping won't help."

He was about to go into the front hall to see if he could get Sergeant Gough to stir up a cup of tea when the intercom buzzed. He answered it.

"Call for you, sir. From Mr. Grey at Special Branch."

Tyler felt a pang of alarm. "Grey? What's he want?" He hoped the man wasn't calling with bad news about Clare. He'd had only one letter from her in three months. He assumed she was still in Switzerland.

"He didn't say. Just that it was important."

"It always is with that bloke. He probably reports his daily bowel movements to Winnie himself."

Gough chuckled. "Shall I tell him you're not in?"

"Good God, no, Guffie. What are you thinking? If the local boffin needs to talk to me urgently, I'd better answer. Could change the course of the war."

He didn't add "and give me something to do," but he had the feeling that Sergeant Gough understood that.

"I'll put him through. And I was just about to make a pot of tea. The wife sent over some fresh-baked tarts for us."

"Now, that is important. You should have said so earlier."

"I was saving the surprise, sir."

Tyler picked up the telephone receiver.

"Evening, Tyler. Beastly weather, isn't it."

"Certainly is, sir." He felt like saying, *It's November. This weather comes about regularly every year*, but he waited for Grey to get to the point. He could hear him sucking on his pipe.

"I'm calling because I have a job for you. There's been an explosion in one of the Brum munitions factories. Rather a nasty affair, truth be told. Some fatalities. Happened earlier today. I had a ring from the inspector at Steelhouse Lane. Name of Mason. He's an old chum of yours, I understand. He said you were stationed in Birmingham at one time."

"I was. Several years ago now."

"He said his officers are stretched thin what with dealing with raids and so forth. He asked if we could spare you to handle the investigation."

"Investigation, sir? I don't consider myself an expert in explosives."

"Don't need to be. It's no different from any other kind of police work. All a matter of common sense, really. You'll no doubt find the blow-up was caused by carelessness, but we want to make sure there was no sabotage involved."

Grey had a way of tailing off the ends of his sentences as if his energy was expiring, like the air from a pricked balloon. With that and the ubiquitous pipe in his mouth, his listener was constantly forced to ask him to repeat himself.

"Did you say sabotage, sir?"

There was a light tap at the door and Sergeant Gough entered, balancing a tray on one hand. Tyler waved to him to put it on the desk.

". . . always a possibility," murmured Grey. "The commies have quite a following in the industrial towns. Not to mention all the nationalists, who are as active as fleas on a dog in these places. If it's not the Welsh, it's the Irish or the Scots. Next thing, every piddling county in England will be demanding its own government."

Tyler nodded to Gough, who poured out a cup of tea and mutely pointed at the jam tarts.

"You are up for this, aren't you, Tyler?" said Grey. "Change of scene is as good as a rest, they say." Tyler had been about to bite into one of the tarts, but he stopped. He wasn't in the slightest bit tired; he wasn't suffering from any bodily fatigue. But Grey said something else, which got lost.

"Beg pardon, sir."

"According to my secretary, there's a train leaving at nine tonight. As this is a special operation, you can put in a requisition for expenses. Keep them reasonable, there's a good chap. We don't have a lot of dosh to fling around. Mason said you can bunk in at the station. They've got spare rooms." He paused and Tyler heard him strike a match. "All right, then? Ring me in a couple of days and let me know how you are getting on. The explosion was probably just what it seems to be – human error. But keep your eyes open. If any of those fanatics have been monkeying around we'll string them up."

Before Grey could disconnect, Tyler said, "Have you had any word from Mrs. Devereaux, sir? I mean, is she all right?"

Grey muttered something that Tyler managed to catch this time. "She is well. We are thinking of having her return to London while she can, but that is up to the ministry. Good luck, Tyler."

The telephone clicked off, leaving Tyler to hang on to that morsel of news like a starving man.

The train was slow and it was going on for eleven o'clock when Tyler arrived in Birmingham. The carriages were unheated, and when he disembarked, he found himself moving stiffly. *Like an old man*, he thought to himself, not pleased.

The fog was pervading even the station and he felt it entering his lungs, dank and sour. Some change of scene! The Shropshire rain, miserable as it might be, at least felt clean. He turned up the collar of his macintosh. Passengers were dispersing quickly, but he paused for a moment to get his bearings.

A man muffled to the eyebrows was leaning against one of the pillars having a cigarette. "Taxi, sir?" His cab was barely visible.

"No thanks, I can walk faster."

"Suit yourself."

"You're taking a gamble, aren't you, mate? Driving in this weather?"

The man shrugged. "Got to make a living, don't I."

Another passenger, a man in an army greatcoat and peaked cap, came through the doors.

"Taxi, Captain?" This time the driver scored a hit.

"Good luck," Tyler called after them. "Now, where were we?" he muttered to himself. He'd brought a filtered torch with him and he snapped on the light. Fat lot of good that did. The beam was simply bouncing back off the wall of fog. He'd have to rely on memory. Not too hard, considering how many times he'd walked his beat in this area. He'd been a police constable for – what was it? four years? After their second child was born, he talked Vera into moving to Birmingham with promises of a better salary, better social life, but she'd never settled down. Finally she gave him an ultimatum: either he returned to Whitchurch with her and the two kiddies or she was leaving him. Tyler had capitulated without much argument. He agreed it would be better for them to grow up in the country. However, he did miss the raw, tough edge of Birmingham life and the challenges of being a police officer there. Tyler sighed. Water under the bridge, that was.

He moved on, gaining more confidence in his route as he did so. The Industrial Revolution had spawned Birmingham, and nobody would ever pretend that this perpetually grimy city was elegant or charming, the way some of the older English towns were elegant and charming. However, people had made their lives here for generations, and the present destruction was distressing to see. Almost every few feet there was evidence of the damage that the recent bombing raids had inflicted. There were craters in the road with police barricades around them as warning. He had to walk around piles of rubble, and his light showed him glimpses of the collapsed walls of houses.

He had just turned the corner onto Colmore Row when a man loomed out of the darkness in front of him. They almost collided but the other man sidestepped nimbly into the road. At that moment a bicyclist shot out of the gloom and, unable to stop in time, crashed into the man, who fell heavily to the ground. The bicycle skidded violently and the rider slipped from the pedals. However, he quickly straightened and, without pausing to see what damage he had caused, pedalled off.

"Hey, look where you're going," shouted Tyler. He aimed his torch but the bike was swallowed up by the fog. He glimpsed only a slight figure wearing a balaclava and dark clothes.

The man was getting to his feet slowly and Tyler went to help him. "You all right, sir?"

"Give me a minute and I'll let you know." His accent was American. He rubbed at his shoulder. "What happened? What hit me?"

"Some idiot of a lad who thinks he can ignore the laws of physics. He was riding much too fast for these conditions."

The American grimaced as he bent down and picked up his hat, which had been knocked off when he fell. "I hope the little brat hits a brick and gets his comeuppance. What the hell is he doing riding around at this time of night, anyway?" He looked around. "You know, I don't have a clue which direction to go in."

"Where were you heading for?"

"My hotel. It's on Corporation Street. But even in broad daylight I'd have trouble finding it. You Limeys insist on changing the name of the street every block or so. And this was way before you thought the Nazis might invade."

Tyler grinned at him. The man seemed a little on the tipsy side but his good humour was infectious.

"I was visiting the auntie of a friend of mine," continued the American. "She kept plying me with her homemade cider. That stuff tastes like apple juice and has the kick of a mule." He moved closer to Tyler. "Are you a warden? You don't have your armband and hat on. You're not a spy, I hope."

"No, I'm not." Tyler pointed ahead of him. "That's the way to your hotel. If you keep close to the curb you should be all right. Corporation Street isn't far. Just go past the next two streets."

The American held out his hand. "My name's Kaplan. If you get hold of that tear-ass bugger, give him a clout for me."

"I will indeed. One for me too."

They shook hands and parted company. Kaplan was walking much more tentatively than he had before. Maybe Tyler should have offered to escort him to his hotel. Good for

Anglo-American relations. Tyler wished he could have nabbed the little blighter, but he'd taken off in too much of a hurry.

The fog swirled in front of him as he trudged on.

***

Jack Walmsley, fourteen years old, a Boy Scout, and an official police messenger, was a lad in deep trouble and he knew it.

"Sod it." He automatically whispered the bad word even though there was not a soul within earshot. He'd skinned his knee badly in the collision with the unknown pedestrian and he could feel a trickle of blood running down his bare leg into his sock. He wanted to go home but he daren't. He had to come back to the gang with something to show for himself.

He started to count the streets, and at the third one he turned, dismounted, and wheeled his bike. Dorset Road had been bombed only a few days ago and he knew the houses were too badly damaged for anybody to have returned to live there. One of those that looked relatively intact had belonged to Mr. and Mrs. Cowan, an elderly couple he'd known since childhood. He'd heard they'd both died in the bombing raid. He shoved aside his feelings of uneasiness. They wouldn't need their stuff now.

He pushed his bike under a remnant of fencing and slipped beneath the police ropes that were festooned around the area. He went to the front door, which was partly off its hinges, opened it cautiously, and stepped into the house.

"People are as thick as planks, Jack," Donny had said to him. "Friggin' stupid, most of them. They have no imagination. They usually leave their bloody money in the back of the wardrobe, in the pantry, or in the living room sideboard, bottom drawers at the back. Look for some sort of tin — biscuits, tea, stuff like that — Aunt

Fannie's po with a lid on. If there isn't any money, scarf the tins of food. Better than bloody silver plate these days. But we can still handle the odd picture frame if it's nice. Keep alert at all times, like a soldier. You don't want to come across a friggin' granny who's bin sitting in the bleedin' pantry waiting out the Jerry. Got it?"

Donny Jarvis had accompanied his question with a painful twist of Jack's ear. He enjoyed doing things like that, and the burn had lingered for a long time after. He'd almost broken Jack's little finger a couple of weeks ago, when he bent it down into the palm until the boy had shouted out in agony.

"Who's the boss here, Jack?"

"You are, Donny," gasped Jack.

"And you love me, don't you?" More pressure applied. "Say yes, like the little pouf you really are."

"Yes, Donny."

"And if I asked you to suck my cock, you would, wouldn't you?"

"Yes, Donny."

The two other boys, Art Fernie and Bert Teale, who were watching, had tittered at this, and Donny thrust away Jack so hard he fell to the ground, cracking his elbow.

"You're disgusting," said Donny. "You're worse than bleedin' shit on my shoe." And he'd wiped his foot on Jack's trousers, going dangerously close to his privates. "Get up, arsehole. Don't come back without that bleedin' rucksack filled to the brim."

Jack started to struggle to his feet, but Donny knocked him back again. "And don't think of running to your old man or Mumsie. They won't help you. Looters go to bloody jail for a long time. We have friends in jail, you little sod, and they would do whatever we asked them to. Got it?".

"Got it," Jack whispered, and Donny let him get up.

They'd been gathered in the air-raid shelter in Bert Teale's backyard. Bert's mother was sozzled as usual and had stretched out under the kitchen table, which she said was as safe as anywhere.

His dad was away in North Africa and Bert had declared one day that they didn't know if he was alive or dead, but as for him, he hoped the bastard was dead. The boys didn't usually exchange such personal feelings with each other, but both Art and Donny had nodded in agreement.

"After the war, I'm going to drive up in my Bentley . . . and I'm going to offer my old man a bloody job working for me."

Donny sported a scar on his upper lip where his dad had knocked him against the stove during one of his mad-drunk fits. Even Jack – who tried to make himself invisible at the meetings and acted as if he didn't see anything – even he was impressed by the implacable hatred in Donny's eyes whenever he mentioned his father.

This cold, foggy November night, he'd gone to Donny's house as instructed. "Fog is the perfect cover," said Donny. "Nobody'll be out and there won't be a bloody raid. Soddin' Jerry won't risk it." He grabbed Jack's hand, ready to twist it. "You won't get lost, will you, little ponce? You know what'll happen if you try to weasel out of this with some poor excuse or other."

Not being able to see more than a foot in front of you seemed more like a real reason than an excuse, but Jack didn't dare say so.

The gang operated like a small feral pack and always went out during an air raid, banking on people to be in the shelters and the streets to be empty. Donny made a point of scoffing at the bombs. "If it's got your bleedin' name on it, you'll cop it; otherwise you won't." The other boys made sure to hide their own fear. They'd had a couple of close calls but otherwise Donny's credo seemed valid. They had hit six houses in succession during the last big raid, early in November. In one place they'd found thirty pounds hidden in the bread box. "Probably saving for Christmas," said Donny with glee.

Usually they worked as a team, two to do the looting, one for a lookout. Tonight Jack was by himself. He was on probation, Donny said.

"You're a friggin' messenger. A Boy Scout. You're a good boy. Everybody thinks the bleedin' sun shines out of a scout's arse. Nobody will question you tootling about."

Jack stood for a moment in the hall. It was totally black and the acrid smell of cordite and dust still lingered. He snapped on his torch, aiming the beam around the hall. Most of the roof was gone and the stairs had partially collapsed. In spite of what Donny had said about the wardrobes, he didn't want to risk going up to the bedrooms.

There was a piece of plywood covering the entrance to the parlour, so he decided to check the kitchen first. Bits of plaster crunched underfoot as he walked down the narrow hallway. The woollen balaclava was itchy on his skin.

The kitchen was small, with yellow sprigged wallpaper that had once been bright and cheery but was now covered with red brick dust. He remembered being in here, sitting at that same table while Mrs. Cowan served him a glass of delicious eggnog. He hoped she couldn't see him now. *Don't think about that. Don't think. Be a soldier.*

He opened the door to the pantry. The neat shelves were lined with tins. All kinds: tinned fruit, stewed tomatoes, peas and green beans, lots of baked beans.

He halted. Several tins had been opened and lay empty on the floor. He didn't know what to make of it but he couldn't back out now. He swung off his rucksack and shovelled in as many tins as he could, until it was bulging. He added a half bag of sugar and the tea caddy. What was that? He paused again, thinking he'd heard something, but it was just the wind blowing through the broken window. The tattered curtains were slapping and flapping like the flags of the dead.

Would this be enough for Donny? Jack couldn't be sure. He'd better check the parlour. People often put their best china

and silver in there, like his mum did. He shrugged the heavy
rucksack onto his back and, swinging his torch from side to
side, he walked cautiously out into the hall.

His heart leapt into his throat.

He was sure there had been a piece of plywood in front of
the entrance to the parlour. It wasn't there now. He could see
it leaning against the wall just to the left of the doorway. His
knees started to tremble so hard he thought he might have to
sit down. His mind immediately started to race with excuses –
*I thought I saw a light in here and thought I'd better make sure . . .
I'm a Boy Scout.*

Oh God, there was somebody just inside the parlour, a
shadow against the lighter window. It moved towards him.

Suddenly a torch light flashed into his eyes, blinding him.
"Stay right there, you little bastard," a man's voice hissed. "One
move and you're a dead man."

Jack turned to make a bolt for it, flinging off his rucksack
as he ran. He hadn't even reached the front door when he felt
the man grab hold of his collar. He was lifted into the air and
slammed down hard on the floor. Then the man knelt on him
so heavily it was hard to breathe. Jack was sure he was going
to die on the spot, but suddenly the weight shifted and the
man got off him.

"Turn over slowly."

Gasping, he did as he was told and the man pulled off the
balaclava. Jack heard the sharp intake of breath.

"Jack. What the hell are you doing here?"

He could just make out the man's face. He was unkempt
and filthy, but unmistakable.

It was his own brother.

***

Eileen Abbott climbed into bed, thrusting her feet between the flannel sheets to find the hot-water bottle, now only luke-warm. Usually the blessed privacy of her snuggery soothed and eased her, but tonight the room felt cold and lonely. Some time ago, when it was clear that she was the daughter who'd be living at home, Eileen had asked to have the front parlour as her own bed-sitting room. She furnished it simply: one armchair, the bed, and a matching wardrobe and dresser. Just enough space for books, her wireless, and a gramophone.

Eileen pointed her toes underneath the covers, something she did without thinking. Her aspirations to be a dancer had long since gone, but every so often when she felt wistful, she would push back the armchair, wind up the gramophone, and dance to a record. Even in that restricted area Eileen prided herself that she could still manage a tight pirouette or two.

She shifted restlessly. Sleep seemed far off. She sat up again and snapped on the bedside lamp. Perhaps writing her report would help her get out of this agitation.

At the outbreak of the war, she'd volunteered to be one of the diarists that the group called Mass Observation had asked for. They also used trained observers to record the voice of the people, as they put it. Typically, these observers noted down overheard conversations and opinions of the general popula-tion. "Good Lord, isn't that what spies do?" her father had remarked when he heard about it. "They're not undercover, just sometimes anonymous," said Eileen. Joe had grunted skepti-cally. Eileen was more trusting. She thought it was a good idea and potentially lessened the gap between the governed and the government. However, she'd gone for the personal diary record. She could hardly use her position as a nurse to note down what were often private conversations with her patients.

Funny thing was, she found writing in the diary was com-forting and she'd stuck to it faithfully. Mass Observation had assured all their volunteers that everything was read even if they couldn't comment.

She unscrewed the top of her Thermos and took a gulp of the hot cocoa her mother had made for her. Then she reached for the notepaper that was on the beside table. Each sheet was stamped across the top: MASS OBSERVATION. DIARIST NUMBER SIXTY. BIRMINGHAM. (PLEASE DATE)

Her hand still didn't feel quite steady and she took a deep breath. Just because she was a trained nurse didn't mean she could be unaffected by the terrible accident that had occurred, but, as always, she forced herself to keep her emotions under control. Getting all weak and teary wasn't going to help anybody.

Sunday, November 24, 1940.

Forgive me for putting it like this, but today was a day from Hell.

There was an explosion at Endicott's this afternoon. Sunday is my day off so I wasn't at the factory when it occurred. My mother and I were in the living room listening to the wireless when we heard it. It could have been anything – an unexploded bomb, a broken gas main – but we both said, "That sounds like it came from Endicott's." Dad had not long before gone in because he was working the afternoon shift, and Mum turned quite white. We went immediately to see what had happened. There were already a lot of people in the street, but it was so foggy some had their hands on the shoulders of the ones in front of them, like blind people do. We plunged into the stream with Mum clinging to my arm, and we were able to move at a good pace. The girls from the factory were standing outside, several wearing the red armband signifying they worked in the Danger Section. Mr. Endicott's secretary, Mr. Cudmore, was trotting up and down like the White Rabbit, trying to get everybody to move across to the other side of the road. He'd come straight from home and he was without his tie, unheard of for him — he is utterly punctilious about his dress. The girls were slow to obey, seeming shocked into paralysis. Fortunately, there were many family members in the crowd that had rushed over, and they claimed their daughters. A light plume of smoke was coming from the roof but there were no flames. Mum and I were highly relieved to see Dad. He was standing with his arm around the shoulders of one of the girls, who was sobbing. He in turn looked relieved to see us. The person he was comforting turned out to be Vanessa, my nephew's wife. Trust her to find an available man to cry all over. Seeing that Dad was none the worse for wear, Mum took over and told Vanessa to buck up, which she did promptly. Nobody had much information except that the explosion had occurred in the B section of the Danger unit. The A section operatives were unscathed. Vanessa and the others had been in the canteen or working on the main floor, which was untouched. Dad said that the fire wardens had already put out any fire and there didn't seem to be any danger to the rest of the factory. The Danger Section is separate from the main floor and has reinforced walls. But Dad said there were injured people inside. I was about to go in when an ambulance arrived. I knew the two men. One's a conshie named Nigel or Neville, something like that. He's a nice lad, really. Works hard. The other is a dour Scot who says he isn't going to fight another war. Everybody calls him Mac. He must be getting on for fifty but he's very strong, physically and emotionally.

They got a stretcher from the ambulance and the three of us entered the building. I stopped only to fetch my

*first-aid kit from the clinic and we went through the
walkway to the Danger Section.*

Eileen paused, remembering. As they entered the shed, the
smell of cordite, blood, and feces assailed them.

*What a sight. Since the bombing raids started, all of us
have had experience in dealing with dead and mangled
bodies, but this was very hard. Probably because I knew
all of the young women. One of them, Tess Deacon, lived
on this street. She was dead, lying like a doll covered
with dust, but not a mark on her. The percussion had
killed her instantly. The worst was Irma Dimble. She
had been eviscerated. Mac stepped forward to deal with
that, bless him. Both of her arms had been severed and
lay, one on each side, a few feet away. I could see that
her ring finger was covered with a piece of sticking
plaster. Funny how you notice irrelevant details like that
in a crisis.*

*I checked on the others. Prue McDermott's throat was
sliced, a raw red gaping mouth of a wound. Her eyes
were open and for a second she focused on me. She tried
to speak but that only made more blood bubble out. I
put a pad on her throat but she sort of sagged and her
eyes rolled back in her head. I knew she was dead. No
time to mourn. Young N. was beside me and he was
stalwart. We went over to the two girls who were still
alive. Sylvia Sumner's right arm had been severed just
below the elbow. It too was lying to one side like a
mannequin's broken limb. Her left hand was a bloody
mess. Poor, poor girl. She had got engaged only a month
ago and she'd come into the clinic especially to show me
the ring.*

The other girl was Audrey Sandilands. Funny, cheeky Audrey. She was unconscious but breathing, although she was bleeding from the nose and mouth. Another percussive injury. Not much I could do for her on the spot. The damage was all internal.

Mac, in the meantime, was examining the two men who had been injured. They must have been working nearby. One of them – Doug Aston – had a deep head wound and the other's eye had been blown out and was lying on his cheek. His name is Peter Pavely and I've known him for years. A kind fellow, a devout Methodist.

I had to decide quickly whom to move first. Audrey, Sylvia, and Mr. Pavely were the worst off. I thought Sylvia and Peter could be saved; I wasn't so sure about Audrey. Fortunately at that moment another two ambulance men arrived and I didn't have to make that choice. I directed them to Audrey and they loaded her onto the stretcher and took her off. I got Mac and Neville to help with Sylvia. She was semi-conscious and moaning softly. I applied tourniquets to both arms and wrapped pads around the wounds. They took her away. I did what I could for Mr. Pavely and Doug Aston until more help arrived.

Eileen gulped down more of the cocoa. She kept some brandy in her cupboard, but she was too chilled to leave the precarious warmth of her bed, so she tugged the covers up higher and continued to write.

Another ambulance arrived and was able to take both men off to the hospital. I stayed behind to organize removal of the three bodies to the mortuary. I asked the wardens who were standing by to assist with the

cleanup – a euphemism if ever there was one for scrap-
ing human tissue and bone from the floor and the
benches and mopping up pools of blood. There were four
wardens, none of them young men, and they were
superb. I knew that two of them had served in the
Great War, the same as my father had, so perhaps they'd
had experience. I know Dad did, although he rarely
talks about it. Dad even got through the police cordon
and came to see if there was anything he could do. I told
him to deal with the rest of the workers, get them to go
home and make sure somebody was with them. He
didn't try to talk me out of my task, bless him. The
factory caretaker, the Polish refugee, came in. He's been
nicknamed Wolf because his real name is unpronounce-
able. He immediately volunteered to fix the huge hole in
the roof with a temporary tarpaulin. He doesn't speak
much English but he was calm and efficient, although he
too looked dreadful. Bless him too. In emergencies such as
these, people going about their business without being
asked are deserving of the George Medal, if you ask me.

I'll try to go to see the Deacons tomorrow. At least
Mum went on our behalf tonight when she heard the
news about Tess. She said the sorrow was almost unbearable. Tess was their pride and joy. Just twenty years old.
We sent her a birthday card two weeks ago. What a
waste of a young life, the promise snuffed out in an
instant. I assume there will be some kind of investigation
into what happened, but with the kind of work those
young women were doing, an accident can happen
anytime. It's both tedious and dangerous, which is the
worst kind of combination.

Christmas will be here in no time. I'm not looking
forward to it. How desolate it will seem with so many

*men overseas and so many families destroyed by the
bombing. It makes you wonder if we can keep going.*

Eileen looked over what she had written and replaced
the notepaper on the table. Was there really somebody reading these diaries? Or was it a futile gesture that mattered to
no one?

She turned off her light and lay awake in the dark.

***

Steelhouse Lane Police Station was an imposing three-storey
building that had an aura of authority reminiscent of the
Victorian era. In actuality it had opened its doors only in 1933.
It was often called grand, sometimes intimidating. Tyler
thought that your opinion was dictated by your conscience.
At the moment, however, its dignity was somewhat diminished by piles of sandbags stacked around the perimeter. Tyler
stepped into the grand arched doorway and pressed the bell.
Alf Mason himself answered the door immediately.

"Tom. Good to see you. Wasn't sure you'd ever get here."

"Sorry. They had to clear the tracks twice."

"You were lucky it was only twice. Come on in." They shook
hands heartily, with some additional thumps on each other's
arms. "Give me your things."

Tyler handed over his hat and coat and Mason ruffled his
hair playfully.

"What happened to the carrot top? You're almost as much
silver as red now."

"At least I've still got some," retorted Tyler.

Mason chuckled, rubbing his own smooth dome ruefully.
"I heard that bald heads were a sign of intelligence."

"The brains burning out the hair, I suppose?"

"Something like that." He snatched Tyler's suitcase before he could protest. "Here, let me take your bag. Let's go up to the common room. I've got a kettle on the boil."

He led the way up a poorly lit flight of stairs and ushered Tyler in. Warmth and brightness welcomed him.

"Thought you'd like a bit of a warm," said Mason. "Mind you, we had to burn some of the furniture to keep the fire going."

Tyler grinned. "Too bad there's a war on. You could requisition some new stuff. Looks like you could do with it."

Heavy use had already softened the furniture and scuffed the wood flooring.

"Go and warm up your cockles," said Mason. He began to gather together the newspapers that were scattered on one of the couches. "That's all my mess. I spend most of my time in here when I'm not working. My house took a hit a few days ago and I've moved in here with the bachelors."

Tyler had obediently gone to the hearth. He turned around. "Good Lord, Alf. I didn't know you were bombed."

Mason shrugged. "Only just happened. Fortunately the girls are both stationed up in Scotland and Yvonne had gone to stay with her sister in the Lake District. It seems the safest place to be at the moment, and she thought she'd be closer to the girls. Not that she's seen much of them by all accounts, and last I heard she says she'd rather risk a bomb than the slow death by boredom that she's currently experiencing." He winked at Tyler. "Yvonne was never one for the beauty of the unsullied countryside. She says there's nothing to do there except count sheep, which puts her to sleep."

"I'm surprised she even agreed to it, knowing your missus."

Mason shrugged. "She's going to give it a trial period. She's only been gone for a month. Course, she wanted to come back when the house was knocked out but I talked her into staying where she was. Everything's boarded up tight." He gave a wry grin. "Truth is, I miss her. Wives! You want them out from underfoot when they're here and can't stand your own company when they're not."

Tyler smiled in response, although Alf was certainly not speaking for him in this regard.

"How's Vera?" Mason asked as he poured some tea from a silver pot on the trolley.

Tyler shrugged. "Bearing up. She doesn't say much."

Mason handed him a cup. "That must be tough for all parties." He pointed. "Do you want me to add a splash to that? I've got whisky – Canadian Club – only good for livening up the tea. We might as well drink it now; there won't be much more where this came from. I think those that say the war will be over by Christmas have got their heads up their jacksies. We're in for the long haul."

Tyler nodded agreement and Mason added a healthy shot to each cup.

"You look done in, Tom. Drink that up and I'll show you your room. You'll find it nice and quiet. There's hardly any of the lads around now and none that you would know. They're all away trying to shore up cities worse off than us. That or they've signed up." He held up the whisky bottle. "More?"

"Thanks."

"With the tea or without?"

"Without. That's goddamn awful char you made, Alf. Did you stew it for a week?"

Mason laughed. "Almost. We just keep adding tea leaves to the pot. The only way to deal with the rationing."

He splashed some more whisky into Tyler's cup and looked over at his friend.

"How're you making out these days, Tom?" he asked quietly.

"All right. Thanks for your letter, by the way. I appreciated it."

"I was utterly stunned when I heard what happened at the internment camp. What a dreadful case! And what came from it must have been hell for you."

Tyler nodded. He didn't want to go into it, not even with Alf.

They sipped at the whisky in silence for a moment, then Mason put down his cup. "I've got to hit the wooden trail or I'll be useless tomorrow. I'm off to Nuneaton to help sort out some administrative problem. I assume you'll be going over to the factory in the morning. The BBC reported the explosion. Did you catch it?"

"No, I didn't."

"They couldn't say where it had taken place – they never do. It was just called a Midlands town. They said there were three fatalities, but one of the injured girls is in critical condition. It'll be four dead soon. Endicott's is closed down tomorrow, so you'll get a chance to have a gander 'round." He tried to stifle a yawn.

"One more thing, Alf," said Tyler. "Our Mr. Grey is wondering if there might be sabotage involved. Communists and so on."

Mason frowned. "I doubt it. All of the workers get security clearance, but we don't clap somebody in irons just because they're on the bolshie side."

"Anybody I should pay particular attention to? Nationalists, for instance?"

"Don't get me started on the bloody Celts. They don't know which side their bread is buttered on. They'll be singing a different tune if Hitler comes knocking on their doors. Do you think he'll welcome them? Fat chance. He hates nationalists of any stripe."

"No IRA sympathizers?"

"Not that I know of. I hope to God we squelched that lot when the last two got the drop for trying to blow up the police station."

"That was back in February, wasn't it?"

Mason nodded. "We haven't heard a peep since then. Good as bloody gold they are. So, sabotage? I doubt it. It's my view that the explosion was an accident. Those gals are rushed through their training. They're young, heads in the clouds. One mistake, one lapse of attention, and *boom*, you're a goner."

He yawned again. "Beg pardon. Long day. Sorry I don't have much more I can give you. I did ring over to the factory, though, and they're getting you a place to work from. Endicott's secretary will meet you and show you around. His name's Cudmore." Mason made a flip-flop gesture with his hand. "He's a good fellow, for all he's a bit limp-wristed. You might not even see Charles Endicott. He avoids trouble like the plague. And he's notoriously tight-fisted. If you do recommend changes to routine, he'll put up a fight if he thinks it'll cost money. Just ignore him or pull rank if you have to. Tell him you're a personal mate of Winnie's. That'll shut him up."

He got to his feet. "If you want to come back here for your meals, just sign up with the canteen. Frankly, you'll get better food at the British Restaurant on Broad Street. It's just opened."

"I'll look into it."

"There'll be some breakfast served here at seven thirty. Not much to write home about these days – toast and tea."

"I don't have to go to morning lock-up parade, I hope."

"We've suspended that for the duration, thank God," said Mason with a chuckle. "At least with this war, justice is swift. Nobody's much bothered with so-called reasonable doubt, which as far as I'm concerned is a crock of shite. You were caught red-handed, matey, off you go to clink. No toffee-nosed lawyer to whinge for you."

Tyler laughed. In spite of his tough talk, he knew Alf was a fair and conscientious copper.

"I won't see you till tomorrow night," continued Mason. "It's going to take an elephant's age to get to Nuneaton if the fog keeps up, so I'm off at the crack of dawn. Ready?"

Except for the fact that he knew it would have embarrassed both of them, Tyler could have hugged his friend. His kindness and matter-of-fact manner were a balm. Mason banked down the fire, then led the way into the hall, snapping off the light behind them.

"I'll say good night then. You know where the loo is. I'm bunking in number twenty-six." Mason looked at him. "Sleeping all right these days?"

"Not bad," Tyler lied.

"It'll take time, Tom."

"To tell you the truth, I was glad to be called up here. Change of scene."

"Thought it would be."

They parted company at Tyler's door with a couple more thumps on each other's arms.

Tyler went into the bedroom. He unpacked the few things he'd brought with him. Two fresh white shirts, a couple of sombre ties in case he spilled something on one of them, warm underwear, woollen socks. He put them into the top drawer of the dresser. The previous occupant of the room had left behind a wrapped toffee. Tyler considered having it but he wasn't sure how long it had been there. He left it alone.

He got into his pyjamas and slipped under the covers. Typical of police-issue furniture, the mattress had known better days. The middle sagged like the belly of an old donkey.

A constable in the adjoining room was playing a record on his gramophone, not loudly, but the music was still audible. It sounded like the weedy American, Frank Something or other. He was singing *I'll never smile again, till I smile at you*. Tyler found the song disturbingly pertinent to his situation. Only three months ago, but it seemed like years since he'd heard from Clare Devereaux, Clare Somerville as she was to him, the woman he had always thought of as his one and only love. He'd had one brief note saying she was still in Switzerland but she hoped she would see him before too long. Rationally, he knew she couldn't say much – her letter would be censored – but he was disappointed that there were no words of love, no endearments. Did she miss him the way he missed her? He'd written three letters but had no way of knowing if they had reached her.

The music from the next room was getting slower and slower. The gramophone must be the kind that needed winding up, and Tyler wondered if the constable had fallen asleep. Frank's voice was starting to drag as if he'd been on a drunken spree.

"*I'm . . . so . . . in . . . lo . . . ve . . . w . . . ith . . . you . . .*"

Finally, to his relief, it stopped completely. *Reminds me of myself*, thought Tyler. *I could do with a good winding up.*

Last month he'd actually gone to the conscription board and tried to enlist. He'd even take a desk job. He couldn't say the men behind the desk had laughed at him. They were rather kind, in fact, but his request had been turned down without preamble. "You're much more valuable doing what you're doing," said one of them. He was a lean, posh-voiced bloke with an eye patch. "We've got to maintain law and order at home, by Jove."

So, by Jove, here he was. Not exactly maintaining law and order but at least trying to sort out accident from intention. His thoughts shifted to the conversation he'd had with Grey. *Common sense, really.* He hoped that was true. An investigation like this wasn't going to be easy. Alf had said there were three fatalities. If he did indeed discover that there had been sabotage, that was three murders.

He snapped off the light. "*Goodnight, Clare, my darling,*" he whispered. "*I hope you're safe.*"

***

Eileen sat up in bed, her heart bumping. *Tap, tap, tap.* Soft yet persistent, coming from outside. *Tap, tap, tap, tap.* She knew the windows were latched and nobody could get in, but it was frightening that at this hour somebody was at her window. She picked up the torch that stood on her table, ready for the times they had to go to the shelter, swung her legs out of bed, and walked cautiously to the window. She lifted aside the thick curtain just a crack and peeked out. Her own shadowy face reflected back at her, but as she pressed closer she could see a shape on the other side of the glass, distorted by the fog and darkness but recognizable. It was her nephew.

Quickly, she pushed up the sash window. "Jack. What are you doing here? What's the matter?"

"Auntie Eileen, I've got to talk to you," he whispered.

"Why are you at the window? You scared the heck out of me. For God's sake go to the front door and I'll let you in."

"Please, Auntie. I don't want Granddad and Gran to get up."

"I'm not going to hold a conversation with you through the window. It's perishing."

He turned away at once, and she closed the window. She slipped on her dressing gown and, torch in hand, went out to the front door.

Jack was on the threshold, and even in the darkness his fear was palpable. She didn't speak, only beckoned, and he followed her into her room. She closed the door behind them and switched on the light.

He looked terrible. His face was covered with dust and

streaked with tears. There was a large bruise on his cheek and one bare knee was badly scraped.

"Just a minute." She went over to her bedside and poured some cocoa into the cup. Then she opened the corner cupboard, took out the bottle of brandy, and poured a generous splash into the cocoa.

"Here. Drink this down."

He did so, coughing and spluttering as the brandy hit his throat. Even then he took the precaution of pressing his sleeve against his mouth to stifle the sound.

"Take your time. Can you get down some more?"

He shook his head. "No, it's awful."

The floorboards overhead creaked and both of them waited, looking upwards.

"It's only Granddad," said Eileen. "He usually goes straight back to sleep."

The creaks retreated and were still.

Jack looked over at her, his face full of misery. "Thanks, Auntie Eileen."

"Are you going to tell me what's going on or not?"

"It's our Brian . . ." he choked.

"What about Brian? Has something happened? Did you get a telegram?"

"No, nothing like that." The boy rubbed hard at his eyes as if he could erase the memory. "I found him in a bombed-out house."

"What do you mean you *found* him?"

It was on the tip of Eileen's tongue to ask what he himself had been doing in a bombed-out house in the middle of the night, but she thought it would be wiser to leave that for now.

"He was hiding. He's gone AWOL, Auntie. He's deserted."

Eileen sat down on the edge of the bed. "My God, Jack. I can't believe it."

"It's true, Auntie. He's been there since Friday."

"Is he going to turn himself in?"

Jack shook his head emphatically. "He said he won't. He won't go back to the front and he won't go to prison." He bit his lip. "Auntie, I think he's gone off his rocker and I think he might do something really bad."

"Does he know you've come here?"

"Yes. He said Granddad and Gran and you were the only ones he could trust. He wants you to come to talk to him."

"Where the dickens is he?"

"In your shelter in the backyard –"

"What!"

"Please, Auntie. I had to do what I was told. He don't seem like our Brian at all. He said if I turned him in, he'd get me, brother or no brother."

Jack's lips were quivering. Eileen tried to make sense of what he was telling her. Brian was her nephew, her godchild, her family. How could he have deserted?

"I'd better go right now and talk to him."

"Be careful, Auntie. He's not himself, honest."

"Well, *I* am myself, so maybe that will bring him to his senses. Stay here." She pointed to his knee. "I'll take care of that when I come back. Let's sort this out first."

She took her overcoat and wellies out of the wardrobe and went through the kitchen to the back door, moving as quietly as she could. She knew what a light sleeper her father was.

She snapped on her torch, waved it in a low circle, then began to walk slowly forward. It helped that Joe had painted the stones that lined the path white. Near the entrance to the shelter, she could make out a dark shape that moved slightly as she approached.

"Brian, is that you? It's Auntie Eileen."

"Come inside." His voice was so hoarse she might not have

known it was him, except she risked flashing the light up to his face. A dark stubble covered most of his face, and his eyes were hollow. It was less than six months since she had last seen him, but any soft boyishness had gone. Brian was twenty-one years old and he looked forty.

Brian held back the entrance blackout curtain for her to step through. In the close space she could smell the acrid stench of his unwashed body. She went ahead into what her father jokingly referred to as the lounge. Brian had lit the oil lamp but kept the wick low. There were deep shadows in every corner.

"So, Brian, what's going on?"

"Just what it looks like, Aunt Eileen. I've left the army. A personally justifiable but nevertheless dishonourable discharge." He stopped. "You don't have a fag on you, do you?"

"I thought you didn't smoke."

"I do now. I told Jack to tell you to bring me some fags. What did you do with him, by the way?"

"He's waiting in my room."

"He'd better not bugger off to the police."

"Of course he won't. Don't be silly."

It was then that Eileen understood what Jack had meant when he said Brian was off his rocker. A muscle in his face was twitching non-stop and he could hardly stand still, jigging like a caged animal, one that would bite without hesitation.

Brian went over to the little dresser that her mother had moved into the shelter for her tea things. The cramped space had Beatrice's signature written all over it: the spirit stove on an upturned painted box, the two camp beds covered with colourful quilts and cushions, an old rug on the floor. Two chairs. An oil heater was in the corner. There was even a photograph stuck on the bare wall of a pugnacious Winston Churchill, whom her mother greatly admired. A green velour curtain discreetly hid the chamber pot in the corner. One of the family jokes was that if Beattie Abbott ever mistakenly got sent to Hades, she'd start fixing it up to make it homely.

"Granddad wouldn't come down here without his roll-ups. Where are they?" asked Brian, jerking open the dresser drawer and scattering the tea packet and cups to the floor, breaking one of them.

"Brian, stop it this minute," Eileen said sharply. "Look at you, you've broken that cup."

He turned around to face her. His expression was dark and wild but her presence obviously brought with it the old authority of aunts over young nephews.

"Sorry," he mumbled.

"There might be some Woodbines in the house. Let's go in there where it's warmer. I'm freezing."

"Then what?"

"What do you mean, then what?"

"Are you going to try to talk me into giving myself up?"

"That might be the best thing to do, Brian."

"I'll die first."

"Oh, don't be so melodramatic. You always did have a tendency to blow things out of proportion."

"I'll be executed if I go back. Hung by the neck until dead."

"Not these days – we need fighting men too badly. You weren't even on the front line. You'll go to jail for a few weeks and that will be it."

"Then I will have to go back to the war."

Eileen sat down in one of the chairs, clasping her hands. "Likely not. You'd probably be given a desk job."

He didn't respond to this. Then he said, "How's Vanessa? Have you talked to her lately?"

"Not since last week. We had tea together in the canteen."

"I should have gone to her house when I got here, but her

parents would have called the police. They never really liked me. She's probably wondering where I am. I wrote and said I had some leave coming."

"Your mum told us that."

He started to fidget. "They cancelled it at the last minute. Rumour was we were going to Africa. To the desert." He flashed her a crooked grin. "You know me, I don't even like going to Blackpool. I decided to take my own leave. Permanent." He fished in his pocket and took out a small bottle. "A bloke gave these to me. Benzedrine. They issue them to the RAF lads to keep them awake."

He was about to shake a couple into his hand when Eileen stopped him.

"I think you should hold off on those things. How long have you been taking them?"

"Since Wednesday. They really work. I thought I'd better stay on the alert. I've been on the run. I couldn't risk having my rail warrant checked, so I've been travelling at night. Jumping on the backs of lorries mostly." He paused. "You remember the Cowans? When I got to Brum, I ended up in their house. Just chance, really. I didn't realize it at first but then I saw them. They were both dead, Auntie. Sitting like statues underneath the stairs."

"So I understand."

"I didn't see them at first. They must have taken cover in the broom cupboard, and in the murk I hadn't noticed them through the slats. They were sitting on two chairs, both covered with plaster dust, both quite upright, and both quite dead."

"They were good, kind people," said Eileen.

"Me and Jack used to go and sing carols in front of their house at Christmas." He burst out in his hoarse voice, "*Please put a penny in the old man's hat. If you haven't got a penny, a ha'penny will do. If you haven't got a ha'penny, God bless you.* And *bang, bang* on the door."

"They were very tolerant."

"You told us finally that they were Jewish."

"That's right. Their real name was Cohen."

"You told us because you found out we were singing the bad version of the song." He shouted again, "*If you haven't got a ha'penny, you're a skinny old Jew.*"

Eileen sighed. "Shush. You're making a lot of noise."

He lowered his voice. "I'm sorry I sang that. They never said anything. Always gave us a shilling and some cake Mrs. Cowan had made. They used to give us homemade eggnog at Christmas. Do you know what, Auntie?"

"Yes?"

"They were holding hands. The wardens had to carry them out together. I hid in the parlour when they came. I couldn't think, so I stayed in the house, hoping something would happen." He made an attempt to smile. "And it did. Jackie found me and here we are."

She got to her feet. "Come on. Let's have a conflab inside."

He didn't protest and Eileen led the way back to her room, both of them tiptoeing like thieves as they crossed the kitchen.

Jack was sitting in the armchair, and he jumped up when they came in, looking warily at his brother.

"Why don't you take that chair, Brian," said Eileen, keeping her voice low. "Jack, is there any cocoa left?"

Jack shook the Thermos. "Some. Here, Bri."

He thrust the drink over but Brian pushed his hand away. "I'm okay. I wouldn't mind a slug of that brandy, though."

Without a word, Eileen poured a hefty shot and he tossed it back as if it were water. She hoped it wasn't going to have an adverse reaction with the Benzedrine he'd been swallowing.

His pupils were dilated and there were flecks of saliva at the corners of his mouth.

He plopped down in the armchair and leaned back. "Whew. Maybe I'm more tired than I realized."

"Why don't you close your eyes for a minute."

"Don't mind if I do." Within seconds he was asleep.

Eileen's heart went out to him. Beneath the frenetic energy he was completely exhausted. She took the quilt off her bed and covered him up.

"What are we going to do, Auntie?" whispered Jack.

***

Even in the pitch darkness, Jack was pedalling dangerously fast. His Auntie Eileen had sent him home, making him swear to secrecy, but he'd dropped his rucksack in the Cowan house and he'd had to retrieve it. Donny had told him that, no matter what the hour, he had to report in when he'd completed his task. He was already much later than they would have expected and he was afraid of what he would encounter. His mind felt numb. He couldn't think of an explanation for the amount of time he'd taken. He was almost out of breath when he reached the street where Donny lived. As he turned the corner, he ran over some debris that was strewn across the road. The jolt threw him forward onto the pedals, banging his already scraped knee. He dismounted to inspect the damage. His shin was stinging and he pushed down his sock so he could see what he'd done. Then he had an idea. He reached for a nearby chunk of brick and, before he could reconsider, he rubbed it really hard up and down the bone, aggravating the scrape and tearing the skin even more. He wanted to yell in pain but bit his lip so hard he drew blood there too. Tears sprung to his eyes. Tentatively he straightened out his leg and got to his feet.

As he flashed the beam of the torch, he could see that a swelling had shot up at once.

He set off again. Would Donny punish him for being so late? Would the loot satisfy him? He wiped away the tears with the back of his hand. What a mess he was in. Donny's house was the end one in a mean row of back-to-backs on Water Street. Jack leaned his bike against the wall. It must have been almost two in the morning, and so dark he might as well have been standing in a coal pit. He didn't dare knock but pushed open the door and stepped directly into the living room. A sharp voice snapped at him.

"Who's that?"

"It's me, Jack."

A pause. Then he saw a figure heave itself up from the floor. Another shape was beside him. Two people had been lying in front of the fireplace, where the embers of a fire still glowed. The second shape said in a drowsy voice, "Wot's up, Donny?" It was a girl's voice. Donny's latest, Thelma, was with him.

Donny poked her hard. "Sit up, slut. We've got a visitor."

She pushed herself onto her elbows. Even in the dim light, Jack could see she was naked. She made no attempt to cover herself. Permission would have to come from Donny first.

"Put the light on," Donny said to Jack, and he obeyed, trying not to look at the girl now revealed. She was his age, only fourteen, but her breasts and hips were already full and rounded. Her eyes were puffy and in the light he could see she had a bruise on her cheek. Whether she'd got it from Donny he didn't know and wouldn't ask.

Donny reached for his cigarette papers and tobacco pouch, which were on the floor beside him.

"Roll us a fag," the girl said.

"No. I only got enough for one left." He was sitting up now

and he quickly went through the routine of rolling a cigarette and lighting it. The sharp smell wafted over to Jack, almost turning his stomach.

"All right, Jacko. What have you got for us and why are you so late? Lucky for you me and my bird weren't in the middle of a shag. Could have been friggin' embarrassing."

"I – I fell and hurt my leg," stuttered Jack. "I dunno, I must have fainted or something. Next thing I knew I was on my way here." He swung his rucksack off his back and put it on the floor. "Got some good swag, Donny."

He opened the bag and tipped out the contents. Donny got to his feet, pulling the blanket that had been covering him and Thelma around his shoulders. He was wearing tight underpants, and Jack couldn't help but glance down. Donny's private parts showed large and defined.

"Oi, Donny, I'm perishing. Give us a blanket." Thelma was whining. Jack knew Donny hated that tone of voice, and he tensed with fear at the retaliation he thought would fall on the girl. But tonight Donny seemed to be in good humour and he let it go.

"Shurrup. I'll come and warm you up in a tick."

He drew on his fag, the red end throwing light onto his thin lips. The old scar was white. He stirred the contents of the bag with his foot.

"Looks good, Jacko. But you're trying to pull one over, aren't you."

Jack tried not to shrink away from him. "No, Donny. Course I'm not."

Donny blew a smoke ring and watched as it dissolved into the air. "Let's put it this way. It's now the middle of the friggin' night. You've had plenty of time to go back and forth several times. But you've only got one sack. What did you do with the others?"

Jack could feel his legs starting to shake. "I told you I fell. I must have been unconscious. I stuffed my bag and came here direct. I swear I did. Just one bag."

"Let's see your stripe."

Jack showed him the goose egg and blood on his shin. Donny whistled softly as if in sympathy.

"I bet that hurt bad."

"It did, Donny. Really hurt."

Donny bent down and brought the end of his cigarette close to Jack's leg. He squinted upwards.

"If I were to stub out my soddin' fag on that there stripe . . . well, it would be pretty bloody nasty, wouldn't it? Especially if I did it more than bloody once."

Jack didn't answer. Oh God. He was afraid he was going to mess his trousers any minute. He could sense that even Thelma was watching them in fear.

Donny straightened up. Jack could see the excitement in the other boy's eyes, the pleasure rising at the prospect of causing pain. Help came from an unexpected quarter. Thelma said, "Look, pet, he's brought some tinned pears. I fancy some."

Jack didn't know if her intervention was an act of courage or if she truly was only interested in the fruit. Whatever the reason, Donny moved away and resumed smoking the fag, pulling down the red-hot tip as far as he could.

"What's it to be then, Jack? The truth or . . ."

He didn't need to finish the sentence. The wound on Jack's shin was already throbbing and he knew Donny was quite capable of following up on his threat.

He opted for the truth and gave up his secret. He betrayed his brother.

LEV KAPLAN TURNED INTO THE NARROW COBBLED lane just past Corporation Street. The telephone booth was at the far end. A sign on the handle read OUT OF ORDER. He glanced around to make sure he was not being observed. The fog had lifted and the Ministry of Information's campaign to make the population aware of questionable behaviour had been effective. He didn't want to arouse suspicion. He squeezed into the booth. It smelled strongly of stale cigarette smoke and cat piss. What did they do, come in to take a leak?

He put a coin in the slot and pressed A.

"Number please?" said a pleasant female voice.

"Cypress 8184."

"One moment, I will connect you." While Kaplan waited he rubbed his painful shoulder. It probably got dislocated when he fell last night. The ligaments were too loose, and a good knock could put it out of joint. *Bloody kid.*

A soft male voice came on the phone. "Identify yourself, please."

"Hitchcock. The lady vanishes."

"Good morning, Mr. Hitchcock. This is John Grey speaking. How is the weather at your end?"

God, the British and their preoccupation with the weather, Lev thought to himself. "Still foul."

"What a pity. We actually are seeing some sun here."

"Jolly good."

The other man gave a genteel cough. "Quite so. Did you have your meeting?"

"Sure did."

"And who was in attendance?"

"Same people as before, with one addition."

"Describe please."

"A youth, barely into long pants but obviously with a heart of steel, forged in poverty and cruelty. I wouldn't want to run into him in a dark alley." He winced as he twisted too quickly. "Come to think of it, I did run into him, literally. Or at least one of his kin."

"What are you referring to?"

"Nothing important."

The man on the end of the phone chuckled. "You Americans have such a poetic way with words. You're saying he's a little criminal already, this tender shoot of the Great Revolution?"

"I'll bet he has a record as long as the Mississippi."

"And his name?"

"His *nom de guerre* is Bolton."

"Ah, how ambitious. One of Birmingham's more famous citizens."

"I'm sure he'd didn't come up with that himself. The ponce assigns our names. He let slip the lad's real name – it's Donny. First name, that is. He is about five-four, thin, pasty-looking, brown hair, and a scar at the corner of his upper lip, right side. Pretty eyes."

"I beg your pardon."

"They're the most distinctive thing about him: light hazel colour, dark lashes. Girl's eyes."

"Is he a homosexual?"

"I'd say definitely not. This little thug is the type that makes a notch on his belt every time he's shagged some poor girl."

"Good. Well done, Mr. Hitchcock. We should be able to trace him quite easily from your vivid description. Our records on the other three men are quite complete now. Do you have something to write on?"

"Uh-huh." Lev didn't even try to get out his notebook. His shoulder was too sore, for one thing. Besides, it aggravated him that Grey didn't trust him to remember. Probably because Lev was a Yank. Not from the right schools, don't you know.

"Ready?"

"Go ahead."

"Cardiff, as you might expect, is a militant Welsh nationalist, real name Ewen Evans. He works at the factory, in the canteen. Arnold, the ponce, as you call him, is a silly boy playing Sexton Blake games. He's in way over his head. He spent one or two terms at Rugby before he was sent down for poor work habits. That's no doubt why he chose the code name he did: Thomas Arnold was a headmaster there in Victorian times. His son was one of our most famous poets. He wrote the exquisite 'Dover Beach.' Perhaps you are familiar with it?"

"That's the one about the ignorant armies having a go at each other on a dark plain, isn't it? Not that much different nowadays, if you think about it."

"Yes, quite. But be that as it may, we were in the midst of discussing Comrade Arnold."

"He giggles all the time. Very irritating."

"His real name is Gilbert Dix. Father a schoolteacher at a third-rate prep school. Patriotic to a fault. The scion is rebelling, I suppose."

"What did you get on Comrade Chopin?"

"He is a bona fide refugee. Polish. He was arrested for so called anti-social behaviour, meaning, in his case, being an advocate of Communism. He was sent to a prison in Dachau for six months. The Nazis are using the term *concentration camp*, meaning they concentrate all the same kind of prisoners in one spot. Easier for administration, I assume. So Germanic, don't you think?"

"Sounds ominous to me." Lev tried without much success to rub at his shoulder and hold the telephone receiver at the same time.

"Apparently our friend had a bad time during incarceration," continued Grey. "It's possible the Abwehr is running him as an undercover agent, or he may be a dyed-in-the-wool true-believer communist. We're not sure yet. His name is Dmitri Wolfsiewicz."

The booth was steaming up, and Lev began to draw little faces on the glass. They all had pipes in their mouths.

"What was on the agenda last night?" asked Grey.

"We had a lively discussion about whether we would cause injury to civilians or not. For the greater good and all that. Means justifies the ends. Neither Chopin nor Cardiff said much. Chopin never does but the Welshman is usually vocal. The runty thug said, 'We're not playing marbles here. Course there'll be dead 'uns.'"

"Did he indeed."

"No, what he actually said was, 'We're not playing fucking bloody marbles. This is bleedin' war. People frigging die.'"

"Foul-mouthed, is he?"

"That's putting it mildly."

"Was this with reference to . . . ?"

"Beg pardon, what did you say?"

"Sunday's incident. Did this have to do with Sunday's incident?"

"Sort of but not directly. Nobody claimed responsibility. I thought the ponce and Taffy were troubled, and maybe the Pole, but I'm not positive. They don't give away much, these fellows. I couldn't tell if they had anything to do with it or not."

"Hmm . . . how interesting. Anything else?"

"The ponce had his big moment. With much licking of his chops, he declared that the chief – that is, Comrade Patrick, not yet seen – wants to close the factory down completely by Christmas."

"How?"

"The very question yours truly asked. He couldn't say right now, says Poncy, but we will know soon enough."

"Is this serious, do you think, or is the young man blowing air out of his anus?"

Lev almost burst out laughing. "I think Arnold likes to pretend to be thick with the boss. He wants to be seen as the lieutenant but I think the real next in line is the Welshman. I didn't get the impression that an actual plan had been formed as yet."

There was a silence at the end of the phone. Lev could hear a sucking sound as if the man were lighting a pipe. He added a Sherlock Holmes deerstalker to one of the little faces on the window.

"Do they trust you?" asked Grey.

"They'd be stupid if they did. I haven't been tested yet. I just have good references."

"Ah, yes, thank you for reminding me. You're going to the factory today, I assume."

"That's right."

"I should tell you there is a policeman investigating the explosion. His name is Tyler, Detective Inspector Tom Tyler. I don't think he'll be a problem, but steer clear of him. He's been seconded from the Shropshire constabulary but he's no country bumpkin. Wouldn't do to underestimate him. We don't want to waste valuable time with his going off on some wild goose chase as far as you are concerned."

Not for the first time, Lev found himself admiring the other man's perfect grammar.

"I'll be the soul of discretion."

Grey gave a disbelieving cough. "Please be. Don't arouse his suspicions. I'll sign off now, then. You can of course reach me any time. We must watch this situation very closely."

Lev hung up the phone. Holding his arm tight to his body, he stepped out of the booth and replaced the OUT OF ORDER sign. The damp air brought on a fit of coughing. *Damn the English weather. Damn the war. Damn ignorant kids.*

***

The three of them were sitting around the kitchen table.

Eileen had waited as long as she could before waking up her parents. Once the initial shock of the situation had abated, they had rallied round, as she knew they would. Brian had gone back to sleep.

"He was always such a good boy. I would never have dreamt he'd do something like this," said Beatrice.

Joe blew on his tea to cool it. His grey hair was sticking up in tufts but his blue eyes were keen and alert. Eileen thought the crisis had invigorated him.

"What on earth caused him to desert?" continued Beattie. She turned to Eileen. "Has he seen Vanessa?"

"He said not."

"Well, I just hope she didn't write him one of those what-you-call-it, John letters. I wouldn't put it past her. That'd send him round the bend if anything would."

"I don't think he knows himself why he did it," said Eileen. "He had a short pass to come home. Rumour was they were going to Africa."

"Africa. Lord help us. I don't blame him." She picked up a skein of wool from the basket beside her. "Hold up your hands, Eileen; I might as well wind this while we talk."

Obediently Eileen did as she was asked and Beattie hooked the ends of the skein over her fingers.

"But like you said, Bea," continued Joe, "other soldiers don't run away from their duty." He sighed. "We have to come to some decision about what to do. It can't be just our responsibility. We'll have to speak to his mother and father. And Vanessa. They are married, after all."

"We're not going to turn him in," said Beatrice. The ball of wool was growing rapidly.

Joe poured some tea into his saucer and slurped it down. "If we don't – which of course goes without saying – but if we don't, what are our alternatives?"

"It's only been a few days. He could still go back, couldn't he?" said Beatrice.

"He's adamant he won't do that," said Eileen.

"I suppose we could send him on his way."

"Don't be silly, Joe," exclaimed his wife. "On his way where? Where can he go?"

"Calm down, Bea, I'm just thinking out loud."

"He's too desperate, Dad," said Eileen. "Frankly, I'd rather report him to the police than have him go off and murder somebody."

Abruptly Beattie stopped what she was doing. "Murder somebody? Why on earth do you say that, Eileen?"

"I'm sorry, Mum, I didn't mean that literally. But he's in such a state, who knows what he could do."

Joe chewed on his lip. "Then the only other possibility is that we hide him until the war is over."

"Which could be years from now," said Eileen.

"True. But I don't know if we have much choice, do we." The two women looked at him.

"No, we don't," replied Eileen.

***

Brian lay on the bed, waiting, thinking. He knew that his granddad, his gran, and his auntie were downstairs discussing what to do. He didn't expect them to understand his reasons for running away. He had a hard time explaining them even to himself. One of the blokes in the bunk next to his received a letter from his girlfriend saying she'd met somebody else. Hodge was furious more than hurt. "You can't trust them, Bri. No matter what tale they spin, they'll hand it all over to some sweet-talker the moment your boat sails." Brian had immediately started to worry about Vanessa. They'd been married only a month before he was called up and sent to Aldershot for basic training. He hadn't seen her for over five months. They'd been separated longer than together. He thought about her constantly, until the need to see her became a consuming hunger. So he'd run away, hidden out in barns and sheds until finally he hopped on a train at Wolverhampton and managed by sheer luck not to get caught.

The train had pulled into the Birmingham station only minutes before a big raid started. He'd hardly got to the end of the street when the warning siren began to scream. The crowd of people around him scattered, most of them heading for the nearest shelter. But the thought of being packed like sardines in a tin repelled him and he kept on, in spite of the warden yelling at him to take cover. Soon he was the only person on the street.

He could hear the rumble of the Jerry bombers overhead. There must have been dozens of them. The searchlights began to rake the sky and he saw planes unload their bombs, which twisted and turned as they fell, as if they were light as sticks. The *thwump*, *thwump* of the ack-ack guns sounded loud and powerful. The barrage balloons, like huge silver fish, shivered on their tethers, and he saw one break loose and collide with some electric wires, bursting into dazzling flames. He had run then, fear propelling him.

Brian rolled onto his back and stared at the ceiling. His Aunt Eileen had used the word *concussed*. The Cowans had been concussed by the force of the bomb blast. There was a knitting bag on the floor next to Mrs. Cowan like the kind his gran had, and Mr. Cowan had a newspaper spread across his knees. Brian wondered at what point Mr. Cowan had taken his wife's hand, and if in those last few moments of life they had known what was happening.

He shoved aside the coverlet and swung his legs out of the bed, realizing he was wearing blue flannel pyjamas that were too large for him – must be his granddad's. He stood up and walked carefully to the wardrobe where the chamber pot was kept. He hated the fact that he had to use it and leave it for his gran to empty in the outside lavatory, but there was no help for it. He daren't go outside.

The linoleum was cold beneath his feet and he shivered as he went over to the window and cautiously lifted a corner of the blackout curtain. The clock said it was nine o'clock but it could easily have been late afternoon. Outside, the backyard looked dreary and dank; the sodden bushes along the path drooped. The fog had lifted but its presence lingered in the dampness and the grey feeble light.

He heard the sound of the front door and his aunt calling goodbye to her parents.

He replaced the chamber pot in the wardrobe. Then he went out into the hall. As he was crossing the landing, his gran's voice came from the bottom of the stairs.

"Bri? Are you up?"

She was standing looking up at him, and her worry came at him like a blow.

"Yes, I'm up, Gran. I'll be right there."

"I've made you some breakfast. Granddad says you can use his razor if you want to."

"That'll be super, thanks."

He continued on to the bathroom. His image in the mirror was shocking. Deep shadows underneath his eyes, a heavy growth of beard, greasy hair. He shaved quickly and scrubbed at his face with a flannel. His clothes weren't anywhere to be seen, but there was a striped terry cloth dressing gown hanging on the back of the door that he guessed was for him.

He went downstairs to the living room. His granddad was sitting at the table, reading the newspaper, his foot on a stool. His gran was in the kitchen.

"Morning, Brian," said Joe. "You're up earlier than I expected. I thought you'd be sleeping round the clock."

"I'm a bit too het up at the moment, Granddad. No work today?"

Joe hesitated. "There was a bad accident at the factory yesterday. An explosion in one of the danger sections. We're closed down for today."

"Good Lord. Was anybody hurt?"

"I'm afraid so. Three of the girls were killed and two badly injured. Two men hurt as well."

Brian stared at him. "Not Vanessa. You'd have told me if it was Vanessa, wouldn't you?"

"Course we would. But you would know one of the girls. Tess Deacon – she lived down the road."

"Tess! My God, that's terrible. She was such a sweet kid."

"She was indeed." Joe indicated the chair closer to the hearth, where a good fire was burning. "Here, sit yourself down."

"Does anybody know what happened, Granddad?"

"Not yet. There'll be an investigation, but it's dangerous material we're dealing with. One slip is all it takes."

His gran came bustling in with a tray, which she put on the table. When she saw Brian's bare feet, she stopped.

"Oh my goodness, we've got to get you some slippers. You'll catch your death walking around like that. I know how cold it is upstairs. We can't afford to light the fires up there."

"I'll be all right. Granddad was just telling me about the factory."

Beatrice nodded. "Dreadful thing, simply dreadful. They've closed down for today but Eileen has gone in. I wish she hadn't but you know how she is. She wanted to make sure everything had been cleaned up as could be cleaned up."

"She had to deal with the mess," said Joe grimly.

"And then to add to her troubles, I came into the picture," said Brian.

"Aye, lad. That you did."

"I'm sorry, Granddad. I didn't know where else to turn. You know how Vanessa's parents are about me. And Mum and Dad . . . well, to tell you the truth" – he tried a chuckle – "you know how Dad is. As a member of His Majesty's postal service, he would probably feel it was his duty to turn me in." Brian was afraid he would start to cry. He was aware that his hands were shaking, and he tucked them under his legs.

Joe cleared his throat, obviously uncomfortable with such emotion. "We had a bit of a talk after you went to sleep, your gran and your aunt Eileen and me. Nobody in this family is going to turn you in, you can be sure of that."

"Thanks, Granddad."

"However – and there is a however – we thought it might be better for you in the long run if you did go back."

Brian burst out, "I can't, I –"

"Calm down, son, calm down. Fact is, you weren't on the front line, so they won't shoot you like they did in my day. You'll get some time in the glasshouse but at least you won't be on the run for the duration. And the sooner you return the better."

"No, Granddad. If they throw you in jail, they make sure you get bad treatment. I know – I've heard all about it. They'd probably put me in solitary. I can't go back." He jumped up, knocking over the chair. "I understand if you can't hide me. I can fend for myself if I have to."

"Don't be daft, our Brian," said Beatrice. "You'll be caught in no time. What'll you live on?"

"Trust your gran to pick up on the important things," said Joe calmly. "Come on, sit down, lad. You're worse than a dog with fleas."

"Finish your tea, there's a good boy," said Beatrice. "Don't forget it's rationed nowadays. You can't waste it."

"And if you're not going to eat that toast, I will," added Joe, pulling the plate towards him.

Brian with some reluctance righted the chair and sat down. His grandfather nibbled on the toast.

"We'll have to find some way to keep you hidden."

"Hidden how?" His voice was high and tight.

"We've got the room, no problem with that. You can stay in the spare, but there is the question of ration books. We're going to have to tell your parents. They'll have to help."

"What about Dad? Does he have to know?"

Joe continued to munch on the toast. Beatrice had taken the other chair at the table and automatically picked up a piece of mending she'd left there. Repairing one of Joe's shirts by the look of it.

"If we put the fear of God into Ted he'll go along with us, I'm sure," said Joe. "Among the lot of us we should be able to support you."

Brian frowned. "I notice you didn't include Vanessa. She is my wife, after all."

Beatrice lowered her head, concentrating on her sewing. She

didn't say anything, but Brian knew what she was thinking.

Joe answered. "Like you said, son, her parents have never taken to you. Do you think the lassie could keep a secret from them? She's young, is Vanessa."

"And a bit on the giddy side, if you don't mind me saying so," added Beatrice, unable to resist.

Brian did mind. But he held his response in check. "I was hoping to see her soon," he said, twisting his fingers around each other.

"I wouldn't recommend that right now," said Joe. "Why don't we wait a bit? You need to get yourself back on track, mentally and physically. Let's take it a day at a time."

"Your granddad has thought of a good hiding place if – if you need it. Tell him, Joe."

"I was looking at the airing cupboard. I can put in a false back. There'll be just enough room for you in there. We'll pile the towels in front and nobody'll be able to tell."

"But Granddad" – Brian struggled to keep his voice level – "you know I've never been too good with small spaces. Remember the doctor that time said I suffered from what-you-call-it – claustro something or other? How'll I breathe in there?"

"Air holes. I'll drill some air holes for you."

Beatrice put the mending back in her sewing basket and got to her feet. "Look at the time. I must get to the shops while there's still something left on the shelves. Your granddad is going to drop in at the hospital."

Brian caught her hand. "Gran, I had a bottle of pills in my pocket. They're good for the nerves. Do you know where they are?"

"No, I don't. I put all your washable clothes in the copper – they had a terrible pong. I didn't see any pills. Eileen must have put them somewhere."

"When will she be home?"

"Four-ish. But she's going to fetch your mum and dad and we'll have a family talk tonight."

"How are you going to get them over here without them wondering what's up? Dad's sure to be suspicious."

"Eileen will tell them it's a surprise birthday party for your gran," said Joe.

Brian slapped his hand on his forehead. "Oh Gran. How could I forget? Many happy returns of the day."

"Thank you, Brian. And don't fret about not remembering. When you get to my age, you want everybody to forget, especially yourself. We won't be more than an hour. Will you be all right?"

"Course I will, Gran. Be careful how you go. Don't bump into a bloody lamppost."

"Watch your language in front of your grandmother," said Joe.

Brian hadn't even realized he'd uttered a rude word. Swearing was so commonplace among army lads.

"Sorry, Gran."

"I've heard worse," she said with a smile.

"You should lock the door behind us," said Joe. "You don't want anybody wandering in. We've always kept an open hearth, as you know, and Mrs. Swann drops in regularly. She's a good old soul but she's always wanting us to contribute to some cause or other. The latest is the Peace Pledge Union. Better if she doesn't see you."

"I'll knock when I get back," said Beatrice. She hesitated. "Perhaps we should have a signal. Three knocks means it's one of us."

"Good."

"You should stay upstairs," said Joe. "Keep the curtains drawn. We've got good neighbours, so they're likely to come over to warn us if they see a light shining."

"I'll be careful."

He was twitching with agitation, finding their slowness unbearable.

Joe wrapped a muffler around his neck and put his cap on. Beatrice had to trot back to the kitchen to get her shopping bag, then she couldn't find her gloves. Brian wanted to scream but he clamped his jaw tightly and stayed in the chair.

Finally they were gone.

***

Alf was right about the breakfast at the station being nothing to write home about, and Tyler saw no reason to linger. The fog had mostly dispersed but the sky was grey and lowering, the air chill. Leafless, bedraggled trees drooped and dripped moisture onto the slick pavements. There were few people on the streets.

When he'd worked in Birmingham previously, Endicott's had been making sporting guns for the gentry. However, even this early in the war, the Ministry of Supply was commandeering every factory it could find that could convert its machines relatively easily to munitions work.

The original owner, unlike many Victorian manufacturers with pretensions, had made no attempt to prettify the building. The factory was dull brick, low and square, no folderols, no grand entrance. It was situated at the end of a cul-de-sac among equally plain small businesses and cheek-by-jowl rundown houses.

Tyler showed his identity card to the guard, a wizened man whose red-tipped nose was holding on to a drop of mucus. He was wearing some kind of dated gatekeeper's uniform that didn't look warm enough. He greeted Tyler with some enthusiasm.

"Morning, Inspector. We were told to expect you. Get this thing sorted out. Everybody wants to get on with work. We can't let the Boche get a lead on us, can we."

"Indeed not."

"I've had instructions from Mr. Cudmore to tell you he'll be waiting inside. Just go along to those double doors."

Tyler entered the lobby. A large clock with its unforgiving stamper dominated one side and there was a glassed-in cloakroom on the other. Only the fine wooden floor and the bevelled glass of the cloakroom gave any indication of the previous age.

The double doors the guard had referred to opened directly onto the factory floor, which held about a dozen machines. A conveyor belt circled the area.

A flight of stairs to his left led up to another glassed-in section, this one contemporary. He could see the tops of tea urns. The canteen, presumably. The rest of the section seemed to be offices. Suddenly he had a brief glimpse of a portly, bald-headed man watching him from the window. As soon as he realized Tyler was looking in his direction he jumped back. At the same time another man, small and neat, in a dark suit, came hurrying down the stairs and trotted towards Tyler, his hand outstretched.

"Good morning, Inspector. I'm Lester Cudmore, Mr. Endicott's secretary. Mr. Endicott sends his sincerest regrets, but he is unable to attend to you at the moment. He has had to leave on other urgent business. He asked me to act in his stead and to make sure you have everything you need."

He covers his employer's tracks very well, thought Tyler. The disappearing man had to be Endicott, a man who, according to Alf, avoided trouble like the plague.

"May I offer you a cup of tea? It's a blamed dismal morning."

"Perhaps later. I'd like to get right down to it."

"Of course. Let me show you where you can work while you are here." He indicated an area that had been partitioned off underneath the stairs. "I do apologize for its smallness but I'm afraid that's all we could do at such short notice."

He opened the door. Tyler had seen larger pantries. There was a table shoved against the wall and two straight-backed chairs. A coat tree. A poster from the National Savings Committee exhorting everybody to buy defence bonds was pinned to the door. That was it.

"I'll hang your coat and hat, shall I, sir?"

Tyler handed them over and waited, looking over the deserted factory floor while Cudmore hung up his things. He probably would have brushed them down, given half a chance.

The secretary came out of the pantry. "I have made myself available if you need me, sir. I am a competent shorthand typist, if you have need of that also." He tapped his coat pocket. "I have a complete list for you of all of Endicott's employees. All those who were present yesterday are in red ink. I have indicated beside each name which shift they were on, where they were working at the time, and so forth."

"Thank you, Mr. Cudmore. Very, er, competent."

The secretary turned pink. He was probably in his late fifties and his face was deeply seamed, as if he'd shouldered too much responsibility from an early age. Everything about him was neat: his smooth, sparse blond hair, his dark, conservative suit and tie. He put Tyler in mind of an undertaker, an impression accentuated by the black arm band he was wearing. But his eyes were shrewd and there was something about him that Tyler liked.

"Where would you like to begin, sir?"

"Perhaps you can explain the usual working procedures first. What happens here on the floor, for instance?"

"This area is where the shell casings are calibrated and buffed. Probably doesn't look like much compared to the big factories, but we keep three shifts running seven days a week. We do our bit."

"The casings are made elsewhere, I presume."

"That's right. They're delivered to the loading dock that you can see in that far left-hand corner. From there the crates are placed on the conveyor belt and carried to each operative. When their particular task is complete, the crates are again put on the conveyor belt and, er, conveyed to the far end. From whence they are all taken to the next stop, which is Section A."

"Keeps everybody busy, I imagine," said Tyler.

"Most of the time, things run along smoothly," said Cudmore with a quick nod. "If anybody does slack off on their part of the job or a machine malfunctions, there is a log jam, of course. Tempers can get a bit frayed when that happens, but I do have to say, Inspector, our workers are for the most part hard-working and conscientious. We're fortunate." He glanced at Tyler. "I do let them know whenever I can. People appreciate a good word now and then, don't you think?"

"I certainly do." Actually, Tyler thought, he himself could do better in that department with his own constables. He should keep it in mind.

"This is not a dangerous area as such," continued Cudmore, "but all workers, even the office staff, are expected to leave any contraband in the cloakrooms when they clock in. That is, cigarettes, matches, lighters, and so forth."

"And do they?"

"I would say so. Everybody is aware of the necessity for these rules."

"Could something get by?"

The secretary frowned. "It isn't likely but I suppose not

utterly impossible. Young women being what they are, the supervisor has to keep a close eye on them. Unimportant things to their minds – a hair grip, a piece of jewellery – but potentially dangerous if they work in the danger sections. Anything metal that might create a spark has to be excluded."

"Have you ever had an accident on this floor?"

"Nothing serious, thank goodness. The odd bit of metal dust in the eye, bruised fingers." He sighed. "The work is tedious. I'm always trying to find ways to keep up the workers' spirits and energy. Mr. Endicott is opposed to piping in music because he thinks it might be distracting. I myself believe it would help relieve the boredom and therefore make everyone more efficient."

"That makes sense. I'm to write a report after my investigation. Maybe I can include that in my recommendations," said Tyler. "Or at least that the matter have some further study."

Cudmore beamed. "Thank you, sir. It would be much appreciated."

"Righto. We can move on."

The secretary led the way to the opposite side of the floor.

"Here are the changing rooms. The female workers are on the right, the men on the left." He gave a sly chuckle. "Perhaps we should have reversed that, given that women are the distaff side of humanity."

Tyler didn't realize what he was referring to at first, but he nodded politely.

"When all the workers have changed from their outdoor clothes, they declare that they are 'clean,' as the expression goes. Section A and Section B operatives, who deal with the fuses, proceed to their buildings, which are outside. Section B, alas, is where the explosion occurred." He indicated the men's changing room.

"We can go through here, sir."

"If you don't mind, I'd like to go by way of the women's room first. Follow in their footsteps as it were."

"Of course, sir. This way." Cudmore actually knocked on the door before he opened it.

The room was spartan, with wire-mesh lockers along the walls and a wooden bench running down the centre. The lavatory stalls were at one end and a communal wash basin in front of them. Blue overalls were hanging on pegs and more than a dozen pairs of black flat shoes were tucked underneath the bench, mute testimony to the absent women. Tyler knew that most of the workers would be returning tomorrow, but there was something oddly desolate about the sight of those empty shoes. He was reminded of the fairy story about the dancing princesses that he used to tell Janet when she was small.

Cudmore seemed to pick up on his thoughts. "The slippers have a way of disappearing. Many of the young women say they make excellent dancing shoes." He indicated a red-painted barrier about six inches high that divided the room just beyond the lockers. "That bar delineates the clean area from the so-called dirty area. As you can see, it's a mental deterrent rather than a physical one. When they're ready, the girls simply step over it and exit through the far door."

"Are the changing rooms kept locked?"

"No, they're not. They were at one time. Mr. Endicott wanted to discourage what he called lavatory-mongering. He thought the women were tempted to linger and gossip with each other."

Tyler could tell by Cudmore's tone of voice this was not a rule he approved of.

"The key kept going missing," continued the secretary. "It became too much trouble to hunt it down if anybody needed to get in. To use the toilet or some such."

Tyler walked over to each door in turn and examined it.

The locks were the old-fashioned kind, requiring a fairly large, straight key.

"No problems with theft, I take it?"

Cudmore shook his head. "We're a small factory. Everybody knows everybody else. We've had no trouble with anything like that."

"Except for the vanishing shoes."

Cudmore smiled. "We've decided to call that normal wear and tear of equipment."

Tyler noticed the secretary had edged closer to the door-way, presumably so he could flee immediately if one of the distaff side did appear.

"Shall we proceed?"

Cudmore stepped over the barrier and ushered Tyler through the door, which opened onto a short roofed passageway. Tyler coughed as the damp outside air penetrated his lungs. It might be more comfortable for the workers if the passage was enclosed. He'd use what clout he could muster and recommend it. Music, covered walkways, pats on the back. What next?

***

Eileen found it strange being in the empty factory. She often went in at odd hours. Ever since the factory had been con-verted to war work, shifts ran day and night. There was always the noise of the machines, the bustle of the workers coming and going. This morning nobody seemed to be in the offices but she wasn't surprised. She'd known Charles Endicott for a long time, and if there was an unpleasant situation he could avoid, he would.

She went into the clinic, which was tucked away at the far end of the main floor. She didn't expect any patients today, so she didn't change into her uniform, but as she was removing her hat she glimpsed her reflection in the mirror. The disturbed night had left its mark. There were dark circles underneath her eyes. *And bags big enough to carry luggage*, she thought ruefully. She was well aware that what she and her parents were proposing to do could have serious repercussions. Most people would understand why, but the government wasn't in the business of understanding. It was against the law to shelter deserters.

Her father's words echoed in her head. *We don't have much choice, do we.*

If there was anything Eileen had learned from her mother, it was the calming effect of work. "When in doubt, do," was Beattie's motto. The medical stocks always needed checking and this was a good time to do it. She opened the supply cupboard. She should order some more tubes of antiseptic. It was costly and hard to come by, but the workers, especially those in Section A, who handled the cordite, frequently got rashes and boils. Prue McDermott had developed dermatitis when she was working in Section A and had transferred only two weeks ago to Section B. Eileen sighed. Lively, glamorous Prue, who loved pretty clothes more than anything in the world. And Irma, solid, dependable Irma, so devastated by the death of her husband. What was to become of her children? No father or mother now. For a moment Eileen thought she was going to cry.

"Hello. Hi. Anybody here?"

She hadn't heard the door open but somebody had come into the clinic. Quickly she closed and locked the cupboard and went out to the waiting room. A man was standing in the doorway. Medium height, perhaps her age, well dressed in a dark overcoat and trilby. He smiled – good teeth, ever so charming a smile – but he was nobody she knew.

"Sorry to disturb you, Sister," he said removing his hat. "I saw your light was on."

"Can I help you?"

"I sure hope so. I've dislocated my shoulder. As I was in the factory today, I thought I'd avail myself of its excellent services."

She could see now that he was holding his left arm tightly against his side.

"Come in. How did you manage to do that?"

The visitor stepped forward. "It happens all the time. Weak ligaments. If you wouldn't mind giving it a good pull, it will go back in place."

"I, er –"

"Don't worry. I've lost count of the number of times I've had this happen. Put your foot in my armpit and give a sharp tug."

Eileen knew what to do, but usually a reduction was performed when the patient was under sedation. She regarded him dubiously. "Maybe it would be better if you went to a hospital."

"Absolutely not. This is nothing to what other people are suffering. I'm not going to take up their time. Some little bastard – excuse the language – on a bike knocked me over in the fog last night and out it popped. I'd hoped I could get it back myself but I haven't been able to." He stuck out his good hand. "God forbid I should forget to introduce myself . . . I'm Lev Kaplan. I'm here to do a film for the Ministry of Information."

She took his hand, which felt cool and firm. She couldn't help but notice he had long musician's fingers.

"I'm Eileen Abbott."

"Glad to meet you, Mrs. Abbott. It is missus, isn't it?"

"No, it's miss, actually."

He gave what she felt was an exaggerated exclamation of surprise. "But some lucky guy has snatched you up, surely."

Before she could say anything, he jumped in. "My apologies. I stepped over the line, I see. Forgive me, it's the Yankee side of me. We're always too brash for English sensibilities. I take that question back. I never asked it, okay?"

"All right. And I won't answer it. Now let's get you fixed up. Will you come into the surgery . . . It would be easier if we could get your overcoat off. Is that possible?"

Lev grinned at her mischievously. "If you can tolerate me screaming. I'm a Yank – we don't believe in stoicism like you Limeys. I find it helps with the pain to yell, unless you have a bullet I can bite on."

"No, I don't. And besides, you might swallow it."

"Too true. All right, I'll be brave. Do it. You look a gentle sort."

"Appearances can be deceiving."

However, she was gentle and she managed to get his overcoat and jacket off with his letting out only a couple of yelps.

"It would be helpful if you could remove your shirt as well."

"Can you cut it off?"

"Don't be ridiculous – it's a good shirt. And we've got clothes rationing here, don't forget."

She helped remove the shirt. In just his undervest, he was unexpectedly well muscled; his shoulders and arms looked strong.

She indicated the gurney. "Lie here, please."

"Best invitation I've had in years," he said and cautiously did as she asked.

She held back a smile. "First of all, I want you to try to relax your shoulder muscles. The arm will go back more easily if you can do that."

"Your servant, ma'am." He took a deep breath as Eileen grasped his hand and forearm.

"Breathe out nice and slowly." She moved his arm to the side and gave one sharp pull, and the shoulder slid back into place.

"Ouch."

In spite of what he'd said earlier, his exclamation was sub-dued. He sat up. "I think that did it. Hardly hurt at all. Thank you." Gingerly he rotated his arm. "Swell. Excellent work."

He had a rather long-jawed, intelligent face and dark brown eyes. His colour was better now, the greyish tinge gone. He must have been in a lot of pain, for all his joking.

"You were very brave – for an American. I've heard much worse from dyed-in-the-wool Englishmen."

"Glad to hear it. I've got British genes, so that must count for something." He began to get dressed. Eileen helped him, finding herself feeling ridiculously shy. *You'd think I'd never seen a semi-clothed man before.*

"Both of my parents were born in the East End of London, to be precise," continued Kaplan. "They met on the boat going over to America. Love prevailed, then marriage, then me. Very proper. I was born in New York."

"Good Lord, what are you doing in England? I would think conditions are far better in America."

"They are indeed, but I was keen to see the home of my ancestors. I came here in thirty-nine and haven't got back yet. It's too risky trying to cross the pond. Besides, my sisters send me food parcels, so I'm okay." He started to ease himself back into his jacket. "I wonder if I might prevail upon you for a cup of tea. I need reviving after my ordeal."

"Of course. I'll put the kettle on."

"I'll come and help."

Eileen burst out laughing. "Now *that* is a dead giveaway that you're not an Englishman. Please stay here; the kitchen area is far too small."

She went into the adjacent office where she kept the Primus stove and tea paraphernalia. "You said you were here to make a film for the Ministry of Information," she called over her shoulder. "What sort of film?"

In spite of what she had said, he had followed her. "Propaganda, I suppose you'd call it. I'm to demonstrate the rewards of working in a factory like Endicott's."

She grimaced. "I'd hardly say we were a good advertisement."

"I'm very sorry about what happened. It must be awfully upsetting for everybody."

His voice was so kind that all she could do was nod, not trusting herself to speak. She was rescued by the shrill whistle of the tea kettle announcing the water had boiled. As she removed it from the stove and poured a splash into the pot to warm it, Kaplan watched with as much interest as if he were an anthropologist studying aboriginal habits in the Dark Continent.

"Go and sit in the waiting room," she said abruptly. "I'll bring it in."

"Yes, Sister," he said meekly.

While she was dispensing the tea, Kaplan looked around. "This room has a nice welcoming feel to it."

Eileen was pleased by the compliment. She had paid a lot of attention to the clinic, wanting to make it as friendly as possible. There was a wool rag rug on the floor that she'd begged from her mother. The two matching chairs and the loveseat were comfortable. She had even hung a couple of prints on the wall. One of them was a stunning photograph of St. Martin's Cathedral, taken at sunset.

"It's a lovely church," murmured Lev as he stood in front of the picture. "Such a pity it got hit."

"One of Birmingham's jewels," said Eileen.

Neither of them spoke for a moment. The appalling devastation that the bombing raids were inflicting on English cities was almost impossible to absorb.

She handed Lev a cup of tea. He waved away the offered milk and sugar.

"Black for me – another Yankee quirk." He sat down on the loveseat. "I'd like to shoot some footage in here. Is that all right with you?"

"As long as I'm not in the picture, I don't mind."

"Of course you must be in the picture. People like to see pretty nurses. It's reassuring."

She raised her eyebrows. "Mr. Kaplan, do all Americans lay it on with a trowel the way you do?"

"'Lay it on with a trowel'? I don't know what that means."

"Never mind. But tell me, how are you going to make a film at Endicott's given what has happened?"

"I understand the factory will reopen tomorrow on a limited basis. I'll shoot some film of the workers on the floor. Needless to say, we need recruits for the war work, but I'll leave it up to the ministry to decide what they show." He put down his cup and stood up, giving his arm another tentative twist. "Good. All hunky-dory. I'd better get going and scout around. Thanks for the most delicious cup of tea I've had since I arrived." He gave a half-bow. "We shall meet again, Miss Abbott. Is it possible that on our second meeting I may call you Eileen? And on our third, may I invite you to come to the pictures with me?"

"Mr. Kaplan, you are moving far too quickly. No first names for at least six months, and certainly no walking out for at least a year."

"Very well. I shall return tomorrow."

He left and Eileen took the tray out to her kitchen. For a few sweet moments the situation at home had receded from her mind.

***

Brian waited to be sure his grandparents had well and truly left him, then he went to his auntie's room.

Where would she have put those pills? He yanked open the drawer of the bedside table. Ha. There they were, together with her Aspirin and a few medical samples she must have brought from the clinic. He poked at them. Painkillers, all sealed.

He took out the RAF pills, twisted off the lid, and shook out a couple into his palm. He gulped them down, not even bothering to get some water. He replaced the bottle. She wouldn't like to know he'd been going through her drawer.

Tap, tap . . . tap, tap.

He froze. Somebody was knocking at the front door. Softly. Surely it wasn't Gran already. She'd said she'd knock three times. Then he heard somebody lift the mail slot and a voice whispered.

"It's me – Jack. Let me in."

Brian went to the door and opened it a crack, enough so he could see his brother.

"Come in. Quick."

Jack stepped forward but another person was right behind him, already inside and closing the door. They both stood in the narrow hall, Jack with his head low, the other fellow, a grin on his face, staring brazenly at Brian.

"Hey, Bri. Fancy seeing you here. Remember me?"

"Yeah. You're Donny Jarvis. You're the shite who stole some of my tools when I was doing a job in one of the back-to-backs."

Donny smirked. "Come on, Bri. Isn't a bloke innocent until proven guilty? I just happened to be in the vicinity. You never knew for sure it was me nicked your things."

"Don't give me that shite. It was you all right. What are you doing here? Don't tell me you've brought back my pliers."

Donny chuckled. "I heard you was in a spot of trouble. Thought I might be able to help."

Jack was looking completely miserable and he had yet another bruise on his chin. "I'm sorry, Bri . . . I –"

Donny slapped him on the shoulder, supposedly playfully but so hard he almost fell.

"Don't blame Jackie. I'm a persuasive kind of bloke. I got him to tell me all."

"So? What are you going to do now you know?"

Brian's pulse was racing so fast he thought he was going to explode. Either that or smack the smirk off Donny's mouth.

The other boy must have sensed what he was feeling, because he shifted slightly out of reach.

"Tell you what, why don't we go where it's more comfy. Jack, you stay here and keep a lookout. If your old gran or grand-dad comes back, stall them."

"But Donny –" pleaded Jack.

Donny pinched Jack's cheek. "Such a mitherer. Give 'em a bloody clout if you have to . . . No, no, silly, I'm joking. We won't be long so they probably won't be back until I finish my chinwag with Bri here. But you're a bloody Boy Scout. You know you've got to be prepared at all times."

He looked at Brian and his eyes were frighteningly cold. Old as death itself. He gestured to the living room.

"Shall we, me old mucker?"

***

Cudmore trotted slightly ahead of Tyler along the passageway, which ended at a fire door. Here a second open walkway branched off to the left.

"That passageway leads to Section A. As you can see, it is separated from Section B and there are two blast walls in between. Good thing too, or I'm afraid we would all have gone up in smoke." He shook his head. "Such dangerous work. I confess to being a coward in this regard, Inspector. I wouldn't do it."

He pushed open the door directly in front of them and they went inside.

"This is where the assembly of the filled fuses is completed. And here, alas, is where the explosion occurred."

Immediately they were assailed by the acrid smell of cordite and burnt wood and the other, more subtle, but to Tyler unmistakable, stink of torn flesh and spilled blood. Not even the overlay of carbolic cleaning fluid could mask it.

The room was long and low-ceilinged, with no windows. Light was filtering through a canvas tarpaulin covering a huge hole in the roof. There were two workbenches. One had collapsed into a heap of blackened shards and splinters. The other was in two pieces and was lying on its side where it had presumably been blown.

Tyler began to walk slowly around the area, which had obviously been scrubbed clean. Not conducive to a crime investigation, but he could understand the impulse.

"What would the women have been working on?"

Cudmore had obviously been anticipating some question of the sort. "I'm more familiar with the administrative side of operations so I thought I'd better write everything down." He took a notebook from his inner pocket and flipped it open. "Perhaps I should start with the work that is done in Section A. As I said, the prepared casings are taken there first, where they are filled with the explosive. Five-grain ASA powder. We tend to use the words *detonator* and *fuse* interchangeably, although that is probably not quite correct."

Tyler nodded. "So far it's clear, Mr. Cudmore."

"The fuses are the vital part of the shells," continued the secretary. "Without a live fuse, the shell casing itself, even with the cordite inside, is inert, not dangerous at all unless you set fire to it, which is what the fuse is supposed to do. Some are timed to explode in the air, where they do their damage by creating shrapnel. Artillery use those."

"I've had experience with that kind of shell, Mr. Cudmore."

"The Great War, I presume, sir?" He sighed. "Who'd ever have thought we'd be embroiled in another world conflict within a generation?"

"Who indeed."

"Well, then, where was I? Oh yes. The shells we fill here at Endicott's are meant to explode on impact. That is why we are dealing with such volatile powders. Section A operatives fill the fuses with the powder. There are usually eight operatives. Seven here in Section B. Yesterday there were three absentees, one from Section A and two from B. I suppose they are considering themselves lucky." He went back to his notebook. "The fuses, which are now filled and therefore potentially lethal, are then conveyed in a special box to the magazine shed, which is located between the two sections." He pointed to the end of the room. "As you can see it is closed off by a fire door. And again I have to say thank goodness for that. The magazine-keeper counts the number of fuses and then they are brought to Section B, where they are finally assembled." He hesitated. "Perhaps I should mention, sir, that when I was speaking to the supervisor, she did say there was some problem with the tally."

"What sort of problem?"

"I'm not sure exactly. The magazine-keeper should be able to tell you. He is Phil Riley. I've underlined his name and written MK beside it."

"Thank you, Mr. Cudmore. Anyway, do go on. We have the operatives in Section B assembling the fuses. How do they do that?"

"The first girl takes fifty at a time from one of the special pots that are in the box. This is referred to as 'traying up.' She attaches each fuse to a plug, which she then hands over to the girl seated next to her. That operative places the plug and fuse into a holder and screws it in place."

"That sounds like a lot of handling for what is, as you say, a potentially lethal weapon."

"Yes, sir, I agree." Cudmore bit his lip. "We probably need more supervision but we always seem to be short-handed. There is one supervisor to oversee both sections. She has to go back and forth. She was in the magazine room when the explosion happened. Normally she would have been in here. She is devastated. Strictly speaking, she is not supposed to let the girls tray up on their own. Obviously they went ahead without her. She feels terrible guilt, the poor woman, terrible guilt."

"I can imagine she would."

"I've marked her name. Mrs. Valerie Castleford. Very decent sort. Tragic all round, isn't it, sir. The families of the dead suffer as well."

Tyler knew all about that. "How are the detonators conveyed from place to place?"

"The dillie man does all that."

"Dillie man?"

"Er, that's what we call him, sir. Don't know why, come to think of it, but he has a trolley with rubberized wheels. That's the dillie. There's a man on each shift. I've marked their names. The one who works the morning shift is Mick Smith. A good, reliable worker who's been with us for three months. He had already left the premises when the accident occurred. The dillie man on the afternoon shift is Joe Abbott, a very experienced worker. He's been with Endicott's for decades. In fact, his daughter is our resident nurse. She was off duty yesterday but she rushed here to help." He couldn't suppress a shudder. "She was invaluable in dealing with the situation."

"Where was Mr. Abbott?"

"He wasn't yet in the factory. In the interest of efficiency, some workers such as the dillie men and the canteen workers don't report for duty until the shift has started. No sense in them sitting around, is there?"

"Not if they are on an hourly wage." Tyler gazed up at the ceiling. "That's a bloody big hole, Mr. Cudmore."

"Yes, sir. I suppose we must be thankful we still have some of the roof left at all."

"How many detonators would be in here at a time?"

"Each magazine box holds six pots, each of which contains five hundred detonators."

Tyler whistled softly. "Three thousand all together. No wonder the hole is that big."

He moved closer to the devastated benches.

"Who was sitting where? Do you have that information?"

"Yes, sir." Cudmore tore a piece of paper from his notebook. "Here is a diagram that might help. There were also two carpenters in the room, repairing one of the benches. I've written in their names." He shook his head. "Nobody is really supposed to be in the working area other than the operatives, but the men had to replace the linoleum on one of the benches. As I understand it, the shift was late arriving in their places so the men probably thought they'd seize their chance . . . They are both in the hospital. One is quite seriously injured, but both survived, thank the Lord."

"You say the shift was late? Why was that?"

"Apparently the door to the changing room was found to be locked and it took a while for a key to be located. I believe the entire shift was delayed by close to fifteen minutes."

"I thought you said the doors weren't usually locked."

"No, they're not. When I spoke to Mrs. Castleford, she had no explanation."

Tyler sighed. "When do you think I can start interviewing people? The sooner the better, I think, if we're going to get to the bottom of this."

"I can have word out to some of the employees to come in this afternoon if you wish, sir. They will be expecting it."

Tyler took another walk around the perimeter of the shattered bench. Funny how smell was so evocative. He had a sudden disturbing memory of the tragedy he'd had to deal with this past summer. There was the same odour of charred wood and, worse, burned bodies, smelling like overcooked meat.

He watched as a puff of dust floated up to the ceiling, as ephemeral as life itself.

Tyler had a look around Section A but it didn't tell him anything new. Like Section B, the building was low and shed-like. No windows here either, just mercury lamps and two benches.

Cudmore, again consulting his notebook, ran through the procedures.

"The explosive powder has to be weighed carefully. Too much and the shell will blow up prematurely; too little and it's a dud. The four operatives on this bench do nothing but weigh and measure. They then pass the containers over to the other bench, where they are emptied into the casings. It is not a complicated procedure by any means, but it does require absolute concentration."

"If anything was wrong at this point, would it be detected?"

"In terms of the correct amount of explosive, there are two operatives who each have the same function, so they act as a double check on each other. If what you mean is could a defective fuse be sent out to Section B, I'd say no. The calibration is inspected here as well as when it first leaves the floor."

"There are a lot of fuses to inspect."

"True, but we are meticulous. Each fuse will go through at least three checks before it gets to Section B."

Tyler rubbed at the back of his hand, which had started to itch. The cordite powder was fine as mist in the air. "I hope the operatives get good wages for this work, Mr. Cudmore."

"They do, sir. Not as much as men who do the same work, mind you, but that's what's laid down and that's what I have to follow."

"Do the women mind this inequality?"

"I've heard a few complaints but mostly they accept it." He smiled at Tyler. "We can't change the world overnight, can we. A lot of the men in the factory were very opposed to having women work here at all. But I think they've proved they can do it."

"The women are fortunate to have such an advocate as you, Mr. Cudmore." *Might as well put into practice the secretary's own labour principles,* thought Tyler. *Praise when due.*

St. Elizabeth's Hospital had been newly built when he was last in Birmingham, but as he approached the entrance he thought it already looked shabby. Maybe it was just his own jaundiced view being projected onto the world. Or maybe it was the war and the grinding down of the spirit that it brought with it.

Like the police station, the hospital had layers of sandbags all around its base.

As he went into the lobby, a young woman came hurrying out. "Beg pardon," she muttered as she stepped out of his path. She wasn't wearing a nurse's cloak but rather a drab mackintosh and felt cloche hat pulled down low. He had an impression of immense distress and he wondered what her reason was for being in the hospital. *Mind your own business, Tyler,* he said to himself. *You should be used to sorrow by now.*

A harried-seeming probationer directed him to the second floor surgical ward, although she tried to impress on him that visiting hours weren't until the afternoon. "Except in extreme cases," she added quietly.

"This is such a case, I'm afraid," said Tyler.

She didn't evince any curiosity. Perhaps all the visitors said that.

The ward held thirty or so beds, all close together. Other than one nurse carrying out a bedpan, it was empty of staff. A few patients were sitting beside their beds but most were lying under the covers. Those who could watched him curiously as he approached the nurses' station in the centre of the floor. The nurse's name plate identified her as A. Ruebotham, RN.

"Yes? Can I help you?" Her tone was cool and polite, the implication clear. *Didn't he know visiting hours weren't until this afternoon?*

He had his identity card at the ready as he introduced himself. She examined the card carefully, satisfied herself he was genuine, and got to her feet.

"Come this way, Inspector. We've put both young women at the end of the ward for a little privacy." She led the way, her shoes squeaking on the linoleum floor. Everything about her struck Tyler as crisp: her white uniform and starched cap, her voice, even the way she walked. The kind of nurse you were always glad to have looking after you. Always certain in an uncertain world.

As they went past one elderly patient, the woman called out, "Sister, Sister."

"Excuse me for a moment, Inspector," said the nurse and she went over to the patient. They had a whispered conversation, which Tyler could tell had to do with him. The nurse straightened up, patted the woman's arm, and returned. He raised his eyebrows questioningly.

"She wondered if you were a doctor."

"She didn't seem to be happy at the prospect."

"She thinks redheads tend to be too excitable," said Miss Ruebotham with a little smile.

"She's right about that," replied Tyler.

The nurse halted in front of a screened-off bed. "This is Miss Audrey Sandilands. I'm afraid she has not regained consciousness. Her condition is critical."

She moved aside the screen. Tyler took one look. It was obvious that Audrey, sustained by tubes, would not now, if ever, be able to answer his questions. He shook his head at the nurse and she replaced the screen.

"The other young woman is over here," she said. "Her condition is serious but she is expected to survive."

She rolled away the screen at the adjoining bed. Tyler stood stock still. He couldn't help himself.

The girl was as pale as her sheets. Deep bruises circled her eyes and there was an ugly cut along her jaw. One arm was hidden underneath a protective frame; the other lay on top of the cover, the hand heavily bandaged.

When he'd last seen her, she had been tanned and blooming with youth and health. She was one of the Land Girls who had been involved in his last case in Whitchurch.

***

Donny had plopped himself down at the living room table. Brian sat down across from him.

"Have a fag." Donny shook out a cigarette and shoved the packet across the table.

Brian ignored it. "What's your proposition?"

Donny took his time, apparently savouring the taste. "Simple really. Dead bloody simple. I don't turn you in and in return you do some work for me."

"Like what?"

"As I recall you were in the electrics business before the army got you over the barrel with your cheeks spread. I'd like you to make me a couple of timers."

"For what?"

"Does it matter?"

"Of course it matters. Timers can do anything. I'll bet you don't want it to flush your toilet. Do you want to make a bomb?"

"You've got it, Bri. Hit the bloody nail on the head."

Brian pushed back his chair in agitation. "You're nuts. What are you going to do, blow up the police station?"

"How'd you guess? No, joke – I'm joking, dope. It's not the sodding police station. That's not what I had in mind. At least, not right away. You've been away so you don't know what it's like here when there's a bleedin' attack. Lots of opportunity for those who can take it. People run out to their shelters, leaving their houses unprotected. As wide open as a whore's you-know-what. Just there for the asking."

"So you go looting. That doesn't involve a bomb."

"Who said anything about a bleedin' bomb? I didn't. Let's put it this way: sometimes it's helpful if you can get something started and you're not there, if you get my meaning."

"No, I don't."

"Never mind. It's not important why I want a bloody timer. Let's just say I do." He started to fiddle with the cigarette packet, and Brian was taken aback to see that underneath the bravado he was nervous. Donny Jarvis nervous? What the hell was he going to come up with?

"You see, I have a good mate – a partner, you might say – who is in need of a . . . demolition expert." Donny blew out a smoke ring and watched it in admiration. "My mate isn't in favour of this bleedin' war and he'd like to do what he can to put a spanner in the works."

"With a bomb."

"Will you stop with the sodding bomb talk? There are lots of other ways to slow down munitions production."

"You're saying he's a fifth columnist?"

"Something like that. Me, I don't give a rat's arse about philosophies, and sod the greater good and what-have-you. I just want to get by."

"Look, you grubby piece of shite," yelled Brian, "you can turn me in if you want to, I don't give a fuck. I'm not getting involved in anything that gets people killed."

Donny's hand went to his pocket. "Fuck me. I had no idea you were a man of bloody principle, Bri. Not seeing as how you left your mates in the bleedin' lurch and all that. But take it easy, nobody will get hurt. We're just going to create a disruption is all."

"So it is a bomb you're planning?"

"Bloody hell, Bri, you're not listening, are you. I've asked you to make me a couple of timers. That's it."

Brian began to pace, hitting his fist into his palm for emphasis. "Let me get this straight. You say you're not a communist and you don't care. What's in it for you, then?"

Donny grinned his feral grin. "That ain't important. You should be asking what's in it for you. And I'll tell, since you need to know. I said I had a bleedin' proposition, didn't I? Fair's fair. Not only will I not turn you in, you do this for me and me mate and in return we'll get you a safe passage to Ireland. You and your missus."

"What!"

"I mean it, I swear on my mother's grave. Your old lady can join you there for the duration."

"That could be years."

"Naw. Six months at most. Jerry's already winning the sodding war."

"You're talking about the occupation of Britain by Nazis."

"That's right. It's bloody inevitable." He smirked. "You've got nothing to lose, if you think about it, and everything to gain. Come on, Bri. If you believed in this war you wouldn't have gone AWOL, would you. Admit it."

It wasn't like that. Brian had no clearly defined thoughts about whether or not this was a just war that he believed in. Nothing so lofty. But deserting and being a traitor were two different things in his mind. Donny was asking him to be a traitor.

"Making a couple of bombs – oh sorry, I mean a couple of timers – isn't going to bring about the end of the war any more quickly."

For a moment Donny dropped the masquerade. "What makes you think it's only going to be a couple of bombs? This isn't a sodding poncey boys' club we're talking about, Bri. We're frigging serious. Look at it like an incendiary. Not so powerful in itself, but when it spreads – watch out. One bomb can set a whole bloody city ablaze, and after that, the country."

Brian guffawed. "My God, Donny, you should hear yourself. That's the worst kind of shite I've heard in a while. Who's your ventriloquist? You couldn't come up with rubbish like that on your own, that's for sure."

Donny's façade cracked, and briefly raw, primitive anger showed through. Brian had scored a hit. He tried to balance his weight so he could be ready for an attack if it came. His heart was pounding and he was giddy.

"No need to insult a pal," said Donny. "Anyways, whether you believe me or not don't matter a piss. I know it's true. So whaddya think? All I want from you is to make the timers."

"People will be killed."

"No, they won't. They might get some plaster dust in their golden tresses, but it won't be serious unless you're the kind of silly bint who considers that the end of the world." Again he gave his funny grin, his scar showing white on his lip.

"Where am I going to get the materials?"

"We'll bring them to you. Jackie, your cheeky little brother, is being most helpful. He can be our go-between."

"And if I say no?"

Donny shrugged. "That's your bloody choice, of course, but that don't make no sense. Here I am offering you freedom: papers that can get you into Ireland. You'll be able to walk about, come and go, just like anybody else. You won't be shut up in a bleedin' house, hiding under the bleedin' bed with the po. But on the other hand, if the frogs did receive a little tip, quietly over the phone, that's it – off you go. They'll throw away the bleedin' key to the glasshouse. That is, if they don't hang you first."

Brian stared at him. He could feel a sour taste in his mouth.

"Ooh, you do have a mad face on, Bri."

"I could turn myself in and blow the whole story."

Donny nodded as sagely as any judge. "You could, Bri, you could. But I know you won't do that."

"How the fuck can you be so sure of that?"

"Her name's Vanessa."

"What d'you mean?"

"I'm sure you'd like to see your wife. What man wouldn't? She's a smasher, that one. You do what I ask and you'll see her soon. You don't and . . ."

Brian sat down and ran his fingers through his hair. His head was throbbing.

Finally he said. "I'll do it."

"Jolly good, old top." Donny stood up and stubbed out his cigarette on the floor. "Like I said, Jackie will be our messenger boy. He'll bring you the stuff you need. No need to wait. Get 'em done right away and Bob's your uncle, off you go to

Paddy land. And Bri . . . don't try to be a bloody hero. It's too late for that. I've told Jackie to get in touch with your Vanessa. He's going to bring her to you tonight. That's nice of me, wouldn't you say?"

"What if she can't come tonight?" Brian blurted out.

"Don't worry. I'm sure she's as keen to see you as you are to see her." Donny actually licked his lips – "From what I've heard, she likes a bit of dock, does your wife."

Brian couldn't hold back. He grabbed Donny by the lapels, almost spitting into his face. "What's that supposed to mean?"

He could see that his outburst pleased Donny. He let him go immediately, but it was too late. Donny had evened the score. He'd hit the Achilles heel.

"Doesn't mean bloody anything other than what you want it to bloody well mean. She's a tasty bit of crumpet and you're still newlyweds, aren't you. She'll have missed getting it. That's all. Now come and see me out before the old lady gets back."

Brian followed him into the hallway. Jack was sitting on the stairs. He was picking at a scab on his knee.

Donny patted his head as if he were a dog. "Good boy, Jack. We've done our business. Your brother will tell you all about it. Ta-ta." He pulled his muffler around his face, opened the door, and slipped away. The fog was creeping back and it lingered on the doorstep, sour as ever.

Brian turned to look at his brother. Jack looked so desperately miserable Brian could hardly feel angry at him.

"Bri . . . I'm so sorry . . ." He was starting to cry.

Brian ruffled his hair. "It's done now. As it is, it might all be to the good. Now you'd better get going. You've got a job to do for me. You're going to talk to Vanessa."

"Right."

"What are you going to tell her?"

"Donny felt it was best if I said you were at home but she couldn't tell anybody until you talked to her. National security."

"Great, she's going to think I'm a frigging spy. Well, never mind. I don't want her coming here to the house. I need more privacy. Tell her to meet me in the shelter. But late. Midnight."

"What if there's a raid?"

"There won't be. Weather's too bad for the bleeders to try tonight."

The boy nodded fearfully. "Ta-ta, Bri." He left.

Brian went into the living room. His throat felt so tight he was afraid he might choke. He sat down and put his head in his hands. They'd know at the barracks by now that he'd gone AWOL. The redcaps would come for him soon.

Could he trust Donny Jarvis? Was it possible to get away to some kind of peace? He and Vanessa? Would she come with him? Oh God, he hoped so with all his heart.

***

Tyler looked questioningly at the nurse.

She said quietly, "Her right arm was severed in the blast and the fingers on her left hand were so damaged they had to be amputated." She sighed. "It's especially hard on girls to lose their ring finger. This young lady had a lovely engagement ring. The ambulance men collected it. We cleaned it up and put it in that dish. Frankly, I'm not sure if that is the best thing to do or not. She hasn't taken in the extent of her injuries yet. Her fiancé is apparently overseas."

Miss Ruebotham indicated that Tyler should bring the one chair as close to the bed as he could. She bent over the girl. "Miss Sumner, Miss Sumner. There is a police officer here who wants to ask you some questions. Do you understand?"

Sylvia was obviously deeply sedated, but her eyelids fluttered and she gave the faintest of nods.

Tyler leaned in. "Hello, Sylvia. It's Inspector Tyler from Whitchurch. Remember me?"

The corners of her mouth turned up a little. "I'm not at the hostel, am I?" Her voice was as faint as a bird's cry on the wind.

"No, you're not," replied Tyler. "I'm working in Brum for now. I've been asked to look into the explosion at the factory. Do you remember it? Are you up to talking to me, lass?"

Sylvia didn't respond immediately. It was as if she were at the bottom of a deep pit and the sound of his voice was delayed before it reached her. Finally she said, "Is Tess all right?"

Tyler glanced at the nurse, who shook her head. "Don't worry about the others now, Miss Sumner. Just do your best to answer the inspector's questions."

"If it gets to be too much, I'll stop," Tyler said softly. "Can you tell me what you remember? Do you know what happened?"

Sylvia ran her tongue over dry lips. "Can I have a drink?"

Miss Ruebotham poured a glass of water.

"I'll give it to her," said Tyler, and he slipped his hand behind the girl's head so she could drink. She sipped a little, then waved it away. He eased her back onto the pillow.

Her eyes looked into his. "Is Irma all right? And Prue and Audrey?"

Again the nurse deflected the question. "Never mind all that for now."

Tyler could see the alarm on Sylvia's face. "They're not dead, are they?"

Miss Ruebotham made a tutting sound. "We can talk about that later. We just want you to concentrate on getting well." She indicated that Tyler should continue.

"Sylvia, was there anything different about yesterday? Any change in procedure or that sort of thing?"

"Prue and Audrey moved . . . our bench . . . two workmen at the other bench. We were late . . . Mrs. Castleford said we could tray up ourselves . . . she had to count something with Mr. Riley." The effort of speaking was rapidly tiring her out. "And Audrey started . . . she's thin as a stick . . . a man touched her in the fog . . ." She fell silent and her eyelids drooped.

"Try to stay awake, there's a good girl," said the nurse, and she snapped her fingers next to Sylvia's ear.

Sylvia blinked. "Is my mum here?"

"She's arriving later today," Miss Ruebotham answered.

Tyler tried again. "Did the explosion happen when you were traying up?"

Sylvia struggled with her answer. "Yes, I think so. There was a terrible bang. And it was hot. So hot. I think my hand got burned." She moved her head restlessly. The memory clearly distressed her. The nurse was making signs to indicate Tyler should finish up.

"Sylvia . . ." He had to wait for her to float once more to the surface of her consciousness. "Sylvia, can you think of anything that might have caused the detonators to go off?"

"Audrey . . . Audrey pulled the pot. I told her to be careful. It was wobbling . . ."

"Is that usual? Have you seen the pot wobble at other times?"

Sylvia didn't seem to hear the question. "My hand hurts." She struggled to sit upright. "What's happened to my arm . . . my hand hurts . . . what? Inspector, what's happened to my arm?"

Miss Ruebotham all but shoved Tyler out of the way. "I think that's enough for now, Inspector."

He stood up and left the matron thrusting a hypodermic needle into Sylvia's arm. Her cries followed him out of the ward.

"What . . . what happened to my arm . . . Where's Colin? Is he dead? Who's died? What's happened? Inspector, don't leave me . . ."

Neither of the two men who'd also been injured in the explosion were able to speak to Tyler. Doug Aston was in critical condition and Peter Pavely could hear nothing except an appalling ringing in his ears. He was sedated.

Tyler decided to walk back to the factory. Not too far from the hospital, one of the streets had been badly damaged in Friday's raid. Most of the houses had been reduced to rubble. Watched over by a solitary constable, some residents were picking through the ruins of their homes. They seemed stoic, almost apathetic, but Tyler knew how much grief and anger lay beneath the surface. He shared it with them.

An elderly woman was sitting on what remained of her front steps. She was bareheaded and dressed in a threadbare black coat. She was stroking a tabby cat lying on her lap. It was obviously dead.

Tyler stopped. "Are you all right, ma'am? Can I do anything for you?"

The woman looked up at him with red-rimmed eyes. "He hated being in the shelter, so I left him in the house when the alarm sounded." She waved at the debris behind her. "We got a direct hit. I was in the shelter but the warden looked for Boots for me. They found him lying by the door. I shouldn't have left him."

At that moment a warden came up who seemed to know the woman. He was carrying a canvas bag.

"Now then, Mrs. Paget. You won't do him or yourself any good sitting here. You'll catch your death of cold. Let's get the moggie properly buried, then we'll go to the first-aid post and get you a nice hot cup of char. There's a couple of ladies there who'll help you see what else you can salvage." He nodded at Tyler. "I'll take care of her." He took the limp cat from her arms and put it gently into the canvas bag.

"I shouldn't have left him," the woman muttered.

Tyler wasn't sure if his stomach was churning for want of food or from a need for warmth and company, but before he returned to the factory, he decided to follow up on Alf's recommendation to eat at the British Restaurant. The place was steamy, noisy, and crowded. He looked around. There were a few men in overcoats and trilbies who were probably from the nearby government offices. A handful of women with baskets on their arms he guessed had been shopping. However, he knew without being told that many of the customers were victims of the bombing raids. Some of them had likely been given meal vouchers by the local wvs. They were the quiet ones who were hunched over, their hands cupped around their bowls of soup as if they could pull the warmth into the core of themselves.

The food was served canteen style and Tyler joined the queue.

"Wot's it to be, sir?" The woman behind the counter held her serving spoon in mid-air. He hesitated. "New here, aren't ya," she said.

He grinned. "How do you know?"

"You've got a country look to ya."

"I, er –" Tyler didn't know how to respond to that.

"Us Brummies get pasty-like. You look like you've been out in the fresh air."

She was a nice-looking woman, close to his own age, he'd guess. She didn't look pasty, but maybe the steam from the hot plates had given her some colour.

"Where you from, then?" she asked.

"Shropshire. Whitchurch."

She beamed. "Oh, I know Whitchurch. Went there a few times when I was a nipper. We had relatives that ran a pub down in Wem. The White Horse. Ever heard of it?"

Tyler shook his head. "No, I haven't. And I thought I knew most of the pubs in the vicinity."

A man standing behind Tyler burst out in exasperation, "You two going to go through your entire life stories or what? Can we get a move on?"

"No need to get riled up," said the server to the other man. "He hasn't been here before." She turned back to Tyler. "You get your complete meal for elevenpence. Today we have shepherd's pie and two veg, which today is peas and carrots, and your pudding, which today is treacle pudding."

"Don't forget he also gets a roll or slice of bread and butter and a cup of tea or coffee," said the man, his voice heavy with sarcasm.

"I was coming to that," said the server. "Is that what you'd like then, dear?" she asked Tyler.

He wasn't about to refuse after all the fuss. "Thanks. Sounds good."

She made up the tray. "Tomorrow we've got Irish stew. It's good and filling. You should come back."

Tyler paid his elevenpence and carried his tray to an empty table by the window.

The man who'd been behind him in the queue followed.

"Mind if I join you?"

Tyler would like to have told the miserable sod to get lost but he just nodded politely. The man sat down and started to unload his tray. He immediately stuffed some of the bread and butter into his mouth, and began talking through unchewed food.

"Blimey, I thought she wasn't going to stop offering what was on tap," he said, spitting bread crumbs as he spoke. "Wish

I could get that kind of service. Must be that good country fresh air you're giving off that attracts them."

Tyler cut into the shepherd's pie. "Must be. Can't think of any other explanation."

"You here on business?" the man asked.

"Sort of."

"I bet I can guess what you do," the man continued, undeterred. "You're an insurance agent. Am I right?"

Tyler stared at him. "What makes you think that?"

"I can always tell. It's the tie, you see. You can tell what a man does by his tie. Yours is quiet, you might say, nothing flashy. Don't want to draw attention to yourself."

Tyler couldn't help but notice that his companion was wearing a brightly coloured tie that appeared to have been liberally sprinkled with brown sauce. Or maybe that was the pattern.

"Besides which," continued the man, "you've got what I'd call a careful look to you. Sizing people up all the time, you are. Well? Am I right? You're in the insurance business, aren't you."

Tyler had to laugh. "Something like that."

Fortunately for Tyler, his unwanted dinner companion soon saw somebody he knew and went to sit with him. Tyler scarfed down his meal and, with a wave to the friendly server, hurried back the factory.

Cudmore was waiting for him outside the cubbyhole.

"Mr. Riley showed up on his own account. Would you like to see him this afternoon?"

"I would. Did you get hold of anybody else?"

"Only two others, I'm sorry to say. I was able to get word to Mick Smith, the dillie man on the first shift. He is here. I asked him to wait in the canteen until you could speak to him. Our second dillie man, Joe Abbott, was not at home. We do have the caretaker, Wolfsiewicz. He is here every day. Mrs. Castleford is under doctor's orders to rest but her husband will bring her in tomorrow. Things will be a little more normal, if I may put it that way, tomorrow and I thought we could cover more ground then."

"More competent thinking, Mr. Cudmore. Right, let's hear what Mr. Riley has to say."

Phil Riley was a short, slim man with horn-rimmed glasses, black hair slicked back from his face, and a pencil-thin moustache. *Fancies himself a bit of a masher*, thought Tyler. The proximity forced on them by the tiny space was uncomfortably intimate. Tyler could smell the pomade that Riley had used on his hair. It looked freshly applied. He'd also augmented his moustache with some kind of black pencil.

"It must have been a dreadful shock to you, what happened on Sunday, Mr. Riley. My job here is to determine what exactly occurred. Just so we make sure it doesn't happen again."

"Good on that," said Riley. He had some kind of accent that Tyler couldn't immediately identify. Maybe North Country?

"I was surprised you came in to work at all today," continued Tyler. "You were given permission to stay at home, I believe."

Riley grimaced. "Yes, we was given permission all right but nobody said we'd get paid, and I can't afford to miss me wages. I've got three nippers at home and a sick wife. I don't have the privilege of staying home."

Tyler made a sympathetic cluck. "I'm with you on that, mate. These toffs don't understand how it works down on the front line, do they?"

Riley scowled. "You can say that again. Nobody docks their wages, do they."

Cudmore melted into the woodwork. Tyler offered Riley a cigarette, which he took and lit hungrily.

"Tell me in your own words what happened on Sunday."

Riley nodded in the direction of the secretary. "No offence, but does Mr. Cudmore need to be here?"

"He's taking notes for me, but he'll leave if you prefer."

"It's just that I don't want anything I say to go beyond this room, if you know what I mean."

"I do," said Tyler. "Mr. Cudmore?"

"Think of me as simply a recording machine."

"Right. Now where were we?"

Riley took a clean handkerchief from his pocket and wiped at his nose. Tyler was rather surprised to see that he seemed on the verge of tears.

"Sorry, sir. Nasty it was." He blew hard into his handkerchief, then folded it carefully away in his pocket. "I was by myself in the magazine shed. It's my job to keep track of the number of detonators that come in and out. Yesterday there was a problem with the count. I was missing fifty detonators. What I had coming in filled from Section A didn't agree with the number that was on the sheet as had been delivered. I was doing a recount. I can't just let the fuses go out without a proper tally, can I."

"And did you find the discrepancy?" Tyler asked.

"Matter of fact, I didn't. We never got back to it, given what happened."

"What did you do when you heard the explosion?"

"I ran out to see what was going on." Riley's shoulders were tense. "It was a horrible sight. I knew all of those girls, you see. Nicer bunch you couldn't hope for." The handkerchief came out again and Tyler waited until Riley could continue.

"I should have been more helpful, I know I should, but I didn't know what to do. Fortunately we've been well drilled on fires and there were men from the floor on the spot. The one bench was burning and there was a hole in the roof, but they had the hose on it. I just made sure the other workers were got out of the building. We didn't know if the whole thing was going to blow, you see."

"Quick thinking, Mr. Riley," murmured Cudmore, and Riley gave him a nod of gratitude.

"Mr. Riley, in your opinion is there any bad feeling among the workers that might lead them to . . . lead them to try to disrupt the work of the factory, for instance?"

"Blimey. You mean sabotage? Fifth-column stuff?"

"You could call it that."

Riley shook his head emphatically. "Not here. Sure, there's the odd whingeing and moaning, but everybody knows we're in this together. Besides, it's too dangerous to play around. The whole damn – excuse me – the whole darned place could blow up if the Danger Section explodes."

He was making a good point, Tyler thought. If it was sabotage, the saboteur was taking quite a risk with his own safety, unless he was able to plan to get out of the way in good time. "And as far as you know, none of the operatives would have been the target of a personal attack?"

Riley stared at Tyler as if he had lost his mind. "An attack? Like an assassination? What we'd like to do on Hitler?"

"Something of that sort."

"How could that be? There wasn't anybody important in that section."

Tyler knew what he meant but he couldn't help thinking about what Cudmore had told him. One of the women had two children. She was certainly important to them.

"Mr. Riley, I'd like to have a look at the actual fuses. Would that be possible?"

"The empty ones are stacked in the magazine shed. You can see those."

"Good. Let's go, shall we."

The shed was situated between the two sections, which were connected to it by short passageways. It was long and narrow but it did have windows, although they were small and high up. Wooden boxes were stacked on shelves that lined one of the walls.

"Walk me through what happens to the fuses, will you, Mr. Riley."

The magazine-keeper indicated a ramp that led up to the door. "The dillie man brings the filled fuses in that entrance. They're in a box such as is on the shelves here. He's picked them up from Section A, where they've been filled with powder. He puts the box down here." He pointed. "I count them and check them against the delivery slip that he gives me. He's got that from the lorry that brings the casings to the factory. While I'm doing me counting, dillie man goes out that exit ramp to Section B with another magazine box that's been marked all present and correct. That's it, really. I divide me time between here and Section A, where I help supervise what's being done."

"The dillie man doesn't wait while you do the count?"

"Not usually. He's coming and going with his deliveries."

Tyler removed a black pot from one of the boxes. It was light, made of some sort of papier mâché, and cylindrical in shape. He placed it on the floor and, squatting down, he tapped it with his finger. It wobbled a little. He gave it a harder tap and it fell over.

"It's not very stable," he said to Riley.

"I know. Mind you, when it's filled with fuses, it's heavier, but I've never thought it was very safe myself."

"The centre of gravity should be higher."

"I think you're right there, Inspector."

Tyler replaced the pot in the box.

Cudmore was standing at the head of the exit ramp, and with Tyler and Riley in the middle of the floor, the space felt cramped.

"There's not a lot of room in here, is there, Mr. Riley?"

"No, there aren't."

Tyler went on. "When you were counting the detonators for the second time, was anybody else with you?"

"What do you mean by that, sir?"

"Earlier you said, *we*. 'We never got back to it.' Was anyone else helping you with the count?"

"No, sir."

"Not the dillie man, for instance?"

"No."

"So you were by yourself?"

Riley slapped at his own head. "Blimey, I almost forgot. I asked the supervisor of the incoming shift to give me a hand. But we'd only just got started when the explosion happened."

"I understand that is Mrs. Castleford?"

Riley nodded. He was looking decidedly uncomfortable.

"Did she go with you to see what had happened?"

"Lord, no. I'd a feeling it was going to be bad. You don't get a bang like that in a munitions factory without it being bad. I made her stay where she was while I went and checked."

Tyler glanced over at Cudmore, whose expression was inscrutable. "Thank you, Mr. Riley. That's all for now. You've been most helpful."

Tyler insisted that Riley go home, and Cudmore promised him he would in fact be paid overtime for coming in today.

"Mick Smith is waiting in the canteen," said the secretary. "Shall I fetch him?"

"Seeing as there's nobody in, why don't I talk to him there. My, er, office quarters are on the tight side."

"Sorry, Inspector. But by all means we can move operations. I can probably make us some tea if you'd like."

"Tea all round, Mr. Cudmore."

He followed the secretary back to the factory floor. A few dim lights were on around the periphery but the place was deep in shadow. The canteen was brighter but also empty except for a man reading a newspaper at one of the tables and a cleaner in overalls who was mopping the floor.

As they came over towards him, the man put away his paper at once and leapt to his feet. Cudmore introduced him as Mick Smith and he and Tyler shook hands. Cudmore explained they would do the interview there in the canteen.

"Fine with me," said Smith.

Tyler indicated the cleaner. "Maybe he could go somewhere else for the time being."

"I'll take care of it, sir," said Cudmore.

He was about to rush off when Tyler stopped him. "Oh, Mr. Cudmore, you said the caretaker was in the factory yesterday. I might as well speak to him next."

"I'll let him know."

He trotted off and Tyler sat down at the table across from Smith. He was probably in his early forties, dark complexioned, with dark, curly hair cut close. There was something of a Gypsy look to him.

Tyler offered him a cigarette. "We'll just wait for Mr. Cudmore if you don't mind. He's taking notes for me."

Smith grinned. "Good secretary then, in'e?" He lit the cigarette and they smoked in silence until Cudmore returned with two cups of tea. Tyler took a swallow, as did Smith.

"Strong enough to stand by itself, as my granny would say."

"And sweet enough to charm any man," added Smith.

Tyler put down his cup and gave Smith more or less the same preamble he'd given Riley.

Smith was quiet for a few moments, concentrating on his tea. "To my knowledge, there was nothing different at all in the routine. I picks up the crates containing fuse casings from the lorry, like I usually do, and puts 'em on the conveyor belt so they can be properly calibrated. Then I drives around to where they're coming off the belt. I picks 'em up and transports 'em to Section A. There I picks up a finished box and brings 'em into the magazine shed to be counted. The supervisor, Phil Riley, has to make sure they is present and correct." Smith's accent was pure Brummie and Tyler had a hard time understanding him some of the time.

"And did he? Yesterday, did Mr. Riley make sure all was in order?" he asked.

"Well 'e did and 'e didn't. We was all right at start, but at the end of shift 'e was in a lather because delivery sheet wasn't tallying with number of fuses that had been filled. 'E kept going on about missing some, or having too many. Sorry to say, sir, I didn't pay 'im much mind. 'E's a mitherer and often keeps me back fussing over the numbers, which always turn out to be wrong. So I just carried on and left 'im to sort out the other stuff."

"Was yours the last box to be delivered to Section B before the accident?"

"It was. The first shift hadn't finished their quota. There's often an overlap between shifts, so that wasn't unusual. Normally the dillie man picks up the assembled fuses and takes 'em back to the loading dock. That's when we have to wave our red flag, because we go through the main floor and we don't want anybody walking into us." He tapped his finger to his nose. "I can see what you're thinking, Inspector. Why go through the main floor?"

"I was wondering about that."

"Because Mr. Endicott doesn't want the expense of building a separate passageway, that's why. Am I right, Mr. Cudmore?"

The secretary pursed his lips. "We are looking into it."

Tyler rescued him. "When you were transporting the magazine boxes, Mr. Smith, did you notice anything at all that was out of the ordinary?"

"Begging your pardon, sir, but like what?"

Tyler waved his hand. "Oh, I don't know. Anything. Did the box seem the usual weight or was it heavier than usual? Did any of the pots look damaged?"

"Like I said, sir, I'd swear on my mother's grave the boxes were no different from the usual. And I don't mess around with that stuff. No, sir. Them's deadly weapons we're dealing with. No, I would have noticed if anything was tampered with . . . which is what you're getting at, isn't it?"

"Frankly, I'm treating this incident as an accident. I'm more interested if you noticed if the pots were badly packed or something like that."

"No, sir, I didn't see that they were."

Tyler finished his tea. "You did say 'tampered with,' Mr. Smith. If such a thing had happened, God forbid, but if it had, do you yourself have an opinion as to how it might have occurred?"

Smith contemplated the question with pursed lips. "Truth to tell, sir, I don't. It's not that the detonators are guarded exactly but they are always somebody's responsibility. I'm not keen to blow myself up, nor I doubt is Phil Riley nor Joe Abbott, who is the afternoon dillie man. 'E does the same job I do."

"You've got a point there. Are the fuses always within your view?"

"While they're on my trolley they are."

"And by the same token, are you yourself always within sight of the other workers?"

Smith had gone back to his cigarette, and he blew out some more smoke. "Come to think of it, there's two places where I'm not. When I get the casings from the loading bay, I'm on the floor with the other workers. But when I've got the finished ones from the conveyor belt, I exit through a fire door to Section A. You can see it from here if you look down. If you think of yourself coming into the main floor as facing north, which strictly speaking you're not, but anyways, let's say you're facing north. The exit to the passageway is northeast. The loading dock is northwest. With me so far?"

"I am indeed, Mr. Smith. Please go on."

"So I go through that fire door with me casings by way of a short connecting passageway, more of a tunnel really – no windows. Yet another door, just to make my life more difficult, and I'm in Section A. Then they all see me and I see them. After that, with a new load, I come back through the same door into the same passage, but instead of going back to the floor, I veer off into the magazine shed for the count. Mr. Riley is of course in there, and unless he's distracted, he sees me."

Smith was speaking slowly and deliberately as if Tyler were a dull pupil. Either that or he wanted to make sure Cudmore was keeping up. From what Tyler had seen so far, the secretary had no difficulty.

"All right so far, sir?"

Tyler nodded.

"So I'd got myself to the magazine shed, hadn't I."

"Yes, you had. Do go on."

"Me, I don't know why we have to have a count at this stage. I mean, where are the fuses going to go to? If they've come in, as they have, from the floor, there should be exactly the same number of them coming from Section A. However, them's the rules and not for me to question why. So, from the magazine shed I pick up a box that's passed muster and is marked as such and I exits through another short tunnel, which connects into Section B."

He glanced over at Tyler. "Now, you asked me if I was always in somebody's sight. Well, truth is, nobody sees me in those two passageways. If I want to pick my nose or scratch my balls, I can. Begging your pardon, Mr. Cudmore."

The secretary managed a smile.

"And how long are you in each passageway, Mr. Smith?" Tyler asked.

"Less than a minute. Seconds, really. But I get the drift of what you're saying, Inspector. If anybody was doing some dirty work, like, where could they do it?"

"And?"

"Can't tell you. Me, I'm not a loonie. This place, you blow up one thing, the whole lot could go. Like I said, I've not got any desire to do myself in. Too much living I want to do."

"Given the routine as you've described it to me, I'd think that's a lot of moving around for such dangerous material."

"I agree with you there, sir. An awful lot of moving around. It should be looked into. Right, Mr. Cudmore?" He stubbed out his cigarette. "When do you think we can get back to work, sir? We mustn't slow down production. We've got to get the weapons to our soldiers or we're done for."

"You're quite right about that, Mr. Smith. But I'm confident we'll never be defeated. Too much toughness in us Brits for that, wouldn't you say?"

"I certainly would, sir."

"Some areas of the factory will be in operation tomorrow," interjected Cudmore.

"Is that it, then, sir?" Smith asked Tyler.

"Yes, it is. Thanks for your help."

Smith got to his feet. "Just call on me if you need to." He turned smartly on his heel and left.

Tyler gave himself a stretch while he was waiting for Cudmore to fetch the caretaker, who'd been relegated to the kitchen. He thought about the two interviews so far. Riley had seemed nervous and edgy. He was covering something up. Tyler sighed. He guessed it was because Riley was having a bit on the side with Mrs. Castleford. Unfaithfulness in marriage tends to sully the conscience, as he knew only too well. Smith, on the other hand, seemed straightforward enough. He'd made a good point about the excessive moving around of the detonators. That should be looked into. But there was something niggling at the back of Tyler's mind about his Brummie friend. He couldn't put his finger on it.

Cudmore returned. "He'll be here directly, sir." He got his notebook at the ready.

"His name is Dmitri Wolfsiewicz but we all call him Wolf. Easier all round. He's a refugee from Poland. He's been here for three months. Good hard-working fellow. Doesn't speak much English. But then we can hardly blame him. English is such a peculiar language, isn't it."

Tyler blinked at him. "Not anything I've given much thought to, Mr. Cudmore, but you're probably right."

The caretaker appeared. He'd removed his overalls and was wearing a brown tweed suit that was too large for him and practically shouted "donation from the wvs." He was young, probably still in his twenties, but his face was thin to the point of emaciation. He moved like somebody much older.

What had happened to him? Tyler wondered.

"I won't keep you long, Mr. Wolfsiewicz," he said. "Just a few questions." The man looked at him in surprise.

Tyler realized he'd made the common faux pas of speaking more loudly than usual, as if Wolf were hard of hearing rather than short of English. He lowered his voice to a normal volume. "I wonder if you could tell me about Sunday."

"What you like to know?"

"Frankly, anything you can tell me. I'm just trying to work out what happened. I understand you are the caretaker here. Were you in the vicinity when the explosion happened?"

Wolf was watching Tyler's lips as if he were indeed deaf. "Yes, I do caretaking. I was in – on the floor." He spoke slowly, enunciating carefully.

"Do you have any idea what might have set off the explosion?"

Wolf shrugged. "All materials very dangerous."

"Were you in Section B at all yesterday?"

"Yes. I do the clean in between shifts. Wipe floor. I wipe the floor to make sure no powder is there."

"Did you notice anything out of the ordinary?" Tyler could hear himself raising his voice again. He didn't think Wolfsiewicz was deaf, but he spoke so carefully and listened so intently Tyler began to wonder if this was a possibility.

"Two men working at that bench. Not usual. Is that what you mean?"

"Anything else?"

This time the cleaner raised his eyes and looked into Tyler's. His eyes were grey-blue and again Tyler had the impression of age. Not necessarily wisdom, but too much life experience for such a young man.

"I cannot help, I regret. I did my work."

"Did you speak to the men?"

Wolfsiewicz paused. "I exchanged only happinesses."

Tyler thought he meant pleasantries, but he rather liked Wolf's version. He tried a different tack. "I understand you are from Poland."

Wolf nodded but Tyler felt the tension that immediately came over him.

"I hear Warsaw is a beautiful city," he continued.

For the first time there was a flash of animation on Wolfsiewicz's thin face. "Not now."

"I'm sorry to hear that."

"Loss of freedom make all things ugly, Inspector."

Tyler was startled by the response, which was unexpectedly poetic. Ironically, a few years into their marriage he'd tried to persuade Vera to go there for a visit, but she refused. Too far, too foreign, strange language, strange food. They ended up going to Torquay. He often wondered if Vera suspected that Tyler's curiosity about Warsaw had to do with Clare Somerville. She was right, of course. Clare had spent time there as a young woman and spoke of it fondly.

He realized the caretaker was watching him warily. Tyler held out his hand. "Thank you, sir. If anything comes to you, anything at all, please let me know."

The Pole's grip was tentative, his fingers cold.

Cudmore watched him leave. "That poor chap always puts me in mind of Father Edmund Campion."

"Campion? Oh, you're right. The Jesuit priest who was executed by one of Queen Bess's lackeys."

"That's the one. He suffered a hideous death. He was one of those hung, drawn, and quartered."

"God, I remember finding a book about martyrs. Illustrated. Ghastly thing."

"Are you a Catholic, sir?"

"Not me. Church of England to the core."

"I read that same book you mention. Foxe's *Book of Martyrs* was the title. I was fascinated by it. I was raised in the old faith, so my morbidity passed for piety," said Cudmore ruefully.

Another surprising statement.

"It all seems such nonsense from our perspective, doesn't it, sir," he went on. "Who has the *true* faith and all that. But I suppose our loyalty is now called upon in a different way. And we punish the disloyal just as severely."

Tyler nodded. He felt at something of a loss. Cudmore was revealing hidden depths.

"Speaking of which, why was Wolf imprisoned by the Germans?"

"I don't really know, sir. He told me he had disagreed with some edict of the Nazis and he was termed anti-social. He might have been a communist, although he hasn't admitted to that. He was lucky he was released, from what I've heard." Cudmore closed his notebook and snapped the elastic band around it. "I'll start transcribing my notes so far. I'll have them ready for you."

"Thank you, Mr. Cudmore. You have been invaluable." Tyler got to his feet. "I'm going to stop by the hospital to see if I can speak to Peter Pavely. We'll resume in the morning."

The matron on the men's ward at St. Elizabeth's was even more formidable than Nurse Ruebotham.

"Mr. Aston is still in a coma, Inspector," she said to Tyler with a frown. "He cannot have any visitors. Mr. Pavely has been seriously injured and must not be disturbed unless it is absolutely necessary."

"Believe me, Matron, I would not disturb him unless, in my humble opinion as an officer of the law, it was absolutely necessary to ask him a few questions."

She hardly yielded. "Very well. But I can only allow ten minutes. These patients are my responsibility."

She led him down the ward. Like Sylvia and Audrey, the two injured men had been put at the far end of the ward and their beds were both screened off.

The matron, whose name tag said she was B. Poltin, pulled back the screen so that Tyler could get close to the bed. Pavely turned his head. One eye was bandaged, the other so swollen it was a mere slit.

"This is Inspector Tyler," said the matron. "He wishes to ask you some questions about the accident. Are you able to do so?"

"Yes, I am." He held out his hand to Tyler. "Glad to see you, in a manner of speaking, that is. Ask away."

"Can you tell me what happened yesterday? From your point of view, that is."

"Wish to hell I knew," said Pavely. "Last thing I remember I was fitting a piece of lino onto the bench. It had come loose and me and Doug Aston were fixing it. That's it. Next thing I know, I'm in this hospital with a bloody bandage on my head." He managed to glance over at the matron, who had stationed herself at the foot of the bed. "I'm not swearing, Matron. That's what it is, a bloody bandage."

Pavely shifted his head so he could fix his good eye on Tyler. "They're keeping very mum about what happened, Inspector, but I gather it was serious."

"Yes, it was."

"Fatalities?"

Before Tyler could reply the matron interrupted him. He was starting to think of it as a nurse's reflex.

"All in good time, Mr. Pavely. For now it's better that the inspector ask the questions."

"I gather that's a yes," said Pavely. "Was it my mate? Did Doug get it?"

Tyler patted the man's hand. "Listen, old chap, the matron will fill you in later. I can tell you, though, your mate wasn't killed."

"Thank God for that," muttered Pavely. "He's a good bloke."

"I'm just trying to get to the bottom of what caused the explosion," continued Tyler. "Do you have any idea why the fuses blew up?"

He thought Pavely had closed his eye but it was hard to tell. "Not the foggiest."

"Do you remember the women doing anything unusual?"

"No. They hadn't come in yet."

Tyler didn't want to distress him any more by revealing the truth. He'd encountered this kind of amnesia before. It was the mind's way of protecting itself. Pavely would hear in good time what had happened.

The bloodshot eye focused on him. "I'm not going to wake up and find out it was my fault, am I?"

Tyler patted his arm. "Not a chance. Now get some rest."

He looked in on Sylvia on his way out but she was asleep. "Resting comfortably," said Nurse Ruebotham. Audrey Sandilands was still on the critical list and the nurse shook her head when Tyler enquired about her. "No change," she said. He thought that was nurse-speak for *We don't hold out much hope.*

If he had been a religious man, he would have said a prayer for the two young women.

***

It didn't seem right to go through the charade of celebrating Beatrice's birthday as if there was nothing the matter, when everything was the matter. Eileen waited until Ted and Phyllis had got settled, hats and coats off, hands warmed, and sitting down.

Then she told them about their Brian. Neither of them said a word at first, then Ted spoke. "Am I hearing you right? You're sitting here cool as a cucumber telling us that Brian has run away from the army and is hiding out in this house?" He jumped up as if he was going to run upstairs and confront Brian on the spot. Joe grabbed his arm and pulled him back into his seat.

"Nobody's cool here, Ted, but going off half-cocked isn't going to help anybody, least of all Brian. We've got to talk about what to do."

"What d'you mean? Isn't he going to turn himself in?"

"He doesn't want to do that, no."

Phyllis had looked up at the ceiling when Eileen said Brian was upstairs but she hadn't moved. She sat, still and pale-faced.

"Dad, did he come here first?"

"He was actually hiding out in a bombed-out house down the road a couple of streets. He'd been there since Friday. Young Jack found him and brought him here."

"Our Jack?"

Joe nodded.

"He never said a word to us," burst out Ted.

"We made him promise not to until we sorted things out," said Eileen.

"Is Brian all right?" Phyllis asked finally. Her voice was flat and expressionless.

"Physically he's well enough," said Joe. "Just exhausted, but mentally he's not too good." He nodded over at Eileen. "Your sister can talk about that."

"Look, Ted, Phyl, I know this is a terrible shock. It was to us as well. But Mum and Dad and me have had a talk. Brian is adamant he's not going to turn himself in. If he's caught and tried as a deserter, it could go very badly for him." She paused, not wanting to be cruel but needing to let them know what was at stake. "The army considers desertion a serious crime . . ."

They both stared at her. Phyllis reached for her husband's hand but he ignored her.

Eileen continued. "We don't know how long the war will last, nobody does. The three of us here are willing to hide him until such time as it's all over. But in the meantime we'll need help with food. We'd have to share our rations."

"Jesus," said Ted. "We can barely make do ourselves. How can we support another mouth?"

"We can do it if we're careful," said Beatrice.

"And I'll thank you to watch your language, Ted," said Joe.

"The question is, do you want to?" Eileen addressed both her sister and brother-in-law, but they all knew it was Ted who had to be convinced.

Phyllis pulled a handkerchief from her sleeve and clutched at it. "Of course we want to. But how did it come to this? What did he say?"

"You can ask him yourself if you like. Shall I call him down?"

"No, wait a bleeding minute," exclaimed Ted. "I'm not ready to talk to him. I've got to get some facts straight first . . . In my book cowards run away from their duty, and I don't hold no truck with cowards. Brian has got a lot of explaining to do, if you ask me."

"Are you saying you'd turn in your own son?" Phyllis cried.

"Don't put words in my mouth, Phyllis. All I'm *saying* is I'd like to hear his story before I make any decision. I'm a government employee, don't forget. Do you realize that if we do cover up for him and he is found, we're going to be in serious trouble ourselves?"

"Yes, we do realize that, Ted," said Joe. "And the three of us here are prepared to take the consequences. You can either leave it to us and keep your mouth shut or you can help out – or you can report him to the authorities."

Ted grunted.

Phyllis turned to Eileen. "Does Vanessa know he's here?"

"Not yet. We thought it best to just start with the immediate family."

"I thought when they took their bleeding vows that made her family," snapped Ted.

It was Joe's turn to raise his voice. "Look, Ted, I can understand you're upset by this news, but I don't allow cursing in this house in front of women."

"Sorry, Dad," muttered Ted.

"Would he stay here?" asked Phyllis.

Beatrice answered that one. "This house is probably the best because we have that spare room."

Ted was leaning forward in his chair, his head in his hands. "He's always been trouble, that boy, but I never dreamt he'd get this low. No moral fibre, that's the problem. I always suspected that was the case and now I know."

Eileen had never been overly fond of her brother-in-law and right now she felt positive dislike. "There are many good men who crack under the strain of war. Perhaps you could hold judgement until you've spoken to him."

"Cowardice, I call it. And then to just land on Mum and Dad's doorstep and expect they will take him in? Pure selfishness. But then he always was Brian first, wasn't he."

Eileen suddenly became aware of footsteps on the stairs, too late to protect Brian from his father's words. Brian opened the door and stood on the threshold. Now that he was cleaned up and shaved, he looked like the boy who had come to stay with them when he was fourteen.

He tried to smile. "Hello, Mum. Hello, Dad. Sorry to be such a trouble." He burst into racking sobs, half turning against the wall. Phyllis flew across the room and put her arms around him.

"Oh, Brian. Don't cry, son. We'll take care of you. Don't worry."

Ted stared at the floor.

Phyllis stepped back. "Oh my, Brian, you're freezing. Come over to the fire and get warm."

Still crying, Brian let his mother lead him to the chair by the hearth. As he passed his father, Ted reached out a tentative hand and patted his back. "Don't take on so, Bri. We're a family. We'll sort it out."

Phyllis knelt beside her son, pressing his head into her shoulder.

After a moment, Eileen went over to them and thrust a handkerchief into Brian's hands. "Buck up, Bri. Where there's life, there's hope. At least we've got you alive." She looked over at her father. "Dad, why don't you and Ted get us some tea? You men can do it for a change. It is Mum's birthday after all, and I think a piece of that cake you brought, Phyl, would be nice."

Clearly relieved to have something to do, the two men rose immediately and went into the kitchen.

"I didn't think Ted'd betray his own flesh and blood," said Beatrice quietly to Eileen.

Eileen hadn't been at all sure which way Ted would jump, but she nodded. "When they come back, why don't you open your presents. It'll take our minds off things for a bit. After that we can go over the arrangements. All right with you, Brian?"

He half grinned. "Thanks, Auntie."

Phyllis shifted slightly. "Ooh, I'm getting a cramp in my leg. I'd better stand up."

Brian clung to her for a moment before letting go, and she slid into the chair beside him. Childlike, he leaned his head on her shoulder. She stroked his hair with one hand and wiped away her own tears with the other.

The two men returned with the tea things, eyeing the women nervously. Neither man was comfortable with too much sloppy emotion.

Eileen brought the presents over to her mother. They all oohed and aahed as each gift was revealed. A pair of knitted slippers from Ted and Phyllis; a box of Cadbury's Milk Tray from Jack; a book from Eileen by one of Beatrice's favourite writers, Georgette Heyer. Beatrice waited until the end to open the present from Joe, which turned out to be a pair of gold earrings.

"Oh, Joe, they're smashing. But where on earth will I get to wear them these days?"

"Turn your card over and you'll get an answer."

She did so and smiled in delight, reading, "'For my wonderful wife, one voucher for two people to the Hippodrome, to be redeemed when she deems fit. Joe.' How thoughtful." She made him put his face close to hers and gave him a kiss.

Eileen and Phyllis exchanged glances and spontaneously they clapped their hands. They knew how much their father disliked going out anywhere; it was indeed quite a sacrifice for him to do this for his wife. "Good for you, Dad. And you might even enjoy yourself."

Joe shifted in embarrassment. "Beattie deserves it. But I'm assuming they'll fix it up before we go." The music hall had been damaged in an October raid.

"I don't care if we have to sit on the bricks. If they're putting on a show, we'll go," said Beatrice. "No excuses for you, Joe Abbott."

As she watched them all, Eileen could feel her throat grow tight with emotion. They still had a lot of hurdles to overcome. Ted had softened for the moment, but she didn't know how long that would last. How long any of them would last, for that matter, when the reality of hiding another human being indefinitely hit them.

***

"Note down the time of your call, sir, and where it's going. All trunk calls have to be reported."

The Steelhouse Lane desk sergeant had obviously been dragged in from retirement for the duration and wasn't happy about it. If he could pass on his resentment to others he would. However, Tyler did as he was asked without comment and waited while the operator connected him to Whitchurch.

Sergeant Basil Gough answered.

"Guffie? Tyler here. How are things going?"

"It's not easy without you, sir, but we're struggling along." As always, Sergeant Gough's delivery was deadpan. "How is the investigation coming?"

"I haven't got much done yet. The factory's closed down today so I only got to interview three people. Technically four, if you include a poor bugger who was working at the site. He's lost his memory and one eye. Basically I've just walked around and tried to get a sense of the procedures. Damned if I could see anything obvious, except it was all bloody dangerous, if you ask me." He paused. "You remember the Land Girls, Guffie? The ones billeted at the Somerville estate this past summer?"

"Indeed I do, sir."

"Well, one of them moved to Brum not too long ago. Sylvia Sumner is her name. She's one of the workers badly hurt in the explosion."

"I'm very sorry to hear that, sir."

"I went over to the hospital." Tyler stopped for a moment. He was glad he was talking to somebody who knew him well. "It was shocking to see her, Guffie. She's not much older than our Janet. Eighteen at the most. Part of one arm and a hand were blown off."

"Poor lassie. Could she shed any light on what happened?"

"Not so far, but she's pretty doped up. I'll go back. But why I'm calling is because I'm going to need some help. The plods here are spread as thin as jam on bread. I want to get young Eagleton over here. Do you think that's possible?"

"I'm sure we can arrange it. The only activity we've had today is Norton's ram getting out of the field. In search of some ewes, apparently. Eager was instrumental in catching him. I'm sure the lad would be glad of more of a challenge."

"Good. Tell him to take the first train he can get."

"Yes, sir." There was a pause, then Gough said, "If you are in need of further help, I myself would be happy to come. I haven't been in the city since I was a nipper."

"What? There's no excitement going on here, I can tell you. Besides, the entire Shropshire constabulary would collapse without you."

Gough coughed. "Not the entire constabulary, sir, but perhaps the Whitchurch division."

They hung up, and under the sharp scrutiny of the sour-faced desk sergeant, Tyler wrote down the time.

"I beg your pardon, Inspector, but there was a message for you from Mr. Mason. He said to inform you he is delayed in Nuneaton overnight."

"Good thing you remembered to tell me, Sergeant. I was prepared to wait up for him."

The sergeant regarded Tyler suspiciously, not sure if he was being reprimanded or not. "I didn't forget, sir. I was just waiting for the opportunity to give you the message."

Tyler grinned at him. "We have an expression where I come from, Sergeant. 'If my aunt could piss standing up, she'd be my uncle.'"

The sergeant scowled. "Yes, sir."

"In case any other messages come in, you will have the opportunity to give them to me in the common room, where I will be spending the next hour."

Tyler left him to contemplate that and went upstairs to the common room. He was tired. He'd been right not to expect a good night's sleep. But he also felt the need for some company.

There was only one man in the room, a uniformed constable who was in the middle of a solitary game of darts. When he heard the door open, he turned and his face lit up. Tyler recognized him immediately. They'd been on the beat together years ago.

"Tommy Tyler, as I live and breathe. Good to see you. The inspector said you were billeted here for a bit. I was hoping our paths would cross. Ben McNaughton here. If you say you don't remember me, I'll plough you."

Tyler laughed. "Forget you? Wish I could, with all the trouble you got me into." He held out his hand. "Hello, Ben. How're you doing? All right?"

They shook hands heartily.

McNaughton was heavier than when Tyler had last seen him and, like Alf, he'd lost a lot of his hair, but he was as boisterous as he remembered.

"Take the weight off your beaters, Tommy. Let me go and rustle up a tot of something from the canteen. We've got some catching up to do."

He was as good as his word, returning in a few moments with half a bottle of sherry and two teacups. "Sorry about these, Tom. Couldn't find the crystal."

The sherry was awful, far too sweet for Tyler's taste, but McNaughton downed it easily. He grinned. "You'd never think I used to be a teetotaller, would you."

"You were pretty strict, as I recall."

McNaughton said, "See what a lot I missed out on." He held out the sherry bottle. "Some more?"

"No, thanks. Save it for the trifle."

"You're right, it is on the sweet side. But beggars can't be choosers." He poured another splash into his cup. "My wife says I have to be careful I don't become a dipsomaniac. She likes fancy words, does my wife, but what she means is that I drink too much. Which is true." He looked at Tyler. "But you know, Tom, lately I find the world looks slightly better through the gleam of a bottle."

Tyler knew what he was talking about but he didn't feel like getting into a warm tub of melancholy at the moment. McNaughton had a good start on him.

"I thought you'd retired, Ben, getting a well-deserved rest on a good pension."

"Ha. Fat chance of either. My wife has been storing up jobs for me for decades, it feels like. Coming back has been a relief. And as for the pension, well, you know what a joke that is."

Tyler grinned. Police wages and pensions were nothing to boast about. "How long have you been back on the job?"

"Since January. They were trawling for officers and they fished up me. I was a reservist."

"How's it been here? We're pretty quiet out in the sticks."

"Bad. It's been bad. There were so many fires in Friday's raid we almost drained the canal."

"No guff!"

"Coventry's had it even worse than us. I was called over there the day after the really bad raid on the twenty-second. The entire centre was virtually razed to the ground." McNaughton downed the last of the sherry. "My mum and dad took me to see Coventry Cathedral when I was a nipper. It was quite a revelation to me. We were chapel, you see, and not given to stained glass windows and such, but even I could tell it was a beauty." He paused. "I remember looking up and the columns seemed to sway like trees reaching up to heaven. I had quite a religious moment. Scared my parents half to death – they thought I might turn papist." He put down his empty cup with a thud. "It's nothing but a shell now. Sodding Krauts. I hope they're getting it as bad."

"By all accounts they are," said Tyler.

McNaughton stood up. "Darn, I'd better get going. I'm on duty in five minutes. Listen, Tommy, let's make sure we have a long chinwag before you have to leave. Go over old times, that sort of thing." He indicated the darts he had placed on the table. "Why don't you get in some practice? I'll take you on tomorrow. I bet I can still beat you."

"You're on. Two quid says you won't."

McNaughton left and Tyler picked up one of the darts. Truth was, he was relieved they had avoided the catch-up. Ben was a good chap in his own way but Tyler had no desire to rake over the coals of the past summer. He didn't know if he'd ever want to.

He aimed the dart and threw it. It missed the mark entirely, hit a wire, and bounced off onto the floor.

***

Brian heard the clock in the downstairs hall chime out the quarter-hour. It was almost midnight. A few minutes and he'd see her. Hold her in his arms. He sat up. Should he go down to the shelter now? Better not. He wanted everybody in the house to be completely asleep.

He could feel his pulse racing and he felt sweaty. The pills. They made it hard for him to sit still. He got off the bed. If he paced too much he risked waking his auntie, whose room was directly below. The house was old and the floors creaked. Maybe he would be better off to go to the shelter now. It would give him something to do. His parents had stayed until seven and, claiming he had a headache, he'd gone up to his room soon after. He'd been lying there ever since, wide awake, mulling over the situation, tight with anxiety. His dad had behaved better than he'd expected but he knew everybody was worried as to whether it would last. Would he go so far as to report his own son? Brian wished he had more confidence that he wouldn't. Oh, sod it. He'd always been that way.

He walked over to the window and, as quietly as he could, he pushed up the sash.

When he was living with his grandparents during those troubled teenage years, he'd found a way to escape the house when he wanted to. Simple: just climb out the window onto the flat roof over the kitchen and slide down the drainpipe. Easy as pie and he'd never been caught, never overused the method. Not that he'd ever got into any serious trouble while he was out on the prowl. Just a bit of minor thievery – sweets, cigarettes mostly, and the occasional tryst with a girlfriend who was willing to keep quiet. Not Vanessa. Not then. She wasn't that kind of girl. She was a virgin when they married.

Night had brought back the fog and it came at him in a wave, making him cough. He didn't mind. It was a blessing. It hid everything.

His gran had fished out some of his granddad's old clothes, and he pulled on a heavy jersey and a pair of plimsolls. He climbed out of the window and was down the drainpipe in a flash. At the bottom he waited for a moment, but the night was dense and silent. He could have been at sea for all the sense of life there was around him. But he could make out the lighter colour of the path that led to the back of the garden, where they'd built the shelter. God, the fog was so thick. Vanessa might not be able to make it in this visibility. Should he go and meet her? Better not. He wasn't sure which way she'd come. He'd just have to trust that she would struggle through.

The bit of exercise had calmed him slightly. He pushed aside the shelter's blackout curtain and went into the narrow entryway. He could risk a fag here. He lit up, taking the smoke deep into his lungs. He hadn't smoked before he'd signed up, but a soldier who didn't smoke was unheard of, and he wanted desperately to fit in. To be liked by the other men. And he was for the most part, although he had to endure his fair share of teasing. "Girlie" sometimes, because of his fair skin and wavy hair. "Lover boy" when they saw how he pined for Vanessa. "Goody Two-shoes" when he worked hard to obey the rules. What would they think now, he wondered. Probably wouldn't believe it. *What? Walmsley the Worm going AWOL? Not a chance.*

Wait! He could hear the soft crunch of footsteps on the gravel path. He lifted the edge of the curtain and peered out into the darkness. A thin beam from a shaded torch was wavering towards him.

"Vanessa? Van, is that you?" he whispered.

The light halted. "Who's that?" a woman's voice answered back.

"Me. It's me, Brian."

The light moved closer and he could make out Vanessa, muffled up against the fog. He jumped out at once and grabbed her in his arms, crushing her against him.

"Nessa. Oh, my love," he moaned into the scarf that she'd wrapped around her face, and with one swoop he lifted her up in his arms.

"Brian—" she protested, but he carried her into the inner room of the shelter and dropped her onto the bunk bed.

"Ow—"

He ignored that, found her mouth, and, forcing open her lips, kissed her deeply.

Finally she managed to break away sufficiently to move her head so she could look at him. "Brian, my God, let me get my breath. What are you doing here?"

"Didn't Jack tell you?"

"Tell me what? He didn't say anything."

"I've deserted."

She struggled to sit up on the bed. "Deserted? Oh my God, Brian, how could you?"

He shrugged. "It just happened. I can't exactly explain it. I was desperate to see you."

"Don't blame me!"

"I'm not blaming you. I'm just trying to explain. But I'm not going back."

"That's ridiculous. If they catch you they'll throw you in prison."

"I don't give a shite. We were about to be shipped away to some godforsaken corner of the world and the thought of not seeing you for months and months, maybe years, was more than I could stand. Jesus love us, Ness, take your coat off. I've got to do it now."

She pushed at his chest. "We can't do it in the shelter. What if there's a raid and your grandparents come out?"

"In this weather? Don't be ridiculous. There won't be a raid tonight."

He started to shove up her skirts with one hand as he undid his trouser buttons with the other.

"Oh, my darling, I can't tell you how many times I've dreamed of this, of being inside you again."

"Brian, for God's sake." But she was more responsive now, slipping out of her coat and pulling down her knickers. He pressed against her but he was too eager, too full, and he spilled himself all over her legs before he could penetrate her. He lay on top of her, panting, and after a minute she pushed him aside, swivelled her hips away, and sat up.

"God, you've messed up my new skirt. Give me my hankie. It's in my bag."

He grabbed her chin and turned her face to him. "I couldn't help myself. There's a lot more where that came from. In fact, I could probably go again in a few minutes. Let's take our clothes off and get under the blankets."

"Bri! What if somebody comes?"

"They won't, I told you. And besides, we're married, for God's sake. Why shouldn't we?"

He tugged off his jersey and trousers and slipped under the blanket.

Vanessa was rubbing at her skirt. "Turn down the light at least. It'll be more romantic."

"No. I want to look at you. I'm starved to see you. Take off your jumper. Good. Now your skirt. Wow, look at you. You *did* prepare for me."

Vanessa was wearing a white lace brassiere and a pair of matching briefs. She shivered. "Course I did, silly. Oh, Bri. Let me get under the covers, I'm freezing."

She was about to climb into the bunk when he stopped her with his outstretched arm. "Hold on. Turn sideways."

"Bri, come on, it's perishing in here."

"I said turn sideways."

Reluctantly she did so.

"Putting on weight are you, Van?"

"Yeah, too many cheese rolls. Besides, you were always on at me to put on some flesh. You kept saying I was a bean-pole. Shove over, I'm coming in." She got under the blanket and snuggled up against him. "Oh, Brian. It's wonderful to see you."

He hugged her closer, rubbing her bare arm to warm her up. "I hope so. When you first come in, I wasn't too sure."

"Don't be such a silly goose. The fog makes everything creepy. I was a bit scared is all."

He kissed her. "You don't need to be scared with me around."

She nuzzled into his neck. "It's all very well to say that, but look at the pickle you've got yourself into."

"I've got plans, Ness. I know a bloke who can get us papers to go to Ireland."

"What? What do you mean, go to Ireland?"

"Shh, shh. Don't worry. We can wait out the war there. You always said you wanted to go abroad. You're my wife. I won't go without you. That's what you want too, isn't it?"

"Course it is."

She lifted up her arm so she could look at her watch. "I've got to go. Mum and Dad will start to wonder where I am."

He caught her wrist. "I haven't seen that watch before. Where'd you get it?"

"One of the girls at the factory gave it to me. Little minx has two soldier boyfriends and they both gave her watches."

"Looks expensive."

"Naw, I doubt it. Just looks like it."

"I don't know if I like you having another bloke's present."

"No skin off your nose, is it. I needed a watch." She pushed back the blanket and reached for her clothes. "I must go, Bri. I'm supposed to be on fire watch. They'll be expecting me. I don't want them to raise no alarm."

He took her face in his hands and looked into her eyes. "You did miss me, didn't you?"

"Of course I did."

"I'm sorry I, er, I couldn't do it properly. I'm too pent up. I'll be all right when we're in our own place in Ireland. It'll be a honeymoon again. Remember how we went at it like rabbits – once, sometimes twice a day? Remember?"

"I remember."

Something had leaked into her voice. He scowled. "I thought you liked it. I thought I satisfied you."

She smiled quickly. "Course you did. It was bloody marvellous."

"Will you be here tomorrow?" he asked.

She was pulling on her jersey and her voice was muffled. "Not tomorrow. It's too risky. Besides I'm too tired, Bri. I work, don't forget."

"While I was away, you didn't visit Mum and Dad much, did you. She wrote me about that."

She wriggled away from him and, sitting on the side of the bed, started to pull on her stockings, carefully so as not to snag them.

"You know they can't stand me. Why should I put up with your mother's looks and secret insults? And your gran's just as bad, you know. You might think butter wouldn't melt in her mouth, but she can be a right cow sometimes."

"Ness, that's not fair. Why do you say that?"

Vanessa imitated Beatrice's voice. "Going out again, Vanessa? Must be nice to have extra money these days. You must have quite a nice bit of savings by now for the house you and our Brian are going to buy."

Brian frowned. "So do you?"

"Do I what?"

"Go out a lot?"

"Why shouldn't I? If you were me you wouldn't want to sit at home with Mum and Dad arguing all night. And him getting pissed. Talk about savings. We'd be living in a palace if we had all the money he's spent on booze. So yes, I go to the pictures whenever I can."

"Who do you go with?"

"Girls from work."

"Like who?"

She stood up abruptly. "For Christ's sake, Bri. You sound like my ma."

She was glaring at him and he swallowed his anger quickly.

"I'm sorry, pet. I know being separated has been hard on you too." He tried to smile. "We won't have to be apart much longer. Can you hold on?"

She moved back a little so she could offer him her lips. "Just about."

They kissed, and when she broke away, she giggled. "Now look what's happened. If you think I'm going to get undressed again, you've got another think coming."

He grinned at her. "That don't mean we can't still do something." He directed her hand. "See, he's good and strong now."

"Oh, all right, then." She began to unfasten her skirt. "But promise you won't shout like you usually do."

***

Donny made his way towards Endicott's factory, walking at as fast a clip as he could. He loathed this weather. His coat was thin and cheap and the damp penetrated to the bone. He had no gloves. He couldn't afford them and they were for poufters anyway. He tucked his chin into his muffler but even that wasn't much help. It was very late but this was the time Comrade Patrick had given him. Personal contact was allowed only in an emergency. You had to mark a certain brick in St. Paul's Church wall. Just your initial was all that was necessary. The Chief answered by chalking a time on another brick.

Donny didn't really mind the darkness. The silence, the emptiness of the streets gave everything a taste of excitement. You never knew what would happen in the night.

In the daytime, this part of Birmingham looked neat and trim; better-class houses, women with pride. But those same women were not above spending a good part of the day queuing up for something or other. When he'd gone out earlier, he'd passed a long line outside the butcher's shop on Broad Street. He'd noticed a handwritten sign in the window. TODAY, FRESH MINCE. HALF A POUND PER CUSTOMER. Rumour had it that the butchers were mixing in horsemeat with the mince, but Donny thought it was stupid to care where the stuff came from as long as it was edible. What was the difference, really?

Dead meat was dead meat. The women in the queue were waiting patiently with their shopping bags and baskets. They were docile as sheep, and he despised them for it.

Donny had met Patrick only once before, also at night. He'd been almost literally dragged there by a black-souled Welshman who'd nabbed him as Donny was coming out of this very church. Taffy had deduced that he, Donny, was up to no good. Not surprising, as it was midnight and he had a suspicious bulge under his coat – the poor box, as a matter of fact, that he'd just nicked. Taffy had given him a cuff across the head and a talking to. Essentially Taffy said he wouldn't throw Donny to the dogs as long as he made himself useful. There was this group of blokes, see, who were against the war and wanted to do whatever they could to make things difficult for the government. Donny could understand that, couldn't he? "I'm no bolshie," Donny had blurted out. Taffy had laughed. "That's not what holds us together, boyo. Some is bolshie, some isn't. But I know we'll find a suitable job for you to do." Donny had no recourse but to agree, and the next day he'd had a meeting with the bloke called Patrick. If Taffy was scary, this man was worse. He hadn't said much, but at the end of the meeting he said, "He'll do." That's it. "He'll do." And Donny felt as if he'd been given a sentence of death. So far he hadn't been called on. Somebody else had done the dirty. But his turn was coming; he knew it was.

Donny had a torch but the battery was fading and the beam was weak. It was bloody dark and he might have gone right past the alcove in the church wall if he hadn't seen the faint glow of a cigarette. He kept on walking as instructed, then at the gate turned around and retraced his footsteps. At the alcove he could just make out the shape of a man.

"Got a light, chum?" he asked.

"Sure."

Still not turning, the man handed over a box of matches and waited while Donny went through the ritual of taking out his cigarette makings, rolling his fag, and lighting up.

"Everything all right, then?" the man asked. He was wearing a workman's cap pulled down over his forehead and the lower part of his face was obscured by a thick scarf that he moved only to drag on his cigarette. Donny didn't think he'd recognize him if he passed him on the street. Even his voice seemed phony, sort of gravelly, unnatural. It was impossible to say where he was from.

"Right as rain," Donny answered. "By the way, don't know where I can get hold of some pliers, do you? I've got a mate who's in the electricity business and he's agreed to do a bit of work for me. He's lost his. Somebody must have bleedin' nicked them." He smirked, enjoying his own private little joke.

He could feel the anger running through the other man's body as if he'd actually touched him, but when he spoke, his voice was the same, low and even. "Is that why you've come here? To ask about frigging pliers? I don't call that an emergency."

"No, right, sorry. What I wanted to let you know was that this bloke can make timers. They're useful things, they are. They'll set off bloody anything you want them to at any time you pick."

"Yes, I know what timers are, sonny."

Suddenly they saw the light of a torch and two men emerged out of the fog. Comrade Patrick shrank back into his alcove and Donny held himself very still. Both of them automatically hid their cigarettes. The men going by didn't seem to notice them. Both had posh educated voices. God knows where they were coming from at that time of night. Or going to, for that matter.

"He's worth listening to, in my opinion. He knows things the government won't tell us about."

"I consider him a traitor . . . pile of rubbish . . ."

They faded out of earshot.

Donny jerked his head, trying to find something to ease the situation. "Stupid ponces. They're talking about that bloody Lord Haw-Haw. He don't know nothing. It's our bloody government puts him up to it, if you ask me. Riles up the bloody people 'gainst Jerry."

The other man shifted slightly. "You've got one more minute, then I'm going. What's on your mind?"

Donny dragged deeply on his fag. "This bloke's in a spot of trouble, see. He's deserted from the army and he needs to get away from here. I told him if he helped me out, I'd get him some papers that'll get him into Ireland."

The comrade coughed, a harsh, dry cough. "My, my, that's big of you. You have access to false papers, do you, then?"

"No, but I thought you might know where I could get them."

Another cough, worse this time. "If I had such stuff I frigging wouldn't hand it over just like that. That's no bargain. Timers aren't that hard to make."

Donny quailed. He'd come to the meeting jaunty, like a young wolf laying his prize catch at the feet of the leader. It didn't seem to be such a prize after all. He fished in his pocket and took out a grubby piece of paper, which he gave to the other man. "Last time there wasn't much damage if you look at it. The bloody factory'll be up and running soon as spit. With my plan, it'll be all over. *Boom*. No more factory whatsoever." He pointed to the paper, which the man was studying. "See, I drew a diagram. We'd only need small bombs. Two at the most. One here, in the boiler room. It's right under the factory floor and would wipe out the machines totally. The second one is here, in the men's changing room. That would be set to go off a few minutes later. And the changing room is right underneath the bleedin' office."

That got Patrick's attention. He half turned towards Donny. "And?"

"That's where we can get lots of lovely moolah." He smirked. "Every cause could do with money, don't you think?"

"You're right about that, Comrade Bolton."

"I made sure I kept my peepers open when I was working there."

Patrick's eyes flickered over to him. "And when was that, sonny?"

"Few months ago. Unfortunately I got the boot. I was accused of being light-fingered, you see."

"Why aren't I surprised."

"Yes, well, they couldn't prove anything, could they? I was in the mailroom. Nice cushy job. Too bad. Anyways, I noticed Endicott always trots off to the bank on the morning of payday. He takes out money and brings it to the office. We don't need to worry about a safe – there ain't one. Just a tin box. At noon, his poncey secretary takes out this same money box, goes into the canteen, and hands out the wages to the first shift. He's always on time. Never fails. It would be easy as pie to time the bomb to go off just as Miss Nancy Boy is walking across the hall. Our comrade, who is all safe and waiting for the bang, could just go and nick it, snip-snap. Stick it in a bag. Nobody's going to notice him in all the botheration that'll be happening. He can walk outside and hand the bag over to . . . to whoever is waiting for it."

Donny was getting excited as he talked. He'd been working on this plan ever since Jack had revealed that his brother was in hiding.

Comrade Patrick was still looking at the sheet of paper. It

was impossible to tell whether or not he liked the idea. Donny felt like rolling another fag but made himself wait.

Finally the other man spoke. "How do you see these objects being put in place?"

"It's easy. First, Comrade Chopin can put one down in the boiler room. He gets out. Tick, tick . . . *boom*. Up it goes. Ta-ta factory. The second bomb, same thing. Comrade Cardiff works in the caf. All he has to do is hide the bomb in his bait tin, put it in his locker, and Bob's your uncle . . ." Donny could feel that a fleck of saliva had appeared at the corner of his mouth but he ignored it. This was almost as good as a bit of shagging. "So what do you think?"

"Sounds possible. I'll have to show it to the Chief."

"I thought that was you."

"Me, I'm just a foot soldier."

Donny didn't know if he believed him, but he didn't pursue it. "We would time it so the two comrades could get well out of the way."

"Maybe."

Donny felt a stab of fear in his gut. He knew what *maybe* really meant.

The comrade stashed the paper in his pocket. "You're a lad who takes the initiative. That could be a good thing or a bad thing. Depends on whether or not you're going off half-cocked. To pull this off properly, we'd need the wherewithal."

"I'm telling you I can get it. Well, at least I can get the timer part. You'd have to come up with the bangers. He's desperate, is this bloke I mentioned. He'll do anything. We'll have the friggin' factory on its knees, and make us a bit of dosh on the side."

"Do you know anything about making bombs, Comrade Bolton?"

"Er, no. But I thought as somebody else would."

The man tapped his arm. "I am starting to like the idea. To tell you the truth, I was casting my mind around for something just like this. Smart lad."

Donny felt himself actually blush with pleasure. Praise indeed.

"But we'll have to move fast. Can your pal be ready with the goods by tomorrow night?"

"Piece of cake. Take him no time at all. He's not doing anything else, is he."

"It'll cost him. Timers are cheap, papers aren't."

"How much?"

"Forty pounds." The man dropped his fag end and crushed it with his shoe. "Meet me tomorrow. Same time. And no word to anybody. The future success of our enterprise will depend on everybody keeping their traps tight shut. Including you, me boyo."

Donny shivered; he couldn't help it. Initially he'd thought this kind of talk was a pile of tommyrot, but he had the feeling that if it suited his purpose, his so-called comrade would wipe out opposition with no more hesitation than killing a fly. Donny also knew without a shadow of a doubt that his own survival depended on his usefulness. Once that was over, so was he. Dead men have a way of keeping their mouths shut.

Patrick moved off. "Two days until payday, Bolton."

CONSTABLE EAGLETON HAD ARRIVED IN THE EARLY hours of the morning, the train having been delayed for two hours. Nevertheless, bright and chipper, he was waiting for Tyler in the canteen at breakfast.

"What do you think you are, Eager? Young?"

"Er, yes, sir. Sorry, sir."

They had weak tea and toast made palatable by the scones Eagleton had brought with him from Sergeant Gough's wife.

"That woman is a national treasure," said Tyler as he munched.

He filled in the constable as to what he had done so far, including his visit to Sylvia Sumner.

"She was a fine-looking girl," said Eagleton. "What a terrible shame."

"Indeed."

"Are we seriously looking for criminal activity, sir?"

"I don't know, but we can't rule out the possibility, not these days. The war has given all the crackpots in the country a chance to play out their grievances. On the other hand, the matter could be personal. Somebody wanting to kill one of the operatives."

"Crikey. Why would they?"

"You don't know much about the ways of love, Eager. Rejection can twist a person inside out."

"Even if you kill many other innocent people?"

"Even that. Anyway, I'm going to set you up in the section where the explosion took place. Go through everything with a sieve. You're looking for anything that might have caused the explosion. Metal, jewellery, that sort of thing. When you take your tea break, go to the canteen and chat up the girls. Young women will always talk to good-looking young coppers like you."

Eagleton looked doubtful. "Do you think so, sir? I haven't had that experience yet."

"This isn't Whitchurch, this is the big city. They're more broad-minded here."

"I suppose it doesn't help that I know virtually everybody in Whitchurch. I'm not new to them either."

"Exactly. Now let's get going. I'm in a cubbyhole on the factory floor. Just room for me and a mouse. Fetch me at once if you come across anything. By the way, lad, it's all right to wear your specs here. I won't tell."

Eagleton blushed. He'd surreptitiously slipped a pair of spectacles into his pocket while they were getting their tea tray.

"Thank you, sir. I only need them for close-up work, but I thought I might get kicked out of the force if anybody knew."

"Not a chance, Eager. Even half-blind you're a better police officer than half the constabulary. I wouldn't allow you to get the chop."

They walked over to the factory. It was another overcast, chilly day. Tyler was beginning to forget what a sunny day looked like. He directed the younger man to the site of the explosion and left him to his task.

He'd just seated himself at the desk-cum-tea-table when Cudmore came in carrying an envelope. He cleared his throat in a self-deprecating way. "Here are my notes from yesterday. I think you'll find them all in order."

"Thank you, Mr. Cudmore." Tyler put the envelope on the desk.

"Did you sleep well, sir?" Cudmore asked.

"Not really."

"Strange bed, most likely. I'm rather like that myself."

Tyler didn't add that he'd also been tormented by bad dreams. Something that should have been getting better but clearly wasn't.

"Did you have the opportunity to interview Mr. Pavely?" asked Cudmore.

"I did but he doesn't remember a thing. His memory literally stops just before the accident happened." Tyler rubbed his hands over his head. "Make a note, Mr. Cudmore. I'd like to know who instructed the men to work on the bench."

The secretary glanced up in surprise. "It was I myself, sir. I got a note about a small tear in the linoleum cover that needed to be repaired. I passed that along to Mr. Pavely, who is our senior maintenance man."

"Did you see the tear yourself?"

Cudmore raised his eyebrows. "I did. I have to ensure that these requisitions are indeed necessary."

"How did the tear get there?"

"I don't understand your question, Inspector."

"As I understand it, no instruments were being used in Section B that were sharp enough to put a hole in linoleum."

"Ah, yes, quite so. This particular damage was at the corner of the bench. The lino was probably not glued down sufficiently and had come loose. It was not a big job but did necessitate the entire cover being removed and re-glued in place."

"When did you receive this requisition?"

"On Saturday, sir."

"And who reported it?"

"Mr. Riley. He discovered it that morning."

"Thank you, Mr. Cudmore. Underline that, will you." Tyler tipped back as far as his chair could go before he connected with the wall. Serious as the subject was, he was rather enjoying this process of dictation. Previously he would have liked it even more if the madly scribbling secretary had been an attractive young woman. But then that was a different Tyler, and in another time.

"Right. Let's just jot down what we're trying to determine here. Question one, first and most obvious: what caused the detonators to explode? Were they incorrectly loaded? Mishandled by one of the girls?" He paused. "There is the rather puzzling fact that the changing room door was locked. This meant a delay in the afternoon shift's getting to their section." He pointed at Cudmore for emphasis. "Question number two, underlined: is this delay significant or irrelevant? Did it put undue pressure on the girls to hurry with their tasks? They should have waited for their supervisor before they trayed up but they chose not to."

Cudmore shook his head disapprovingly.

"If the operatives had got to their benches on time," continued Tyler, "the workmen would not have been allowed to remain. Did they somehow contribute to the explosion? If so, how? I told Pavely it wasn't his fault. They couldn't have caused a spark with what they were doing, and they weren't handling the pots."

"But their presence did mean the women who were normally at Bench Two had to move over," said the secretary. "That might have caused undue congestion."

Tyler paused and pinched the bridge of his nose. A familiar throb was beginning its tune in his temples. "Too many bloody variables, Mr. Cudmore. I feel like a dog chasing its own tail. I'm going in circles, with nothing to show for it but a dicey smell."

Cudmore peered at Tyler. His blue eyes were sharp. "There is one thing that might be added to the mix, as it were, Inspector. With this new quota system that Mr. Endicott introduced – with the best of intentions of course . . ."

He paused while Tyler nodded his support for Endicott's intentions.

"He said he would give a bonus of five pounds to whichever shift produces the most work by the end of the month. The competition among the employees has become intense. I wondered to myself if somebody from the Red shift – the first shift, that is – I wondered if one of the young women had locked the door so that the Blue shift would be delayed and fall behind on their quota."

"Ah, a good thing to wonder about, Mr. Cudmore. I'd better have a word with those girls. Did they all come in today?"

"Not all of them, but I can fetch the ones that are here and send word to the others."

"Let's do that, then. Where is the changing room key usually kept?"

"I keep all keys in my office for safety."

"Would everybody know that?"

"I believe it is common knowledge, sir."

"Any missing?"

"No, sir, I checked. They're hanging on hooks by my desk, all present and correct. On Sunday it was Mr. Riley who took the key and opened the door. He obviously returned it."

"Right, let's start setting up interviews. It's a bit cramped in here but that can't be helped."

"People are getting used to being squashed these days," said Cudmore. He unfastened a piece of paper from the back of his notebook. "I have this list prepared for you. It is the same one I gave you yesterday. The letter P beside a name indicates that they are in the factory today and thus available for you to speak to."

He handed the sheet of paper to Tyler.

"Mrs. Castleford is already here, sir. She is still quite distraught. It would be kind if you could start with her."

"Very well, Mr. Cudmore. Let's be kind."

***

So far the clinic hadn't been busy but Eileen was expecting she'd be receiving workers as the day went on. She was glad she'd stocked up recently on sleeping draughts. With the horrendous events of Sunday and the drubbing the city had taken the previous week, she knew she'd be asked to dispense them. Fortunately, her requisitions were usually approved by Mr. Cudmore, who was only too happy to sign off on such things. Endicott, who periodically stuck his fat finger in, never liked to see evidence of what he called high-strung females.

The waiting room door opened and Lev Kaplan entered. He was carrying a brown paper bag, which he thrust at her.

"Good morning, Sister. My thank-you gift . . . No, no, don't refuse until you see what it is. Then I know you will have to accept."

She peeked into the bag. It smelled of coffee.

"I know you Limeys love your tea, but if you ever had a chance to taste real American coffee you would change your entire way of life."

"We have coffee here," Eileen answered, exasperated.

"Camp Coffee Essence is not remotely like the real thing. It's like comparing sludge to single-malt Scotch. This coffee is soluble in water, so it's fast and easy to make and it's almost as good as brewed coffee. I assume you don't own a percolator, do you?"

Eileen laughed. "You are quite right, Mr. Kaplan, I don't have a percolator. I'm not even sure what that is."

"Would you mind calling me Lev? Only my bank manager and the Ministry refer to me as Mr. Kaplan. It puts a distance between us."

"That might not be a bad idea."

"Too pushy, huh?"

"Far too pushy."

"How long will I have to wait until you feel you know me well enough to spend a few hours in my company? Come on, what's the worst that can happen? You will be bored to death? Offended beyond human endurance? Either way it's only four hours out of your life, and who knows how long anybody has these days." He made his face serious but his eyes were laughing.

"What four hours are you referring to?"

"I would like to invite you to a dance at the Jewish Association fundraiser. Tomorrow night."

"I couldn't possibly—"

He interrupted her. "I know we haven't known each other very long—"

"Twenty-four hours, to be exact."

"These days, that's loads of time. Do say you'll come. It's a most worthy cause."

"I . . . er . . ."

"You don't have to give me an answer right now. I'll be back soon to do some shooting."

"What do you mean, shooting?"

"I thought I'd do some filming with Mr. Endicott and you."

"What!"

He looked around the clinic. "Like I said, this is a nice, friendly space. It will go down well. I have to do something with him that looks inviting, so I thought I'd bring him here."

Her expression obviously betrayed her feelings about her boss.

"See it as an act of patriotism," said Lev.

"Really, Mr. Kaplan, I'm sure you could find better subjects from among our workers."

"You are far too modest, Miss Abbott. I cannot think of another person who better conveys kindness and competence all nicely blended together."

She regarded him doubtfully, not sure if he was teasing or laying on insincere dollops of flattery. Neither seemed to be the case.

"That's settled, then. Enjoy the coffee. I'll be back later." He left.

Eileen was still holding the paper bag. She inhaled deeply. It was true she hadn't had much coffee in her life, but if that wonderful aroma was anything to go by she was going to enjoy it a lot.

A sharp little voice spoke at the back of her mind. *And that isn't all you think you might enjoy. Don't lie to yourself, Eileen Abbott.*

***

Mrs. Valerie Castleford was a short, plump woman still on the hopeful side of middle age. Normally probably attractive in a lush way, today her eyes were red and swollen and her skin blotchy. Nevertheless she'd taken care with her appearance and she was dressed in a smart, snug-fitting tweed suit and matching hat. Like Cudmore, she was wearing a black arm band. Her husband appeared to be some years older and was grey to her blonde. He seemed at a complete loss as to how to help her and could only pat her arm periodically, a gesture she ignored. She pulled a handkerchief from her handbag and burst into tears as soon as she sat down.

"Take your time, Mrs. Castleford," said Tyler. "I know what a dreadful shock this has all been. It would help me if you just tell me in your own words what happened, from the time you first arrived at the factory until after the explosion."

The very word seemed to make her flinch. "There was nothing but confusion when I arrived. The changing room was locked, nobody knew where the key was, and the girls from both sections were in the cloakroom area, waiting. Normally I'm there first, you see, but wouldn't you know it, on this one Sunday of all Sundays, I was a bit late. I sing in the choir at my church and the organist wanted to speak to me afterwards."

"She has a lovely voice, does our Val," interjected her husband.

She threw him a rather irritated look. "The inspector isn't interested in hearing that, Sid. Like I said, the girls were all outside instead of where they should have been, getting changed. They said as how they couldn't get into the room. I went to see if we could find a key. Finally Mr. Riley opened the door for us."

"Did he have his own key?" Tyler asked.

She shook her head. "Us supervisors we probably should have our own sets, but we don't. The only persons to have master keys are the caretaker and Mr. Cudmore here. We've been told it's safer that way. It meant Phil had to go and get the set from Mr. Cudmore's office."

The secretary was looking upset but wisely didn't try to defend the policy.

Mrs. Castleford cast a quick glance at her husband. "At this time Mr. Riley told me that there was some kind of mix-up in the number of detonators that had been delivered. He was fifty short – that's one pot. We had to sort it out. You can't let fuses go unaccounted for. I said I would help with the recount. When the girls were all settled, I went to the magazine shed." She dabbed at her eyelids. "They should have waited to tray up while I talked to Phil, that is, Mr. Riley. Like I said, that was most important." She hiccupped.

"Did you tell them to start on their own?"

Mrs. Castleford initially looked as if she was going to deny it, but she said, "I suppose I must have. They were always in such a hurry. Young girls are impatient."

She fell silent, miserable in her guilt.

"So you left them?" prompted Tyler.

"I didn't think I was going to be long. As it was, I had only just got into the shed and was getting the lowdown from Phil when the explosion occurred. Phil told me to stay where I was and he ran to see what had happened. But I couldn't just stay there, could I. I went to follow him, but I tripped."

"She bruised her knees bad," said her husband. "Show him, Val."

Obediently Mrs. Castleford hitched up her skirt, revealing the injuries. Nothing too serious as far as Tyler could tell.

"I could hear somebody screaming. I knew something terrible had happened. There was so much smoke and dust. Then Phil reappeared. 'Don't come in, Val,' he says to me. 'We've got to get the ambulance.' There was girls from the floor coming out now to see what was happening. Phil stands in front of the fire door and stops them." She paused, unable to mask her admiration. "Brave he was. I mean, we didn't know if there was going to be more explosions. 'Go outside at once, girls,' he says to the women. 'We've had fire drill lots of times, so they were good. They all left quietly." She started to weep again and her husband patted more frantically. "I blame myself. They were not supposed to tray up by themselves, but they wanted to reach their quota so badly." She moaned. "I feel so responsible."

"I don't like her working here, I never have," said her husband. "She could have been killed herself. I had to get the doctor in to give her some pills."

"Somebody's got to do the job," she muttered.

"You didn't know the changing room door would be locked, though," said Tyler. "That delayed you and put everyone under pressure. Any idea, by the way, as to why it was locked?"

"No. I haven't thought about it really. I just thought it was some new order from Mr. Endicott."

Tyler looked over at the secretary. "Mr. Cudmore?"

"I would have passed any such order along to the supervisors. No such command was issued."

"Mrs. Castleford," continued Tyler, "when you first came into the section, was everything normal?"

"Except for the two men who were fixing the bench. They weren't supposed to be there but they said as how they wouldn't be long." She halted. "They were both badly hurt."

"Do you know how the table came to be damaged?"

"Not really. Phil was the one who noticed the lino was peeling off. Not installed properly, most likely."

Tyler waited a moment. "Anything else that was different about the section?"

"No . . . yes, there was. The magazine box wasn't in its usual place. Is that the sort of thing you mean?"

"Where was it?"

"On the floor between the two benches. The dillie man usually puts it at the end of the second bench. It's easier for me to get to it that way. But Mr. Aston said it was on the floor."

"Did he say who put it there?"

"Not that I remember. It was left over from the previous shift. They hadn't finished. I was just glad we had work to do. Doug helped me move the box to the bench so the girls could get started. I'm always so careful to make sure they tray up properly."

"But in this case your care was overridden by the necessity of counting the fuses . . . with Mr. Riley."

Mrs. Castleford shrank down into her chair and Tyler felt like a bully. "That's correct. And I knew I wouldn't be gone long . . ."

Her husband removed his comforting hand. She wiped hard at her eyes.

You're not going to scrub away your guilt like that, thought Tyler. *While you were after having a bit on the side, your charges went ahead and got themselves killed. That's something you're going to have to live with.*

But would they have been killed anyway, whether or not Mrs. Castleford had supervised the traying up herself, as she was supposed to? That's what he had to get to.

"Mrs. Castleford, I am assuming that the explosion was a tragic accident, but . . ." He hesitated. "If in the unlikely instance it was deliberately caused, is there any one person, or group of people, who in your opinion might be capable of such an act?"

Both Castlefords stared at him in horror. "Are you saying fifth columnists did it?" asked Mr. Castleford.

"No, I'm not saying that at all. I'm just making sure all possibilities are dealt with."

"Oh no," gasped Mrs. Castleford. "Never. They're all good girls as far as I'm concerned."

Tyler smiled reassuringly. "I'm sure that's true, Mrs. Castleford, but as supervisor, you are privy to the less public aspects of factory life. Discontents, complaints, that sort of thing."

Mr. Castleford seemed glad to be going in that direction. He nudged his wife. "Tell him, Val. You've often carried on to me about some of those girls. Just the other day you mentioned that Pat woman and the one with the double-barrelled name, Mary Something or other – she's said right out that she was a communist."

Tyler checked the list Cudmore had given him. "You are referring to Miss Mary Ringwald-Brown, I presume? She was working on the first shift."

"Yes, that's right."

"And Pat would be Miss Pat O'Callaghan?"

"They're both malcontents, if you ask me," said her husband. "Tell him, Val."

Mrs. Castleford pursed her lips. "Miss Ringwald-Brown is a funny duck. She's quite la-di-da, really, but says she wants to be in a factory with the workers. The *poletarys*, or something like that. She's always urging them to go on strike over the slightest thing. Not enough hot water, not enough tea time, too long hours. I don't hold with it myself. There's a war on. Our boys are over there giving up their lives; we can put up with a bit of inconvenience." She puffed out her chest, her misery temporarily forgotten.

"Do the others listen to her?"

"Not them. They can't stand her. She's very unpopular."

"Is Miss O'Callaghan the same?"

"No, not in that way. She's common as muck, excuse my language. Irish, and you know what they're like. No, she won't admit to being a commie; says she's Labour and that's different. But she's also against management most of the time, no matter what they do. So what's the difference, if you know what I mean."

Again Tyler consulted the list. "I gather that two operatives who were supposed to be on the afternoon shift in Section B were absent. One was Miss June Lipton and the other was Miss Ringwald-Brown, who had already worked the early shift."

"Yes, sir, that's correct. The girls will sometimes take on two shifts in a row if they're a bit short. If the hubbie is coming home on leave, for instance, and they want a nice new frock to wear. Not that Miss Ringwald-Brown has a hubbie or would buy a new frock. She's not like that."

"Did she mention why she signed up for a double?"

"No, she didn't say. She's not one to confide in anybody else. As far as I know she doesn't have a man friend."

"Sounds fishy to me," chimed in Mr. Castleford.

Tyler didn't want any rumours starting, so he said rather sharply, "Not necessarily." He turned back to Mrs. Castleford. "Other than the fact that Miss Brown has communist sympathies, do you yourself think she is capable of sabotage?"

Mrs. Castleford hesitated. "I'd say no, right off the bat, but these days you never know what people are capable of. The world's gone off its rocker as far as I'm concerned."

Tyler couldn't have agreed more, but he just nodded. "And with regard to the other young woman, Miss June Lipton, do you know why she was absent?"

"She did show up initially but said she was not feeling well and went back home." Mrs. Castleford lowered her voice. "She's a very nice young lady. It's just that she has trouble at a certain time of the month."

Cudmore kept his head down.

"By the way," Tyler asked. "Did you and Phil – Mr. Riley – ever sort out the problem of the missing detonators?"

Again the telltale blush. "No, we didn't. Sometimes it's the bill of lading that's wrong. After the explosion it slipped from my mind."

"Not surprising, that." He smiled at her. "I think that's about all the questions I have for now. You've been a big help, Mrs. Castleford. But I do want you to keep all this under your hat. Mum's the word."

Cudmore opened the door to usher them out. Castleford was behind his wife but didn't touch her. Poor bugger. What do you do with a wife whose affections lie elsewhere? Tyler sighed. He knew what it was like to be in the other shoes. He sat for a moment ruminating. He took his cigarette case out of his pocket and snapped it open. Clare had given it to him for his twenty-first birthday. The inscription gleamed at him reproachfully. *Love forever, C.* It was a love forever. At least for him it was.

Suddenly the door was thrust open and Cudmore popped his head in. "Dearie me, sir, you'd better come. The girls are all in the canteen. They're threatening to go on strike!"

The secretary was almost twittering with nervousness. "Word just came through that Audrey Sandilands has died.

The employees were on their tea break and one or two of the, er, more *difficult* women have taken advantage of the tragedy and want to call for a strike."

"I don't really have any jurisdiction here," said Tyler. "Legally there's nothing I can do unless they start to vandalize the place. In which case we'd have to call in the local police."

"I thought perhaps your presence here would calm things down."

"Or inflame them," said Tyler.

"Oh no, Inspector. They're not like that. It's because they're all so upset. They just need to hear the voice of reason. I'd be much obliged if you would look in on it."

"All right, let's go."

There was a lot of noise emanating from the canteen. Cudmore tried the door but it was locked. However, when he rapped it was opened immediately. An attractive young woman with long blonde hair greeted them.

"Mr. Cudmore. Come with a message from the boss, have you?"

"No, not exactly, Miss Tomlin. But I would like to hear what you have to say. On his behalf."

"Who's your chum?"

"This is Detective Inspector Tyler. He's investigating the explosion."

"Oops, sorry, sir. I didn't mean to be cheeky."

Another woman appeared behind her. "What's going on, Frankie?" She was older, tough as leather. The hair left exposed at the front of her turban was a telltale orangey blonde.

"This gentleman's a police officer, Pat."

Tyler gave them what he hoped was a disarming smile. "I understand you're thinking of coming out on strike."

Pat, clearly the leader, answered. "That's right. We're fed up with the treatment we've been getting." She had a strong Irish brogue. "We're still at the discussing stage, so you can't object."

Mrs. Castleford's husband had referred to her as a malcontent but that was not Tyler's first impression. She didn't seem "common as muck" either. Just a woman of conviction with a no-nonsense attitude.

"I am here to find out what happened on Sunday," he said. "Perhaps our two concerns will coincide. I'm sure nobody wants to delay production any longer than necessary, and we all want to make sure the factory is safe."

Pat appraised him with a skeptical *I've heard blarney before* look. Then she nodded. "Let them in, Frankie."

"Mr. Cudmore as well?"

"Sure, why not. He's a good bloke. He'll tell the boss what we're thinking. Right, Les?"

"Quite right, Miss O'Callaghan."

The blonde opened the door and they entered the canteen. There were about two dozen workers seated at the tables. As far as Tyler could tell they were all women, but he noticed Mick Smith, the dillie man, standing against the far wall. There was one other man, a short, dark-haired bloke in an apron, behind the serving counter.

Everyone went quiet as they entered and curious eyes gazed at him.

"Come up," said Pat. "You can sit at the head table."

There was a minuscule stage at the far end of the canteen and she led the way towards it.

"Shove over, you lot," she said to the women sitting there. "This is Detective Inspector Tyler. He wants to be part of our deliberations."

"Why should he?" demanded a woman at the far end. "We are not doing anything illegal."

She had a cultivated accent and a sallow, long-jawed face. Must be Mary with the hyphenated name that Mrs. Castleford had mentioned. Rather to his surprise, Tyler recognized her as the woman he'd passed on his way into the hospital yesterday. Whatever distress she had been experiencing then was no longer apparent. She looked sour and belligerent.

"He's investigating Sunday's explosion," answered Pat before Tyler could reply.

"We are dealing with other matters at the moment."

"For God's sake, Mary, we've got to get that sorted out. Women were killed, or didn't you notice?" Pat's voice was tart. She'd obviously had previous run-ins with Mary Ringwald-Brown.

"Workers are dying every day and have for centuries. They will continue to do so unless we take steps to take control of the products of our own labour."

"Jesus love us," exclaimed Pat. "Will you stop with the spouting? Let's deal with one thing at a time."

One of the other girls looked up at Tyler. "You can share my chair if you like, Inspector." She was what he'd call a smasher, fresh-faced and full-lipped, with an abundance of fair, curly hair. Many of the other women were still wearing their restrictive turbans. Not this one. She was a hair-tosser if ever he'd met one.

He might have had no choice but to accept her offer, but Mr. Cudmore had already procured a spare chair.

"Thank you, Mrs. Walmsley," he said briskly. "I think the inspector will be more comfortable on his own chair."

Tyler sat down.

Pat had got up on the stage. "Quiet everybody. Quiet. Shut up. Now you all know Mr. Cudmore here. The gentleman with him is Inspector Tyler. He's here to get to the bottom of what happened on Sunday." She looked over at Tyler. "Do you want to say a few words?"

Not really, thought Tyler. Public speaking wasn't quite his forte. Nevertheless, he thought he should take advantage of the gathering. He got up and joined Pat on the stage.

"First of all, I want to express my deepest regret that Audrey Sandilands has succumbed to her injuries. You are all doing a most important job and we don't want anything like this to happen again."

"Too true," called out Mary Ringwald-Brown in a loud voice. "The owners don't want to lose their peasants."

Various groans greeted this. Tyler sympathized with them. The woman's comments were tasteless, given the circumstances. She didn't seem to have a lot of support among those same peasants.

"I'm not speaking for any owner," said Tyler. "I'm a police officer. It's my job. Any and all equivocal deaths have to be investigated. I'd like to be able to count on your help."

At that moment the canteen door opened and a man tiptoed in. He was carrying a camera and a tripod. He was trying to be unobtrusive but that only served to draw glances in his direction. He looked familiar but Tyler couldn't place him.

Pat drew their attention back to the matter in hand. "What would help you the most from us, Inspector?"

"I'd like to hear your opinions concerning safety in the factory," said Tyler. He nodded at the secretary. "Mr. Cudmore will take notes and what seems relevant, I promise, will be presented to Mr. Endicott. My job is not only to determine what happened on Sunday but to make sure there is no recurrence."

"Hear, hear," Mick Smith called out.

One of the women in the front row raised her hand. Tyler nodded at her.

"Go ahead, Miss . . ."

"Lipton. June Lipton. I think I am speaking for all of us here when I say we want to do our bit for the war effort. My fiancé is overseas and I want him to come back in one piece, and soon."

There was a murmur of sympathy from the others. "The problem to my mind is that we are too rushed," she continued. "Too much is expected of us. We're not machines."

That brought a burst of clapping. Somebody else, not waiting to be acknowledged, called out, "We need more break time."

"Inspector?" The blonde girl who'd been keeping the door waved at him. "We all get tired at the end of our shift. That's when accidents happen. We'd like to have some music to keep us awake. We could pipe in the BBC."

More agreement from the other workers. They were all livening up. Cudmore recorded it in his notebook. Tyler could see that the latecomer was setting up his camera in a corner of the room. Pat noticed at the same time.

"Oi, you. What do you think you're doing?"

He smiled at her. "I'm here from the ministry to make a film about the factory."

Suddenly Tyler realized who he was. The Yank. The man in the fog.

Mary Ringwald-Brown sprang to her feet. "We cannot allow this. We have not approved this man. What is the purpose of this film?"

"He is quite legitimate," interjected Cudmore. "The request to film footage of the factory came in before the dreadful tragedy occurred, but Mr. Kaplan has assured me he will be very sensitive as to what he photographs."

Mary was still standing. She virtually shook her fist at Cudmore. "The government doesn't give a fig about us. We're just fodder for the cannons." She addressed Kaplan. "You want us all to be smiling and cheerful, don't you. You want the lie."

"I apologize," said Kaplan and he immediately removed his camera from the tripod. "I had no intention of doing anything other than record what you have to say. As the inspector has pointed out, we must make sure this factory is a safe place to work."

Mary looked as if she wanted to continue the fight, but Pat took charge again. "Let's get back to it then. Just don't take any photos right now, mister." She scanned the crowd. "What else do people have to say?"

"Management treats us like children half the time," said a woman at the back of the room. She was a Liverpool lass, a good, tough Scouser, tall and curvaceous in her snug overalls. A smattering of applause to that. "Women aren't men," she continued.

"Thank goodness for that, look you," called out the man behind the counter. Some laughter.

"I'm serious, Taffy. For instance, we women have, on occasion, a need to go to the wc quite suddenly. We can't wait for tea break and we don't want to have to get special permission to leave our stations."

That received a big ovation. Cudmore did his *I have no idea what you're referring to* head duck. Tyler could see the women around him casting covert glances in his direction to see if he understood what Scouse was talking about. He did.

Frankie spoke up next. "I agree with Lily. So what if we stay a few minutes longer in the lavatory?"

"We need better towels, by the way," interrupted the Scouser. "The ones that are provided are a disgrace."

"And the water is never hot," said the smasher beside Tyler.

The door at the rear opened again and a woman in a nurse's white formal uniform entered.

"Hold on a minute, you lot," Pat called out. "Miss Abbott has just come in. Let's give her a seat."

Frankie stood up. "Over here, Sister."

Looking slightly discomfited by the attention, the woman made her way to the front and slipped into the chair. She had a good face for a nurse, Tyler thought, intelligent and kind. Their eyes met briefly as she sat down. Like everybody else she was curious about him, but he thought for a moment he caught an expression of anxiety.

"We're just getting things off our chest," Pat said.

"I'm glad to hear it."

Mary was still standing. "May I point out that Miss Abbott is part of management? I don't think she should be allowed in the meeting."

"This is not an official union meeting, Mary," replied Pat. "We don't even have a bloody union. Miss Abbott has gone to bat for us many times. I'm not turfing her out."

"Let's put it to a vote," said the other woman.

"No, we will not," answered Pat in exasperation. "We were talking about important things and this is the first time we've had the opportunity. Let's go on."

"Why do the men earn more money than us when we do the same work?" asked June in a rather timid voice.

"Good question, ducks," called out Smith. "If you can do what we do, you should get the same."

"You've got a point, June," said Pat. "But for now we're probably better off concentrating on the issue of safety. We can't change the whole world in one go."

"Tell Mr. Endicott we don't appreciate the lav doors being locked on us," said Frankie.

Cudmore looked up. "There was no such directive issued by management."

"So why were they locked on Sunday, then? It put the next shift in such a rush."

"They probably hurried too much," interjected Lily. "That's why the accident happened."

Tyler could see how disturbing this notion was to the women around him.

"The bloody doors didn't lock themselves, Mr. Cudmore," continued Frankie. "If you weren't the one who gave the order, who did?"

"I'm afraid I don't know," answered the secretary.

The Welshman stepped out from behind the counter. "Beg pardon, ladies, but I'm after wondering if there's any point to this question. Shouldn't you be talking about the state of some of the machines, for instance? They've been here since the factory was making muskets, if you ask me. Mr. Endicott should cough up and have them replaced."

"If you don't mind another bloke putting in his tuppence-worth," said Smith, "I'm in agreement with Taffy 'ere. And while we're at it, why can't we get the stoves updated? No offence, Taffy, but the food here leaves something to be desired."

"I know it, look you. And I'm the one gets the blame."

Lily called out, "That's all very well, but the men's loo wasn't locked. Why not?"

Pat turned to Tyler. "Any ideas, Inspector? You're the detective here."

Tyler shrugged. "I took a peek at the changing room doors yesterday and they can only be locked with a key. As I understand it there was no key in the door when the Blue shift arrived," said Tyler. "Mrs. Castleford had to send for one."

"Mr. Cudmore?" asked Lily. "You should know the answer to that. Who has the bloody keys?"

"I have a set, Miss Johnson. As does the caretaker. I have already explained this to the inspector. My keys are kept on a board near my desk. Mr. Riley knows this, and he picked up the one for the changing room."

"I can't see Phil messing about with locking doors and what-not," said Frankie. "Why would he? Why would anybody?"

Tyler didn't particularly like what he was about to say, but he felt he had to. "It has been suggested to me that perhaps somebody on the first shift deliberately caused a delay so that the second shift would be late getting to work."

"Because of the bonus?" said Pat.

Tyler nodded.

The room was suddenly silent. One of the women at the back started to weep. They all understood the implications if such a thing had occurred. The nurse was staring down at her hands. Tyler had the sense that she, like Cudmore, had been opposed to the introduction of a bonus.

Pat's expression was grim. "If that was indeed the case, we need to get to the bottom of what happened so we don't lose anybody else."

All eyes were on Tyler. "As far as I can figure it out, the only time somebody could have locked the doors was in the fifteen-minute period between the first shifts from Sections A and B leaving and the second shifts arriving." He took out the sheet of paper that the ever-helpful secretary had given him. "I have a list of who was working in those sections. I'll read the names of those who have come in to work this morning." He did so. Four of them were sitting at the head table. "Am I missing anybody?"

Silence.

"Does anybody know who was the last to leave the changing room at the end of the first shift?" Tyler asked.

Mrs. Walmsley, the smasher, pointed towards Pat. "You were. You and Francine. I distinctly remember. I was going to the canteen and asked if you'd like to have a cuppa but you said Frankie had lost her scarf and you were going to look for it."

"Me mum give it to me, and she'd kill me if she thought I'd lost it," said Frankie in agitation.

"As it turned out," said Pat, "it was under the bench."

Tyler spoke to Pat. "So you and Miss Tomlin were the last women to leave?"

"I suppose we were. I wasn't paying attention."

"And obviously the door wasn't locked or you wouldn't have been able to get out."

"No, it was bloody not," said Frankie with some indignation. "And neither me nor Pat has a bloody key. There was nobody else in the room. It was empty. We didn't touch nothing. Just got me scarf which belonged to *me* and then we went to clock out."

Miss Abbott spoke up. "If you think this is important, Inspector, you can check the time sheet."

A burst of talk, and Tyler could see that his communist friend, who had been quiet during the back-and-forth, was flushed with rage. She glared directly at him. "You are trying to turn us against each other. Worker against worker. Those other women are our comrades. You are working for management. You're trying to shift the blame on us in the most insidious way. Typical."

Bedlam erupted. Some girls were yelling at Mary to be quiet and others were calling out agreement. As far as Tyler could tell the two men were staying out of it, as was the Yank.

He held up his hands. "Ladies, please. I realize my line of enquiry is distasteful to you but we might as well settle it once and for all. The fewer loose ends, the better. Mr. Cudmore, could you get the time sheet from yesterday for us?"

Cudmore hurried away.

Frankie had been looking very agitated during this exchange. She turned to Mary. "You were going to work a double on Sunday, weren't you?"

"I decided I was too tired and I changed my mind."

"Lucky thing, that."

"It's appalling what you are insinuating."

"Just asking," said Frankie.

"Hold on," said Lily. "Mary normally belongs to the Blue

shift. She wouldn't want them to fall behind. Wouldn't do her no good to slow them down."

"Precisely. Thank you, Lily."

Pat was still on the stage but she looked scared. Tyler addressed the women.

"While we're all waiting for Mr. Cudmore, why don't you get a refill. And more buns. It's on me. All right with you, Taffy?"

"Come and get it, my lassies," said the Welshman.

There was a hustle and bustle as they availed themselves of Tyler's offer.

"I'll get one for you, Inspector," said the smasher with a captivating smile. She brushed against him as she went by.

In the midst of all the activity, Kaplan came over to the table. He held out his hand. "Inspector, good to see you again. Recognized you right away."

"You seem recovered, Mr. Kaplan."

He beamed at her. "I'm swell, thanks. My shoulder had popped out but Miss Abbott put it right back."

"Only too happy to oblige, Mr. Kaplan."

"Cor blimey," said Lily, who had returned with a tray of cups of tea. "I can't see how filming this cock-up is going to help recruit new workers. If it was me, I wouldn't touch this place with a barge pole . . . locked doors, missed counts, fatal explosions – blimey."

Cudmore re-entered the canteen carrying a bundle of time sheets. He handed them to Tyler, who riffled through them. He waited a bit longer for the tea to be gulped down, then went back to the stage. He didn't have to ask for attention. There was silence immediately.

"All right, then. According to what I have here, the first person to leave from Section B was Miss Johnson, who clocked out at a half past two."

"I had to get home," said Lily. "I live with me mum and she was poorly."

Tyler checked the list and read out loud, "At two forty, Miss Francine Tomlin clocked off, and at two forty-one, Miss O'Callaghan."

He paused. The last name was a bit of a surprise. Aware of the possible consequences, he rechecked the list. No, it wasn't a mistake.

"At two forty-five, the last person working on the shift clocked out. That was Miss Mary Ringwald-Brown."

The women turned to stare at Mary. She had left the table when Cudmore entered and was standing by the food counter.

"Oi, oi," said Pat. "Did you forget to mention it, Mary? You were after us, then. Frankie and me weren't the last."

Mary shrugged impatiently. "It is all so unimportant."

"According to the inspector here, it might be very important. You could have locked the door yourself."

"Please don't be ridiculous," said Mary, her voice like a knife.

Tyler interceded. "Miss Brown, Miss O'Callaghan has said that when she and Miss Tomlin left, the changing room was empty. Yet the evidence is unmistakable that you clocked out after the two of them."

She scowled at him. "Evidence? I didn't know I was on trial. And my name is Ringwald-Brown."

"I beg your pardon. Do you have any explanation for this odd discrepancy, Miss Ringwald-Brown?"

"You are putting me into a very embarrassing position."

Pat burst out, "You're for sure hiding something. What were you doing?"

Mary started to fidget. "If you must know, I was in the toilet. I had, er . . . oh, this is so humiliating . . . I had started my menstrual cycle, and yes, I was in the toilet fixing myself up. I didn't feel like making a public announcement about it."

"Did you lock the door?" Pat asked bluntly.

"Of course I didn't. First of all, I'm a mere peon and I don't have a key, and second, why would I? And don't spout that lie to me about trying to stall the next group. I've been against the quota system from the beginning. You can ask anybody here."

"True. She's telling the truth about that," said Lily.

"I was right behind O'Callaghan and Francine," continued Mary. "The door was definitely not locked when I left."

"And when you did leave, was the changing room empty?" Tyler asked.

"As far as I know. I suppose there is a possibility that some other poor woman was lurking in the stalls, but I didn't check. I had no reason to. Besides, if there was such a creature, she would have had to clock out as well. You, Inspector, and you, Mr. Cudmore, appear to have gone to a lot of trouble to show that I was the last to do that."

Funny how she has the knack of making everything seem underhand and suspect, thought Tyler. *As if there was a conspiracy building against her.*

"Quite so. Well, thank you, Miss Ringwald-Brown."

Tyler knew there was no way to prove whether or not she was telling the truth, but he had a strong feeling she was lying. If so, why? What had she been trying to do? Slow everything down probably, meddle with the capitalist system. On the other hand, he suspected this delay might have put too much pressure on the Blue shift. Was that why Mary had looked so distressed at the hospital? Were the deaths of four young women on her conscience? He looked over at her. She was standing straight, her head held high. *The stance of a woman prepared to be a martyr*, thought Tyler.

***

Brian lay for a while, not sleeping, just thinking. Finally he decided to venture downstairs. He knew his gran would bring him his breakfast if he didn't, and he was desperate to get out of the tiny room. He used the commode, got dressed in the old jersey and too-big pants of his grandfather, and went down to the living room.

As he'd expected, Beatrice was waiting for him. She was sitting at the table knitting, her fingers fast and nimble. The wireless was turned down low but he could make out some organ music wailing away; the BBC seemed intent on boring the British population out of their minds. She greeted him anxiously as he came in, searching his face for messages as to his mood. He dragged up a smile.

"Morning, Gran. Sleep well?"

"It's me should be asking you that. You look exhausted, Bri."

"I'm all right. There'll be lots of time to get caught up later."

She put down the knitting. "Your granddad and Auntie Eileen have gone off to the factory. It'll be a short day today, I'm sure. I was just waiting to see the whites of your eyes before I put the kettle on."

He patted her on the shoulder. "You stay right there, Gran. I'm going to wait on you for once. No, I insist. I didn't have a present for your birthday but at least I can give you a bit of fuss."

He went into the kitchen and lit the gas. He knew that Beatrice kept small change in a biscuit tin in the cupboard. Quietly he took it down. There were a couple of shillings, three pennies, and a sixpence. He took one of the shillings.

The kettle came to a boil and he poured the water into the pot. It was an old brown one that his grandmother had had for years. He'd bought her a fancy china pot for Christmas once but she never used it, claiming the brown Betty made the best tea. There was a slice of cake left over and he put it on a plate. He opened the drawer of the sideboard, found a used candle, lit it, and fixed the shilling to the bottom of the plate with the melted wax. Piling everything onto a tray, he went into the living room.

"This is belated but I'm going to sing anyway." Somewhat off-key, he sang "Happy Birthday."

He placed the tray on her lap. "Now make a wish and blow out the candle."

She tried to go along with the game, but not too successfully. Brian knew what her wish was, and she'd have to blow out a town full of candles before it could be granted.

"Look under the plate."

She found the shilling. "Brian, I don't want this."

"You can't give back a present, it's not polite. I want you to buy some of your favourite sweeties at Kenny's. Now, shall I pour the tea?"

"Not yet. Let it steep a bit more. Aren't you having anything?"

"Later."

"It's early to be eating cake," she murmured. Nevertheless she took a bite.

Brian plopped down in the chair opposite her. "Will you read my tea leaves, Gran? Remember how you used to do that? You were always a proper Gypsy."

"I don't know, Bri. I haven't done that since the war started. Frankly, I was afraid what I'd see."

"Please. Just this once. You were always so good. Uncanny, really."

She smiled at him, pleased. "All right. Drink your tea and drain your cup."

He did so in a hurry, the hot tea almost scalding his throat.

"That's it. Now hold the cup in your left hand, swish the leaves around three times counter-clockwise, and put it upside down in the saucer. Good." She picked up the cup by the handle and peered into it.

"What?" He asked impatiently. "What do you see?"

"Well, there are some clouds. They are on both sides of the handle, so that means they are behind you but you're not yet through."

"That's for sure."

"But there is a bird here . . . no, maybe more than one, which means good news." She twisted the tea cup back and forth. "I see a journey coming up. Across stormy water, but you will reach the other side safely." Another turn while Brian listened intently, as he always had. "There are some scissors—"

"Uh-oh, that means a quarrel, doesn't it?"

"Yes, a quarrel. It's right next to a volcano, so you have to watch you don't lose your temper."

"Let me see. Where is a volcano?"

Beatrice pointed to a cone-shaped clump of tea leaves. "There."

"Looks more like a mushroom to me, and I know that means change."

"Who's reading these leaves, you or me?" said Beatrice, lowering the cup.

"Sorry, Granny, you are. Go on. What else?"

"Hmm . . . I see a visitor, a man perhaps, but it's not clear – could be a woman. This person needs your help."

"Can't be the MPs, then."

She glanced at him nervously and he grinned reassuringly. "Any more birds? I like them."

She examined the teacup again. "No, just those two."

He too looked into the cup. "Is that a V? Is Vanessa in the tea leaves?"

"It could be a V."

"Is it next to the mushroom?"

"Not really. It's closer to the pair of scissors."

"Which is a quarrel."

"Possibly." She returned the cup to its saucer. "These leaves are hard to read; they're too clumped up together. You should have drunk more of the tea." She leaned forward and kissed his cheek. "I'm sure we can arrange for you to meet Vanessa soon. We just have to be careful, that's all."

He lowered his eyes, not wanting her to see the truth. "You know what, Gran, you're right about the travel. I, er, I'm thinking I can get to Ireland and wait out the war there. The Irish government won't extradite anybody who's on their soil, because they're a neutral country."

She looked at him in astonishment. "But how would you get to Ireland?"

"I'll find a way, don't worry."

"Oh, Bri, I don't know . . ." But he could tell that the possibility was a relief to her.

"I only have to hide out here for a few more days at most. That'll make it easier for Dad's conscience to stomach, don't you think? He seemed to be having trouble with it."

"Don't be silly. He wants what's best for you." She sighed. "It would certainly be easier in terms of the rationing."

"Settled, then. I'll need your help a bit, Gran. You know how Granddad is. He'll want to know all the details – how I'm going to get there and so on, but I can't share those with him. You understand, don't you?"

She looked at him, puzzled. "No, I don't really, Bri. Are there other people involved?"

"Lord, no. Just me. But it'd be better if my plans weren't known . . . MPs might come here, for instance, and you know what a terrible liar you are."

He jumped to attention and imitated a ferocious-sounding military policeman. "Mrs. Abbott, have you seen your grandson recently? Answer truthfully or God will strike you dead." He mimicked his grandmother with a high-pitched voice and wrung his hands guiltily. "Er, why no, Officer, not recently, at least, not that I know of."

She laughed. "Get out of here. I wouldn't sound like that."

"Yes, you would. You are transparent as a pane of glass. Remember that time when Dad came here to find me? This was before I'd moved in, but I'd come over that night bawling my eyes out like I was a babbie. He asked if I was in the house and you said no and even if I was you wouldn't tell him anyway. Not while he was in a mood like that. I could hear you from upstairs, and I knew he didn't believe a word."

"He left though, didn't he."

"True, but that was out of respect for you. He knew all the time I was here."

"Regardless, it did give him a chance to cool off, and the next day we had a family talk and he was quite reasonable."

"You're being kind, Gran. He wasn't reasonable at all. He was only too glad to get me out of his hair."

Beatrice reached for his hand and held it briefly. "He does love you, Brian. He just has a hard time showing it."

He shook his head. "See. I said you were terrible at telling fibs."

***

Joe Abbott was grey-haired, tall, and on the thin side. He had innate presence – a quality Tyler had seen in some ncos in the army. It had nothing to do with education or social status and more to do with character. Tyler noticed that he walked with a limp.

When they shook hands, Abbott's was cool and firm.

"Please sit down, sir."

Abbott took the chair Mr. Cudmore had offered. "You've got a gammy leg, I see," said Tyler.

"Legacy of the last war. Gas ulcer," said Abbott. His gaze was wary.

"Right. Let's start then, shall we? Mr. Cudmore is taking notes for me. Hope you don't mind – my handwriting is terrible. By the way, I assume the nurse here at the clinic is a relative?"

"She's my daughter."

"Thought so. There's a strong family resemblance."

"She's better-looking."

Tyler chuckled. "Aren't they always. Thank goodness my daughter inherited her mother's hair, not mine."

Abbott smiled politely but seemed to relax a little.

"Your counterpart, Mr. Smith, has described the nature of the job, but I wonder if you wouldn't just run through what you did on Sunday afternoon. I'm particularly interested in whether there was anything out of the usual routine."

Abbott tightened his lips. "To tell you the truth, I hadn't even started. Management feels there's no point in us dillie men being here before quarter to three. First shift leaves at two thirty, but we have the fifteen-minute changeover break and there isn't any work for me to pick up right away. I was just coming up the road when I heard the explosion."

"Mr. Abbott, I tell you frankly I am treating this incident as a tragic accident, but in the unlikely event that it was not . . . that is, if some kind of sabotage was involved, do you have any idea how that could have occurred?"

"No, I do not."

"I asked Mr. Smith this question, Mr. Abbott – were the fuses always within your sight? Nobody could have tampered with them, for instance?"

Abbott stiffened. "No, Inspector."

Tyler tapped ash off his cigarette. "I understand there are

two places on your route where you are essentially on your own and out of sight of any other worker."

Abbott frowned. "Not sure what – oh, the corridors between the magazine shed and the doors to the two sections. Is that where you mean?"

"That's what Mr. Smith said."

"Technically he's right, but they're only a few feet long and the operatives do come back and forth sometimes. If they have to go to the toilets, for instance. We can't be assured of privacy, if that's what you're getting at."

"Right. I have one last question. Is there anybody in the factory that might be capable of an act of sabotage? Anybody at all? Take your time to answer."

Abbott hadn't been in the canteen when suspicion was directed at Mary Ringwald-Brown. Tyler was curious as to what he would say.

In fact, Abbott looked angry. "I don't need to take my time, begging your pardon, Inspector. I don't know anybody who would intentionally cause the death of four blameless young women. Nobody."

"Well, thank you, Mr. Abbott."

Tyler shook hands and Abbott left.

While Cudmore went to fetch his next interviewee, Tyler made a list in his own notebook:

1. Check further into the Yank, Lev Kaplan. Was he too eager to photograph what was happening in the canteen? Images of discontent like that could be destructive for morale. Some newspapers of the leftist bent would make hay with them. See if indeed the ministry did hire him.

2. See if there are police files on Miss Ringwald-Brown and Miss June Lipton, who both so conveniently missed the explosion at the last minute.

3. Not to mention Miss O'Callaghan and her friend. Also Mick Smith and Joe Abbott – both with easy access to the magazine box.

4. Talk to Alf Mason about looters. Does he have anybody in his files who fitted the description of the lad on the bike?

5. And finally, check on the background of the competent secretary, Mr. Lester Cudmore.

Sorry, Les, thought Tyler. *Nothing personal. Just the habits of a copper who's found it pays to trust almost nobody.*

***

Beatrice had gone off to the shops. She and Phyllis had worked out that if they both bought more of food items that were not rationed, such as cabbage and potatoes, they could fill out the meals. But that meant Beattie had to go farther afield, where she wasn't known. Brian knew she'd be gone for a while.

He couldn't sit still. He went to the window and risked a peek through the curtain. His gran was right. It was dismal outside. Somebody was coming down the road and he dropped the curtain quickly. He couldn't bear to go back to the upstairs room. His thoughts shifted and roiled in his head. Donny Jarvis, Vanessa, the army mates he'd left.

The clock on the mantel chimed the quarter-hour. The morning seemed interminable. Brian felt a curious mixture of exhausted and wide awake. He wondered if his aunt had some sleeping pills, something to calm him down. Probably. He got up and went to Eileen's room. The door was locked. Shite. It hadn't been locked yesterday. Had she realized he'd been having a look around? What was she trying to keep away from him? The pills in her drawer probably. He gave the door a kick.

He prowled into the living room again. Granddad had said not to turn on the wireless, but if he kept it really quiet it might be all right. He snapped it on, keeping the volume low. Same insipid organ music. He turned it off. Damn. His hand was shaking like an old man's. He tried to hold it steady, but that didn't help either.

What are the other lads up to? he wondered. They'd know by now he'd done a bunk. Would they be talking about him? Ridiculing him? Nobby Clark would. He'd made it clear he despised Brian, but a couple of the others – Shorty Green and Podge – would understand. Maybe they were all on board ship by now, heading for Africa.

He put his head on the table. Oh God. What had he done?

He must have actually fallen into a short sleep, because he was jerked awake by knocking at the front door. *One, two, three.* Repeated. *One, two, three.* He waited, holding his breath, until the mail slot opened and a voice whispered, "*It's me – Jackie.*"

Quickly Brian went to the door and let him in, making sure he stayed hidden. The day was overcast and gloomy but the safety of the fog had gone.

Jack held out a net shopping bag. "This is for you. From Donny."

Brian grabbed it and looked inside. There was a box wrapped in newspaper.

"Stay here." He ran up to his room and thrust the bag underneath the bed. He didn't know if it would be ultimately safe from his gran's housekeeping, but it would have to do for now. When he returned to the living room, Jack was sitting at the table, not moving, just waiting.

"Gran should be back soon," said Brian. "Do you want a cuppa?"

"No, thanks. I'm supposed to be at school. I'm going to get another late detention."

"Hold on a bit. I wanted to have a chinwag while we could."

"I'd better not stay too long, Bri."

Brian shook out a cigarette from his packet and offered it to Jack. "You smoking yet?"

"Not yet."

"Smart lad." Shakily Brian lit a cigarette and drew in a lungful of smoke. "I was curious as to how you got into the clutches of that rotten sod Donny Jarvis."

Jack shrugged, not looking at him. "He saw me coming out of one of the bombed-out houses."

"God, Jackie, don't tell me you were looting."

Another shrug. "I suppose so."

Brian caught his arm. "No, Jackie. Not suppose. Either you were or you weren't."

The boy tugged himself free, shrinking away from him. "The people were dead so they didn't need it anymore, did they."

"What'd you steal? I'm curious."

"Some money. They'd left it in a jam jar. It wasn't much."

"How much?"

"'Bout ten bob."

"And for ten shillings you sold your soul to Donny Jarvis?"

Jack was on the verge of tears. "I didn't know what to do."

"Why didn't you go to Dad? Or better yet, why didn't you talk to Granddad? He knows how to deal with rubbish like Donny."

"I can't. Donny'll hurt me bad if I tell anybody and if I don't do what he says."

"That where you got your bruise?"

Jack nodded, his face abject. "I didn't want to say anything about you, Bri, but it sort of all came out. Donny's like that. Nobody stands up to him. He broke his last girlfriend's nose because she cheeked him. He doesn't just threaten – he does."

Brian chucked the boy under the chin. "No good crying over spilt milk. I'm going to take care of Mr. Jarvis before I go."

Jackie looked at him, round-eyed. "What'll you do?"

"Never mind about that." He stubbed out his cigarette. "Do you know what's in the bag he gave you?"

"No."

"Good. Keep it that way." He grinned. "If you think Donny Jarvis can hurt people, he's got nothing on me when I get riled up." He pushed back his chair and stood up. "Don't know about you, but I need that cuppa."

Jackie glanced over at the clock on the mantelpiece. "No, I've really got to go, Bri."

"Not yet. There's something else I want to talk to you about."

Brian went into the kitchen, leaving the door open. "How're you doing at school?" he called over his shoulder.

"All right."

"Did you get Mr. Lishman this year?"

"Yeah."

"He's a bit of an arsehole but he makes you learn."

"Yeah."

Brian stood in the doorway. He said, ever so casually, "I saw Nessa last night. She made it in spite of the fog."

"Good. That must have been nice for you." Jack's eyes were lowered.

Brian stepped closer. "What did you tell her exactly when you gave her the message?"

"That you were here and would meet her at midnight in the shelter. Just like you told me. Why? Did she get the time wrong?"

"No, no, she was right on time. Funny thing, though, she seemed surprised to see me. I mean to see *me*. Almost as if she was expecting somebody else."

Jack didn't look at him. "Don't be daft, Brian. How could she be?"

"That's what I wondered. So I thought I'd better ask what you said exactly." His lips twisted into his ferocious grin. "Maybe you said some film star was waiting in the shelter."

"Course I didn't."

"Michael Wilding, for instance. Or Leslie Howard."

"Not likely."

"When you said it was me wanted to see her, and that I wasn't in the army anymore, she must have been quite taken aback."

"Course she was."

A piece of coal fell in the fireplace and Jack jumped. Brian didn't take his eyes off his brother's face.

"Was she glad? When you said I was home and waiting for her, was she glad?"

"Course she was, Bri."

Brian came to the table where Jack was sitting. "It's a relief to know what you just said, Jackie."

"Sure, Bri. Anytime."

Brian turned his brother's head towards him. "Because I don't like fibbers, Jack. In fact, I hate them."

After Jack had left, Brian felt even more restless. His grand-dad had said they should keep the curtains closed at all times. A lot of people did these days, so it wouldn't seem so strange. They were heavy blackout curtains; he had to turn the light on when he was in the room. He would love to go out and get some fresh air but he knew he couldn't. He wasn't going to be outside in daylight for a long time. What if Donny let him down and didn't bring him the passport and identity card? Well, he wasn't going to stay here. He'd go stark, raving mad. He'd find a way to get to Ireland himself. Even if the absolute worst happened and Vanessa couldn't come with him right away, he'd go regardless. The war couldn't last forever. He'd have to wait it out.

He went back upstairs and pulled out the bag from underneath the bed. He decided to take a chance on his gran's being out for a couple of hours and decided to use the living room.

He emptied the contents of the shopping bag onto the table. There were two alarm clocks without the outer casings, a couple of batteries, two tiny light bulbs from a torch, and some wires. That was it. He hadn't made a timer before but it was a simple matter really. Connect the wires from the battery to the clock, then to the light bulb. Set the alarm for a certain time. When it switched on, it would connect with the light bulb, which would start to heat up. So much for Donny's protestations about no bombs. This type of timer was intended to connect with some kind of explosive substance that would react to heat. It was small but it didn't have to be big. Everything would fit in a shoebox.

"No casualties," Donny had said, but who was kidding whom? Well, he couldn't think about that. This was survival of the fittest. Let those who can survive. He couldn't take care of everybody else.

Suddenly the front door opened and in walked Mrs. Swann, the next-door neighbour. "Beattie, I'm off to the shops. Do you—"

Seeing him, she stopped in her tracks. "Brian, what are you doing here? I thought you were off in the army."

His mind froze. He could easily have told her he was on leave, but he could see she was peering curiously over his shoulder.

"Is Beattie in?"

"No, she's gone shopping."

Something must have showed on his face, some expression that alarmed her. She began to turn towards the door.

"I'll just drop off this pamphlet, then."

He was on her in a flash, grabbing her thin arm. "Mrs. Swann, stay here."

"Brian, what's wrong with you?"

She tried to push him away and get out the door but he jerked her hard and she fell to the ground. Her head connected with the bottom step in a sickening bounce. The breath had been knocked out of her body and she lay gasping on the floor, one leg splayed out at a grotesque angle. Brian was paralyzed. She was going into seizures and it was obvious from the sudden stench that she had involuntarily voided her bowels. She moaned and her eyelids fluttered.

It was the moan that broke Brian's immobility. Terror swept through him. Without a thought, wanting only to stop the sound, he seized one of his granddad's brass-topped walking sticks from the stand.

She was a fragile old thing and it didn't take much to silence her, only two savage blows.

Brian started to talk out loud. "Got to get her out of the hall – quick."

He was panting as if he'd been running. Mrs. Swann's hat had tilted over her forehead and a halo of blood was spreading around her head.

"Don't think about that now. Get her out of here. The shelter. I'll take her down to the shelter."

He grabbed the hall rug and wrapped her in it. His grandfather's mac and old cap were hanging on the coat stand. Trembling, Brian put them on.

"If anybody sees me, they'll think it's Granddad."

Mrs. Swann was frail and small, but she was now a dead weight and he had to heave to get her over his shoulder.

He stumbled towards the back door, his knees shaking so hard he could hardly walk.

"You would have told. I know you would have. It was an accident. I didn't mean to pull you like that."

He managed to open the door a crack and peeked out. Nobody was in sight and a thin rain had started, darkening the already gloomy day. He kicked open the door and, making himself walk briskly, he strode down the path to the air-raid shelter. Now his burden seemed light, although the smell was sickening in his nostrils.

There was a green chenille curtain hanging across the far corner of the shelter. Behind it, offering some cramped privacy, was a chamber pot, a jug of water, and a pile of extra blankets. There was just room between the blankets and the wall to dump the body, although he had to fold her up like a rag doll. He pulled away the rug and loaded the grey blankets around and on top of her.

"I'm sorry, but you shouldn't have walked in like that," he whispered. "Look at it like this. A bomb could have dropped on you. We don't know what God's plan was for you, do we. You've lived your life. Mine's just starting."

He dropped the curtain. Nothing looked disturbed. Good. He just hoped they wouldn't be using the shelter tonight.

He pulled his granddad's cap tightly onto his head. "Come on. Walk casually."

He went back to the house carrying the bloodied rug, the rain wetting his face.

When he got inside, Brian felt his strength leave his body like air out of a balloon. He could have lain down and gone to sleep right there and then. But he had to clean up.

He filled the kitchen sink with water and dumped the rug in. The water turned pink immediately. Then he got a wash rag, mop, and bucket and went back to the hall. Bloody hell. He'd been standing close enough to the old lady to catch some of the blood spatter, and his jersey was sticky all down the front. And the walking stick. He had to clean the walking stick. He pulled off his jersey and used it to wipe the stick, then replaced it in the stand. He was trying to move as fast as he could but the sensation was like moving through water.

Everything was an effort and he couldn't get his thoughts in order.

He started to wash the floor . . . no, wait, he mustn't be found here in his undervest with the blood-stained jersey at his feet. And the timers. He had to get them out of the living room.

He scrambled up to his room, using hands and feet as if he were a dog. He shoved the jersey in the shopping bag with the other stuff. He didn't dare spend time washing himself off but he couldn't see any stains on his skin – his clothes had absorbed the blood. But everything smelled bad. Had some of her shit got on his trousers when he picked her up? He checked frantically but couldn't see any. Maybe it was on the jersey. He'd have to throw it out as soon as possible. Fortunately his gran had given him a couple of extras. He grabbed one from the drawer and pulled it on. The shit smell lessened but not that much.

He went back downstairs, slipping on the last two steps in his haste and banging his tailbone painfully. On the linoleum was a large red stain flecked with bits of whitish grey stuff that must be brain matter. He dragged over the bucket and started to mop it up, trying not to gag.

The rage that had overtaken him seemed far off. He could hardly remember hitting Mrs. Swann. Had he always had such a temper? He'd been angry at times like anybody else, but he'd never lost control in this way before. But war changed men. The timid became bold and the apparently brave crumpled in the face of danger. That's what they said.

But you haven't been at war, said a cold voice in his head. *She was an old, helpless woman who never did you any harm.*

He whimpered. Mrs. Swann had given him sweeties when he was a child and even a pair of socks she'd knitted herself when he had a birthday. She'd always been kind and interested in his welfare. For a moment he experienced a rush of such grief and remorse that it actually made him feel as if he would collapse.

Maybe she wasn't dead.

He considered making a dash for the shelter just to make sure, but he might be seen. Besides, he knew she was dead. His act was irrevocable.

He heard a quick three taps at the door, then the key in the lock and Beattie came in.

"Brian," she exclaimed. "What are you doing?"

He was surprised how easily he could lie to her. "Gran, I'm so sorry. I tripped and spilled my tea all over everything. I'm so sorry."

"That's all right, Bri. What did you do with the rug?"

"I put it in the sink to soak."

"That was the right thing to do." She began to take off her headscarf and her coat. "Come on, cheer up, it's not the end of the world. That rug's had a lot more than that spilled on it over the years." She sniffed. "What's that bad smell?"

"Oh, Jackie dropped in this morning. He must have stepped in some dog dirt."

"Ugh. Why wasn't he at school?"

"He was skipping off, I suppose."

"I'm worried about that boy. He's not himself at all."

She tidied her hair in the mirror of the hall stand. Their eyes met.

"Bri . . . should you be downstairs?"

"Please, Gran. I'm going stir-crazy."

"Oh dear, we can't have that. Just stay away from the windows, there's a good boy. And the door wasn't locked. We must be so careful." She picked up her basket. "I did well with the veg. I went over to Stebbings and he had a new delivery of potatoes in. I bought some extra carrots as well. I told him I was shopping for Mrs. Swann, so I'll have to give her a bundle in case she says something." She bent down. "What's this?" She fished out a card that had got shoved under the coat stand. "Why, it's one of Maisie's Peace Pledge cards. How did that get here?"

"She must have dropped it through the letter slot and it got swept over there."

Beatrice put the card in her pocket. "If this war goes on much longer, I'll join myself. Anyway, I'll just pop out and take her the carrots or she'll be coming over. Won't be long."

Don't. Don't go. He swallowed hard so he wouldn't actually shout those words to her. He heard the back door click shut and he rushed to the window to see what she was doing. She crossed the back garden, went past the shelter, and opened the gate of Mrs. Swann's garden, where she vanished up the path out of sight. He waited. There was a bread knife on the draining board by the sink and he picked it up. For what? He didn't allow himself to contemplate the answer to that. Within a few minutes Beatrice reappeared. She was walking calmly down the path, not running, not looking bewildered or afraid. *Go past the shelter. Don't go in there.* She didn't, and in another minute she was at the house.

"Did Mrs. Swann like her carrots?" Brian set the knife back down

"She wasn't home. I left them on the counter." Beatrice shook her head. "She's getting a bit doddery in her old age. She'd left her kettle on the stove. Good thing I came in when I did. It had practically boiled dry."

Beatrice went to the sink and started to squeeze the rug. "You did make a mess of this, didn't you."

"Sorry."

Beatrice glanced over her shoulder at him, then came over and drew him into her arms. "It's not important, Brian. It'll wash out."

***

For the rest of the afternoon Tyler worked non-stop, interviewing as many people as he could before the end of their shift.

A very clear picture emerged of a factory ridden too hard. Morale was low and it wasn't just because of the explosion, which all the workers thought had been an accident. The dead girls had been well liked, and both Tyler and Cudmore had to proffer handkerchiefs at regular intervals. Mary Ringwald-Brown's name came up frequently. A shadow had descended over her that she wasn't easily going to dispel.

She herself refused to be interviewed. She claimed to have said everything there was to say in the canteen interrogation – note the word – and unless he was going to charge her with the crime of being a natural woman, he had no legal grounds to insist on her presence. Cudmore delivered this message, voice neutral, manner neutral. He'd have made a good diplomat, Tyler thought. As for himself, he thought the woman's attitude was provocative but he didn't want to give her fuel for her fire by throwing his weight around. He decided to leave her be for the time being.

"We should stop soon," he said to the secretary, who was looking bleary-eyed. "How many more people are there to see?"

"That's the last of those who came in today, sir. I shall send word to the absentees and ask them to come in tomorrow."

"Mr. Cudmore, you are a brick."

"Thank you, sir. I shall have these notes ready for you by tomorrow morning."

Tyler got up. "I'll go and see how my constable has made out."

Eagleton was covered in dust and looked hot and tired, but he'd accomplished a lot. He'd brought in a table and was standing in front of it putting the shards of the papier-mâché pots together. A neat pile of debris was beside the shattered bench.

"You look like a desert rat, Eager. Time for a cuppa, I'd say."

"Thank you, sir. This dust gets in your throat something awful."

"Did you get some lunch?"

"I did, sir. A tasty bowl of veggie soup." He removed his glasses and put them in his pocket. "I'm afraid there's not a lot to report, sir. There's too much damage to the pots to determine if they were originally faulty. As you thought, the explosion seems to have occurred right here." He pointed to a spot directly in front of the stool once occupied by Tess Deacon. "This person got the brunt. There were a few remnants of her tray but I would say that all the other fuses in the pot were ignited. That in turn must have set off the fuses in the magazine box, which was at the end of the bench."

Eagleton had placed markers at the spots where the girls had been seated. He continued: "The injuries each girl sustained are consistent with their proximity to the primary explosion. Miss Sumner got caught by flying shrapnel from the fuses in the box."

On his table he'd also put various ragged pieces of cloth, each labelled. Tyler went over to have a look. All were stained with blood.

"As best I could, I matched the material with the position of the operative at the bench," said Eager. "They're all scraps, sir. Nothing identifiable except for a bit of a collar with an initial embroidered on it. Letter A, so I'm assuming it was part of Audrey Sandilands' uniform."

There were five black felt shoes lined up.

"I haven't matched the slippers to the owners, sir. I haven't got information on the identifying characteristics of the women. Shoe sizes, that is. I'm assuming the missing shoes went with the victims."

"Thank you, lad, you have been most conscientious. I take it nothing has turned up that is unexpected?"

"No pins or jewellery, sir. Nothing metal at all. I've sieved through everything. No accelerants to indicate arson." He gave Tyler a shy grin. "That course you sent me on was useful. First thing I looked for."

He held out his hand. "I did find two loose buttons. They're regulation issue, so I assume they came from the overalls. But there was also this." He pointed to a small silver medallion.

"Looks like a Saint Christopher medal."

"Isn't he the patron saint of lost causes," said Eagleton.

"You're right about that, lad. Put them in an envelope and let's store what we can in boxes. If any boffins from Special Branch want to verify your findings, they can. I'll tell the management; they can get to work on repairing the area by tomorrow."

"If you'll excuse me saying so, I for one would like to see us getting back at the bloody Jerries as soon as possible. Only wish I could be fighting them myself."

Tyler patted him on the arm. "I'm not sure you could hit the side of the pyramids, Eager. But leave this for now. Any tittle-tattle you picked up from the canteen?"

"No, sir. I did sit myself at one of the tables but the girls were all chatting about film stars. I tried to steer the conversation round to the explosion but they said they didn't want to talk about it. They're taking up a collection for the funerals and they dunned me for half a crown."

"Include it in your expenses."

"Oh, I wouldn't do that, sir. It's a private donation." He gave a self-deprecating cough. "Might I have permission to go to the pictures tonight if there is no further work for me, sir? There's a George Formby film on and I haven't had a chance to see him before. Everybody says he's very funny."

"I might come with you, Eager. I haven't seen him either. A laugh would do us good."

"Yes, sir." The constable couldn't hide the expression of chagrin that flitted across his face.

Tyler chuckled. "I get it. You want to go with a lass, not your old inspector. Did you ask her already?"

"Sort of, sir. As it turns out, I was acquainted previously with one of the girls. Just before the war I happened to be in Birmingham and we met at a roller-skating rink." He grinned. "We ran into each other literally. She's very good, but I was a beginner."

"Well, before you go off gallivanting there's a bit of work I'd like you to do. If you come with me to my pantry, I'll give you the list. You can use the telephone at Steelhouse Lane to make the calls. Don't be put off by the desk sergeant. He thinks we country cops don't understand modern technology. Go along with him – it'll make him happy."

Tyler was thinking of turning in. He wasn't particularly tired but the station was empty, Alf Mason wasn't back yet, and Eagleton had gone off to the flicks with his roller-skating friend. Tyler had hurried off from Whitchurch without bringing anything to read, and except for newspapers, the station seemed to have a dearth of reading material. He was about to go in search of something when the door opened and Mason came in. He'd removed his coat and hat downstairs but he looked damp and cold.

"Come on over to the fire," said Tyler. "I'll stir it up a bit."

"You do that and I'll fix us a drink," said Alf. "Single malt be all right?"

"More than all right," said Tyler.

Mason was carrying a briefcase and he snapped it open, removed a bottle of Scotch, and poured some into two of the glasses on the sideboard. He brought one over to Tyler as he tossed back the other. By the time Tyler had taken his first appreciative sip, Mason was pouring himself a second. He smacked his lips. "That'll warm your cockles, Tom. As for me, I feel as if a whole bottle won't do."

Mason plunked himself into the chair close to the fire. "Tom, this is a rotten bloody war. I thought I'd done with it, done with wars, but we never learn, do we. I had to sit with a man for a couple of hours today who'd just heard his only son had been killed in a plane crash. Lad was nineteen. A training run apparently, nothing heroic. He's a good bloke, is Sam, one of the best. But he went to pieces when he heard the news. Hard to take. We were in the station. His wife rang. She probably should have told him just to come home and given him the news there, but she didn't." Mason poured his third whisky. Tyler hadn't even finished his first.

"You never know how blokes are going to react, do you." Mason continued. "I mean, you'd have thought Sam was the stiff-upper-lip type. He is normally, but he just sat down on the floor. Not even a chair – the floor. And he cried. I thought he'd never stop."

Mason swished the Scotch around in his glass and Tyler could feel himself going still. The last thing he wanted was to draw attention to his own tragedy. He'd cried only once and Clare had held him as if he were a child. But he'd also thought he'd never stop.

He got to his feet and went over to Mason. "Listen, mate, why don't I get you some grub from the kitchen to go with that firewater? The last thing you need is a hangover tomorrow."

Mason looked up at him. His expression was bleak. "To tell you the truth, I'm getting used to it."

***

The evening had fallen early and dark, with a steady drizzle. The four of them were all huddled close to the fire, listening to the wireless. It was Beattie's favourite program, "It's That Man Again." At least they could still laugh at "That Man" Tommy Handley. Joe, who looked exhausted, was dozing in his easy chair; Eileen and Beattie were both knitting. Beattie was good at socks, while Eileen stayed with the easier task of a khaki-coloured muffler. Brian seemed to be alternately paying attention to the wireless and then to his own tormenting thoughts.

There was a knock on the door.

Joe woke up at once. "Hide him," he said to Eileen, who lifted the tablecloth.

"Quick, Brian, get under here." He scrambled to do so.

There was a second knock.

"I'll get it," said Eileen. She waited to make sure Brian was truly hidden. Both her parents were regarding her anxiously.

Eileen switched off the light in the hall before she opened the front door. It was so dark that she didn't immediately recognize the girl standing on the threshold. She'd tied a scarf around her head and turned up the collar of her raincoat, but she still looked wet and miserable.

"Hello, Auntie Eileen. Can I come in?"

"Vanessa, we weren't expecting you . . . I, er . . ."

"It's all right. I know he's here."

"Do you indeed? Then you'd better come inside."

Vanessa stepped into the hall and Eileen closed the door behind her.

"Let me take your coat."

"I didn't think to bring a brolly. Stupid me." Vanessa giggled nervously. "He sent word to me through Jackie."

"He's in the living room," said Eileen.

The girl hesitated for a moment. "How is he?"

"As you might expect. Nervous. He's got himself into a lot of trouble."

"Don't I know it," Vanessa answered. "I wish he'd had more sense."

Eileen led the way into the living room. "It's Vanessa," she said.

Brian scrambled out from underneath the table, almost dragging the cloth with him. He came over to the girl immediately and kissed her.

"Hello, sweetheart. My God, your cheek is like ice. Come over to the fire and take my chair. Here, let me rub your hands. Where are your gloves?"

"I've lost them somewhere," said Vanessa.

Beatrice made room in front of the fire and mustered up a polite smile, but there was no mistaking her disapproval.

"Hello, Vanessa," said Joe.

Brian was warming his wife's hands but she soon withdrew them. "We thought it best if you knew that I knew . . ." She giggled again. "That sounds a bit funny, doesn't it."

Beatrice put down her knitting. Eileen went to the table to check if there was any tea left. When in doubt, pour tea.

"We got together last night," said Brian. "In the shelter."

Both Joe and Beatrice stared at him.

"You do understand the bad position Brian is in, don't you, Vanessa?" said Joe. "If anybody discovers he's here, he'll be sent back to his regiment and put in jail."

"I'll help out," said Vanessa. "I can bring rations as well."

"We can manage," said Beatrice. "He's hardly eating more than a bird as it is."

"Thanks for thinking of me, Ness," said Brian, and he brushed a strand of hair away from her face, a gesture so naked in its passion that even Eileen turned away in embarrassment.

Beatrice was fidgeting with the knitting on her lap. "What do you think, Joe?"

"I'm sure Vanessa will be careful."

"Course I will . . . But, sorry, I wasn't going to stay long. Just wanted to say hello and let you know the lie of the land. I'm on fire-watch duty tonight and I need to get a bit of shut-eye before I check in."

"You can sleep here," said Brian. "I've got my old bedroom."

"I'd better not, Bri. Mum and Dad will wonder."

"We'd best not get them suspecting anything," said Joe.

Beatrice couldn't help adding, "And your parents have never been partial to our Brian, have they."

Vanessa didn't answer. She stood up.

"I'll see you to the door," said Brian.

Eileen caught his arm. "No, you won't, my lad. I will. You've got to keep away from the windows and doors at all times."

Brian nodded, pulled Vanessa to him, and kissed her. She squirmed and broke away.

"Bri – not here. I'll try to come tomorrow. In the evening. Ta-ra, Nana Abbott, ta-ta, Granddad Abbott."

In the hall, Vanessa stopped to check her appearance in the mirror. She took a lipstick out of her handbag. "That was quite a scene in the canteen today, wasn't it. I've never been partial to Mary. Do you think she was responsible for locking the doors?"

"I don't know," said Eileen.

"The detective was sweet, I thought. And good-looking for a man his age. The Yank too. He can take my picture any-time." She applied a new layer of crimson to her full lips and made a kissing gesture to seal the lipstick, then pinched her cheeks to bring some colour to them.

"This situation with Brian must be very difficult for you," said Eileen. "We need to stick together. If you want to drop by the clinic and talk to me anytime, you can."

The girl looked at her, eyebrows raised and wariness in her eyes. "Thanks, but I'm hunky-dory. I'm over the shock now."

She checked the mirror again, studied herself critically for a moment, then fluffed up her hair. The rain had made it curlier than usual. She wiped a smudge of lipstick from her front teeth. "Well, I'm off, then."

She reached for her wet raincoat and shrugged herself into it. The buttonholes were straining.

Before she could open the door, Eileen stopped her. "You're pregnant, aren't you," she said quietly.

"What? What are you talking about?"

"Come on, I'm a nurse. I'd guess you're about two or three months gone. Brian has been away for five months. It's not his."

Vanessa shrugged off her hand. "That's a load of bollocks."

"You've been seen with an airman on more than one occasion."

"Says who?"

"Phyllis saw you going to the pictures. She said you two were very chummy."

"She must have made a mistake. Weren't me."

"Vanessa, Brian will know. He can count as well as the next man."

"Good thing he come home when he did, then." Vanessa's voice was spiteful and Eileen felt her sympathy evaporating.

"I had no idea you were so callous."

"I don't know what *callous* means but I can imagine it's not too nice. I'm not any of those sorts of names. I just know how to get through life."

"What if he guesses?"

Vanessa scowled. "I'll make sure he don't."

Eileen knew that was as close to admitting the truth as Vanessa was going to come. Eileen removed an umbrella from the stand. "Here. It's still raining. Take this."

"Naw, I won't melt. I'm not made of sugar."

Eileen took the usual blackout precautions and Vanessa stepped out into the rain and hurried away.

Suddenly a wave of exhaustion swept over Eileen. What with the events at the factory, not much sleep, and worry, she felt as if the weight of the world had descended on her shoulders. What was it Churchill had said? "We can take it." Easy for him to say. He should come and walk in her shoes for a while, not to mention the people who'd been bombed out. "We can take it." Of course.

***

Donny hurried to the meeting place. Nobody was around. The night was so raw and chill, everybody who could stay at home had done so. Comrade Patrick had got there first as usual and was standing, almost invisible, in the shadowy recess of the church. Donny went through the ritual of asking for a fag and a match.

"Parcels all delivered as ordered, comrade."

The other man didn't answer and Donny raced on. "When can you have the passport and visa to Ireland?"

"What passport?"

"I told him we'd get him out of the country."

"Not a chance. He's a liability. As soon as we get those timers made, you've got to deal with him."

"What d'you mean, deal with him?"

The man stabbed the end of his fag in Donny's direction. "You want to play with the big boys, Donny, you've got to use your noggin. I'm not going to spell it out to you. Your pal's the kind of man who'd blab out everything the moment a copper got hold of him. He knows who you are. He doesn't know me, but I'm not taking any chances."

Donny could feel his heart beating faster. He himself could be seen as a liability. He was in the know as well. His throat went dry.

Suddenly the man gave him a slap on the shoulder. "Don't worry, lad. You are very useful. I'm not referring to you. Anyway, let's take things a step at a time. I want those timers right away. Tomorrow. No reason to delay. The factory's still weak."

Donny felt as if his bowels were loosening. It was one thing to bash a man or two, rob some houses, make plans on paper, but this was seriously big-time. It scared the shite out of him.

Patrick's eyes, just visible above the muffler, seemed to crinkle. He looked almost friendly. "You're playing with the grown-ups, Comrade Bolton. Do you think you can handle it?"

"Course I can. But after the, er, the incident, when are you going to get out of here?"

"Not right away. Too suspicious. But I will have to get another job because there won't be one at Endicott's. I'm thinking of applying at BSA. More money, bigger group to get lost in."

"Are they going to get the same treatment?"

"Of course. Endicott's is our dress rehearsal."

Donny shivered. "What about the Chief? Is he getting out too?"

"Nice of you to think about that, lad. The Chief will do just fine. Oi, you're going to get perishing pneumonia if you don't get indoors soon. Meet me tomorrow and bring me the timers." The man reached out and stuffed a pound note in Donny's pocket. "Here's some payment in advance." He ground his fag underneath his boot, then turned and walked off.

Donny leaned against the wall. He took the pound note from his pocket and sniffed at it. Lovely smell. What would he do with his share of the money? Maybe he could buy passage on a ship for America. It was risky he knew that, U-boats like bleedin' wolves, but some were getting through and he'd heard there were good places over there. Better weather, better food . . . a sharp lad could make himself a good living if he put his mind to it.

***

Brian could hear his granddad snoring. It was one o'clock. He rubbed his head hard. He was having trouble keeping his thoughts straight. He'd have to ask Donny for more details. Where should he head for? Donny had mentioned contacts in Ireland. Who the fuck were they? Brian hoped they weren't IRA terrorists. He just wanted to disappear until the war was over. Just him and Vanessa, maybe on a farm somewhere. Blending in.

He turned off the light in the room, went over to the window, and lifted the curtain. It was black as a coal hole outside. Not a wink of light anywhere. No bombers tonight, thank God. He was pushing his luck. He had to move the body from the shelter before it was discovered. He fished out a heavy, dark jersey from the dresser. Wait a minute, didn't he see his old balaclava in the back of the wardrobe last night? Yes, grand – there it was. He pulled it on. Whew, it smelled of camphor. His gran was always strewing mothballs around. He pushed up the window and climbed outside. There he had to wait for a minute until he got more used to the darkness, then crawled along the roof to the drainpipe, swung his legs over, and climbed down.

At the entrance to the shelter he paused, drawing in his breath in a half-sob. It was almost as if there was a running commentary in his brain. *Got to be done. You've got to move her now, before it's too late. Remember, it was an accident. If she wasn't so old, all that would have happened was she'd get a goose egg on her noggin. You lost your temper, but that happens to people.* But he couldn't shake off his feelings of shame and regret.

He steeled himself, went inside, and lit the lamp, keeping the wick low. The air inside the shelter was stale, damp, with a hint of something else that he didn't want to acknowledge. He pulled aside the green curtain. The smell was stronger here and he almost gagged on it. He moved aside the stack of blankets. There was the body now, already stiffened with rigor mortis. He'd folded her up and she'd stayed in that position, so she looked tiny and almost childlike now. He dragged her out, rolled her in one of the blankets, and picked her up. She was too stiff to put on his shoulders, so he had to hold her as if she were indeed a child. A child he was carrying to bed, perhaps, the way his mum had carried him when he was little. He couldn't remember his dad doing it. He kicked the remaining blankets into place as best he could, blew out the light, went into the passageway of the shelter, and pushed open the door.

The inner commentary started up again. He thought for a minute he was speaking out loud but he wasn't sure. *No point in crying over spilt milk. Get her buried. Nobody will ever know and you can get on with things. Soldiers have to keep going no matter what they've done.*

He headed for the bombed-out house where he'd first holed up. The streets were completely deserted, the houses dark, but he found he had no trouble seeing where he was going.

If you try to shrink into the shadows or if you act like you've got something to hide, you'll draw suspicion. Shoulders back, brisk walk, march like a soldier.

His burden felt light. Her foot was sticking out from the blanket. She had lost her shoe somewhere. Where? God, it didn't matter. Nobody would be looking for it. He turned the corner and into Dorset Row. So far, so good. There was the Cowan house. Everywhere around him was quiet as the grave. He struggled over the rubble that was in front of the door and got inside. Once in the hall, he gently lowered the body to the floor and pushed it against the wall. Should he hide it any more than that? The wall had been loosened by the blast and was leaning in at an angle. One good shove would bring it down. He did just that, and in a cloud of dust the wall collapsed, partially covering the body.

Not a good move, Brian. What if somebody heard?

This time he did speak out loud, answering himself. "Walls are always collapsing after a raid. Besides, there's nobody left on the street."

He scrabbled with the rubble and completed the job. Mrs. Swann was quite hidden.

He stepped back. *Maybe you should say a prayer for her.*

"What sort of prayer?"

The Catholics say, "May God have mercy on your soul." Say that at least.

"All right."

Buck up, Brian. It's all done now. You'd better get back before anybody misses you.

He slipped out into the darkness.

WHEN EILEEN ARRIVED AT THE FACTORY, SHE FOUND Mr. Cudmore waiting for her in front of the clinic.

"Miss Abbott, Mr. Endicott has come in today and Mr. Kaplan has persuaded him to take part in the film he's putting together. Mr. Kaplan suggested a good location to start might be here in the clinic." He allowed himself a little smile. "Mr. Endicott is not quite comfortable being photographed and we thought something on the active side might help him relax."

"Good heavens. What do you mean, active?"

Before the secretary had a chance to elaborate, Lev Kaplan appeared carrying a heavy-looking camera on his shoulder.

"Good morning, Miss Abbott. Ready for stardom?"

"Perpetually. Do come in."

Endicott was trailing behind with obvious reluctance. She ushered them into the waiting room.

"I'll just take this opportunity to check in with the inspector," said Cudmore, and he disappeared.

Lev grinned at Eileen. "Thank you for giving us your time, Miss Abbott. We won't take long." He started to set up his tripod. "I thought I'd do a pan of the waiting room first. It's so cozy."

Eileen felt almost sorry for Endicott, who was fidgeting with his tie like a schoolboy on a first date. "Yes, very nice, very nice," he muttered.

"Now then, Sister," said Lev. "Pretend Mr. Endicott has just come in. Open and close the door. Good. Start talking. We'll do a voice-over later, so don't worry about what you say. Just be as natural as you can. Good. Go into the surgery and show him the equipment. Smile. Talk it up."

Eileen produced a smile and Endicott grimaced fiercely with what she presumed was his equivalent. In fact, his awkwardness brought out her professional side. She was used to men who collapsed into shyness in the presence of a nurse.

"Miss Abbott, perhaps you can demonstrate how you handle blood donations," Lev called out. "Mr. Endicott, would you just lie on the bed for a moment?"

"Do I have to?" asked the other man, and he twisted his moustache frantically. "I wasn't expecting to be donating today."

"Think of it as a contribution to the war effort. It won't hurt. I can guarantee Miss Abbott is very gentle."

Endicott climbed reluctantly onto the cot.

"Yes, that's it. Now cover him over with your pretty quilt, Miss Abbott. Good. Nice smile, now. That always does wonders."

Eileen patted Endicott's arm. "Will you remove your jacket, sir. Now roll up your sleeve. I'll just take your blood pressure first." She tightened the cuff around Endicott's arm and pumped up the pressure.

"Hmm, 170 over 95. Rather high."

For the first time Endicott became engaged in the process. "What does that mean?"

"I suggest you check with your GP. He will probably recommend a regimen of diet and exercise for you. You might have to cut out any alcohol."

"Oh dear, do you really think so?"

"It isn't something to be ignored, sir. However, one reading isn't conclusive. The circumstances might have elevated your pressure. A lot of men react in a similar fashion."

"That's nice," said Lev. "Very nice. Mr. Endicott, perhaps you wouldn't mind lying back again and we can do a repeat."

"Perhaps I shouldn't donate blood today, Sister," said Endicott as he lay back.

"Miss Abbott, will you stroke his head, soothe him – do something comforting. Mr. Endicott, you can smile up at her appreciatively."

Eileen's encounters with Charles Endicott had been minimal. He was the factory owner, she his employee. She wanted to tell Lev he was being too American again. Take his blood pressure, all right, but stroke his forehead? No, thank you. However, before she could do anything one way or the other, they heard loud screams and cries from outside the clinic.

The door burst open and Cudmore rushed in.

"Sister, Sister, come quick. There's been an accident on the floor. One of the girls has been scalped."

Tyler and Eagleton had just arrived at the factory when they heard the screams. They ran through the lobby and shoved open the doors to the factory floor. One of the women was half sitting, half lying in front of her machine with her hands to her head. Blood was streaming through her fingers and had already soaked the front of her overalls. She was sobbing and moaning. A small group of workers was hovering nearby, clutching at each other, unable to look away but terrified by what they saw.

Tyler could see Miss Abbott kneeling beside the injured girl, the top of whose head was a red, jellied mess.

Eileen bent over. "Francine. Francine. Let me have a look. Take your hands away."

The girl hardly seemed to hear her. She was uttering loud, frightened cries.

Tyler crouched down as well. "Come on, lass. Let the nurse have a look."

Francine's sobs subsided slightly, but when she removed her hands and saw the amount of blood on them she let out a high-pitched wail.

Tyler nodded at his constable, who went over to the other women.

"Come on, ladies, step back if you please."

They shuffled away a few feet. Tyler saw several of the women from the canteen among them. The photographer was standing nearby, not intervening, apparently waiting to be called upon if necessary.

Eileen had a medicine bag beside her from which she took a sterile dressing. She unwrapped it and placed it on the girl's head. Almost immediately the cotton turned scarlet.

"Do you want me to hold it in place?" Tyler asked.

Eileen nodded. "Now, Francine," she said to the girl. "Scalp wounds always bleed a lot, so this seems much worse than it is. You'll be all right when we get you stitched up." She looked over her shoulder. "Mr. Cudmore, will you go and telephone for an ambulance."

The secretary hurried off to do her bidding and Eileen slipped her arm around Francine's shoulders.

"We're going to get you to sit up on the bench, Frankie. You'll be more comfortable . . . I'll need your help, Inspector."

Kaplan stepped forward. "We'll do that. You keep pressure on the pad."

"All right. You take her under the hips. Inspector Tyler, get her shoulders. On the count of three swing her onto the bench, gently as you can. One . . . two . . . three."

They got Francine up and sitting. Without being asked, Kaplan took another pad from the medical bag and handed it to Eileen, who replaced the sodden one. Tyler heard a whimper from one of the other girls but it was quickly suppressed.

The nurse addressed Pat O'Callaghan. "Go to the clinic. Bring me the packet of ice that's in the refrigerator. And a pillow and a blanket."

Pat took off.

Francine's face was grey-white. Tyler could see her eyes were starting to roll up in her head.

Eileen spoke firmly. "Francine, sit up straight, there's a girl. I'm going to put a bandage on to keep the dressing in place. Do you think you can hold your head up while I do so?"

"I'll help her, Sister."

Tyler was rather surprised to see it was Mary Ringwald-Brown stepping forward. She came over, grasped Francine by the chin to hold her steady with one hand, and pushed down on the pad with the other. Eileen took a triangular bandage from the bag.

In spite of the pressure Mary was putting on the wound, the amount of blood still flowing was horrific. Eileen started to wrap the pad in place.

Cudmore came hurrying back, Pat at his heels. "The ambulance will be here right away, Sister."

Pat handed over the ice pack and Mary held it on top of the bandage.

Eileen took a long syringe from the bag, which she thrust through the seal of a small ampoule.

"Pat, roll up her sleeve for me . . . Francine, make a fist, there's a good girl." She plunged the needle into the swelling vein. Francine yelped – there had been no time for finesse. Fortunately the tranquilizer was fast-acting, and within moments she became quieter, although her body continued to shudder like a motor car running out of petrol.

Eileen covered her with the blanket and propped a pillow behind her head.

"What happened?" Tyler asked.

"Apparently her hair got entangled in the wheel of her lathe."

At that moment the scream of the air-raid warning siren tore through the room. Tyler had heard it only once before, when Whitchurch had run a practice. It was a horrible sound, the rise and fall of the wailing like some strange animal in agony.

Eileen straightened up. "Oh God, that's all we need." She addressed the girls. "All right everybody, to the shelters. Hurry."

"What about Frankie?" Mary asked.

"We'll be fine here. I don't want her moved."

"I'll stay," said Pat.

"No, you won't. We'll be all right. Get out of here."

The siren continued to wail.

Eagleton had already got the group mobilized. "Everybody to the shelters. Come on, hurry."

They had been well drilled and began to move to the exit.

"Pat, Mary, get going," commanded Eileen.

Reluctantly Pat obeyed. Mary followed. Her hands were stained with Francine's blood and she was wiping them, unheeding, on her overalls.

"Good heavens, I'd better check on Mr. Endicott," said Cudmore.

"Speaking of which, where is he?" Kaplan asked. "He must still be in the clinic."

"I'll have a look," said the secretary and he scuttled off. The siren continued.

Eagleton returned. He looked nervous. An actual bombing raid was new to him too.

"Eager, go with the women, there's a lad," said Tyler. He looked at Eileen. "I'll stay here. If we have to move her you'll need help."

Francine was out for the count by now.

"I'm not going anywhere either," said Lev. "Yanks can tough it out with any Limey."

In spite of the situation, the others had to smile.

"All right. Let's at least get ourselves underneath one of the machines," said Eileen. "It'll give us some protection if the ceiling comes down. We'll reverse what we did before."

The two men picked up Francine and shifted her as carefully as they could so she was lying underneath the lathe. Eileen squeezed in beside her.

She waved her hands at the two men. "Take cover."

Tyler thought the best thing to do was cram himself in the space under the nearby machine. He slid into something wet. Then he saw, just above him, a long swatch of once-blonde hair dangling from the wheel. A piece of scalp was still attached.

***

Lev gave the password and was admitted. As always, from his American perspective, Comrade Arnold seemed formally dressed for a mere evening at home. He was wearing a navy blue blazer, striped tie, and grey flannels. His shoes were highly polished. Only his canary-yellow socks appeared out of place.

"Who's here?" Lev asked.

"Everybody but Comrade Cardiff."

"Has the new guy, Bolton, arrived yet?"

"Yes, he has. They are all a little concerned about your message."

Lev had chalked *Hitchcock requests meeting tonight* on the church wall.

Arnold led the way down the hall to his room. "I do hope this is necessary, comrade," he said fussily. "It really isn't safe to meet other than at our regular times."

"I'd think it was the opposite. Being unpredictable has always seemed a much better course of action. However, who am I to say? I'm just an ignorant Yank."

He received the customary giggle as a response.

As with the previous meeting, the room was already filled with tobacco smoke. Nobody was talking. Comrade Bolton was sitting just inside the door with his cap and overcoat on; Chopin was by the fireplace, also wearing his outdoor clothes and fingerless gloves, his hands outstretched to the low-burning fire. He nodded a greeting to Lev, but Comrade Bolton glared at him in such an obvious, provocative way that Lev felt a surge of anger. How that lad had got to this age without somebody killing him was a miracle.

"Sorry, I don't have any tea to offer you," said Arnold. "Rationing, don't you know." He pulled forward a rickety-looking chair just as they heard a knock on the door. "Ah, that must be Comrade Cardiff. I'll let him in."

Lev could hear the faint sound of music from the upstairs room. The invisible landlords were home. Who were they, and what did they think was going on in their parlour? he wondered.

Arnold returned, the Welshman behind him. Cardiff looked angry.

"I'm on the night shift, comrades. I'd like to get this over with quickly. What's so urgent?"

"I'll be working at Endicott's for a while longer," said Lev. I want to know what the plans are. As you can imagine, comrades, I have no desire to be present in the factory if it is going to get blown to smithereens."

Chopin looked up, startled. "What you mean? Who said so?"

Lev shrugged. "It's as obvious as the nose on your face something is in the works. Incidents like today aren't enough. They only slow down production for a short while." He looked over at the Pole. "Were you the one responsible for the so-called mishap?"

Arnold jumped in with surprising firmness. "Better not to ask questions like that, comrade. Who does what shouldn't be part of general parlance."

"Hey, I'm a Yank, don't forget. We don't use ten-dollar words if we don't have to. I assume you're telling me to keep my trap shut."

"Quite so."

"Suit yourself. However, what's been done so far is piddling – a woman injured, no general strike, no significant halt in production."

"Sunday not piddling," said Chopin without turning his head.

"According to you lot, that was an accident. Lucky for us, unlucky for those women."

Nobody spoke. Even Comrade Bolton was still.

Lev continued. "What comes next has to be major and we all know that. Let's not kid ourselves. I assume our esteemed leader, Patrick, is planning another 'accident.' And soon. Am I right, Comrade Arnold?"

Arnold had lit his pipe and he sucked on it hungrily. "I'm not able to answer you at this time, Comrade Hitchcock. I am awaiting orders."

Cardiff spoke out sharply. "I'm with our Yankee comrade, look you. I don't want to be killed either. I'd like to live another day and continue with our work. I want to know what the plans are. And do they involve me or not?"

Arnold shrugged nervously. "All I can tell you is that Comrade Patrick has something in mind that is very close to being executed. But until all is worked out, it's better you not know."

"Christ almighty," said Lev. "Are we talking about days? Tomorrow? Next week?"

Bolton spoke up. "Don't get your knickers in a bleedin' knot, comrade. It will happen soon, I promise."

"*You* promise. Why is it you promising? I thought we had an equal stake in this mission. Why do you have special privilege?"

The youth sneered at him. "Let's say I'm currently acting as Comrade Patrick's lieutenant."

"Really? I find it hard to believe, our illustrious leader would rely on a kid like you. You've hardly let go of your mommy's titty."

He was doing everything he could to needle the youth, but Bolton had a lot of self-control and one of those dead faces that revealed little. Only his eyes seemed to grow darker.

Cardiff grinned. Chopin hardly seemed to have heard or understood.

Arnold fluttered his pale, fat hands. "Please, Comrade Hitchcock. This is quite unproductive. It is not relevant. We must await our orders."

"I need to know who my orders are coming from," said Lev. "Why should I risk everything for an invisible man?"

Comrade Bolton nodded. "You have a point, Yank. But don't worry. Everything is in place for our little party. And it's going to be bloody spectacular."

"When? Or is that too difficult a question for a mere lieutenant to answer?"

"Let's say you will be given warning."

"But I need to have some idea when these fireworks are going to happen. As well as everything else, I'm a legitimate filmmaker making a legitimate film. I have no desire to have my hard work go up in smoke. Besides, as our Welsh comrade says, I too want to live to fight another day. When are you and 'the boss' planning this, and what do you mean by spectacular?"

Cardiff lit up one of his home-rolled fags, drew on it deeply, and picked a piece of tobacco from his lip. "If our American friend here is going to be in the clear, what about us two, Comrade Chopin and me? Will we have a job to do or is it better if we are absent that day?"

Arnold did another flutter. "You will be receiving your instructions within the next day or two. You are part of the plan, an important part. Both of you."

"But not me?" Lev managed to make his voice sound sulky. A man who was being passed over in favour of inferiors.

Comrade Bolton answered. "You'll be needed afterwards."

Lev raised his eyebrows. "I get it. I'm to film the destruction part. Pan over dead bodies and that sort of thing. My secret other film to show the people what a lousy job their government is doing."

"That's right. You've hit the nail on the head."

"I thought we had agreed there would be no civilian casualties. You're suggesting there will be, and a lot of them."

Comrade Bolton bared his teeth in a sort of smile. "Minimal, old chap. Fucking minimal."

Lev turned to the Welshman. "How do you feel about the civilian damage, comrade?"

Cardiff hesitated. "Like we've said previous, you can't win a war without spilling blood, and we're in a war."

"But these are innocent young women we're talking about," said Lev.

Cardiff dragged on his cigarette. "Let's put it this way, comrade. The English have a long history of not giving a damn about the innocent when they want something."

"What do you mean?"

"Yeah, comrade," interrupted Bolton. "Tell us your own sad story. And then I can add mine and Chopin here can tell his. I bet he has a doozy. Except for Comrade Arnold, who grew up in the lap of luxury with a silver spoon in his arse. I bet we can all turn on the bloody spigot. Maybe even the Yank has got a sob story tucked away."

"Comrade Chopin," Lev interjected. "How do you feel about what's being planned? This so-called spectacular show."

The other man didn't move. "We have to stop the sickness in the world."

Before Lev could press him as to what the hell he meant by that, Cardiff spoke up.

"If you must know, my father, both of his brothers, and my oldest cousin all worked in the mines in Wales. What else is there to do for a living in that godforsaken place? They worked for a pittance. Most of them had too many children, most of them had black lung. Those men – my own flesh and blood, look you – all died in the mines. Typical happening. One of the shafts collapsed and twenty men died a slow and lingering death. They had no pensions, of course, except what the benevolent society could pay out. The English owners didn't give a shite. Nobody came to the funerals and they docked the wages of the men who did attend. Nobody asked if something could be done to prevent accidents like that."

Cardiff's voice was low. He was looking at the floor. "I was eleven years old when my pa died and I became the breadwinner for the family. Seven wee ones, me the oldest. One day I saw one of the owners drive by in his motor car with his wife in furs beside him. My mam didn't have furs. She went without clothes and food so her kiddies could have something to stop the pain from the cold and the hunger. She died when she was forty. The doctor said the cause of death was pernicious anemia. I say she died because she was worn out."

His bitterness and white-hot rage were spilling into the room, so palpable they could burn the skin. "I'm sorry if civilians have to die, but if this is one more step on our journey to bring down the English and return the Welsh land to its rightful owners, I consider it necessary. No matter what the price."

"I gather that was a vote in favour," said Lev.

Cardiff flushed. "That's right. And sorry I am for the long speech. Mind you, I'd like to know sooner rather than later when I might expect it all to happen."

Arnold was clearly so relieved to have Taffy's support that he blurted out, "It'll be before the week is out." Realizing he had said too much, he stopped. "But that is for your information only."

Bolton looked at Lev. "Can we all trust you to keep your bleedin' mouth shut, comrade?"

"What do you take me for?" Lev answered irritably.

"Good bloody question. Unless I read you wrong, you're very interested in saving your own bloody skin. That, or you've got another reason for wanting to know when the party will happen."

"What the hell is that supposed to mean?" said Lev and he took a step forward. In the small parlour that meant he was almost nose to nose with the youth.

Cardiff put out a hand between them. "Not a good time to fight among ourselves, comrades."

Lev could feel the strength of Cardiff's forearm and he moved back.

The clock on the mantelpiece chimed. A pleasant, melodic sound that seemed to belong to a world of china teacups and freshly toasted crumpets, not this squalid, dingy room filled with murder.

"I've got to go," said Cardiff. "Comrade Hitchcock, do you have an answer to your questions?"

Lev shrugged. "In a way. But I do want to go on record that I hate being kept in the dark like this."

"Objection noted," said Arnold.

The Welshman held out his hand to Lev. "In case I don't have a chance to shake your hand at a later date, I wish you well, and here's to the revolution."

They shook hands. Cardiff waved at the others. "I shall await my instructions, Comrade Arnold. Usual method of communication?"

"Quite so."

He left and there was an uneasy silence for a few moments. Lev knew it would be impossible to get any more information. Nobody trusted him. The doors had closed. He wasn't even sure who was in the know. Not Chopin, and presumably not Cardiff as yet. The little thug was, and obviously Arnold. For a moment he felt a wave of desperation. How the hell was he going to find out what they had planned? Even if he had them arrested he didn't know who the leader at the plant was, and that was the man he wanted. Otherwise he would have simply lopped off one of the heads of the Hydra. More would grow.

***

It was almost midnight and Eileen knew she should get to sleep, but she was too agitated to even try. She took out her Mass Observation diary.

> *Lev Kaplan asked me to go to the pictures with him. He said I deserved it after what had happened this morning. I immediately said no, I couldn't possibly, but he pressed me. "Why not? It's no disrespect to Frankie and the other girls if we try to grasp at whatever pleasure we can while we can." Words to that effect anyway, although he put it more elegantly. He has a way with words, does Mr. Kaplan. He's right. At least I think he is. Francine is going to be all right, but she will have some*

*disfigurement for the rest of her life. Poor girl. She was
always so proud of her lovely long hair.*

Eileen paused. What she wanted to write about she was
reluctant to share with Mass Observation. She decided to continue anyway.

*I can hardly remember what the film was about. Michael
Wilding doing something or other with Anna Neagle.
The only seats left were in the back row and I felt some
misgivings about sitting there. Lev seemed oblivious. Is
this just an English custom — the back-row courtships? It
was soon apparent nobody was there to see a film. I felt
quite ridiculous. The man seated next to me was virtually moaning as he kissed his girlfriend. His hand was
clearly in a very intimate place. I was trying to cut him
out of my consciousness and concentrate on the film but it
was almost impossible. Then Lev whispered in my ear,
"If we can't beat them, let's join them." He turned my
chin and kissed me.*

Eileen stopped writing. What a sweet, long kiss it had been.
His lips were soft. Had men's lips always been that soft? There
was more tenderness and exploration than passion in that kiss.

*I couldn't shake off my self-consciousness. I'm over forty,
for heaven's sake, not fourteen. But the cinema was dark.
I hoped nobody would see us. I wanted him to kiss me
again, but he didn't right away. He turned back to the
film although he kept hold of my hand. He seemed
comfortable in a way I wasn't at all. He laughed at some
antic on the screen. All I could think of was when he
would kiss me again. He must have read my mind,*

*because after a while he turned again. I could see his
smile. "Are you okay?" he asked. I wanted to say, "No, I'm
not. I want to go somewhere where we can lie naked
together, where I can feel you inside me. I don't care if
we've only just met. We could be dead tomorrow and I
would never have known the bliss of being made love to
by a man like you." But of course I couldn't say that and
simply nodded and gave his hand a squeeze. He did kiss
me again, but it wasn't like the first kiss. This time there
was more intensity to it. I could hardly breathe. The man
next to me must have had his orgasm, because his groans
were stifled. His girlfriend was giggling and he was
jerking. I didn't want that. I didn't want to be acting
like a teenager. I suddenly felt cold and removed. I didn't
want to kiss anymore. The film wasn't over yet but a
couple a few rows in front of us got up and left. "Let's
take their seat," I said to Lev. I didn't give him much
chance to answer and I stood up with my coat. I was
almost afraid to go past the noisy couple on my left but
they were both lighting cigarettes and didn't seem to be
aware of me at all. The girl couldn't have been more
than sixteen, the boy hardly any older. We did go and sit
in the other seats and it was better, although if my life
depended on it, I don't think I could recall the plot of the
film. Lev had brought chocolates with him and I ate
more than I should. I regretted it later.*

*About seven thirty, just before the film ended, there
was an air-raid warning. The second one today. The
film was stopped and the little nervous manager came
out to tell us we could leave for the shelter. They couldn't
give a refund as more than half of the film had been
played. Those who wanted could stay at their own risk
and watch the rest. Only a few people left, and after a*

brief consultation, Lev and I decided to stick it out. We didn't hear any bombs dropping, so either it was a false alarm or the bombers were heading somewhere else, the way they did this morning. Bristol or Liverpool probably – surely Coventry can't get hit again. Poor people. It was even more difficult to concentrate with half an ear on what was happening outside, but even though I couldn't see anybody in the dark, I felt as if we were all connected by the invisible bonds of fear and defiance. At least it took me away from my agitation, so I'm thankful for that. The all-clear sounded half an hour later, almost at the same time that THE END *flashed on the screen. We laughed at that. Then the lights went on and we filed out, smiling and chatting to each other like old friends as if we had cheated the Nazi war machine, which I suppose we had in a way.*

The night was so overcast we thought we were probably safe from another raid and we actually found a café open. I'd never been in it before and it looked decidedly seedy, but I didn't want to go home yet and neither did he. And it was seedy, the air heavy with stale grease that clung to my clothes after. But the tea was all right and they had some scones left. They were rock-hard but we took them anyway. Lev said, "Eileen, forgive me for the back-row thing. They were the only seats left. I think I embarrassed you." I didn't want to lie, so I just said, "Well, we're not teenagers, are we?" I wasn't going to say how much I still felt that kiss. Then he leaned closer so nobody could hear us. "I would like to make love to you properly. Is there any possibility that could ever happen, dear Miss Abbott?"

My God. What could I say? I made a feeble joke that it was all right to call me by my first name now that

*we'd kissed. The café was filled with men in uniform
and their girls. All younger than us, of course. I seemed to
be surrounded by love, or certainly a desperate lust.*

*"I'd like that," I said. The words were out of my
mouth before I knew it.*

*So that was more or less that. He said he's going back
to London soon. He has digs there. But he said that Mrs.
Cooper goes to her daughter's in the country every weekend. Perhaps we could work it out for me to come and
stay. I agreed, although I don't know how I'm going to do
that. Not with the Brian situation hanging over us.*

Again Eileen stopped writing for a moment. The house was
silent, everybody asleep except her.

*Things were very bad before I went out. Brian was
desperate and couldn't sit down for more than a minute.
He's upset that he can't see Vanessa. I made him take a
sedative to calm him down. I don't know how she is
going to deal with that pregnancy. Over tea, Brian told
Dad and me what he'd already told Mum, that he might
be able to get papers to get him to Ireland. It will cost
money but we're willing to pay if we have to. He says
Jack can be the go-between and nobody questioned that.
Later perhaps we will take our respective heads out of
the sand where that boy is concerned.*

She closed the diary and replaced it at the back of the
drawer. Her room was chilly but it was too late to build up
the fire. A needless extravagance. Her thoughts leaped to
being in bed with Lev. It had been such a long time since
she had experienced sexual intimacy, and that last time hadn't
been particularly fulfilling. She had imagined herself in love

with one of the office managers at Endicott's. She knew he was married but he said he was separated. Not true, as it turned out. But they had gone to a hotel in the country for a weekend. The lovemaking had been rather perfunctory. Indeed, she had to say *dull*. He had spent most of the time complaining about his wife and kids, who were feckless. What she had seen in him she couldn't imagine and she was glad when he moved away to Nottingham. And now there was Lev. And she had never in her life felt like this about anybody before.

She turned out her bedside lamp, got out of bed, and went over to the window. She pulled back the blackout curtain. It was so dark outside she could hardly see past the end of the front garden, but she caught the tiny flash of a torch. The air-raid warden was making his rounds. She knew him – Reg Anderson from the next street. He was too old to be doing this but he insisted. Watching his slow progress, she felt absurdly weepy.

She went back to her bed. How could she have been day-dreaming about loving a strange man when all this life and death was on her doorstep? Another war within her lifetime. Another time when young, vital men lost their lives. Another time when women wept.

***

Tyler was sitting with Alf Mason in the common room. They'd had a decent enough meal and were now into the cigar-and-brandy stage. "Like gents," said Alf. "Drink up, it's the last bottle." There were three constables – one of them Eagleton – playing a spirited game of darts, and the wireless was broadcasting some BBC light music program. Tyler could actually feel himself relaxing.

Eagleton hit a bull's eye and let out a loud cheer. Considering he wasn't wearing his spectacles, it was quite a feat.

Mason turned back to Tyler. "Do you remember when we used to hide our duty arm bands and pretend we were off-duty so we could go into the pub? You were darts-mad in those days and you were always on the lookout for a match."

"Not to mention a pint," added Tyler.

"That too."

Tyler grinned. "We must have had wool for noggins. We could have got dismissed on the spot if we'd been found out."

"Might not have been such a bad thing. I would have bought my own pub and been a wealthy man by now instead of an underpaid copper."

"True."

They lapsed into the comfortable silence of old friends.

Alf flicked off some cigar ash. "What's your take, then, Tom? Are you chalking up this latest incident to another accident? More carelessness?"

Tyler blew out some of the rich cigar smoke. "It is looking like that. I examined Francine's lathe but those machines were built decades ago. The guard had come loose and slipped down between the wheels. Francine was also apparently in the habit of leaving some of her hair out of her turban. Thought the turban was ugly."

"Sounds like a contemporary morality play. The fruits of vanity."

It was Tyler who swished around his brandy this time. "They're young girls, most of them. A bit of vanity is allowed, wouldn't you say?"

"You're talking to somebody who has two daughters, Tom."

"The wheel should have stopped immediately when her hair got caught, but it didn't," continued Tyler. "Apparently there's been more than one of these accidents. Nobody has been scalped before, thank God, but there have been badly bruised fingers."

"Endicott should have them replaced," said Alf. "The lathes, I mean."

"I agree. The workers have been asking for new models since the factory was commandeered, but so far Endicott has been dragging his feet."

"He's got a reputation of being a skinflint."

Tyler stabbed the air with his cigar. "I'm going to make it part of my recommendations. 'Replace decrepit machines.'"

Alf laughed. "You're enjoying the chance to throw your weight around, aren't you, Tommy. I always knew you were a bit of a bolshie."

"Me! You, more like."

"Not so. But the older I get, the more I get fed up with the privileged few ruling the roost."

Tyler raised his glass. "I'm with you there, Alf. My fighting ancestors go back a long way."

Alf clicked his glass against Tyler's. "Here's to the revolution."

They both sipped the brandy, Tyler making noises of appreciation. "Good stuff, Alf."

"Savour it, mate. Like I said, that's the last bottle I've got. Everything's vanishing into the black market." He scowled. "I hate profiteers like poison."

Tyler nodded. He hadn't told Alf that in the summer he'd been on the point of arresting his own father-in-law for dabbling in the black market.

"Speaking of which," continued Alf, "did Endicott have any reaction to the incident?"

"He vanished. His secretary whispered in my ear that the poor man has a phobia about blood. Faints dead away at the very sight."

Alf grinned. "That could be convenient or inconvenient, depending on your point of view. Anyway, with regard to the other matter, wish I could be of more help."

"No, you have been, Alf. Just the chance to run things by you has been grand. And getting access to the police files without having to go through red tape."

"None of those on your list have police form, I gather."

"Not one. All clean as whistles."

"Like I said, we're pretty thorough about screening the munitions workers."

"Young Eager over there did manage to check out the Yank I mentioned," said Tyler. "He seems bona fide. Commissioned by the Ministry of Information to make documentaries. I'm glad he's cleared, to tell you the truth. He seems like a good bloke. He was right there when needed. Very steady. Besides which, I think he and the nurse fancy each other. I'd hate to see her hurt."

"I wish the Yanks would get off the po and join us," said Alf. "Don't say I said this, but I'm not sure England can survive without them."

Tyler nodded. "It's looking grimmer every day, Alf."

"So, back to what we were saying. Come to any conclusion about Sunday yet?"

"Not quite. I read over the most meticulous notes that Mr. Cudmore typed up for me but I couldn't see any patterns. No inconsistencies in the statements that jumped out and bit me on the nose."

"Ah, that kind. Either people are becoming better liars or I'm getting too old for this job," said Mason. "I don't seem to catch those things."

Another good throw by Eagleton, and the resulting excitement distracted them. Tyler put down his brandy glass so he could clap.

Alf turned back to face Tyler. "So what's your doubt about the explosion, Tom? You've got one, I can tell."

Tyler shrugged. "You and I both know how many people died in the last war because of so many factors. Stupidity on their part; even worse stupidity on the part of the top brass; or the weather turned; or a mechanical part broke down. Nothing you could control except perhaps the ignorance." He sighed. "In this case, the combination of pressure to go fast – management's fault; perhaps the lust of the two supervisors, who left the girls to start on their own; the chance that the men were working when they shouldn't; the fact that somebody locked the changing room door and made them late. All those factors added up. Remove any one of them and you might not have had the explosion. At least not on that day."

Mason swished his brandy around in his glass before swallowing the last of it. "Why would somebody lock the doors?"

"It's my guess the culprit was a woman named Mary Ringwald-Brown. Clearly upper class but she says she's a member of the Communist Party. She's an ignorant woman, I have to say. Stopped thinking years ago. She talks like a pamphlet. I could see her trying to disrupt production and convincing herself she was justified." He mimicked Mary's nasal voice. "'It's not a war of country against country. It's a war of the owners against the proletariat.'"

"Cor blimey. I can't even spell proletariat."

There was yet another shout of triumph from the direction of the dartboard. This time it was one of the Brummie constables who'd hit a bull's eye.

"Come and join us, Inspector Tyler," called Eagleton.

"No, thanks, lad. I'm for bed."

"Me too," said Mason. "Another bloody early morning call." He stood up. "You lads make sure the fire's tamped down before you leave."

They all exchanged good-nights and Tyler went to his room. It was funny how quickly he'd slipped back into the old routine. Alf had joked about being a publican but he wasn't serious. Once a copper always a copper, as far as Tyler was concerned. He started to undress, unlacing his shoes and placing them side by side underneath the bed. Shite – that was what had been niggling at him. He'd been drilled when he was in the army to keep his kit neat and tidy. Clothes hung up, boots together out of sight. All the men learned this until it was instinct. All drill became that way.

When Mick Smith had got to his feet at the start of their interview, he'd automatically stood at attention. He'd also been about to salute, Tyler would swear. When he left, he'd made a sharp turn as if he was on a parade ground.

Mr. Smith had been a soldier.

Tyler turned back his covers. Was that significant? There were lots of ex-soldiers around, including himself. Joe Abbott, for instance, had made no bones about being in the army during the Great War. Smith could have served then. There was no real reason to mention it. He'd ask Cudmore in the morning.

But Tyler remembered what Alf had told him. The Irishman they had hanged for planting a bomb in the Coventry police station had claimed to be a member of the Irish Republican Army. He'd emphasized that he was a soldier. The IRA trained their men to think and act like that. Smith certainly didn't appear to be Irish, but it was something else to take note of. Alf was right – Tyler did have doubts. He hadn't finished nosing around yet.

EILEEN DIDN'T KNOW WHICH HAD COME FIRST, THE banging on the front door or her mother shaking her by the shoulder.

Beatrice, still in her nightclothes, was standing over her, her voice hoarse with fear. "Eileen, get up. The redcaps have come for Brian."

She was awake and jumping out of bed at once. "Where is he?"

"Your dad is getting him into the airing cupboard."

More banging.

Eileen grabbed her dressing gown from the hook on the door. "Go into the kitchen, Mum. I'll stall them. Try to act natural."

Beatrice was shaking but she nodded and hurried away. Eileen stuffed her feet into her slippers and went to the door. It was not yet light but she could make out two husky young men in the uniform of the military police standing on the doorstep. One touched his fingers politely to his forehead but there was no softness in his face. The other soldier looked even tougher.

"I'm Sergeant Carson, madam. Who are we addressing?"

"I'm Eileen Abbott. What is the problem, Sergeant?"

"We're trying to locate an individual by the name of Brian Walmsley. We understand his grandparents live here. Are you a relative?"

"Brian is my nephew. Why do you want him?" Eileen couldn't believe how coolly she spoke.

"He is absent without leave from his regiment."

"Are you certain? We just heard from him. He is getting leave soon."

While she was talking to the sergeant, she could see the corporal was on the alert for any sign of a running man. She had no illusions that she was fooling them. They had entered into an unspoken game, a dance where each understood the rules and which would soon come to a conclusion.

"We have reason to believe he might be hiding here."

"What? Don't be ridiculous. There's just myself and my parents."

"I'm sorry, madam, but we have authority to search the premises."

"My parents are elderly. This will be most upsetting for them."

The sergeant moved closer. He was losing patience. "Please step aside, madam."

Then Eileen heard her father from behind her. "Let them in, Eileen. They're only doing their duty."

He touched her shoulders. "Go and wait with your mother. I'll show these gentlemen around."

Eileen walked back to the kitchen, aware that her heart was thudding in her chest. Beatrice was sitting at the table clutching a cup of tea in both hands as if it were a lifeline. Eileen sat down opposite her and covered her mother's hands with her own.

"Don't worry, Mum."

She had left the kitchen door open and she could see Joe and the two soldiers. Her father was a tall man, but a little stooped now and skinny. The two young military policemen dwarfed him. There seemed no room in the hall for all three of them.

"I'll take a look in here, please, sir," said the sergeant, indicating Eileen's room. Joe opened the door and the corporal went into the room. Eileen hoped he wasn't going to overturn anything; common sense should tell him there was no place for a man to hide. She was right; the soldier soon emerged. The two of them came into to the kitchen.

"Morning, ma'am," said the one who was doing the talking. "We're looking for a deserter, Private Brian Walmsley. It's my understanding that he is your grandson."

Eileen gave her mother's icy-cold hand a squeeze. Beatrice nodded.

Carson looked over at Joe, who was in the doorway. The corporal stood outside at the ready.

"You do understand that it is a criminal offence, punishable to the full extent of the law, to give shelter to or to aid and abet a deserter?"

"Yes, we understand," Joe replied.

The sergeant nodded at the other soldier. "Check the back garden, will you, Andrews. There might be a shed. And make sure he's not in the lavatory."

"There isn't a shed and he's not in the lavatory," said Eileen, who felt impelled to resist them. They weren't in fact being particularly bullying or rude, but the sound of their boots, their guns at the ready in their holsters, their peaked caps with the red bands all created a sense of menace.

Her remark went unheeded and the corporal walked past them and out the back door.

Nobody spoke while they waited for him to return. Carson was listening for any sound that would indicate somebody else was in the house. Eileen could see how alert he was. What would happen if Brian was discovered? She was praying that he wouldn't panic and try to make a run for it. She was still clutching her mother's hand. She let go, afraid she might draw more suspicion onto them. Why were the redcaps there? Had they already gone to her sister's house? To Vanessa's parents? But it was barely light, and she sensed they had come there first. Why?

Andrews re-entered and shook his head. "All clear out there."

"I'd like to see upstairs, please, Mr. Abbott," said Carson. Again he did the deferential touch-to-the-forehead gesture but he didn't apologize. Eileen knew they hadn't fooled him. God, she hoped Brian's hiding place was safe, and she thanked their lucky stars that Joe had had the foresight to prepare the warming cupboard.

There was a carpet on the stairs but the house was old and the floorboards creaked. The three men went upstairs, and to Eileen they were thundering.

Lie still, Brian, lie still.

She couldn't just sit passively, she couldn't. She smiled reassuringly at her mother and went to the bottom of the stairs.

Joe opened the door to the spare room first. Eileen ran up to the landing and stood watching. This time the men were both more thorough. As Carson flung open the wardrobe, Andrews actually drew his revolver and stepped to one side, ready to fire if need be. The sergeant moved aside the few clothes that were hanging there: Joe's old clothes and a couple of Beatrice's frocks. He even sniffed at them.

"Somebody been smoking?"

"That's me," said Joe. "I like me pipe. Sometimes I sit in here and smoke it because it bothers the missus."

Then Carson squatted down and pulled out the chamber pot from underneath the bed. There was urine in it.

"This pot has been used recently," said the sergeant.

"That was me, too. I spent the night in here. Fact is, my wife snores something fierce . . . Don't tell her I told you – she considers it unladylike to snore."

Carson didn't answer. He flung back the quilt on the bed and ran his hand over the mattress.

"This is warm."

"Yes, it would be," said Joe without a blink. "You blokes got us all out of bed."

"Can I see the other bedroom?" said Carson.

Joe led the way across the short landing to the main bedroom. The sergeant went through the same procedure, checking the wardrobe and looking underneath the bed. There was a chamber pot there, which was empty. Eileen felt an absurd flash of relief, as if it were a matter of being house-proud. See, they weren't a dirty family.

The bathroom adjoined this bedroom and in between was the airing cupboard. Eileen's mouth was dry with fear. She marvelled at how calm and confident her father appeared.

Carson opened the door to the airing cupboard.

There was a pile of towels inside. He lifted them aside cautiously and tapped hard with his knuckles on the wall. To Eileen it seemed obvious that the wall was hollow, but the sergeant didn't appear to pick up on it. He replaced the towels and closed the door.

"You've seen everything except the bathroom," said Joe. "Toilet's outside, more's the pity. One of these days, after the war, I've promised my wife we'll have an indoor loo."

The young sergeant actually smiled. "My parents keep saying the same thing. My mum would like nothing better than not to go outside in the freezing cold."

He stepped into the bathroom, but it was obvious at a glance that there was nowhere a man could hide. There was just the bathtub, open shelves where Beatrice had put extra soap and knick-knacks, and a small basket for dirty clothes. Carson took the lid off the basket. Oh God, thought Eileen again, but Beatrice had followed Joe's instructions rigorously. She hadn't put any clothes in the hamper that belonged to Brian.

The two soldiers exchanged glances.

"Is that it, then, Sergeant?" Joe asked.

"Yes, sir, it would seem so. I must remind you that if Private

Walmsley does contact you or show up at your house, you must notify the police immediately."

"I understand that."

This time the soldiers went down the stairs first and Eileen and her father trailed behind. Closer to Joe she could tell how hard-won his composure had been. He smelled of sweat.

Eileen let the men out and closed the door.

Joe put his finger to his lips. "Wait," he whispered. "Make sure they have well and truly gone."

Eileen looked out through the side window. The men walked smartly in step down the path. At the gate they turned right. She knew what Joe was getting at. The redcaps could easily be trying to trick them – they could return.

Beatrice emerged from the kitchen. "I'll stay here and keep a lookout. You two go and see how Brian is."

Joe went back upstairs, Eileen close behind him. He opened the airing cupboard, pulled the towels and linens onto the floor, and with one tug pried away the false wall.

Brian was crouched in a tight ball. He had stuffed a flannel into his mouth to stop himself from screaming.

***

Jack woke up suddenly, fear propelling him into consciousness. Every night he had a nightmare, usually that he was trying to run away from a Nazi who was out to kill him, but his legs were like lead and he couldn't move fast enough. He managed to force himself awake just as the murderer was grabbing him by the neck. Jack didn't need a head doctor to interpret the dream. He knew he was running away from Donny and his gang, and even when fully awake, he had the same feeling of helplessness as he had in his nightmare. He didn't know how he was ever going to get away.

He could hear his mum moving downstairs and for a moment he wanted to throw himself into her arms as if he were a little boy. But what could she do? She'd tell his father, for sure, and he would bring in the police. Even if Donny was sent to jail, eventually he'd get out, and woe betide the one who had betrayed him.

He thought he heard sounds from his parents' bedroom. His dad might be getting up. He got into his trousers and jersey and went down to the kitchen.

His mother was standing at the counter, cutting some bread for toast. "Morning, Jack. You're up with the sun. How come?"

She smiled at him, but he'd seen her unguarded expression and was shocked to see how sad and tired she looked.

"No reason. I was awake. Is Dad up?"

"Just about. I thought I'd cook us up some bacon for break-fast. Do you want your egg today or save it?"

"Today, please." He slid into a chair at the kitchen table.

"Are you going to go to Holy Communion today?" his mother asked.

Jack hesitated. His grammar school was an old-fashioned one, still affiliated with the Church of England. The pupils were expected to attend matins and to take Communion on a regular basis. The truth was, Jack was afraid to go. Even though he was old enough to know better, he was afraid that God would send a sign of His disapproval. Strike him dead in the middle of the service. Old Mr. Perry had been a mean blighter and he'd been struck down one day when he knelt to say his prayers. *Crash.* Gone, just like that. God had got vengeance.

"I don't think so, Mum." Before he could come up with a plausible excuse, there was a loud knocking at the front door. She looked at Jack in alarm.

"Who can that be at this time of the morning?"

Jack felt himself go white. None of their neighbours would knock like that on their front door. Friends used the back entrance.

Phyllis wiped her hands on the pinafore. "Fetch your dad. They've come about Brian, I'll bet."

There was another heavy pounding.

Phyllis caught him by the sleeve. "No, wait. Run to your granddad's house and warn them. Go out the back way. Quick."

"What about Dad?"

"God help us, we'll have to hope he can keep his mouth shut. Run, Jack. Run."

Jack opened the back door as his mother went to the front. He heard a deep masculine voice say, "Mrs. Walmsley? I'm Sergeant Carson, Military Police. We're looking for your son, Brian Walmsley."

As soon as he reached the back entry, Jack took off. A part of him was flooded with relief that they had come for Brian, not him.

***

"It's all right, Brian. It's all right," Eileen repeated. "They've gone. You're quite safe."

"Come on out, son," said Joe, and together he and Eileen helped Brian crawl out of the tiny space. He was shaking so violently he could hardly stand up. His pupils were so dilated the irises had almost disappeared.

"Dad, get me the stool from the bathroom," said Eileen. Joe did so at once and she made Brian sit down. "Put your head between your knees and take some deep breaths." She put her hand on the back of his neck. "That's it. Good. Another one. Good boy."

Joe's face was expressionless but Eileen could feel his tension. Redcaps were one thing – he could deal with them, concrete objects – but this kind of hysteria in a man he was at a loss as to how to handle.

"Let's go downstairs to my room," she said.

Joe took Brian's arm and slipped it across his shoulders. They looked like two comrades coming off the battlefield. Eileen was right behind them.

Beatrice silently opened the door to Eileen's bed-sitting room and all of them went inside.

"I'll make us some tea," Beatrice said and hurried off to the kitchen. Joe sat his grandson in the armchair by the fire.

Eileen took her shawl and covered him, then went to her dresser and took out the bottle of brandy. She poured a big shot into a glass.

"Here, swallow this down. You've had a shock."

Brian didn't need to be told twice. He gulped back the brandy, wiped his mouth with the back of his hand, and leaned back in the chair.

"I can't go in that cupboard again. I'd rather die."

Suddenly they heard Beattie talking to somebody at the back door. All three of them froze.

"Stay here," said Eileen. "Brian, if you have to, get under the bed."

She opened the door and looked into the hall. Jack emerged from the kitchen, Beatrice behind him.

"The redcaps are looking for Brian," he burst out breathlessly. "They came to the house just now. Me mum said to come and warn you."

"They were here already," said Eileen. "We got Brian hidden just in time. We're all in my room. What did your mum and dad say to the redcaps?"

He shook his head. "I don't know. They were at the front

door and Mum told me to run and warn you. I went out the back way."

"Did anybody see you come here?"

"Nobody, Auntie. Nobody's about."

Just as well, she thought. One glimpse of Jack's face and everybody on the street would be at the door, wondering if the Abbotts had received a telegram.

She turned to Joe. "What do you think's the best thing to do, Dad?" She kept her voice low so Brian couldn't hear them.

Her father rubbed at his face. "We can't hide him again like that. He won't be able to stand it. Let's hope Ted kept quiet."

Eileen tapped Jack on the shoulder. "I want you to get over to the factory. Find Mr. Cudmore and tell him I won't be in today."

"What if he asks me why?"

"He won't. Don't say any more than that, for God's sake."

Jack started for the door and she stopped him. "Wait." She went back into her room and got a piece of paper from her desk. Brian was sitting with his eyes closed, utterly still. She scribbled out her note. *Dear Lev, I won't be able to meet you tonight. Not feeling well. See you tomorrow.*

She stuffed the note into an envelope and went back into the hall.

"Here, Jack. I want you to give this to a man by the name of Lev Kaplan. He's making a film at the factory. If he's not there, leave it with the guard at the gate. It's important that he gets it. Got that?"

"Yes, Auntie."

"Come straight back here when you've done that. And don't run. We've got to act as if everything is as usual."

The boy nodded and Eileen let him out the front door. She was aware that both Joe and Beattie were regarding her curiously.

"The American was supposed to be taking photos of the clinic this afternoon."

Her dissembling came so glibly she felt a pang of shame. But however much she loved her parents, Eileen did not feel ready to share her new tender, tumultuous feelings. Especially not right now.

She smiled at her mother. "Now then, Mum, how about that tea you were going to make?"

Eileen and Joe went out into the hall.

"We've got to get him out of here, Eileen. He's going to crack completely if we don't. We need those identity papers he was going on about, and we need them soon. Now, it's my feeling that our Jack and Brian are in on something together. Frankly, at this moment I don't want to enquire too closely. What's your feeling?"

She nodded. "I agree totally."

Joe grimaced. "Eileen, my pet, I never dreamed we'd ever be in a position like this. Redcaps stomping through the house, us all telling lies like we were criminals . . ."

Eileen came over and put her arms around him. "Me neither, Dad. But you know what? I'm proud of you."

***

When Tyler arrived at the factory, an immaculate Cudmore, smooth-haired and close-shaven, was waiting for him.

"You're a great morale booster, Mr. Cudmore."

The secretary turned rather pink. "Really, sir? How so?"

"You manage to convey order even in the midst of chaos."

"Thank you, sir. I do think these things are important, even in wartime. I should say, especially in wartime. Polished shoes can do wonders for the spirits."

"Right." Tyler took his place behind the desk. "Speaking of

shoes, I wonder what you can tell me about Michael Smith, the dillie man. Do you know if he was ever in the army?"

Cudmore looked puzzled. "I'm not sure, sir. I can look at his application record. He's only worked here for three months, so I'm sure we still have it on file."

"Excellent. So what have you got for me?"

"There are a few more workers in today that you haven't spoken to. I assume you will be wanting to interview them."

"Thank you, Mr. Cudmore. By the way, has Miss Ringwald-Brown clocked in yet? I thought I'd have another try at talking to her."

"No, sir. I did check before you arrived. I believe the young lady in question has called in to say she is not well and won't be at work today."

"Do you have her address? Perhaps if she's under the weather I should go to see her instead."

"That would be in my files, sir. I shall bring it for you."

Tyler noticed that there was a Thermos on the desk. "For me?"

"Yes, sir. I took the liberty of making you some tea. That way you won't have to bother going to the canteen."

"Thank you, Mr. Cudmore."

In fact, Tyler would have been more than happy to join the workers on their break. Professionally, as he'd said to his constable, mingling with the crowd, listening, paying attention could pay dividends.

The secretary stepped back into his usual position by the door and close to the wall. "Mr. Endicott sends his apologies, sir, but he won't be in today. He has urgent work to attend to on his estate." He gave a small cough. "He's quite highly strung, appearances to the contrary. He was dreadfully upset by what happened yesterday."

"Not half as upset as the poor girl who's lost her hair," retorted Tyler.

"Quite so. I did take the liberty of ringing the hospital this morning. Miss Tomlin is out of danger but still in isolation for the time being." The cough again. "I was going to take it upon myself to collect money for some flowers and a card to send to her."

"Good idea, Mr. Cudmore. Add this." Tyler fished in his pocket and found a couple of shillings, then he began to unscrew the Thermos lid. "All right, let's get going. I'd like to wrap this up today if it's at all possible."

***

Jack was seated at the dining room table between Joe and Eileen. He was fiddling with a spoon, twisting and turning it in his hands. They had talked Brian into going back upstairs.

Joe shifted his bad leg. "Now, son, I'm not going to pry any more than I need to, but you can see what a heap of trouble we've got on our hands. We've got to get our Brian out of here, and the sooner the better. Now, he was talking to us about getting hold of a passport so he could get to Ireland for the duration. Do you have any idea where he was thinking he might get such an item?"

Jack shook his head. Too quickly and too hard. "No, Granddad."

"I'd ask him, but he's in no condition at the moment. So I thought if there was any way you could help out, we'd all appreciate it. Maybe he let slip a name, for instance." Joe's voice was quiet, but as usual he conveyed an authority that was unmistakable.

Jack was looking so terrified that Eileen couldn't help herself. She reached over and covered his hand with hers. "Jack, you don't have to be scared of us. We're your family. But Brian was positive he could get a passport for himself and Vanessa. Is it true what he believes?"

"I think so, Auntie."

"Who's getting it for him? We might be able to speed things up." Joe leaned forward slightly and Eileen saw her nephew flinch.

"He did sort of mention somebody . . . I don't know him myself but . . . he lives in one of the back-to-backs near Water Street."

Joe scowled. "Why aren't I surprised about that? Go on, son. Could you get in touch with this person, do you think?"

"I could try, Granddad."

"Will he want money?"

Jack nodded.

"Any idea how much?"

"No, Granddad."

Joe turned to Eileen. "What do you think? A false identity these days – what are we talking about? Two quid? Ten? Twenty?"

"I don't know, Dad. They probably take as much as they can get."

Joe stood up and went to the sideboard. "Let's start with that, then, and if we have to we'll come up with more." He reached into a drawer and, fishing about at the back, took out a tin that had once held toffees. "We're going to have to borrow from your gran's housekeeping for now." He stirred the pile of coins in the tin. "A bit short of three pounds."

"I have a couple of pounds in my purse," said Eileen. "I'll get them."

"All right." Joe took an envelope from the drawer. He tipped the money from the tin into the envelope, then paused and removed a couple of shillings. "I'd better leave her something for shopping."

Eileen returned with the two pounds and Joe added them to the envelope. He handed it to his grandson.

"That's five pounds altogether. See if you can find this fellow. We need to get things in motion right away."

Jack stashed the envelope in his pocket.

"Off you go, then," said Joe. "Fast as you can. Come back here as soon as you've seen him."

"Yes, Granddad. I'll just let our Brian know I'm going."

He scurried off upstairs before either Joe or Eileen could protest.

Brian was lying on the bed with his eyes closed, dragging on a cigarette. The small room was thick with smoke.

"I'm going to take some money to Donny for your papers . . ." Jack's voice tailed off as he waited to see how his brother would react.

Brian shot bolt upright. "There's not supposed to be money exchanged. What did you tell them? Did you mention the timers?"

"Nothing, Brian. Nothing, honest. I don't even know about timers or anything. Granddad and Auntie Eileen just thought they'd have to pay."

"So they will," said Brian, letting out a deep breath. "Knowing Donny Jarvis, he wouldn't keep his end of the bargain if his life depended on it. Of course he'd want money as well as − forget what I just said about timers, Jack. It's nothing like that. He just wanted me to fix something for him."

"Yes, Brian."

Brian lit another cigarette from the butt of the first. "My end's done. The bag is in the wardrobe. You can take it to Donny."

Jack went to the wardrobe and removed the shopping bag that he'd delivered what seemed like eons ago.

"Hide it under your coat," said Brian sharply. "You don't want anyone asking difficult questions."

Jack tucked the bag inside his jacket.

"How much money are you taking him?" asked Brian.

"Five pounds."

"God, that's nothing. Donny will laugh his head off."

"That's all Granddad and Auntie Eileen could come up with for now."

Brian scowled. "Tell Donny we'll get some more. But tell him I've got to get out of this house soon or I'll blow the whole thing. I don't give a shite."

Suddenly he jumped up and grabbed his brother's arm. "Got that, Jack? Donny Jarvis isn't the only one with power here." He gave Jack a pinch. "Are you clear? Do you know what you're going to say?"

"Yes, Brian."

"Repeat it back to me."

"We can come up with more money but Donny has to hand over the papers before he gets it."

Brian burst out laughing. "Well done, little titch. That's it. Now off you go. Report back to me."

***

Bert Teale opened Donny's door. "Well, if it isn't the little pansy. What you want, missie?"

"I need to talk to Donny."

"Did you bring stuff?"

"No, I—"

"Well, he don't want to talk to you lessen you bring stuff." He started to close the door but a voice from inside the room called out.

"Let him in, Bertie. Didn't you hear him? He needs to talk." Donny giggled, which Jack found very odd indeed, coming from him.

"Come in then, pansy," said Bert. He yanked Jack into the house by the collar.

Donny was lying on the couch, and curled up on the floor beside him, like a dog, was Thelma. She appeared to be asleep. Jack hoped desperately that she wasn't dead. The room was filled with smoke, strange and acrid-smelling, but not unpleasant. Donny was puffing on a long tube attached to a round pot on the floor that was making funny bubbling sounds. He actually smiled at Jack. "Welcome, you little sod. What is it you want?"

Jack didn't know if he should say anything in front of Bert and Thelma, but he was too afraid to consider much beyond the immediate task. "I was wondering if you, er . . . had them goods you were going to give me for my brother. I've got the bag . . ." His voice tailed off.

"Bert, go take a piss," Donny said. Thelma didn't stir.

Bert knew better than to protest, although he looked sullen and flicked Jack hard on the cheek as he went by. Donny settled back on the couch. His eyelids drooped.

"Now then, our Jackie, you have to be careful what you say. Careless talk costs lives. How *is* Brian doing, by the way?"

"Not so well, Donny. He'd like to leave as soon as possible. He says to tell you he wants you to keep your end of the bargain."

"He does, does he?" Donny waved the pipe contraption in the air, then sucked on it deeply, holding his breath before blowing out the smoke. "It's dear to get what he wants. Very dear. Say, fifty pounds. Tell him if he can come up with that, I'll get him the goods."

Jack took the envelope out of his coat. "I don't have that much. But you can have this now and the rest later." He had no idea if Brian would be able to get the money, but that wasn't his problem. At least, he hoped it wasn't.

In spite of his drowsy state, Donny was alert enough to count the money in the envelope. He dropped it on the floor. "That's a joke, that is, little Jackie. Your Brian won't get a pot to shit in for that."

Thelma stirred. Donny moved his foot and rested it on her haunches.

Jack tried to avoid looking at the girl. "Sorry, Donny. I'll try to get the rest for you. When can he have the stuff?"

More drawing on the pipe. More bubbling. Then Donny waved the mouthpiece in Jack's direction. "Tell him you've got to make the drop at the Cowan house, right after blackout. You have the money, he can have the goods. Simple as that. You can put it in the oven."

"Thanks, Donny." Jack placed the bag gingerly on the floor and turned to go.

"What's your hurry?" said Donny. "Take the weight off your beaters. You've been a good kid, all told. Here . . ." He held out the pipe. "Take a puff. You'll like it."

"No, no thanks, Donny. I'd better get back."

"Suit yourself."

"What is it?" Jack couldn't help but ask.

"Just baccy. A rather special kind of baccy, mind you. A friend got it for me in return for a couple of favours. It comes from darkie country. It's called ganja."

He took another drag on the pipe. Jack seized his chance and sidled to the door. "I'll pass on the message, Donny. Tonight after blackout. Put the money in the oven. Fifty pounds."

Donny didn't seem to hear. Jack opened the door and stepped out into the courtyard. Bert was leaning against the wall, hunched into his coat. Jack didn't give him another opportunity to slap or pinch but took off into the street. The funny tobacco smell clung to his clothes.

***

At Tyler's request, Cudmore had provided a thick swatch of employee files. They had set up young Eagleton at a desk in the office. He looked a little daunted when Tyler told him he had to go through them.

"Just pull out any that you think we should examine more closely. You don't have to go back further than three months, but see if there's anybody who's been moving around from factory to factory. Also, make sure as best you can that the references are genuine. Let me know if a letter is signed by somebody calling himself Goebbels. Or Churchill, for that matter."

"Yes, sir."

"And Eager – you can wear your specs. Makes you look like a boffin."

"Yes, sir. I presume that's a good thing."

Tyler left him to it and began the final interviews. There was a steady flow of workers but he learned nothing new. None of them thought the explosion was anything but an accident.

"Fifth columnists? Sabotage? Never. We're all Englishmen here," said one wizened bloke who worked the night shift. "If it was done on purpose, how'd anybody do it?"

Good question.

He asked all of them for suggestions as to improvements in the future, and most had a lot to say.

"Management should come into the canteen sometimes and show us they're human."

"We should go on a tour of the airdrome and see the bombers. We don't even know where our shells go."

"Me, I work here so I can do my bit for the King and Queen and the little princesses. My own girl is the same age as

Princess Elizabeth. I want to make sure that madman in Berlin doesn't ever get to them."

"Mr. Endicott should give us more credit for brains, not to mention patriotism," said a woman with a thick Brummie accent. She looked as if she'd had a tough life but that didn't stop her from being astute. "I work the lathes. We need a break in the middle of the shift. Everybody gets the sags after tea time. We'll work better."

That complaint had been voiced yesterday when the women were contemplating going on strike. Tyler was feeling something of the sags himself by now and he sympathized.

Cudmore wrote everything down. Tyler was glad that at least he'd been able to give the workers a chance to vent their frustrations.

After the last interview, Tyler said. "Mr. Cudmore, take a note, if you please, and make sure Mr. Endicott receives it. 'By the authority vested in me by His Majesty the King and the chief minister of the realm, Winston Churchill, I hereby declare all of the suggestions herein recorded be implemented as soon as possible, on pain of death.'"

Cudmore didn't bat an eye. "Quite right too, sir."

Another alarm sounded in the late afternoon, but no raiders, and Tyler followed the lead of the seasoned Brummies and stayed where he was. *Move only when you hear the bombs dropping.*

The secretary had found Smith's file and gave it to Tyler. There was no record of his being in the army. He'd come from Manchester to work at Endicott's. Better pay was the reason given. He had a good letter of reference from the supervisor at the factory where he'd worked previously.

"Did anybody check on this?" Tyler asked.

"Oh dear, I'm afraid not, sir. We were hiring a lot of people all at the same time. I wasn't able to follow up on any of the references. We did place him on the usual probationary period of two weeks. He has shown himself to be a reliable worker. He's never late. No absenteeism."

Tyler hesitated. He knew the secretary was overworked.

"There are a couple of other workers who have been in the army," added Cudmore. "Mr. Abbott was a corporal with the Royal Lancers of Leicester. He was invalided out in '17 with a gas-caused ulcer. A good man too. Most reliable. The other man is Phil Riley, who joined the reserve army in '38. He is a part of the home defence now." Cudmore regarded Tyler anxiously. "Is this important, sir? I'd vouch for all three of them."

"Just tying up loose ends," said Tyler. "Maybe I'd better talk to Smith again. Just to satisfy myself."

Cudmore became even more flustered. "He's not in today, sir. I told him he could have the day off. He was complaining of a touch of lumbago, and seeing as he had talked to you yesterday, I didn't see the harm."

"I'm sure that's quite all right, Mr. Cudmore. It'll keep." Tyler got up stiffly from his chair. "I thought I'd drop in at the hospital. Who knows? Perhaps Peter Pavely has regained some of his memory."

"I'll get on to typing up these notes right away."

"Thanks. And don't forget to give me Miss Ringwald-Brown's address. I thought I'd pay her a visit. As she won't come to Mahomet, the mountain will go to her."

"Beg pardon, sir?"

"Never mind. Just a turn of phrase." *Definitely an afternoon sag*, thought Tyler.

He looked in on his constable, who actually seemed to be enjoying himself. He had a dozen files set aside.

"Good work, Eager. This could keep us in Brummagem for a month at least. Are you being astute, I wonder, or does your diligence have anything to do with a certain collision-prone roller skater?"

"Good heavens, sir. I wouldn't dream of being so devious."

Tyler ruffled his hair. "Glad to hear it, son."

***

Phyllis had brought over an extra pork chop and some potatoes. She deposited them on the kitchen counter. Jack had come with her, but not Ted.

"The post must go through," said Phyllis in answer to her mother's query. "He's working overtime."

"Go and sit in the other room," said Beattie. "I'm going to cook up something for us shortly."

Phyllis went into the living room with Jack. Joe was sitting close to the fire, his leg on a hassock. Eileen was reading a book and Brian was at the table fiddling with an old jigsaw puzzle.

"Crikey, you're a cheery lot, aren't you," said Phyllis. "I've been to livelier funerals."

Brian looked up. "Did you get the money?"

"And hello to you, Brian."

"Sorry, Mum. Hello."

"Come and have a warm, Phyl," said Eileen. "Shove over a bit, Dad."

"Thanks." Phyllis went to her son and dropped a quick kiss on his head. "And yes, Brian, I did get the money. I took out forty pounds from our savings. That's all there is." Her eyes were red and puffy from crying but Brian didn't seem to notice or care.

Joe moved his chair and Phyllis went to stand beside him. "We've already given the bastard five pounds, so all we need is five more," he said.

Beattie came in from the kitchen. "Here's another pound. I was keeping it for emergencies."

"And I've got two more," said Eileen. She winked at her mother. "I'd forgotten I even had it. It was in *my* emergency tin."

"Let's put everything on the table," said Joe.

Phyllis rummaged through her handbag. "I thought . . . yes, I knew I did. Here's a pound in change."

Joe pulled some coins from his pocket. "Four bob. Five pennies. Two halfpennies." He added them to the collection.

"I've got sixpence, Granddad," said Jack.

"Might as well throw it in," said Joe. He poked at the pile of money. "Four pound, five shillings. That'll have to do. The bastard won't renege for want of a few shillings, will he?"

Brian had watched the proceedings without a word. Then he muttered, "Thanks everybody. I'll pay you back, I promise."

Joe beckoned to Jack. "You might as well take this now. It'll be dark soon."

"I'll go with him," said Eileen.

"No, I'll go," said Phyllis. "I'm his mother, after all."

Joe went to stand up. "I should be the one to go if anybody does. We don't know what this rat might get up to."

"No, Dad. You're not going anywhere. Look at you. Your face is as grey as a flannel shirt. Your leg's bothering you, isn't it."

"I'm all right."

"No, you're not," interjected Beattie. "It's best that Eileen goes. She's used to dealing with problem people."

"Mum –" Phyllis started to object.

"No arguing, either of you. Phyllis, you should spend some time with Brian. Joe, I'm going to put fresh ointment on your ankle. Eileen, you should get going."

The Abbotts weren't a particularly demonstrative family but Eileen couldn't help herself. She gave her mother a kiss on the cheek. "I never knew you could be such a battle-axe," she said affectionately.

"I need to be sometimes with this lot," said Beattie.

Brian swivelled towards Eileen. "Auntie, I need to get a message to Vanessa. We'll leave as soon as I get that passport. She's got to be ready."

"All right, I'll go to her house after we drop off the money."

Eileen put her hand on her other nephew's shoulder. "Come on, Jack. Let's go."

He smiled up at her and she could see the relief in his face. He was just a sprat, thin, pale-skinned like his mother. His bony shoulder blades were prominent under the woollen jersey.

"Please be careful how you go, Eileen," said Beattie. "Make sure you have your torch with you."

"I will, Mum." Eileen turned to Jack. "Why don't you start getting your coat on. I'll get an envelope for the money."

They both went out into the hall. Joe began to fold the notes. Brian could have been on another planet for all the interaction he was having with them.

Beattie addressed Phyllis. "Maisie Swann has vanished."

"What do you mean, vanished?"

"Her daughter came by this afternoon. Maisie hasn't been home since yesterday by all accounts. They're afraid she got caught in the blackout and has fallen into some crater. It's been known to happen."

"Oh dear, I hope she's all right."

"Winifred is going around to all the hospitals to see if they have any patients fitting her description. She said she'd come later and tell me."

Brian looked up.

"Don't worry," Beattie said to him. "We can get you upstairs if we have to."

Eileen returned with a large envelope in her hand. "This is all I could find."

Joe slid in the coins and the pound notes and sealed the envelope.

"Phyl, there's a bottle of pills in the bedside table drawer in my room," said Eileen. "They've got a blue label. Give Dad two with a glass of water. The ointment is in there as well. You don't need much, and it soothes the pain."

Joe flapped his hand. "Will you women stop fussing. I should have sired boys – make life much easier."

This was a long-standing family joke and the two sisters hissed at him.

"I've been like a son, haven't I, Granddad?" Brian burst out. His intensity destroyed the momentary mood of playfulness.

"Brian, for goodness sake," said Phyllis, her voice sharp with impatience.

"It's all right, Phyl," said Joe. He reached over to his grandson. "Yes, you have, Brian. Both you and Jack have been like sons. Now let's do what we have to do so we can put all this behind us."

Brian caught his grandfather's hand and held it tightly against his chest. "What if we can't, Granddad? Put it behind us, I mean. What if we can't?"

Eileen had her hand resting lightly on Jack's shoulder as they walked. She directed her torch at their feet, but with the overcast sky and no lights anywhere, it was hard to see. They kept close to the hedges for guidance.

"Jack," she said quietly, "how do you know this man who's supposed to get the passport?"

"I dunno, Auntie. I just met him somewhere."

"What's his name?"

"I dunno."

Eileen stopped so she could look straight into his face. "Jack, I'm not interested in punishing you. As a family we're in a right pickle. We've got to help Brian, but it's not as simple as that. We're doing something that's totally against the law. I'm prepared to do it, though I wish I didn't have to. I hope to God this war doesn't last much longer and that Brian and others like him will be all right."

The boy was avoiding looking at her and she could feel he was shaking.

"Can you tell me what's wrong, Jack? What have you got yourself into? You seem terrified of your own shadow." She brushed away a tear that had spilled from his eye. "Buck up, lad, you're a big boy now. You're my own flesh and blood and I want to help you."

"You can't, Auntie. Nobody can."

That sounded so melodramatic that in spite of herself she smiled. "Try me. Come on, before we get to the house. Tell me what's going on. Is somebody threatening you?"

Jack nodded but didn't speak.

"You've been looting, haven't you."

Even now Jack seemed about to deny everything, but she pressed on. "Was he with you? Is that what's going on?"

"Yes, Auntie," Jack whispered. "He . . . he saw me. He saw me going into one of the houses. He said he'd tell the police. He said I'd go to jail and he knew people in jail who'd get me . . . They do awful things to boys in jail, Auntie. Awful things." The words were tumbling out now, and Jack couldn't stop crying. "I agreed to be part of his gang so he wouldn't rat on me."

"When did all this happen?"

"A few weeks ago."

"What's this man's name?"

"Donny Jarvis. He lives in one of the back-to-backs on Water Street."

Eileen frowned. "I know him. He was sent to the public clinic by the truant officer when I was doing a stint there. He's just a lad, not a man."

"He's sixteen. He hurts me, Auntie. He hurts me if I don't bring back enough stuff."

Eileen took a handkerchief out of her pocket and handed it to her nephew. "Here, blow your nose. You're beginning to sound like Oliver Twist."

She waited until Jack had subsided, lingering sobs coming out of his throat like hiccups.

"I'm not surprised Donny Jarvis has turned into a bad apple. His home life was as rough as it could be. He'll remember me, I'm sure. Maybe I should talk to him."

Jack almost squealed. "Please don't, Auntie. Nobody is supposed to know. He'll kill me."

"All right, all right. One thing at a time. Let's do our errand and go back to Gran and Granddad's. Once Brian has gone we'll talk about what to do with the wretched lad you've got yourself tangled up with."

But Jack was not to be so easily comforted. "He'll kill me if he finds out I've told on him."

Suddenly Eileen stopped. "Hold on – I'm being slow on the uptake here. This fellow Donny, is he the one who's supposed to be getting illegal papers for Brian?"

Jack nodded.

"How's he getting them?"

"I don't know, Auntie."

Eileen bit her lip. While Jack was talking it had been at the back of her mind that she would report Donny to the police. But the family needed him right now. She couldn't turn him in just yet.

They were at the bombed house now. It had been a pretty, well-tended house, and now it was destroyed. Eileen blinked away a tear. The Cowans had been good people, salt of the earth.

She halted. "I'll keep watch. You deposit the money. Hurry, Jack."

***

Tyler was greeted at the entrance to the ward by Nurse Ruebotham. Her manner was only slightly less intimidating this time around. She seemed harried.

"We're frightfully short-handed so I'm going to have to trust you to be sensitive to Miss Sumner's state. Don't overtire her."

"I'll be careful."

"Physically, she's improving – the young are resilient. But she's quite despondent. She knows what has happened to her."

She moved aside the screen around the bed. The adjacent bed, where Audrey Sandilands had been, was empty.

"I'll leave you, Inspector. No more than ten minutes."

Tyler pulled up the chair close to the bed and sat down. The nurse had said Sylvia was improving, but to his eyes she looked worse than when he'd last seen her. The bruises on her face were darker, her skin even whiter.

"Sylvia. It's Inspector Tyler."

She opened her eyes and looked at him. "Is Colin here?"

"I don't believe so. But I'm sure he's been sent for."

There was a small movement from her bandaged right arm, as if she was trying to reach over to him. Tyler saw an expression of fear flood her face.

"They said I've lost my arm, but it doesn't feel that way. I keep thinking I can move it. Isn't that odd?"

"I understand that does happen sometimes," murmured Tyler.

She turned her head away from him. "I'm going to release Colin from our engagement. He shouldn't have to be tied to a cripple for the rest of his life."

"Sylvia, look at me. Come on, look at me."

Reluctantly, she did so.

"What if Colin was the one to get injured? Would you break up with him because he'd got knocked about a bit?"

Her eyes were filled with tears. "You know I wouldn't. I'd love him just the same."

"And his feelings for you won't change one bit." Tyler hoped this was true.

Again she turned away. "You don't understand, Inspector. I've lost all my fingers. I won't be able to wear his wedding ring."

"What's important is that you're alive. That's what will matter to Colin."

She was silent.

"That's what would matter to you, wouldn't it?" continued Tyler softly.

She turned back and studied him for a moment. "You have a kind face, Inspector. You have a daughter, don't you."

"Aye, lass. She's a bit younger than you."

"She's lucky to have you for a dad."

"It's more the other way around, if you ask me."

The screen was moved aside and Nurse Ruebotham poked her head in. "I'd say that's it for today, Inspector."

Tyler got to his feet.

"Did you want to ask me something?" Sylvia whispered. She was becoming drowsy.

"Just one thing. We found a St. Christopher medal amongst the debris in your section. Do you know who it might have belonged to?"

"No, I don't. Not allowed to bring in stuff like that."

"Inspector, time's up," said Miss Ruebotham.

Sylvia's eyelids were drooping. "Thank you, Inspector."

Tyler's heart ached for the girl.

He was able to see Peter Pavely, who still had no further recollection of the explosion. "No, Inspector. Like I said, the last thing I remember is walking into the shed."

"And there was nobody there, I gather."

"The workers weren't in yet, if that's what you mean. Phil Riley was checking to see how many fuses were left over from the previous shift." He hesitated. "At least I think he was there. It's all a bit fuzzy. He always has to check at shift change. Maybe it was a different day I seen him. I went in on Friday to have a look at what had to be done. Maybe that's when I seen him." The effort to remember was clearly upsetting him.

"Don't worry, mate. I'll check it out," said Tyler quickly. "That's it, then? Maybe Mr. Riley?"

"The cleaner, the foreign chap – we might have passed him in the passageway." He rubbed at his head. "I'm not positive. That might have been another day too. He has to clean around the floor when shift changes."

"Nobody else? No dillie man making a delivery?"

"I don't think so." A look of terror came across his face. Tyler had seen a similar expression on Sylvia's. "Is this going to go away?" Pavely said loudly. "I've got terrible ringing in my ears and my mind is jumping all over the place. Do you know, when you sat down, for a minute I thought you was my brother, Dan. Could have sworn it was him. But then I remembered he's dead and gone a long time ago. First war." His one eye focused on Tyler. "You're not Dan, are you? You're not Dan come for me?"

Tyler stood up and patted Pavely's shoulder. "No, I'm not. It's the sedation playing tricks. Try not to worry. You're going to be all right."

Pavely caught him by the arm. "When is somebody going to tell me what happened? I keep thinking I was to blame and you're all keeping it from me."

"That's not the case, Mr. Pavely. Tell you what, why don't you lie back in bed and try to get some sleep? I'm going to have the nurse look in on you."

Obedient as a young child, Pavely slipped down under the covers. Tyler tucked the sheet up close to his chin.

"Hush, now. You're going to be all right."

***

Donny Jarvis was hiding in the shadows of the house next door when Jack and a woman approached. He recognized her right away. When he was in second form, he'd contracted a bad case of scabies and a shocked and repulsed teacher had sent him to the local clinic. The nurse had been kind, soothed his maddening itch with some ointment, shared her lunch with him, and wrote a note to his parents. Bloody laugh that was. His father had clipped his ear for causing trouble and his mother had gone on a rant about them interfering. Nothing came of the letter – no better food, even less cleanliness.

He supposed he was grudgingly grateful to the nurse. She'd tried, and she at least had treated him like a human being. Her name was Abbott, he remembered, and Brian and Jack were related to her. Too bad it was her family he'd got in the squeeze.

Jack made the drop while she waited outside, then Donny watched them walk away.

He collected the money and went to the meeting he'd arranged with Comrade Patrick. As he entered the gate, he felt uneasy. In early November a bomb had landed in a churchyard and bones and bits of ancient corpses were spewed all around. Live blokes Donny felt he could handle; bloody stiffs were something else. Funny he didn't worry about getting killed himself. In fact, he found the raids exciting. And of course there were rich pickings after. During a raid he often went into the middle of the street to watch the action. He loved the roar and crackle of the blazing fires, the *thwump*, *thwump* of the bombs landing, the sharp rattle of the ack-ack guns. He breathed in the smell of cordite and burning wood like somebody else breathed in the fresh smell of pine trees.

He might even consider signing up when he was older. Nothing to do with love of country. As far as he was concerned, the government could stick their flag up their arse as far as it would go. They'd never done anything for him. But he sort of fancied being in a battle. Having a big, deadly gun. You could just mow men down with one of them. And a bayonet. He'd seen a newsreel at the pictures of soldiers training. They stuck the bayonet into a stuffed dummy, all looking very chuffed and calm about it. The dummy didn't look anything like a real man. No blood gushing out, no terror on the face of the dying. Not like it really was. But it was all legit. All paid for by the government.

He went to the appointed place, the alcove sheltered by an overhang of the church roof. There was a row of ugly shapes along the roof edge, heads with twisted features. Why people would decorate a church with those things Donny couldn't fathom. He stamped his feet, which were getting cold in spite of his wool socks. He'd nicked them from Lewis's department store on one of his little excursions.

He wondered if he could risk lighting a fag. He didn't want some nosy air-raid warden seeing him. They came out after dark like gnats at twilight.

Finally he heard the soft crunch of footsteps on the gravel path. Somebody was coming. He slipped his fingers into the knucks in his coat pocket, just in case. A man's figure emerged out of the gloom. He was whistling softly, a popular tune, "Run Rabbit Run." It was Patrick. Donny stepped forward a couple of feet so he could be seen. Patrick stopped.

"Evening, lad. You're nice and punctual. Seen anybody?"

"Not a bleedin' soul. There's just me and the corpses."

"Good. Let's tuck in here for a minute, then."

Patrick moved ahead to the darkest place along the wall, where there was a shallow depression. He wasted no time. "Have you got the stuff?"

Donny handed over the shopping bag. Patrick set it by his feet. "And the money?"

Donny fished inside his coat and took out the envelope. Patrick had a small torch with him and he snapped it on, focusing the beam on the contents of the envelope. He riffled through the notes.

"There's only thirty-five here. I said forty."

"That's all they could come up with, I suppose," Donny replied quickly.

He thought the other man smiled, thin and cold, but he couldn't be sure. As usual, most of his face was hidden by a muffler. "Too bad. I was going to give you a fiver for yourself but I won't be able to do that now."

"'S all right." Donny could actually feel himself sweating in spite of the cold. He thrust his hand into his pocket again and felt the reassuring smooth weight of the knuckle-duster. "When can he get the papers?"

Patrick chuckled. "Don't be an idiot. Where would I get forged papers? I'm not the Secret Service."

"Right, course . . . so our friend is going to be disappointed?"

"'Fraid so."

"What shall I tell him?"

"Tell him whatever you bloody well like."

"Do you want to get more dosh out of him, then?"

"No, we're going to get plenty of money soon. But your pal is a liability. When he knows he's paid for nothing, he's likely to go into a sulk. You never know what he might take into his head to go and do. We've got what we wanted."

"And the plan is in place?"

"It is. Won't be long now."

Donny decided to risk rolling a fag and lighting it. He took the packet of papers from his coat but Patrick caught him by the hand. "Don't do that yet, Bolton. Wait till I've gone. I don't want anybody coming for a look-see."

Donny could feel the other man's breath on his cheek, slightly sour-smelling. "Is there anything more for me to do, then?"

"No, I'll take it from here. You know the drill; you'll get notice when I want you."

"Wait. What shall I do about my friend?"

Patrick was already walking away. "Deal with him any way you bloody well want. Like I said, he's a liability. Don't mess up, me boyo. Tomorrow will be our Guy Fawkes' Day."

The darkness swallowed him up almost immediately. Donny took out his cigarette makings. That had been a close shave. He'd been stupid to think he'd get away with keeping back a fiver from the money Patrick was expecting. Good thing he'd factored in what he considered to be his commission from the start. He'd picked up almost fifteen quid. Not bad.

He struck his match and lit the fag, drawing the tobacco deep into his lungs. He'd mixed in a little of the remaining ganja with the regular tobacco.

"Deal with him," Patrick had said.

You *dealt with* rats. You *dealt with* the odd yowling tomcat that came into the back entry. You *dealt with* blokes who thought they could put one over on you. It was one thing to have a dust-up with some sod from another gang, say, or whack your girl, or hurt a kid like Jack. But to actually kill somebody in cold blood, that was a different story.

Shit. Bloody hell. What was he going to do?

***

Eileen sent Jack back to the house to report that they had delivered the money and she went on alone to Bennett Street, where Vanessa's parents lived. A gust of wind hit her face; bits of newspaper wrapped around her feet. She could see the headlines: "High-Explosive Bombs Drop on City Centre. Many Lives Lost." That had happened only a week ago. She knew another attack was probably coming soon. The moon had appeared, trailing clouds. In the past, before the war changed everything, she'd loved to see the moon grow full. Now the sight brought dread. It was a deadly beauty. She wondered if Lev had been disappointed by her note. Maybe he'd gone ahead and invited some other woman to go to the dance. Some younger, prettier woman?

"Get a grip on yourself, Eileen Abbott. *Miss* Eileen Abbott," she whispered out loud. She was glad when her torch picked out the numbers on the gate of 62.

She went up the path and knocked. No answer. She knocked again. Did she have the right number? She contemplated the arch of a rose trellis over the doorway. Frost-seared, marooned roses. Vanessa's mother liked gardening, she recalled. What was her name? Joan? June? They'd only met once, at the wedding breakfast. Jane. That was her name. Beattie had referred to her as "Jane, ever so plain."

She was about to knock again when the door opened. It was Jane herself.

"Good evening, Mrs. Wainwright, Eileen Abbott here. Is Vanessa at home? I'd like to talk to her for a minute."

Jane Wainwright was wearing a flowered housedress, a shapeless beige cardigan, and down-at-heel slippers, and she had a fag between her stained fingers. She could have been the model for the cartoon character Sally Slattern, who appeared in the *Daily Mail*. She also smelled strongly of booze.

"Oh yes, Miss Abbott. Didn't recognize you for a minute. It's dark on them steps. The landlord won't fix the bulb no matter how often I ask him. It's the blackout as will kill us, if you ask me. Nessie's upstairs. She's going to a flick with one of her mates from work. I wish she wouldn't, but you can't keep young girls shut up all the time, can you. Especially when we might all be dead tomorrow." Jane Wainwright had a perpetually disgruntled way of speaking, as if early in her life she'd been given the short end of the stick and felt hard done by ever since.

She stared at Eileen as if she expected some kind of answer. Eileen nodded at her. "Indeed not."

"I'll tell her you want her. Hold on."

She yelled over her shoulder. "Vanessa, Miss Abbott is here to see you. Brian's aunt." She stepped back. "Would you like to come in for a cuppa?"

The invitation was given with such reluctance that Eileen wouldn't have accepted if she were dying of thirst. "Thanks, but I won't. I don't want to be out too late. I just want to talk to Vanessa for a minute."

"Nothing wrong, is there? With Brian, I mean. He's not dead or missing, is he?"

"No, he's not."

Mrs. Wainwright waited for Eileen to deliver more information, but Vanessa appeared in the doorway behind her. She eyed Eileen warily. "Auntie Eileen. This is a surprise."

"I won't stay. I just wanted to have a word with you."

"I was on my way out, to tell the truth. I'm going to the flicks with one of the girls." She was rather dolled up for a mere trip to the cinema with a mate. High-heeled shoes, smart frock.

"I did ask her in, but she wouldn't," said her mother. The original invitation had been given ungraciously, but now Jane seemed aggrieved that Eileen had turned it down.

"I was ready to leave anyway, Ma. Don't wait up."

"Be careful, my girl."

Vanessa grabbed her coat off the peg in the hall. "You'd better close the door quick. You're showing a light."

Her mother went back inside with a flounce.

"Let's walk to the end of the road," Vanessa said to Eileen. "Ma can be a right cow sometimes. She always wants to stick her nose in my business. You lead the way."

At the corner Eileen turned to face her. Vanessa's blonde hair gleamed in the moonlight. She smelled of violets.

"We have given money to the man who is to bring the passport. As soon as he's got it, Brian wants to leave for Ireland right away. You'll have to be on standby."

"I see." Vanessa's voice was as tiny as a child's.

"Do you intend to go with him?" Eileen asked bluntly.

Vanessa began to shuffle her feet. "Brr. It's freezing. I need a fur coat."

"Do you intend to go with Brian to Ireland?" Eileen asked again.

"Bri thinks it's going to be easy, but it won't. I don't want to be on the run. And Ireland, for Pete's sake. I've heard they don't even have electricity or proper toilets. I don't fancy it."

Eileen had expected this and swallowed her impatience. "I don't think it's that bad. But you've got to make up your mind right away. He can't stay here. He'll break down. He's on the verge now as it is."

Vanessa's voice was sullen. "I don't know why he can't just turn himself in. They need soldiers. I asked a bloke and he said as long as he wasn't on the front line and getting others into danger, he won't get the full monty. Just a few months in the glasshouse."

"At the moment even being in jail would be too much. He feels he can't continue to serve in the army." Eileen hesitated. "It has a lot to do with you, Vanessa."

"Me? That's ridiculous. I'm not to blame if he's nervy. He always has been. It's got nothing to do with me."

"He's very attached to you. It might help if you talk to him. Persuade him to go back to his regiment. Assure him you'll still be waiting for him."

Vanessa bent her head so that her hair curtained her face. "That's easy for you to say. You can't take anything for granted these days, can you."

Eileen knew at that moment that if Vanessa had ever been in love with Brian, she was so no longer. "You're right about that. Not even marriage vows, it seems." Eileen knew she was being harsh but she couldn't help it. Her own pent-up feelings made her impatient. She wanted to shake the girl. "So, am I reading this correctly? You don't intend to go to Ireland with Brian?"

Vanessa shivered and pulled her coat closer around her. "What would my mum say? I wouldn't be able to write to her or anything, and who knows how long this sodding war will last. She'd be broken-hearted."

Vanessa hadn't demonstrated a great deal of tender feeling towards her mother, but Eileen let that ride.

"I can't go, Auntie Eileen. I just can't. He'll have to go back to the army or go to Ireland by himself." She caught hold of Eileen's arm. "I'm scared of him is the truth. He's changed. I'd be afraid to be with him, just him and me."

Eileen could feel her stomach knotting. Vanessa was right. Brian *had* changed, and the man he had become was disturbing. Her anger towards the girl evaporated and she touched her hand. "There's also the matter of the baby. No, there's no use denying it . . . What are you going to do about that?"

Vanessa let go of Eileen's arm and stepped back. "If there was a kid on the way, which I'm not agreeing there is, it'd be better if he wasn't here."

"Easier to make up a story, you mean?"

Vanessa glanced over her shoulder as if she was afraid her mother might be close enough to hear her. "He should just go back to his regiment. He'll be all right."

Eileen frowned. And then the penny dropped. How could she have been so thick? She raised the torch so the light was shining in Vanessa's face. Her eyes were glistening with fear.

"You informed the military police where he was, didn't you. That's why they came to us first. They knew where to look."

Vanessa tried to move out of the light but she had her back to the hedge and couldn't move. "No, no, of course I didn't. I'd never do anything like that." Her nose was running and she wiped away the mucus with the back of her hand. The tough, brash young woman vanished and she became a child, lost and overwhelmed. "Honest, Auntie. Honest I didn't."

But Eileen knew she was lying. She lowered the torch. "I don't believe you, Vanessa. But right now Brian is the top priority. I'll have to pass along what you just said about not going with him—"

"No, wait," interrupted Vanessa. "I didn't say that exactly. I've got to think about it. Don't tell him anything yet. Please."

"Very well. But if we get another visit from the MPs, you are going to be in royal trouble. Do you understand me?"

Vanessa nodded.

Eileen pulled a handkerchief out of her pocket. "Here, wipe your nose. You'd better get going. You'll be late."

Vanessa blew into the handkerchief as if she were a child. "I'm sorry, Auntie. I'm so sorry."

"Not half as much as I am, Vanessa."

***

Mary Ringwald-Brown lived in a rooming house a few streets over from the hospital. Tyler walked there, glad of the opportunity to clear his head, not to mention his heart. He'd told Sylvia he was the lucky one to have Janet for a daughter, and he'd meant it. He considered he'd been a bloody failure as a husband, but he thought he'd been a decent father. Most of the time, anyway. Could have done better with Jimmy, he knew that. But it was too late now. He had to push that thought away.

The moonlight was bathing the houses, softening the shabbiness of this stretch of road. Number 220 was a narrow, tall Victorian house squeezed in between two newer houses. He knocked on the door, and after a long time it was opened by Mary Ringwald-Brown herself.

She looked the way she had when Tyler had first encountered her at the hospital, a woman under duress. She was dishevelled, her print frock unironed. However, when she saw who it was, her expression immediately became guarded and hard. "Inspector Tyler. What can I do for you?"

"I'm just following up on a few matters to do with the explosion at the factory. Do you mind if I come in?"

She hesitated. "I'm, er, I'm expecting guests."

"Nice. I won't keep you."

She glanced over his shoulder, then stepped back so he could enter.

"I'm on the third floor. I hope you don't mind stairs."

"Good exercise."

She led the way up the dingy staircase. At the second landing, a door opened a crack and Tyler glimpsed a beady eye looking out.

"It's all right, Mr. Merrick. Just the meter man," said Mary.

The door closed at once. "He's so nosy I wonder he doesn't get stuck in the crack," said Mary, not bothering to lower her voice.

Her room proved to be as Tyler might have expected. Ugly furniture, probably belonging to the landlady, no softening pillows or personal touches. The walls were plastered with posters, all of them communist propaganda. Hefty workers with fists raised as they slogged towards their salvation. The air was permeated with the smell of cooking fat. Mary didn't offer him a chair, nor did she sit down herself. Tyler sat down on the sagging couch anyway.

"Miss Ringwald-Brown, I won't beat around the bush. There is no doubt in my mind that you were the one who locked the doors to the women's changing room. I can't charge you with mischief as I don't have enough proof, but it might help my investigation if you would tell me the truth. One less thing for me to pursue."

An ugly flush spread across her face. "I've already told you I had nothing to do with that incident. How many times must I repeat myself?" Her voice had got higher and even more shrill.

"I don't think the delay caused by the locked doors directly contributed to the explosion," said Tyler, choosing his words carefully. "It may have put the workers under pressure, but as far as I'm concerned it was an accident that could have happened at any time."

Mary sat down on the wooden chair across from him. "Inspector, I have never hidden my involvement with the British Communist Party. I know that many people think it strange that I, who have been more privileged than most, should feel so keenly for the working classes, but I do."

"I share your sentiments, Miss Brown. Everyone deserves a break in life."

She viewed him with suspicion but he revealed nothing. "Sometimes good has to be wrested from evil, even if the cost is high."

"Sounds like our reason for going to war, if you ask me."

"I don't mean that exactly. If you were afflicted with a cancer, for instance, you would endeavour to cut out that cancer before it spread and destroyed your life. The surgery might be painful but it would be worth it, don't you think?"

"I'm glad to say I've never been in that dilemma, Miss Brown. But is that how you justify your actions on Sunday? You were intending to promote the greater health of the factory?"

That struck a nerve, and she got to her feet abruptly and went to the door. "As I said, Inspector, I will not be held responsible for what happened on Sunday. It was an accident. Now if you don't mind, I am expecting a guest and I should tidy up a little."

Short of handcuffing her and taking her to the police station, there was nothing he could do. He stood up. "If you do happen to change your mind about helping me to resolve this tragedy, Miss Ringwald-Brown, I would greatly appreciate it. I am at the Steelhouse Lane station."

She glared at him. "That will not happen, Inspector. I have said all I am willing to say."

As soon as he was outside on the landing, she slammed the door behind him. He made his way downstairs. The door on the second floor opened a crack and the eye of the unseen occupant followed him on his way out.

***

Brian was staring at the ceiling. It needed plastering – there was a fine maze of cracks that had been there for a long time. He was playing at make-believe the way he had when he was a boy and had slept in this same room. In those days he was riding on a horse, a tireless black stallion. He'd have to travel along the London Road, gallop on the narrow, twisting path to the castle – top right-hand corner of the ceiling. There he would kill the wicked sheriff, save the princess, and be the hero of the land. He was forcing himself to play that old game, but it wasn't working. He couldn't remember when he'd felt calm. Felt normal. He'd forgotten what it was like to sleep.

Robin Hood didn't kill old ladies who wouldn't hurt a fly. Robin Hood wasn't a deserter.

There was a tap on the door. "Brian, there's a letter for you."

He sat up at once. "Come in, Gran."

Beattie entered. She handed him an envelope. "Somebody dropped this through the letter slot. I don't know what time. I only just noticed it."

One look at the handwriting and Brian knew it was from Donny. The large scrawl was like the boy himself: barely literate, rough, aggressive, taking up most of the front of the envelope. He tore open the flap and took out a note, a single sheet of torn-off paper.

Put another fiver in the Kowan house. or the deal is off. I'll tell you when.

"Who's it from?" asked Beatrice.

"The bloke who's bringing the ID papers. He wants another five pounds."

Beattie's face crumpled. "Oh no. I don't know if we can come up with that much more money. Not right away."

He looked at her. He'd already made up his mind what he was going to do. "Don't worry, Gran. I'll take care of it."

"How? How will you?" Her normally soft voice was shrill.

"I'll talk to him. You can't get blood out of a stone. He's being well paid as it is."

"What if he won't go for it? What if he won't wait? Oh, Brian, what are we going to do?" She sat down on the edge of the bed as if her legs wouldn't hold her up any longer.

Brian folded the note and stuffed it into his trouser pocket. "Don't worry, Gran," he repeated. "I'll get the necessary and I'll be out of your hair as soon as I can, I promise."

Her eyes were filled with tears. "I just want you to be safe."

He put his finger on his lips. "Shush, no more crying. I will be all right." He flexed his arm so that his biceps swelled. "See? Me strong man."

He came around to where she was sitting. He dropped a kiss on her head. "Why don't you go downstairs and make us some tea. I'll come down in a minute."

Beattie got stiffly to her feet. As she left, she was wiping at her eyes.

How dare that little son of a bitch think he could wring more money out of them?

He went over to the wardrobe. His granddad had bought the wardrobe some years ago, then found that one of the boards was loose. He'd reinforced it, not worrying about how it looked, as it was in the back of the wardrobe. When he was living with them, Brian had discovered there was a small space between the old board and the new. He hid things there. Nothing much – a packet of fags when he was supposed to be too young to smoke; a couple of dirty pictures a boy at school had sold to him. Then, before he left to go back home, he'd hidden a switchblade that he'd picked up in the market. He knew his gran would never find it – the hiding place was too good. As soon as he'd taken over the room this time, he'd checked the spot, and there the knife was, waiting like an old friend.

He took it out and flicked the spring. The blade shot out, sharp and deadly. Frigging Donny Jarvis was taking on more than he bargained for. It wasn't an extra five pounds that Brian was going to give him.

***

Tyler decided to head back to the police station, where he could look over his notes and start writing his report. There wasn't any more to do at the factory for now, but as he passed he stood for a moment at the gate. It was already blackout time and he could see a few dimmed torches bobbing as people made their way home. A tram rattled by, headlamps low, no lights showing inside. He felt he was in a city of ghosts.

"Inspector. Inspector Tyler."

It was Lev Kaplan. "I'm going your way. I'll walk with you partway," he said.

At that moment the by now familiar wail of the siren started. Searchlights immediately sprang into action, fingering the sky. The barrage balloons gleamed as silver as fish when the beams caught them.

"Damn," said Kaplan. "I was afraid they might take advantage of the moon, and they have."

Tyler could hear the bang of high explosives. They must have landed only a few streets away. Immediately the sky was aglow as fire leaped into the air. The ack-ack guns spat, the searchlights criss-crossed, trying to pin the bombers in their sights. A warden, his tin hat askew, was frantically blowing his whistle.

"We'd better get to the shelter," said Kaplan. "There's one down the road. Come on, follow the arrows."

He set off at a trot. Tyler followed close behind him.

They heard the clanging of the fire engines. More *thwumps*. Even closer this time.

The warden stopped blowing his whistle long enough to wave them into the shelter. "Hurry, get inside. It's going to be a bad one."

They went into the shelter. The walls, floor, and ceiling were concrete, the benches that lined the walls had wooden slats. The space was permeated with a stale, unpleasant smell: too many people engulfed in fear and sweat had been forced to sit in here. The only light came from two oil lamps hung from hooks in the ceiling. A dozen or so people were already seated on the benches and they eyed them curiously as they entered. Six men, similarly dressed in cloth caps, mufflers, and tweed coats, were sitting together on the opposite bench. One of them slid over and patted the place next to him.

"Here you go, then," he said. He had a Welsh lilt to his voice. Kaplan sat down and Tyler took the remaining space opposite, next to a woman with two young children. The girl, who looked about three, was clinging to her mother like a little monkey and crying frantically. The other child, a boy, was struggling to be a big boy, but he too pressed close. The girl was wearing a red pixie hat and a matching coat. Her brother and mother also looked as if they were in their good clothes. God knows where the woman had been going when the raid started. Seated next to her were two young women, sisters by the look of them, who flashed friendly smiles in Tyler's direction. The door opened again and a man and a woman scrambled in. He was well dressed – dark formal overcoat, trilby, a white silk scarf around his neck. She was wearing a lush fur coat and matching hat. The man smiled politely at the gathering. "Good evening. Looks like we're in for a bit of a bashing." His voice was cultured, educated.

"Evening," murmured the rest of the little group, and the mother with the children moved to make room. The newcomers sat down, and the woman, who was perhaps in her forties, stared into space as if by ignoring everybody she could make the whole unpleasant situation disappear. The steel door opened again and the warden poked his head in.

"That's it for now; we're full. Stay here until you hear the all-clear. If it's urgent that you have to do your business, there's a bucket behind that curtain, but nevertheless, we prefer it if you can hold on until the all-clear."

He disappeared. Lev said cheerfully, "I appreciate how considerate the English are about bladder relief."

That drew slightly embarrassed smiles from the rest. Then there was a horrendous crash, so close they could hear the patter of debris on the roof. Tyler stood up and squatted on his heels so he could be on a level with the little girl.

"Those bangs are very scary, aren't they. But you know what? We're safe in here, and they aren't nearly as scary if we make some noise of our own. Why don't we all sing together? I bet you know some good songs." The kiddie stared at Tyler as if he were utterly barmy, and he thought for a moment he might have made things worse. But at least the surprise of a strange man talking to her had temporarily stopped her howls.

"Answer the nice gentleman, Muriel," said the mother. "You know some songs, don't you."

"I do," interrupted the boy, not to be outdone, even *in extremis*.

"What songs do you know?" Tyler asked.

His bluff called, the lad hesitated. "'God Save the King.'"

Tyler glanced around the shelter. All eyes were upon him, none of them looking particularly partial to singing the national anthem at this moment. Then one of the Welshmen spoke up. "Look you now, little fellow, what's your name?"

"Fred."

"I tell you what, young Fred. 'God Save the King' might be a good song for later on. In the meantime, why don't my mates and me give out a bit of a singsong. You can join in if you know the tunes. All right, lads?"

There was a rapid consultation in Welsh among the six of them. The first man gave them the note and they plunged into a vigorous rendition of "Men of Harlech." Even when another bomb landed nearby, the men were so lively they managed to distract everybody, including the two children. When they finished, the man in evening dress grinned broadly. "Oh, I say, jolly good." Even the woman beside him dragged up a smile. Lev led the applause. The Welshmen immediately started another song.

And so it went on for the next several hours. Whenever there was a bit of a lull, the Welshmen would sing. The unrelenting noise of explosions and guns continued.

The people in the shelter, initially complete strangers, eventually got to know each other. The Welshmen worked together in Nichol's, a local factory that was making uniforms. They were part of a church choir and had been singing together for years. They had come to Birmingham because the wages were better there than back in Aberdovey, where they were from. Tyler asked them if they knew his mate Jones, who played on the police soccer team. They didn't know that particular Jones, look you, but there were lots of others.

The woman with the two children was Mrs. Doreen Latimer, on her way home from visiting her mother when she'd got caught in the raid. The two sisters, Josie and Irene Meadows, had been at the pictures and thought they could get home in time but had been caught by the raid.

The well-to-do couple completely melted and became quite human. He was Aubrey Wilson, who worked for Lloyd's. She was Blanche, his wife. They had been on their way to attend a concert put on by the Birmingham Jewish Association. "Quite marvellous what those people can do in the area of music," said Blanche. She actually allowed the child, Muriel, to stroke her fur coat, which the girl loved.

As for Lev Kaplan, to Tyler's mind he was the hit of the night, in spite of stiff competition from some champion Welsh singers and a fur coat. First of all, he was a Yank, something never encountered before by any of the others. Even the upper-crust couple confessed that, whereas they had met two or three Canadians, they were not previously acquainted with an American. Not only that, Lev turned out to be an expert with sleight-of-hand tricks. He made pennies appear and disappear into ears and hair. The children weren't the only ones who loved it – Tyler laughed with everybody else. Who'd ever have thought sitting on an uncomfortable hard bench for hours while bombs dropped all around could be enjoyable, but it was.

The noise of the attack went on relentlessly. The children had to use the bucket behind the curtain, and then, in spite of the noise, they fell asleep. Muriel slumped against Tyler's shoulder and he stroked her hair gently. Janet had often slept like that when she was a child. Everybody finally fell silent and tried to get some sleep. The Welshmen did, but the others were constantly being startled awake by another series of explosions. Tyler dozed off and on. This was what the cities had been dealing with ever since August.

***

At the first sound of the siren, Beatrice and Joe automatically gathered together what they called their shelter kit, an old cloth bag of Beatrice's that she kept packed for a long stay in the shelter. A flask of brandy; a large Thermos of water; a bag of sweeties, jealously guarded to be eaten only under these circumstances; her leather purse with the special papers they might need in the event they were bombed out of their house.

Everything else – blankets, extra clothes, books, and games – was already in the shelter.

Beatrice went to the bottom of the stairs and called to Brian. He appeared on the landing.

"Get down to the pantry, Bri. We've got to go out to the shelter."

"Will do, Gran. Don't worry about me."

The ack-ack guns had opened up, and they could hear the thud of exploding bombs. It sounded as if a heavy raid was already beginning. They hadn't got very much notice.

Joe appeared beside her. He too looked up at Brian. "All right, son?"

"I'm fine, Granddad. Get out of here."

Still Beatrice hesitated. Joe nudged her. "Come on, old gal. We've discussed all this."

Brian had put on his coat and was coming down the stairs. He gave his grandmother a kiss on the cheek. "Is there anything in the pantry I shouldn't touch?"

She managed to smile. "Have whatever you want. I wish there was more."

Joe picked up the shelter bag and they went to the back door. Fires were already blazing, not too far from their street by the look of things.

"Let's make a run for it," he said, and they scurried off.

Brian stood at the window, watching them through the crack in the curtain, until they were safely inside. He couldn't bear the thought of hiding in the tiny, dark pantry. Joe had fed electric light in there, but what if there was a direct hit and he got buried, or the light went out, as it often did if the lines were hit? Even thinking about it made Brian break out in a sweat. He peeked out the window again. The sky was lit up from the fires and the searchlights fingering the sky. He could see the outline of the Jerry bombers as the lights caught their underbellies. He felt no hatred for the men inside. There were men in those planes as afraid as any one of ours. They might be married as well.

An explosion hit so close he felt the floor tremble, and he went to the pantry. His grandmother had put a chair in there, tucked under the sloping ceiling. Just enough room for one person. He felt a rush of bile into his mouth as he looked at the dark space. He'd rather take his chances in the living room. He went over to the table where he knew he should take cover, but he couldn't stand it. He got up again and ran up the stairs to the bedroom. He rummaged in the back of the wardrobe, where he had been storing all his clothes since the redcaps had come. He took out his army overcoat and cap and put them on. The coat was heavy – not practical really, not warm enough, not flexible enough to permit much action – but he felt comforted by the weight of it, by its legitimacy. He hurried back downstairs through the kitchen and slipped out the back door. He was taking a risk of being seen but he didn't care. He had to get out. He had to do something.

Keeping close to the wall, he trotted around to the front of the house. The street was completely deserted. The siren had stopped howling but the noise of the explosions and the flak was horrendous. He actually saw the stick of black bombs tumbling out of one of the Jerry bombers, falling through the beams of the searchlights. Then the ground shuddered as the bombs landed.

He started to run. At the corner of the street an air-raid warden popped out of an archway.

"Get under cover, you bloody idiot," he yelled.

Brian ignored him and just ran faster, until he could run no farther. His chest was hurting from the exertion and he was forced to slow down. Suddenly there was a huge blast of fire as one of the barrage balloons floating near the Bull Ring burst into flames. He couldn't see if an aeroplane had collided with it or if the ack-ack guns had caught it by mistake. It was falling to the ground like a giant burning ember.

One more street and he was at the canal. The flames of a burning building were reflected in the water so that it looked as if it too were on fire. A couple of firefighters were focused on trying to bring the blaze under control. The heavy hose looked barely manageable. One of them saw him and called out something over his shoulder. Brian didn't hear what he said but the meaning was clear. They desperately needed help.

"Soldier, we could use a hand here," shouted the man. His face was red in the glare and he was not young.

"What do you want me to do?" Brian asked.

"Help us raise the hose. We're trying to train it on the upper windows."

Brian grabbed hold and the three of them were able to lift the hose sufficiently to train the water on the burning house.

"Let's hope we don't run out of water tonight, like we did before," said the man. "It's already bad – the main line got hit. Good thing we've got the canal."

Brian couldn't believe how hot it was this close to the flames. He felt as if the skin on his face was being seared. But as he leaned back like a man in a tug-of-war, the fire was awakening something within him, a strange sensation, as if he were no longer human, as if he had superhuman strength. If the other two men let go of the hose, he would be able to hold it up on his own. Earlier he had seen the underside of a bomber and felt only pity for the anonymous crew. Now he felt as if he hated all the Jerries, all those men who had willingly dropped their explosives on this street; he hated all those who had created such destruction.

"Did everybody get out in time?" he yelled at the fireman in front of him.

"Let's hope so, 'cos if they didn't, they're goners by now."

Brian was almost sorry. If necessary he would have run into the heart of the fire to rescue anyone who might be trapped there.

He had completely forgotten about the woman he had himself killed not so very long ago. He was not Brian the murderer, the deserter, he was Brian the saviour, the protector of the innocent.

It must have been an hour before the firemen could eventually let Brian go. He waved his farewell and he half ran, half walked in the direction of Water Street. He knew Donny Jarvis lived in one of the back-to-backs, the end house, and he went straight to it. He didn't knock – nobody would hear him anyway – he simply tried the doorknob. It opened at once. People didn't lock their doors in this area of town. All comings and goings would be noticed. Except, he hoped, in the midst of a raid.

Donny was by himself, lying on a couch in front of the low fire, smoking one of his ever-present fags. He sat up when Brian burst in, wary, testing the air like an animal.

"What the fuck – Brian. Didn't recognize you for a minute with the gear on. Come in, why don't you. Come for a cuppa and a biccy?"

"No, I fucking well haven't. I want those sodding papers I've paid for."

Donny drew a steady, deep inhale of smoke, never taking his eyes off Brian. "There wasn't enough money. It'll cost you another fiver."

"Fuck you. You got plenty of bloody money."

A violent shudder shook the house and they both had to wait. A shower of dust drifted down from the ceiling.

"Good thing Ma and everybody's gone to the shelter," said Donny. "Me, I figure it's either got your name on it or it hasn't. What do you think, Bri?"

"I don't give a fuck." He reached into this pocket and took out the knife. "I tell you what, though. This *has* got your bleeding name on it unless you cough up those papers." He flicked the button and the blade jumped out.

Donny went very still. Some animals do that when they're threatened. It doesn't mean they aren't dangerous.

***

It was after five in the morning when they finally heard the all-clear siren. Tyler had been dozing but he woke up and looked at his watch. The raid had lasted nine hours. After a few minutes, the door opened and their warden looked in.

"All clear. You can go now. I suggest you get home as fast as you can. This might not be over yet . . . Be careful where you step. There'll be a lot of debris."

Stiffly, like people alighting from a long train ride, they got to their feet and began to shuffle to the exit. Little Fred had been asleep for the past hour, and Lev picked him up to carry him outside.

One by one they emerged from the shelter. Tyler felt as if they had stepped into Hell's inferno.

Houses in the street behind them were burning, and smudge flares, intended as camouflage, were lit along the side of the road, making the air thick with choking smoke. The guns were temporarily quiet, the raiders had passed, but the streets were filled with noise – the crackling of flames; the horrendous crashing sound of buildings collapsing; the constant scream of the ambulances. For a moment they all stood on the steps, held motionless by the horror of it.

Gently Lev put the boy down. "Where do you live, Mrs. Latimer?" he asked the mother. "My friend and I will see you home."

"I actually live in Church Stretton. I was heading for the station when the siren sounded," she said.

One of the Welshmen heard her. "So was we, look you. We'll accompany you, if that's all right, missus. Come on, laddie. Upsadaisy." He hauled Fred onto his back. His weight was nothing for a man accustomed to carrying sacks of coal.

"Do you want a lift too?" one of the other men asked Muriel. She nodded shyly and he hoisted her up the same way.

The warden had been waiting. "Hurry up, folks."

"Bin nice knowing you," said the leader, and the little pack of short, bandy-legged men trotted off at a good clip, the young mother in the middle of them.

"I hope there's a train running," said Lev.

The two sisters said their goodbyes and dashed away. They'd withstood the raid very well, Tyler thought.

The Wilsons lingered for a few moments. "Goodbye. You were quite splendid," Mr. Wilson said to Lev. "And you too, sir," he added. "Kept us calm, I must say." They all shook hands.

"Cheerio," replied Lev.

Mrs. Wilson had resumed her cool demeanour. The unexpected intimacy of the night was already gone. It would become good fodder for dinner anecdotes, thought Tyler. But he'd liked them. Liked all of them, these unchosen companions of the night. He gave himself a little shake. God, he was getting to be quite sentimental. If he went on like this for the duration, he'd end up like mush.

"Where to now, mate?" Kaplan asked him.

"I thought I'd go to one of the first-aid posts. They might need help."

"I'll come with you. I've done a St. John Ambulance first-aid course."

"Good Lord, Kaplan, you are full of surprises. Your list of accomplishments is endless."

Lev shrugged. "Just good old Yankee know-how."

There was a lot of debris littering the street, dreadfully recent. They went past a house on fire, the firefighters holding the hoses as steady as they could. The heat was almost unbearable. Only the shell remained of somebody's home. All their precious, irreplaceable things gone.

Neither Kaplan nor Tyler spoke. There was nothing to be said.

They helped out a nearby first-aid post for a couple of hours. The more serious cases were sent to the hospital, so their task was mostly to bathe scrapes and bruises and offer cups of strong, sweet tea to the fearful and shocked.

The nurse at the post was a cheery old bird, called out of retirement by the current crisis. Her name, she said, was Sweeney, like the notorious barber.

"Good to see you chaps helping out," she said. "Can't just leave all the mopping up for us women."

"But you do it so much better," said Lev, who seemed to consider it his mission in life to charm women. Tyler had to admit he was very successful at it.

Mrs. Sweeney was not one to mollycoddle the less seriously injured. "There's others worse off than you," she said more than once to anybody who was inclined to moan and groan.

Dawn was creeping across the sky when the flow of people to the post finally stopped.

"I can manage now, gentlemen," said the nurse, "but I can tell you where you'd be really needed if you're up to it."

"Where?"

"The mortuary."

Tyler and Kaplan set off up the hill. The sun was barely breaking through the dark clouds and it was damp and chill. Some fires were still not under control but the fire wardens had mostly subdued them into black smoke. The air was thick with the smell of burning. Rubble was everywhere. They passed a bus that had been hit by an explosive. It was on its side, partly buried, in the middle of the road. Tyler hoped that the passengers had got out in time.

People were still emerging from the shelters. A grocer was sweeping away the shattered glass from the front of his shop. The windows and door had been blown off. His assistant was scrawling a message on a piece of wood. COME IN, WE'RE OPEN.

As they reached the gates of the mortuary, a voice hailed them. "Inspector! Mr. Kaplan!" It was Eileen Abbott. Tyler didn't miss the expression of delight on Kaplan's face.

"I called in at Number Four first-aid station," said Eileen. "Mrs. Sweeney said you were on your way here."

"We'll be glad to help out if you need us," said Tyler.

She looked doubtful. "It won't be pretty."

"I'm sure it won't," answered Tyler.

"Don't worry about me," said Kaplan. "I'm tougher than you might think."

She gave him a brief smile. "Come on, then."

They went inside. As she had warned them, it wasn't pretty.

All the bodies recovered so far had been placed on cots packed closely together. Only a few were covered. It seemed as if the ambulance men had run out of coverings after a while. Despite regular mopping of the floor with carbolic detergent, the air was starting to get bad. Brick dust, burned bodies and clothing, dead flesh.

An exhausted looking wvs woman was walking between the rows of dead with a clipboard, making a record of the tags that had been tied to the cots.

Eileen went to her and gently removed the clipboard from

her grasp. "Miss Mady, I'll take over now. You get yourself home right away. It must have been a terrible night."

The other woman was no longer young. "I've only done four rows. They started bringing them in as soon as the all-clear sounded. We're running out of room."

"Don't worry about that. We'll make do," said Eileen. "And these gentlemen are going to assist me."

Miss Mady reluctantly surrendered her task. "One of the police reservists, Constable Baker, has been helping. He just went upstairs to the reception hall with a list."

She left, walking slowly, as if she might awake the dead that surrounded her.

"Give me the clipboard," said Tyler. "I'll do the recording."

"Thank you, Inspector. Mr. Kaplan, would you go upstairs and start questioning the relatives. They'll be coming in by now, anxious for news. Ask for the address of the person they've come about and, most important, get as exact a description as you can of the missing person."

"Will do." He paused for a moment. "Feeling better?"

Eileen looked at him blankly. "I, er, yes, thank you."

Lev took the register she handed him and followed Miss Mady up to the reception hall.

"We have to match up the bodies to that list," Eileen said to Tyler. "The really hard part is when we bring family down for a formal identification."

"I can imagine that is difficult," said Tyler. It was something he'd experienced.

"Generally people are good and don't make a fuss."

The swinging doors opened and two stretcher-bearers entered. They were covered with dust and dirt and had obviously been working for hours. They deposited the stretcher on one of the few remaining gurneys. Tyler felt his heart sink. The mound underneath the blanket was ominously small.

"Do you have an identity for the casualty?" Eileen asked the first man.

"Yes, Sister. She'll likely be Daisy Marsden from 65 Granite Street. She were in the cellar. House took a direct hit."

Tyler made a note.

"Approximate age of victim?" Eileen continued.

The man took a notebook from his pocket and opened it up. "According to the warden's list, she's five."

"Colour of hair?"

"Brown, I'd say."

"Eyes?"

The man glanced at his partner, who had sagged against the wall and was staring at the floor.

"Brown," said the other man.

Tyler wrote down the details.

"Is the whereabouts of next of kin known?"

The first man consulted his notebook. "Parents are Henry and Ethel Marsden. One child, Daisy. Missus was pulled out but she's badly hurt, as I understand. He's overseas. Poor sod. What a thing to come home to."

He looked on the verge of tears and he pinched the bridge of his nose to keep them back. He was short and skinny, looked to be call-up age, but was probably in a reserved occupation and doing night duty as an ambulance driver. His eyes were red-rimmed, the pupils dilated. He was shaking. Tyler had seen that look before. The poor sod was in a state of shock.

Eileen was keeping her voice crisp and professional. "Is the body intact?"

"Not a mark on her. I don't understand it."

She lifted the canvas sheet. Tyler recoiled. He couldn't help himself – the body was so tiny and doll-like. It was completely covered with red brick dust but there were no visible signs of injury except for a thin line of blood from the corner of the child's mouth.

"She died from concussive impact," said Eileen to the stretcher-bearer. "Typically the lungs burst, but sometimes the heart is crushed inside the ribcage."

She took a handkerchief out of her pocket and wiped away the blood and some of the dust from the cheek. Tyler could see that when the alarm sounded, the child's mother had prepared her to go into the shelter, her warm clothes probably at the ready. Daisy was wearing a green wool coat over her nightgown, white socks, and neat black shoes with a V strap. She had been a pretty child. Tyler was glad to bury his head in taking down the facts. He felt a lump in his throat. What a tragedy for the father to come back to. If he came back, that is.

"Thank you," Eileen said to the two men. "You can put the stretcher in the number thirty-seven spot." She noted down their numbers, which were on their arm bands. She smiled at them both. "There's a tea urn upstairs. Go and help yourself."

"Don't mind if I do," said the first man. They nodded their thanks, lifted their all too light burden, and trudged off.

Eileen and Tyler exchanged glances, not speaking.

The doors swung open again and a man came in. He was stooped and was wearing a shabby overcoat, but his badges of authority were his yellow arm band and the tin helmet of an ARP warden. He was carrying something at arm's length that was wrapped in a blood-soaked flowered frock. Eileen intercepted him.

"I'll take care of this," she said to Tyler, who had been about to join her. Obedient to her tone of voice, he stopped in his tracks and waited.

"What have you got, John?" Eileen asked the warden quietly.

"Leg, ma'am. Left. Male. Found on the pavement on Fleet Street. There was a dress shop blown out just across the road and I snatched up the first thing I could find to wrap it in. Didn't seem right to just leave it lying there."

Eileen unwrapped the fabric so she could take a look. The severed leg had little resemblance now to anything living. Only the dusty raw flesh and bone at the hip end indicated that it had once been part of a human being. The remnants of the trousers were grey flannel. The foot was intact, still in its black leather shoe and, rather incongruously, bright yellow socks. Not a lot to go on when they tried to identify the corpse.

She rewrapped the leg. "Thank you, John. I'll deal with it now."

"I almost forgot . . . you will need this." The warden handed her a piece of creased paper. "It's a list of all the occupants registered on that part of Fleet Street. Numbers 82 and 84 are the worst hit. They're on fire. Funny thing was, the bomb didn't drop on them. Maybe it was a delayed-action kind." He shrugged. "Who knows? Bombs do funny things. I'll go back and see what's what as soon as I can hand this over."

Eileen carried the gruesome object to the back of the room, where all the severed body parts were screened off.

"An undertaker will try to match the parts to the bodies," she said to Tyler. "I'll see if there's anyone else in the hall."

She opened the entrance doors and beckoned to two stretcher-bearers. She waited while they put the stretcher on top of the gurney.

"Do you have a positive identification?"

"Yes, Sister, we do." The ambulance driver was succinct. He'd gone through the procedure too many times already. "The body was retrieved from a house in Water Street. Direct hit with an HE."

"Give me the details," said Tyler, his pencil poised. One of the men checked his slip.

"Body of a male. Formerly one of the residents at 70 Water

Street. According to the registration list, his name's Donald Jarvis."

Eileen frowned. "What the—" She lifted the canvas cover sufficiently to reveal the face. "My God!" Her face went white and she stared down at the body in horror.

"Sister, what is it?" Tyler asked.

"There's some mistake. His name isn't Jarvis. This is my nephew, Brian Walmsley."

Eileen Abbott was not the fainting kind, but she sat down abruptly on a nearby chair. "Where did you find this body?" she said to the stretcher-bearers.

"Like I said, Sister, he was caught by a direct hit on his house. Water Street. Number 70."

"Why is he identified as Donald Jarvis?" Tyler asked.

"That's the name I was given. The rest of the family was in the nearby public shelter and were not injured. His ma said her son had stayed behind in the house. We took him out of the front room."

"Did the parents make a visual identification?"

"No, they was too busy looking after themselves. We said we were bringing him here and they could come later."

Eileen was sitting motionless, her eyes unseeing. Tyler went over to her. He touched her on the shoulder. "I suppose there's no doubt this is your nephew?"

"None at all."

Tyler nodded at one of the men to replace the cover over the corpse's face.

"Where did your nephew live?" he asked Eileen.

"I, er . . . he's a soldier. He was stationed in Aldershot. We heard he was coming home on leave." She looked at Tyler. "We were expecting him at our house. It, er, it . . . we have more room than his parents."

"Could he have been visiting the Jarvises on Water Street?"

"No. At least, I don't believe so . . ." Her voice trailed off.

Tyler wondered why she was lying to him. He turned to the stretcher-bearers. "Thanks, chaps."

"We'll get back to the hospital, then."

"Grab a cuppa from upstairs. You'll find a Yank up there helping out. Tell him to come down here, will you?"

They walked away wearily.

Tyler addressed Eileen. "I can continue on here, Miss Abbott, if you want to leave."

She got to her feet, her self-control shaky but in place.

"Thank you. I must tell my family." She paused. "Brian was twenty years old, Inspector. He may not have died in the line of fire, but he is a casualty of war just the same."

The door to the upper level opened and Lev Kaplan came hurrying down. He went straight to Eileen and took her in his arms. She did not resist.

"The ambulance men told me that they had just brought in your nephew. I'm so sorry, Eileen."

She allowed herself to be comforted for a few moments, then moved back. "I must get home."

"I'll take you," said Lev.

"No! I'll be all right, thank you. Inspector Tyler is taking over for me. I will come back as soon as I can and conclude the formalities."

She gathered her coat and hat. As she went past the gurney, she touched it lightly, shaking her head. "Brian, what were you thinking?"

Lev walked her as far as the door. Tyler waited until he returned.

"What rotten bad luck," said Lev. "They told me there was some sort of mix-up in the identity. What happened?"

"I'm not sure," Tyler answered. "The nephew must have

been visiting the Jarvis chappie who lives in the house that got it. I didn't want to upset Miss Abbott, but there's something I want to take a look at."

He pulled back the sheet. Brian was wearing an army greatcoat, which was unbuttoned. Underneath he was dressed in a woollen Fair Isle jersey, the front of which was soaked with blood. His trousers were not army issue either and looked far too big for him. The shocking thing, however, was a long, deep gash across his throat. Tyler leaned in to take a better look.

Kaplan peered over his shoulder. "That isn't a shrapnel wound," he said quietly. "I've seen this sort of thing before. His throat's been slashed."

Tyler nodded. "Certainly looks like it."

"Any ideas as to who did it?"

"Not yet. It appears he was in the front room of the Jarvis house. The parents thought this was their son Donny."

"Good God. Jarvis. Donny Jarvis." He stared at the corpse. "That's definitely not him."

"How d'you know?"

In answer, Lev reached into an inner pocket in his jacket and took out a card. "There's something I should tell you, Inspector. Read it. It's legit."

Before Tyler could do more than assimilate the actual profession of the supposed photographer, the upper door opened again and the constable came hurrying down the stairs. "Is there an ambulance man here?" he asked Tyler. "Apparently the gas main has broken at the house on Water Street where they took out that body. They found out there's a bloke trapped in there. They need to get him out quick."

Lev looked at Tyler. "Do you think that's Donny?"

"Could be. Let's go find out." He tapped Lev's arm. "Come on. It'll be faster if we go on foot."

—

He was right. They arrived at Water Street in a few minutes, bypassing the clogged streets.

The destroyed houses were still sending up trails of smoke and a group of people was gathered not far away, being watched over by a florid-faced constable.

Tyler went over to him. "I'm DCI Tyler, working out of Steelhouse Lane. I'm looking for a bloke named Donny Jarvis."

"Sorry, sir. He's a dead un. He was packed off to the mortuary not so long ago."

"That wasn't Jarvis. Case of mistaken identity. We're looking for the real Jarvis. We heard there's a bloke still trapped in the rubble. That might be him."

"If it is, he's an unlucky sod. The upper floor collapsed into the living room. That's where we got the other bloke. The entire house was more or less pushed into the cellar. They should have been in the shelter, but there you go, too late now. Go and have a word with PC Markle, sir. He's been talking to somebody over there."

"The lad who's buried – is he still alive?" Kaplan asked.

"Apparently. One of the wardens just now made contact. He's gone to fetch the poor bloke's mam. See if she wants to say goodbye."

"Goodbye?"

"There's gas leaking into the space he's in. Nothing we can do at the moment. He's a goner. Matter of time. You can hear he's getting groggy."

"Come on, Kaplan," said Tyler.

He showed his police badge to the constable at the barricade, who lifted the rope so they could duck underneath. They crossed the littered backyard and went to where the original door had been. Tyler shoved aside some bricks, knelt down, and put his face as close as he could to what had once been the living room floor.

"Hello! Hello, Donny? Donny Jarvis? Can you hear me?"

He pressed his ear against the boards and heard Donny's voice, thin and faint.

"When the fuck are you getting me out of here?"

"Let me talk to him," said Kaplan, and he bent over the small space.

"Donny, it's Comrade Hitchcock talking to you. The police are working on getting you out but it's going to be difficult."

"Tell them to fucking hurry up. I can smell gas. It's making me feel sick."

"Donny, what happened? The police pulled out a man called Brian Walmsley. His throat had been cut. Did you kill him?"

Tyler could hear a chuckle floating up. "It was him or me, stupid sod. Comes at me with a knife. I'll plead self-defence. Then the bleedin' bomb landed, so I probably needn't have bothered. We was buried." He coughed. "God almighty, this is getting worse. How's the digging coming along?"

"Slowly. Listen to me, Donny, truth is there's not much chance of getting you out before the gas gets to you. You're probably starting to feel nauseated and sort of sleepy. Am I right?"

"What the fuck are you telling me? Can't you make an air hole or something?"

"Can you move over this way? I can try to get a pipe down to you."

More coughing. "No, you dumb sod, I'm trapped. The entire fucking upstairs fell on me. I can't move a bleedin' inch. Shit, shit, my legs have gone." He choked again. "You know what, Yank? You're dead jammy, you are."

"Why is that, Donny?"

"You're getting a nice package from America. Made it myself, with a little help. But it doesn't look like you'll be the one to open it. Which is just as well, if you get my meaning."

"Who else was getting a present?"

"The ponce. Couldn't be trusted either. He'd have shot his mouth off if the police had come to call."

"What about Chopin and Cardiff?"

"No packages. Don't need them."

Lev put his mouth to the boards again. "Donny. Were any of the comrades responsible for the explosion at Endicott's?"

"One of them was."

"How?"

"The Big Bad Wolf dropped a trinket in Little Red Riding Hood's basket. Made the pots all shaky." Another chuckle. "They blew themselves up. What a bloody joke, getting Endie's own workers to do the job for us. Bet nobody'll catch it."

"Damn," muttered Kaplan. More loudly he said, "Do you believe in God, Donny? Because if you do, now's the time to clear your conscience. At the meeting we talked about a new act of sabotage. Spectacular, you called it. Is there something planned, Donny? Is there?"

"Course there is. A big one."

"When?" Lev asked.

"Today." The word came drifting up to them.

Tyler began to make wild signs to Kaplan that he wanted to speak, but the other man forestalled him.

"If you tell me the plan you can save a lot of lives. They're innocent girls, Donny. They don't deserve this. Please, I beg of you, tell me what's supposed to happen."

There was a silence, and Tyler seized his chance to shove Kaplan out of the way. He leaned over the narrow crack in the floorboards.

"Donny Jarvis? This is Inspector Tyler talking to you. Can you hear me?"

He was afraid for a minute that Donny had already slipped into unconsciousness. Then, in a much fainter voice than before, the boy spoke. "I might have known the fucking frogs would gather."

"For once you got something right, Donny. And let me tell you this. Mr. Kaplan here is a good bloke and he's being nice to you. I'm not. But out of the goodness of my heart, and seeing as how you're not feeling too comfy, I'll make a deal with you. If we do get you out alive, you won't go to the clink as long as you co-operate. If you don't and you die anyway, I'll make sure your entire family is put in jail as accessories to major crimes and I'll throw away the keys. Do you understand me, Donny?"

Kaplan was shaking his head and mouthing, *It won't work.*

But Tyler knew his subject. "It's a promise either way, Donny."

The voice was almost inaudible by now. "Is me mum here?"

Tyler looked over his shoulder. A woman, thin and scrawny in a shabby navy coat, was standing at the front of the crowd, watching. Behind her was a man, equally poorly dressed, with the red, puffy face of a habitual drunk. He seemed sober at the moment but wasn't moving.

"Yes, she's here. If you answer my question I'll let you talk to her."

"Fuck that. Mum won't have anything to say anyway. No trade-off, copper."

Tyler heard retching from the trapped boy.

"Shite. I've been sick all down myself."

"Donny, who, then? Do you want to talk to your father?"

"What for? The old bastard won't do me any good, never has. Is me mum crying?"

Without even looking, Tyler knew the answer. This family didn't cry. "Of course she is."

"Crap. You can go fuck yourself. I want to talk to the Yank."

Kaplan had heard this and there was no choice. Tyler changed places, shuffling back in the rubble so he could still hear.

"Donny, it's Hitchcock here."

"Good. Listen. I don't trust that copper, but there's something I want you to do for me."

"Okay."

"There's a girl name of Thelma. She's just a kid but I think I knocked her up. If you promise you'll look in on her I'll tell you what you want to know."

"I promise."

"Is that a Yank promise?"

"No, it's a Jewish promise. They're solid."

Another silence, then the faint voice. "What time is it?"

Lev checked his watch. "It's almost a quarter past seven."

"You're going to have to get a move on . . . bombs in the factory . . . going to go off at half-past . . ."

"Where are they?"

"Mm . . . men's changing room . . . We were planning to lift the payroll . . . Good scheme . . . Mine."

"Are there others?"

"Boiler room . . . My idea again."

Lev yelled, not caring if the onlookers could hear him. "Donny, who's the head man? Who's Comrade Patrick?"

The whisper floated up to him. "Go fuck yourself, Yank . . . I don't know . . . wouldn't tell if I did."

There was a choking rattle of breath, then silence.

Tyler jumped to his feet. "For Christ's sake, let's get over there."

They scrambled back under the barrier. Tyler grabbed the constable. "Get the alarm out right away. There've been bombs planted in the Endicott factory. We've got to get the workers evacuated immediately. We've only got minutes."

The constable pulled out his whistle and blew several long blasts.

Mrs. Jarvis shouted out to them. "How's Donny? Why aren't you getting him out?"

"Is the young man still alive, sir?" the constable asked.

"No, he's not." Unexpectedly, Tyler felt a pang of pity for the miserable end that Donny Jarvis had faced.

Kaplan clearly didn't share that emotion. "He's probably being welcomed into Hell at this moment."

Tyler caught hold of Kaplan's arm. "Come on, we'll take the ambulance."

**

Chopin looked at the big clock on the wall. Twenty minutes past seven. Four more hours to go. Placing the bomb had been easy. It was in a wicker lunch box, identical to the one he usually carried. There was a label on the top that read THIS IS THE PROPERTY OF DMITRI WOLF. Carrying the duplicate box, he had gone down to the boiler room. Nobody went down there, and if they did, they would assume he was coming back for his sandwiches, a habit he had already established. The bomb had fit comfortably into the lunch box. Once in the boiler room he had simply removed the wrapped package carefully, placed it in the bottom of the bucket, and added the tightly sealed false bottom. Comrade Patrick had already visited him and assured him everything was ready to go. He mustn't tamper with it.

The ticking of the timer was audible but muffled by the seal.

The plan was to place both mop and bucket against the boiler and leave them there. Patrick had been insistent about that. "We don't want anybody to suspect you. You're too valuable to us."

According to Patrick, the timer was set to go off at a half past eleven, when the workers on the first shift were having their tea break. The factory was not at full strength yet, so there weren't likely to be casualties. The aim, Patrick said, was always to disrupt production, not to destroy their workers. Wolf didn't really care. He'd lost his own will to live more than a year ago, in the concentration camp. He cared about revenge, and that was it. Casualties were to be expected in a war. The glorious end was freedom from all capitalist oppression, and this justified the means.

Taffy too had followed his instructions to the letter. He had placed his lunch box in his locker.

***

Tyler's experience of driving on rutted country roads stood him in good stead. He had switched on the ambulance alarm, but even if they wanted to, the few cars on the road could hardly move out of the way. For what seemed like endless minutes they were stopped behind a fire truck, the firefighters all trying to subdue a blazing shop front. Lev was about to get out and run to the factory, but Tyler inched around the truck, bouncing over the hoses, and sped along the centre of the street. Endicott's wasn't far, and although it seemed a terribly long time, they were soon there.

On the frantic ride, Lev had filled in Tyler. Two saboteurs that he knew of, Wolfsiewicz and Taffy Evans.

"The caretaker and the man who works in the canteen?"

"That's them. Good cover, I must say."

"But you don't know who's the brains behind all of this?"

"No. Wish I did."

"You said his *nom de guerre* is Patrick. Is he IRA?"

"Possibly. Or that could be just a red herring. I'm not even positive he works at the factory, although that is likely."

"And you're with the Security Service?" Tyler asked.

"That's right. I've been what we call infiltrating."

"Haven't been very effective, have you," said Tyler, speaking out of fear. He regretted his words when he saw Kaplan's expression. The American didn't need his reproach. He was excoriating himself.

Lev gasped with relief when they pulled up in front of the gates. They could see a stream of workers hurrying from the building. The message had got through in time. They were being evacuated.

Suddenly Lev opened his door and yelled out, "Stop that man. He's a saboteur. Get him!"

Tyler saw that he was pointing at Taffy Evans, who was exiting with a group of women. Sizing up the situation immediately, the Welshman turned and started to run back through the crowd into the building.

Constable Eagleton was escorting the workers out of the factory. Tyler shouted to him, "Eager, go after him!"

Eagleton understood and set off in pursuit. Both men disappeared through the entrance doors. Kaplan jumped down from the ambulance and did his best to shove through the crowd after them. He was hindered by the panic infecting the women, who began to scatter, discipline forgotten, but he got through, and he too vanished into the factory.

Tyler started to shout, "Clear the area. Clear the area as fast as you can."

Nobody seemed to be listening, but at that moment two other officers arrived on bicycles. "Move everybody as far away from this building as you can," commanded Tyler. "Now! We've got an unexploded bomb in there."

One of the men blew his whistle and the other started to move towards the women, his arms outstretched as if he were herding sheep.

Tyler saw some familiar faces. June Lipton and Pat O'Callaghan were in the crowd. Lily Johnson and Phil Riley were behind them, both being guided out by Mick Smith, the dillie man.

Tyler ran over. "Have any of you seen the caretaker?"

"Wolf? He was heading downstairs to the boiler room last I saw him," answered Pat.

"What's going on?" asked Smith. "Do you need some help?"

Tyler waved him off and turned and ran to the entrance, now empty of people. Once inside the hall, he paused long enough to take stock. Eagleton, Kaplan, and Taffy were nowhere to be seen or heard.

He looked up at the clock with its large black hands. He had three minutes.

It was one of the few times in his career that he wished he was armed. He headed straight for the boiler room. He half slid, half tumbled down the stairs.

The room was deserted except for one man. Dmitri Wolfsiewicz, alias Comrade Chopin. For a split second Tyler thought the man had lost his senses – he seemed to be mopping the floor. Then, even as Tyler burst in, he saw the cleaner lift a package out of his bucket and place it on the ground close to the massive boiler, which squatted in the centre of the room.

He yelled out, "Wolf. Wolf, stop."

Wolfsiewicz turned around in surprise. The rubberized linoleum had obscured the sound of Tyler's footsteps.

Tyler forced himself to slow down, to breathe. He didn't want to frighten the man into some kind of precipitous action. He stopped a few feet away from him.

"Comrade, plans have changed."

Chopin frowned. "How do you know?"

"Comrade Bolton has been killed in an air raid. I was there. Before he died he told me everything. I know you're going to plant a bomb. You can't go ahead. It's not right to involve innocent people."

"Tell that to Hitler and Churchill," answered Wolf with a

grimace. "Tell that to landlords who have exploited us for centuries."

Tyler took a step forward. "It's you, mate, who are being exploited. You might not know it, but the bombs are due to go off in exactly two minutes."

The other man shrugged. "So what? Important thing is factory will shut down completely."

"Don't be an idiot. Do you think Comrade Patrick gives a shit about the revolution? He was planning your death and the Welshman's. Bolton's dead, but he confessed they were intending to steal the payroll. That is the whole point of the explosion. They have no loyalty to anything except money."

"All revolutions need money. I knew that was plan."

"Don't you care that your comrades were intending to kill you?"

"It does not matter now."

Without warning, Wolf grabbed the handle of the bucket with both hands and swung it violently, aiming for Tyler's head. Tyler got his arm up in time to deflect the blow, but the rim split his wrist to the bone. Immediately Wolf swung again and connected with Tyler's jaw. He spun away but was able to catch hold of the bottom of the bucket with both hands. Using it like a battering ram, Tyler knocked the other man to the ground. Wolf staggered backwards, frantically trying to regain his footing.

Tyler was upon him. Just as Wolf had swung at him, so now he whipped the bucket down on the other man's head as hard as he could. Wolfsiewicz collapsed and was still.

Tyler picked up the package and carried it to one of the buckets of water that lined the room. His wrist dripped blood behind him.

The bomb in the changing room exploded.

—

Tyler was awakened by a man's voice shouting in his ear.

"Inspector? Tom? Are you awake?"

He opened his eyes. He seemed to be in bed. A hospital bed by the feel of it. Lev Kaplan was leaning over him.

"Thank God you're still in the land of the living, Tom, old chap. I wasn't sure for a minute. You look like Marley's ghost with that bandage."

Tyler opened his mouth to answer but an excruciating stab of pain shot through his jaw. He got out some guttural noises.

Lev understood. "Don't try to talk. The doctor put some contraption in your mouth to keep your jaw immobile, but we need to debrief. Perhaps you could wag your finger, once for yes, twice for no. Okay?"

Tyler lifted his heavily bandaged arm, which also hurt. He wagged his finger once.

"Great. In case you're wondering, when we got you out of the factory you were unconscious and you had a wicked gash on your arm and a broken jaw. Chopin was also senseless, but I guess he was the one who did that before you clobbered him. Am I right?"

Tyler indicated yes.

"Cardiff's bomb did go off."

Tyler pointed. The American's arm was in a sling.

Lev shook his head. "I wasn't hurt by that. My shoulder's dislocated. I tripped just before we could nab him, so I wasn't in the direct line of the blast. Cardiff was killed. He went for the bomb he'd planted in the men's changing room. It exploded in his hands. God knows what he was planning to do. Save or destroy?"

Tyler managed to mutter, "Eager? Is he all right?"

"He is. The Welshman absorbed the full force. Your poor constable got splattered with guts and gore but other than that he was unhurt. He's been hanging out in the corridor waiting for you to come to." Kaplan hesitated. "Your wife hasn't yet been told you were injured. I thought you'd be the one to decide what to tell her when you were more able."

Tyler made noises of agreement.

"Thanks to you, Tom, the whole factory didn't go up and everybody got out in time. The bomb in the boiler room would have done immense damage. I understand you dropped the damn thing in a bucket of water."

"Mm-hm."

"By the way, I had a bit of a natter with our mutual friend Mr. Grey, and he'd like us to keep everything low-key. No sense in frightening people with stories of what a close call it was. The official word will be that there were fifth columnists working in the factory but they've been apprehended." He smiled. "You're going to get all the glory. I shall remain in the background, just a lowly photographer who came to help. Not that I won't accept hugs and kisses if offered. Not from you, don't worry. I was thinking of somebody with a softer cheek."

Tyler twirled his finger indicating Lev should continue. The American's expression grew serious.

"The cell I was attempting to infiltrate is no longer. The head man had obviously decided it was safer to silence erstwhile allies. The body of Comrade Arnold was found in his house, minus a leg, I might add. It wasn't Jerry that dropped the bomb on him. That was delivered by hand. Seriously injured his parents, who lived upstairs. They claim they didn't know what he was up to. Thought he was working for the government and they were proud of him." Lev fished in his pocket and took out a packet of cigarettes. "Want one? They're American."

Tyler gave a one-fingered wag.

Lev lit up and put the cigarette between Tyler's lips. Drawing on the fag hurt like hell but Tyler didn't care. Lev waited for a moment for him to exhale.

"There was a parcel waiting for me at my hotel," he continued. "God help us, it was a dud, but I would have opened it, expecting it to be a food parcel from home." He glanced at Tyler. "Okay so far? Want another puff?"

Tyler wagged his finger. Lev helped him with the cigarette.

"As I was saying, the commie cell is no longer. Bolton's dead of course, Cardiff and Arnold all mincemeat. Comrade Chopin is also a goner."

Tyler struggled to sit up in the bed, but Lev pushed him back gently.

"Calm down, Tom, you'll hurt yourself. No, you didn't kill him. He was carted off to the station unconscious but alive. We discovered later he had a cyanide pill in a hollow tooth. When he came to, he bit on it. Pouf. Gone in seconds."

Tyler made noises.

"I know what you mean, Tom. Poor benighted soul that he was." Kaplan offered the cigarette again but Tyler declined. Lev smoked it himself. "One of the women from the factory, Mary Ringwald-Brown, committed suicide."

Tyler groaned.

"She hung herself from the light fixture in her room. Her landlady found her early this morning."

"Leave a note?" Tyler managed to croak out.

"Not just a note, a veritable tome, apparently. Inspector Mason filled me in. She actually addressed the letter to you but we thought you wouldn't mind if we read it."

Tyler tried to nod but thought better of it. "What say?"

"Nothing much really, if you strip away all the cant. She was sorry for what she did. She didn't mean to hurt anybody. What was she referring to? According to our guttersnipe, Bolton, Comrade Chopin was the one who sabotaged the pots."

"Locked doors to changing room. Set tragedy in motion."

"Did she do it of her own accord or do you think she was following instructions from our very own Comrade Patrick?"

"Not sure. Certain suicide?"

"Looks like it, but we can make doubly sure if you want us to?"

Tyler wagged his finger.

Lev stubbed out his cigarette. "The real trouble is we haven't caught Comrade Patrick and that, frankly, scares the bejesus out of me. We've got to find him otherwise we've only scotched the snake not killed it, as the Bard put it. I understand you've got your lad, Eager, going through employee files. I've asked Inspector Mason to assign some constables to help. That's one way we might be able to trace him. I'm betting he worked at the factory. I might be good with invisible ink and codes and all that stuff but I think good old-fashioned police know-how is called for here."

Another wag from Tyler. Lev grinned. "I see you agree." He stood up. "I'm going to let you get some rest, Tom. I'll be back later."

Tyler mimed writing.

"You want some paper? Hold on." Kaplan reached in his pocket. "Oh, shoot, Tom, I almost forgot. There was a letter for you at the station." He handed it to Tyler, who scrutinized it briefly, turned it over, and indicated to Kaplan he needed a pencil. Hastily, the American fished one out of his pocket and Tyler managed to scribble a few lines on the back of the envelope.

Kaplan read what he'd written. "*Mary's house. See Merrick.* You think we should go and have a look there?"

"Yes."

"I'll go over right now – I assume Merrick's another lodger. I'll take your constable with me, he needs something to do."

Tyler wagged an agreement.

Lev put the packet of cigarettes on the bedside table. "I've got it on the best authority that King George will be visiting the hospital tomorrow. You can offer him a good American cigarette. I hear he smokes like a chimney."

Tyler made two wags.

"It's true. It's just not public knowledge." He looked down at Tyler. "Hope your letter is good news, Tom. I see it's postmarked Switzerland. Cheerio, as you Limeys say." He left.

Tyler tore open the envelope. And it was good news.

Dear Tom. A very brief note to let you know I am finishing up a few loose ends here before I return to London. I shall be in touch as soon as I can. Yours, Clare.

Tyler closed his eyes. Maybe it was the dulling effect of the morphine, but all he could really think of was his investigation. He knew he was useless at the moment, but he had no intention of lying around beyond tomorrow. He had work to do. As Kaplan had put it, good old-fashioned police work was called for if they were going to catch Comrade Patrick. Loose ends, indeed.

He pressed the note to his lips briefly, then he fell asleep.

EPILOGUE

MR. MERRICK DRESSED CAREFULLY, PUTTING ON HIS navy blazer and sapper's tie. He didn't like having to talk to strangers, but he'd sat and pondered long enough. The information he had was very important.

Mr. Merrick had hardly exchanged more than a few words with Miss Ringwald-Brown since she had moved in. He thought she was toffee-nosed and couldn't for the life of him understand why she was living in a flea pit like this. He had no choice, what with his paltry army pension, but he could tell she was well off. He was also quite aware she saw him as a nosy parker. In a manner of speaking, she was right. He took a certain pride in his own powers of observation, and living in the rooming house offered him a great deal of scope to practise. Take the red-headed man she'd led upstairs only yesterday. "The meter man," she'd called him. As if he, Merrick, was a dumb idiot. The man wasn't in uniform for one thing, and Merrick could tell just by the way he held himself he was a copper.

Same with the other lodger, the Chum, who lived in the house. Merrick had overheard Miss Ringwald-Brown use the word *comrade* when speaking to the new fellow, hence his own nickname Chum. The Chum had moved into the rooming house three months ago and had lost no time in getting in good with Miss Ringwald-Brown. He wasn't from the same social class as her, Merrick knew that. The Chum had a lower class Brummie accent, very thick, nothing at all posh like hers. But Merrick had noticed that some women found the rougher type of men attractive. And this man was rough all right. Fit and hard muscled. Sallow as an Arab.

Last night, Merrick had seen the Chum go up the stairs and he'd overheard voices, a lot of crying from her. It had been quite late when he'd heard the Chum leave again. Then, lo and behold, the poor woman had hung herself. The police and the ambulance men had come and gone but nobody had stirred in the room that the Chum occupied. Merrick assumed the Chum had gone to work before the catastrophe was discovered, but you never knew these days.

When things quieted down, Merrick decided he should check on the Chum, just in case he hadn't gone to work, in case something else had happened. Merrick knocked and went inside. The door was locked but he had a key. He'd lived in the rooming house for a long time and the landlady trusted him to take care of small repairs if needed. He could come and go as he pleased. Merrick was respectful of other people's property. He never ever took anything that wasn't his. He was just curious, that's all. How they lived, what they did.

He could tell at once that the lodger had fled. The room was tidy as a monk's, and the Chum's clothes were gone from the wardrobe. The dresser was empty. He'd taken his precious wireless with him. He liked to listen to it at all hours, Merrick knew that. The walls of the old house were paper thin.

Merrick returned to his own room, to think about what he ought to do. The more he sat and pondered, the more he came to believe he owed it to the Public Good to go to the police.

He checked his image in the spotty mirror and straightened his back. What he particularly wanted to tell the police was that the dead woman's lover had been a soldier at one time. Not a soldier of the King, Merrick was sure of that. But a soldier nonetheless. Unfortunately they might have a bit of trouble tracking him down because his name was as common as he was.

Smith. His name was Michael Smith.

Author's Note

This is a work of fiction based on fact. Endicott's did not exist as I have depicted it, but similar factories did. Very soon after the outbreak of the Second World War, the British government commandeered factories throughout the country and adapted them for the making of munitions. The work was frequently dangerous and usually tedious, a combination that made matters doubly hazardous. The male population was diminished by the need for fighting men, and women were recruited to fill the gaps in the factories, on the buses, in the fields. Initially there was resistance to this shift in gender roles but eventually the women won respect. Only a die-hard stick-in-the-mud could ignore how essential this new labour force was to the war effort.

When peace finally arrived in 1945, most women returned to the life they had been living before the war – if they could. Returning soldiers had been guaranteed their old jobs, but the following years were ones of huge adjustment for everyone. The rigid class (and gender) divisions that had throttled British society had begun to dissolve. Once the bird is out of the cage, it isn't easily put back. Eventually, a grocer's daughter would become Prime Minister of Britain. Who'd ever have thought that possible in 1945?

If I have interested my readers in learning more about this amazing seismic shift in British society, I am satisfied.

The title of this book is from *A Christmas Carol* by Charles Dickens. When the Ghost of Christmas Present appears to

Ebenezer Scrooge, he reveals two wretched children who have been sheltering inside his robe. They are the children of Man, says the Spirit. "This boy is Ignorance. This girl is Want. Beware of both of them . . . but most of all beware this boy, for on his brow I see that written which is Doom unless the writing be erased."

When I first read the story as a child, these words burned into my mind and ever since, the notions of ignorance, closed-mindedness, and fanaticism have been anathema to me. For example, against the war in the beginning, willing to foster acts of sabotage and dissent, the British Communist Party did a complete about-face after Hitler attacked Russia. The bad guys – the British and the Allies – became the good guys and the BCP became fervently pro-war. Of course, nobody was willing to admit that Joseph Stalin had already shown himself to be as terrible a tyrant and murderer as Hitler himself.

On the other hand, during this long season of darkness, there were many instances that revealed the astonishing fair-mindedness people are capable of.

Acknowledgements

As always I owe a big debt of gratitude to my school chums from Saltley Grammar school. Jessie Bailey led us around (and around) Birmingham city centre so I could find a suitable location for Endicott's factory. Pam Rowan and Enid Harley are always willing to search out information when I need it. We all grew up in Brum, and their support and encouragement are precious to me.

There are so many wonderful sources that I consulted to get my facts right, but I owe a particular debt to Carl Chinn's book, *Brum Undaunted: Birmingham During the Blitz* (2005).

Thanks to Donald Adams, who steered me to several useful sources concerning policing in Birmingham.

Especial thanks to my indefatigable, ever-patient editor, Lara Hinchberger. And to McClelland & Stewart, who gave me this opportunity to write the book I have always wanted to write.

Finally, a huge thanks to Deb Drennan, who, one afternoon, kindly asked what book I was working on. We discovered we both had a deep passion for the lives of the women who worked in the munitions factories during World War II. Deb because her grandmother had worked at a huge munitions factory in Toronto, Canada, during the war years, I because I was in the midst of this book. One thing led to another and from this concept has come a TV series, *Bomb Girls*.

I feel immensely privileged to have gone on this journey with so many terrific people.

If you enjoyed **Beware this Boy**,
treat yourself to an excerpt from the
new Tom Tyler mystery
No Known Grave
coming in November 2014.

And don't miss the first
Detective Inspector Tom Tyler mystery
Season of Darkness

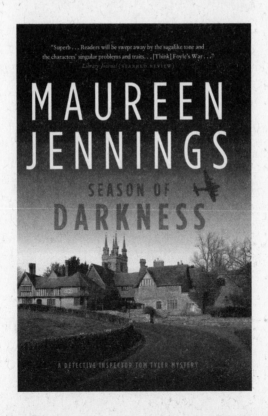

JULY 15, 1942

*There is no moon, no light showing at all. It takes a few moments
to become accustomed to the darkness but the pigeons are easy to
locate, cooing softly, rustling in the straw of the coop. They are
used to being handled so it is easy to pick one out, a sleek brown
speckled male. It doesn't protest when the capsule is fastened on its
leg. Death comes swiftly and painlessly with a hard twist of the
neck. Then the soft, warm body is removed.*

. . .

Sergeant McHattie and his family occupied one of two cot-
tages which nestled into a gentle slope about a hundred yards
behind the main building. As Hughes approached the little
cottage, he felt a sharp twinge of uneasiness. He could see that
the blackout curtains were still drawn in all of the front windows. He knew that Mrs. McHattie and her daughter always
visited her family in Wem on Tuesday nights and wouldn't be
at home, but where was Jock? It was so unlike him to be sleeping in. The two young laddies perhaps, now that it was the
school hols, but not the sergeant. Hughes glanced at the other
nearby cottage, where Mrs. Fuller, the cook, lived with her
son, Alfie. Hughes had seen her earlier serving breakfast in

the dining room, and as he would have expected, her curtains were pulled back and the windows were wide open.

He stepped up to the front door of the McHattie cottage and knocked. No answer. Had the Sarge indeed been taken ill? He knocked again. Silence. He tried the door knob, which turned easily. He pushed open the door and went inside.

The place was in darkness.

"Sergeant McHattie? Jock? Are you home?"

There was no response.

Hughes switched on the overhead light.

"Anybody home? It's me, Hughes."

There was no wireless playing, no dishes on the kitchen table, no sign that anybody had been up and about. Jock's bagpipes drooped over a chair.

Suddenly, something yowled and ran out from the kitchen.

"Shite," Hughes gasped. "Bloody hell, Blackie. You gave me a fright there."

The cat immediately started to wrap itself around his legs. He went to scratch its head but it darted away up the stairs. Hughes followed it up to a small landing. There was a night light here, barely penetrating the gloom but sufficient for him to make out two partly open doors.

He sniffed. There was a sour smell in the air.

Cautiously he peeked into the first bedroom.

"Jock? Jock, you in here?"

The blackout curtains were closed here as well and it was pitch dark. He snapped on the light.

Even though the orderly was used to the frailty of the human body, what he saw made bile rush into his mouth. Sprawled on the floor between the door and the bed was Jock's young son, Ben. He was lying on his back, his arms flung out to the sides. He was dressed in his pyjamas, the front stained with blood which had also streaked his face in dark rivulets.

Jock McHattie was in the bed, still under the covers. He had a halo of blood around his head and there was a large ragged tear in the pillow. Bits of white substance had spread everywhere. Brains or feathers, it was hard to tell.

Although Hughes knew there was nothing he could do for either of them, he had to make sure. He stepped closer to the boy, crouched down, and touched Ben's hand. It was cool. There was a large, black-rimmed hole in the middle of the boy's forehead. He had been shot at close range.

Slowly, Hughes straightened up and went over to the bed. Like his son, Jock appeared to have been shot. There was an identical wound in his temple. His skin was also cold. Death for both of them must have occurred some hours earlier.

The cat was meowing loudly and rubbing itself against Ben's body.

Hughes backed away onto the landing, but just as he did so he heard a sound, so soft he almost missed it, coming from the second bedroom. His knees were shaking but he made himself go and look. Again he had to turn on the light. There was another whimper. It was coming from underneath the nearest bed. He bent down. The terrified face of a young boy stared out at him. It was Charlie, the younger McHattie boy.

"Mr. Hughes," he whispered. "Please help me, Mr. Hughes."

Iden Ford

Born in England, MAUREEN JENNINGS emigrated to Canada as a teenager. The first Detective Murdoch mystery was published in 1997. Six more followed, all to enthusiastic reviews. In 2003, Shaftesbury Films adapted three of the novels into movies of the week, and four years later the *Murdoch Mysteries* TV series was created; it is now shown around the world, including in the UK, the United States (as *The Artful Detective*), and much of Europe, as well as on Canada's national broadcast network, CBC TV. The Detective Inspector Tom Tyler series, set in World War II-era England, got off to a spectacular start with 2011's *Season of Darkness*, followed by *Beware this Boy* in 2012. Maureen lives in Toronto with her husband, their two dogs, Varley and Murdoch, and their cat, Willie. Visit www.maureenjennings.com.

D/K
22/9/23